The
Things You
Do for Love

Rachel Crowther is a doctor who worked for the NHS for 20 years, and the mother of five children. She dabbled in creative writing between babies and medical exams until an Arvon course prompted her to take it more seriously. She's also a keen musician and cook. This is her second novel.

Also by Rachel Crowther

The Partridge and the Pelican

The Things You Do for Love

Rachel Crowther

Rachel Crowther

ZAFFRE

First published in 2016 by

Zaffre Publishing
80–81 Wimpole St, London W1G 9RE
www.zaffrebooks.co.uk

A CIP catalogue record for this book is available from the British Library.

ISBN: 978-1-7857-6184-3

also available as an ebook

1 3 5 7 9 10 8 6 4 2

Printed and bound by Clays Ltd, St Ives Plc

Zaffre Publishing is an imprint of Bonnier Zaffre,
a Bonnier Publishing company
www.bonnierzaffre.co.uk
www.bonnierpublishing.com

For Clemency, Katie, Toby, Daphne and Rowena
with love and thanks

All the things you do for love –
  Are they the things you do for pleasure?
All the things you do for love –
  I've got to ask you whether
All the things you do for love –
  Are they the things you're gonna treasure?

Mia van Arlen, 'Tough Love'

Prologue

London, May 2014

Face to face with the statue, Kitty felt the air in her lungs turn to stone. Half human and half rampant vegetation, this figure was utterly different from everything else in the exhibition. One hand clasped a staff wound with ivy that snaked up his arm and around his neck; the other held a pitcher overflowing with grapes. Kitty recognised the trappings of Bacchus, a haggard and ramshackle Bacchus, but she recognised something else too in this representation of him. The wild tangle of his hair was dismayingly familiar, but it was his face, the curl of his mouth and the line of his nose and even the trace of a teasing glint in his eyes that triggered such a jolt of disbelief.

As Kitty stared, the noise of the crowded gallery dropped away. Somewhere in the room were her mother and her sister, other people she knew, who should see this, but she couldn't drag her eyes away from the sculpture. The carving was exceptionally delicate, the marks of Alice's chisels and rifflers polished away until the texture of the marble was as smooth as skin, the features all-but-alive. Vines spiralled from his shoulders and leaves furled across his chest, but the foliage drew back from the shocking lesion near his heart: a crusting, carbuncular mass that thrust up through the skin and sprawled across the broad ribcage.

Kitty felt the floor lurch beneath her feet, the solid world turning suddenly treacherous. Somewhere in the ether she heard someone say, 'Are you all right? You look terribly pale, can I . . .?'

At the same time a woman's voice cut shrilly across the buzz of concern.

'Good Lord,' she said, 'it's Henry Jones. Look at Bacchus' face: he's the absolute image of Henry Jones.'

1

PART I

Greville Auctioneers, Friday 12th December 2014

Paintings and drawings by Nicholas Comyn, from the collection of the late Henry Jones

Lot no. 1: Family Portrait, 1995

This sketch represents something of a mystery. Donated anonymously, it is the only work in this sale that does not come from Henry Jones' personal collection. It has the appearance of a preliminary study for a painting, but it is not known whether the finished work was produced before Comyn's untimely death in May 1995.

According to the donor, the family depicted here is Henry Jones and his wife, the surgeon Flora Macintyre, with their two daughters Louisa and Kitty, but the figures are not drawn in sufficient detail to make it possible to identify them. The background is barely sketched in, giving only a vague impression of an interior space in which the four figures stand in a somewhat uncomfortable relationship to each other and to the viewer. The younger child is in her father's arms, while the older one is placed between her parents. The mother's hand rests on her daughter's shoulder, but her face is turned slightly towards a window which can just be seen on the left hand side.

The composition does not appear to be a formal pose, but neither is it entirely naturalistic. The subjects seem almost to be on the move, as if this were a still from a film sequence that has caught them in a brief, artificial moment of proximity and stasis: it begs the question of what might have happened in the moment after this scene was captured. If this were a preliminary study, it might well be one of several needed to shape the artist's conception of the planned work and of his subjects. Nonetheless, it has considerable emotional power.

Despite the questions surrounding its provenance, this sketch is certainly by Comyn: it bears his signature, and his style is readily detectable in the clean lines and deft shading. Given that the Jones family were on intimate terms with Comyn, it seems likely, too, that they are the subjects. The viewer can draw their own conclusions about the resemblance between these figures and representations of the Joneses in other pictures in this collection.

1

English Channel, May 2014

Leaning over the rail that bounded the grimy strip of deck, Flora watched the miles disappear in a hurtle of grey water past the bows of the ferry. It was the middle of May, and despite the heavy clouds the scent of summer was discernible in the air. Salt spray speckled her face and she could hear the distant squeal of children, raucous and cheerful above the noise of the engine. This was a moment, Flora thought, when she should feel glad to be alive.

But almost in the same instant, it occurred to her that it would be quite possible to manoeuvre herself over the side of the boat and into that churning sea. Quite simple, in fact: it was a short drop to another strip of deck below, and beneath that nothing but water. There was no one else about and she was lithe enough to manage the vault easily. If she wanted to, she could be gone before anyone noticed.

For a few moments Flora stood very still, letting the throb of the engine rise through her body like a thunderous heartbeat. The idea of simply disappearing had never occurred to her before, and it shocked her, but she could see that it would be a logical solution – one logical solution – to the problem posed by her situation. And it could feasibly be passed off as an accident, sparing others the guilt or regret they might otherwise feel obliged to bear. She gripped the rail tightly, feeling a surge of emotion too complex and contrary to disentangle. Grief, fear, exaltation – even amusement, a shred of it, at the pickle she found herself in.

It would take time, people said, to adjust to all that had happened in the last six months. She should give herself time. But it seemed to Flora that it was time itself she couldn't adjust to. The sudden having of time:

the way it stretched before her, empty and expectant and oddly unyielding. It was as if she'd stumbled into one of those echoing Elizabethan galleries where ladies could walk and talk to pass the idle hours. Not the kind of place she was accustomed to, Flora Macintyre the surgeon-mother-wife-authority. The do-er of good, mostly: the do-er, at any rate. What on earth was she to do in this unfamiliar territory?

She was on her way home, just now, after spending a week in Alsace with a well-meaning cousin of Henry's who'd guessed that she had few people to offer her this sort of reprieve after the funeral. That was exactly what the week had provided, Flora thought – a reprieve, but nothing more. She could hardly say how she'd filled it, even. She'd got through it, but it was only a week, and there were hundreds more of them to come. She was only sixty; she might reasonably expect to live another twenty-five years.

She gazed out, marvelling at the emptiness of the horizon. The ferry seemed to be trundling through nothingness: an unrelenting grey stretched in every direction. But then, as she stared, something appeared in the distance – something she couldn't make out at first, but which took shape gradually as a boat. Straining her eyes, she could see it bobbing and swaying in a way that suggested there was no one on board to steer it. A tug, perhaps, that had broken free of its moorings and drifted out to sea.

Her attention was so absorbed that she didn't hear anyone approaching.

'Do you think it'll hit us?'

Flora turned. She recognised the young woman who'd climbed the stairs ahead of her half an hour before, between a pair of blonde children already red-faced with unsatisfied demands. She was alone now, holding a cigarette awkwardly as though she wasn't accustomed to smoking. Like a child pretending, Flora thought, and the image caught her interest.

'Do you think it might?' she asked.

The woman lifted the cigarette to her lips and sucked at it briefly, blowing the smoke out almost at once.

'It looks out of control to me,' she said. A pleasant Scottish accent, mixing consternation and amusement.

They stood side by side, gazing at the approaching tug. Its course veered steadily towards the ferry, as if drawn by the magnetic pull of the larger vessel.

'They're not built for collisions, these,' the woman said. 'Do you remember one nearly sank a few years ago?'

Flora didn't remember, but she could be persuaded that she did. She glanced again at her companion – a striking face, she thought, despite the weary lines beneath her eyes. For a moment it seemed possible that this was some younger version of herself, an alter ego conjured from the emptiness of sea and sky to share this drama with her.

The tug was small, but the ferry certainly wasn't capable of deft avoiding swerves. Any moment, Flora thought, a warning siren would sound and instructions would come over the tannoy. But there was silence, apart from the chug of engines and the whisper of water – as though there were no one else on board, no one but the two of them to witness the unfolding scene. As the tug came inexorably closer, Flora's mind filled with an exhilarating sense of disbelief: the terror and release of an impending crisis she could do nothing to avert. Like being a passenger on the *Titanic*, she thought, watching the iceberg loom into view.

And then at the last minute, almost in slow motion, the danger receded. The tug seemed intent on its course until it was nearly upon them – until it was lifted by the rush of water down the side of the larger boat, hesitated for a moment with its nose in the air as though appraising the situation, and finally, quietly, ducked away. Nudged aside, Flora thought, by a great metal whale, gently insistent, and too vast to brook dissent.

As the tug made its giddy escape and the ferry sailed on with majestic indifference, Flora's first thought was that she had been cheated of the thrill of calamity. But her second, insinuating itself before she could stop it, was that she was glad to have survived unscathed. The flame of life, she thought, selfish and indomitable or simply bloody-minded, was not to be extinguished so easily.

'Well,' said the woman. She threw her cigarette over the side of the boat. 'That was exciting.'

Her voice had the same quality of eager flatness you might use to conceal from a child the scale of a crisis narrowly avoided. Flora glanced at her, and she laughed suddenly.

'I really thought it was going to hit us,' she said.

'Yes,' said Flora. 'So did I.'

'A *folie à deux*,' the woman said. 'How funny. What's your reason for courting disaster?'

Caught off balance, Flora smiled. 'I'm not sure how to answer that.'

The woman looked at her with a curiosity Flora found she didn't mind. It was easier with strangers, she thought. There was no obligation to dissemble – and still less to tell the truth.

'Are you travelling alone?' the woman asked.

'Yes.'

'Been on holiday?'

'Not exactly.'

'Oh?'

Her smile banished the shadows around her eyes, and Flora saw that the cigarette and the attempt at raffish gaiety had been misleading: this woman was a provider, well versed in service to others. Even the peculiar circumstances of the last ten minutes couldn't deflect her from making pleasant conversation with a stranger.

'I've retired,' Flora said. 'I'm . . . I have plenty of time to travel now.'

'How lovely. Lucky you.'

How lovely, Flora thought. *Lucky you.* She felt once more the twitch of readjustment that caught at her sleeve several times a day. She was fortunate, that certainly seemed beyond question. She was a member of the last generation who'd be able to retire at sixty. She'd have enough money, even if Henry had left less than she'd expected: her NHS pension was more than adequate. Certainly there were blessings to count as well as losses – and yet; and yet.

As she hesitated, her companion grasped abruptly at the railing.

'Oh dear,' she said. 'That cigarette was a mistake. I thought it might help.'

Flora looked beyond her to the sea. It was rougher than it had been a few minutes before, the waves surging and billowing.

'Serves me right,' the woman said. 'I shouldn't . . .'

She groaned as the boat dipped and lifted, and Flora saw her shoulders tense. She felt a wave of sympathy, and with it a whiff of consolation, the sense that there was some reassurance in suffering among others – but it was followed by something exactly opposite: the familiar surgeon's instinct to distance herself; to rise above sickness and misery.

And then, out of the blue, another thought: Henry was always a bad sailor. Henry would have been out here looking green, too.

Watching this stranger gasp in lungfuls of salty air, Flora was assailed by a dizzying spasm of grief. She stared at the horizon in an attempt to steady herself, but the blankness around her seemed overwhelming now. Nothing to cling on to, she thought; nothing to navigate by. The moment when she'd seen her way clear to clambering over the side of the boat came back to her vividly, and she felt a flash of regret. Might she have done it, if this woman hadn't come along?

'I was never like this before the children,' the woman said. 'I was terribly sick with both of them, and it's as if . . .' Her voice trailed off.

'Maybe it'll get better again,' Flora said. Not a Flora thing to say: she despised such platitudes, as a rule. She looked again at her companion, young and healthy despite her current affliction. When they reached

Dover she would rejoin her family and disembark, pink-cheeked with relief. She didn't need the pity of a stranger.

Flora pushed herself back from the rail. Perhaps she'd go and see what the café had to offer, she thought. But then the woman spoke again.

'What did you do?' she asked.

'I beg your pardon?'

'You said you'd retired.' She looked very pale still, the attempt at conversation an effort.

Flora hesitated. 'I was a doctor,' she said. 'A surgeon.'

'Goodness.'

There was usually something more at this point – the story of a relative's operation, or an apologia for full-time motherhood – sometimes a half-hearted display of interest in Flora's field. Perhaps it was only the clutch of nausea that prevented the woman from taking any of these courses, but Flora was grateful, nonetheless.

'I retired in January to look after my husband,' she heard herself saying. 'He died six weeks ago.'

'I'm sorry. And that's why you're . . .'

Flora nodded. Despite the urge to escape, to forget all about the imagined collision and the indignity of seasickness, something held her back. This encounter, the drama of the tug, seemed – oh, a test case, she thought, for what anything might amount to now, for her. Was that mere superstition, a foolish falling-back on signs and coincidence, or was she opening her mind – as she should, as she must – to a different way of doing things: a new kind of life?

'I wonder what I'd do in your position,' the woman said.

'I beg your pardon?' Flora turned sharply. It occurred to her, with a jolt of chagrin, that the woman had been watching her earlier and might have guessed what had been on her mind.

'I don't mean to – but the idea of being able to do anything . . .' Her companion smiled, sheepish now. 'You could turn round and go back to France if you wanted to. I can't imagine that.'

'No.' Not the right answer, Flora thought. She felt unaccountably shaky; partly with relief, but there was something more painful too.

'I mean, not that I don't want to go home, but . . .'

The younger woman fell silent. Flora remembered the children flanking her an hour before, the patience of her voice. She wished she could think of something to say, but she couldn't. It was surely too late now to acquire the habit of small talk, or the kind of empathy other people seemed to find so easy. Glancing up, she saw that the first streak of land had appeared: the chalky Dover cliffs, symbol of home even to those who'd never seen them before. The other woman looked at her watch.

'I'd better go,' she said. She smiled again – which was more than she deserved, Flora thought. 'It's been nice meeting you.'

Watching her companion disappear through the door to the cabin, Flora felt strangely bereft. It wasn't that she'd wanted to continue the conversation; simply that there had been a connection between the two of them for a little while, and now it was at an end. Perhaps she should expect this, she thought – that every insignificant parting would hurt a little, and every small loss would invoke the larger losses she'd suffered. She remembered, then, saying goodbye to Landon after the funeral, thanking him for his eulogy and feeling, at that moment, a greater grief for his departure than for Henry's death. Remembering that other funeral, of course, and what had come after it, although she'd fought the memory down – and must again, she told herself, as another bewildering tide of emotions rose in her throat. How could she deal at once with the complications of the past and the future? Oh, damn Henry for dying: at least he had understood her. Whatever secrets they'd kept from each other had been outweighed, vastly outweighed, by the comforting certainty that they understood each other, and knew how they fitted together. How was she to explain herself to the world now, when she barely understood herself?

As the Dover cliffs came steadily closer, Flora forced herself to consider her situation. Six months ago she'd been at full stretch as clinician and teacher and researcher. Now here she was, retired as well as widowed; entirely without occupation. It seemed to her suddenly that she'd found herself in this position unwittingly: almost – almost – against her will. Flora the clear-thinker, the maker of rational decisions, outmanoeuvred by Fate in some sleight of hand she was still narrowing her eyes to spot.

She shifted slightly, turning away from the approaching port as she examined this thought. She certainly wouldn't have retired at sixty if Henry hadn't been dying. She might not have done if they'd had a different sort of marriage all those years. She was grateful for those last few months, though. That much was true: she didn't want to come to regret them. But she needed to manage the next bit of life gracefully. She couldn't bear people to look at her with pity – or worse, with that shifty look she'd seen on several faces at the funeral.

And then she heard the echo of the other woman's voice: *You could turn round and go back to France if you wanted.*

It was a mad idea, of course. But she thought about Alice's private view that evening; about seeing her daughters and Landon – quite possibly Landon – and the well-meaning questions she would be asked. She thought about Orchards, half-empty after the furious clearing-out of the last few weeks. She thought about signs and coincidence; about the oppression and the opportunities of free choice; about the flame of life burning stubbornly inside her.

When they arrived at Dover and her fellow passengers joined the crush to get back to their cars, Flora hung back. When the stream of traffic headed out of the port and towards the motorway, Flora circled round, and without thinking very hard about what she was doing, she bought a ticket on the next ferry back to France.

March 1995

As Flora drives away from the hospital, her mind is full of heroism. Waiting at the traffic lights, then heading out onto the dual carriageway, she relives the hours under the lights, the glint of instruments, the counting in of swabs – all the rites and pageantry of the operating theatre, brought to bear on the body of one ordinary citizen. She conjures up the face of her patient, a young man with a faint tinge of green in the hollows of his cheeks, being coaxed back to consciousness among the reassuring paraphernalia of drips and drains and monitors.

And then she remembers the size of the tumour, the length of gut they had to remove, the bleakness of the prognosis. As the orderly lights of the ring road give way to unlit country lanes, Flora feels the adrenaline ebbing away. There is always this moment, this crunch of reality, when the elation of exercising her craft evaporates and the patient comes back into focus, a person with a life that has been interrupted by medical catastrophe. She never deceives herself about such things, but it's necessary to put them away while you get on with the job, focussing on the gaping abdomen before you.

Flora slows for a difficult corner then picks up speed again, shifting into fourth for the straight run along to the final crossroads. But, she tells herself, it's the person who wakes up in the recovery room, whom she'll see tomorrow morning on the ward, that she's made a difference to. She has done what she can to help him beat the odds. She thinks again of the hours of concentration and the expertise of her team: five hours multiplied by five, six, seven people. It's more than going through the motions, surgery. It's always more than that; always a battle fought to the last ditch. This afternoon they halted two hours in, wondering whether to abandon the resection, but they were right to go on. There are always the cases that turn out better than you dare expect, she tells herself, as well as those who do worse.

The village is quiet this evening, but the lights are on in the house, and a cheerful glow filters through the curtains as she turns into the drive. Flora thinks of Henry and the girls inside, cooking supper or watching television or finishing homework.

But in the moment between turning off the engine and opening the car door, the complications of home creep back into her mind: an almost tangible shift from comforting allegory to untidy reality. She recalls last night's row, left hanging this morning, and her earnest assurance to the children that she'd be home early tonight. It's her birthday, she remembers. They promised her a cake. She glances at the clock on the dashboard – it's almost nine. Will Kitty still be up? Will Lou be sulking by now?

There's no one around when she opens the door, just a hushed murmur of voices which she takes for the television. But in a moment Lou rushes down the stairs and throws herself against her chest.

'Mummy! You're back!'

Lou is twelve, and not much given to throwing herself at her mother anymore. Holding her tight for a moment, Flora can feel her small heart thudding.

'I'm so sorry I'm late,' she says. 'I really meant not to be, today of all days.'

'It's OK,' Lou says. 'We've got . . .' She draws away now a little awkwardly, as though she's not sure how she found herself plastered against her mother. 'Daddy's in the kitchen,' she says. 'I was on look-out.'

Flora catches a note of something – warning? – in Lou's voice. Her eyes sweep round the hall, halting for a moment on the portrait of her husband that hangs at the bottom of the stairs: a handsome boy of nineteen, drawn by his friend Nicholas Comyn during a tour of Italy, smiling at the world in the assurance of a warm reception.

'Is Kitty still up?' she asks – but before Lou can answer, Henry appears from the kitchen, carrying a bottle of champagne and some glasses on a tray. Henry resplendent in silk shirt and cravat, every inch the elegant host, the eminent critic, the reassuring Radio Three voice-over.

'Darling,' he says, 'Happy Birthday. Has Lou . . .?'

He leans forward to kiss her, swinging the tray to the side so he can get close enough to reach her lips. Last night's row hovers between them, less easy to dodge than the tray. Flora can smell wine on his breath, and can detect it, too, in the flush across his cheekbones. The soft skin there is a reliable barometer for excess consumption of several kinds.

'Sorry I'm late,' she says. 'Unavoidably detained at the operating table.'

'You're here now,' he says. 'Let me pour you a drink.'

Flora's eyes are caught now by another picture, another Comyn, of Kitty and Lou on the beach last summer. Something about it lights a fuse inside her: the image of happy family life. The same image she almost allowed herself to believe in a few minutes ago. She's been fobbed off too often with a glass of wine, she tells herself. She glances towards Lou, but Lou has vanished again. She's become an expert at vanishing, Flora thinks, with a flash of pain.

'Wait,' she says, as Henry moves towards the sitting room door. 'We need to talk.'

Henry halts, but he doesn't turn to face her. 'Not now,' he says, his voice almost jovial.

'Why not?' Anger has flared more quickly than usual, provoked by the way Henry's dress and demeanour speak of an evening of celebration, and by her guilt about Lou. By the too-familiar chain of complication and compromise. The last vestiges of surgical adrenaline urge her on. 'It's always "not now",' she says. 'Perhaps this is the moment, Henry. We can't simply –' She raises a fist, half-clenched – not as a threat, not exactly, but as evidence of her strength of feeling, her seriousness of intent.

And then the sitting room door bursts open. The murmur of voices swells suddenly and Kitty flies towards her, pink tutu fluttering, full of the wildness of a not-quite-three-year-old allowed to stay up beyond her bedtime.

'We've got a party for you!' she shouts.

The room behind her is full of people, looking nervously, smilingly, in Flora's direction. The smell of festivity is unmistakable: wine and perfume and the pepperiness of hot breath billow out into the hall.

Caught in the dismay of an ill-timed surprise, Flora can't muster the appropriate response. Memories of her mother's parties swim into her mind, and she feels suddenly very tired. Henry looks at her, raises an eyebrow infinitesimally, and then he goes on into the sitting room, and there is nothing for it but to follow him.

'What a nice surprise,' Flora says.

The guests – mainly from the village: not many of them friends, to be honest – are clearly embarrassed by the anticlimax, after keeping quiet for so long. They glance at Flora as though they know they should be pleased that their hostess is here at last, but are not sure they are. Why on earth has Henry invited them? To create a party, she thinks. A diversion. Because it would be hard to muster a houseful of people, otherwise, with whom they could go through the motions. Goddammit: and it's she who looks ungracious now. Heartless, even. Well, she'll show them. She scoops Kitty up and swings her round, kissing her hot little face.

'My darling,' she says, 'how beautiful you look.'

'You haven't got your party clothes on,' says Kitty. 'Have you been in the hospital all the time?'

'All the time.' Flora settles Kitty on her hip and turns away from Henry, who is coming towards her with a glass of champagne. 'All this long time. Now, Kitty, come and help me say hello to everyone.'

Flora hears the phone ringing, but for once it doesn't call her to attention. She's talking to a feisty octogenarian who lives opposite the church, but she hears Lou answering the phone and registers a flicker of pride at her daughter's self-assurance as she says yes, and who is it, and hang on a moment. Then she sees Lou coming towards her – and there, belatedly, is the catch in her chest.

She takes the call in the kitchen. It's Paul Briggs, her Registrar. In the instant before he speaks she glances at the clock and calculates the possibilities.

'We need you to come back in,' Paul says, his voice deadpan as always. 'We need to take him back to theatre. Cal Nevitt's getting him prepped right now.'

Lou is hovering beside her, and when she's put the phone down Flora pulls her in close. She smells of apples and milk, a little girl scent still, without the pungency of adolescence. Flora shuts her eyes, extending the moment as long as she dares. But when she opens them again the party, the noise and colour and warmth of it, looks like a film, something happening at one remove.

'I have to go, darling,' she says. 'I'm so sorry. The lovely party and everything.'

Lou takes Flora's hand and squeezes it, and then she lifts it away from her shoulder, gently, as though prising a toy out of her mother's grasp. 'I'll tell Daddy,' she says. 'I'll tell him you won't be back till late.'

'Not too late, I hope,' Flora says, but she knows it'll be hours before she's home again. She knows that Lou knows, too. She hesitates a moment, thinking of the party guests, the flush in Henry's cheeks, her fist stalled in mid-air.

'I'll go out the back way,' she says, 'so I don't cause any fuss.'

She kisses Lou, thinks of Kitty, hesitates again.

'Will you put Kitty to bed?' she asks. 'I really can't . . .'

'I'll tell her it was a murgency,' says Lou, employing Kitty's word to make her mother smile.

Flora feels tears pricking then, not so much at Lou's competence as at the need for it; the need for a twelve-year-old to smooth things over for her parents. She wants to say she'll make it up to her, wants to believe she'll have the chance.

Her car keys are still in her pocket. Once the door is shut behind her she runs round the side of the house and slides into the driving seat. The last waft of merriment from the party trails behind her as she backs out of the drive and heads away up the lane.

2

Leaning against the wall in the far corner of the gallery, Lou shut her eyes as another wave of nausea flooded through her. The air was thick with stale breath and perfume: she longed for an open window, for a glass of water, for her bed. Where was Kitty, she wondered, and Flora? Where was Alice, for that matter? She could see Alice's sculptures dotted around the room, but she hadn't paid proper attention to them yet, and she certainly hadn't given more than a glance to any of the other artists' work.

A waft of spiced oil reached her nose, and Lou made a soft crooning sound, something between a moan and a murmur of regret. This upheaval in her body seemed too violent for the cause – the few cells multiplying hopefully inside her. These should surely be the symptoms of something malign, aggressive, heart-stopping: something like the cancer that had killed her father, not the foetus conceived, with what now seemed such distasteful timing, two weeks before he died. She had hardly acknowledged the existence of that tiny creature yet, and this was absolutely the wrong moment for it to make its presence so compellingly felt.

Lou forced herself to survey the room, a cavernous space dense with people. The banner strung along the opposite wall matched the one outside, across the portico of the Taelwyn Gallery. The distinctive font trumpeted style and consequence: *Morris Prize 2014*, it said, and in smaller letters below, *Open daily 10-6, 17th May – 21st June*. Lou registered a flicker of the pride she'd felt when Alice was shortlisted, tempered now by something less straightforward. She scanned the crowd again for her mother and her sister, but there were only the faces of strangers, blurring into each other. The noise was considerable; the particular social pitch, Lou thought, of bohemian privilege, or artistic aspiration, or whatever phrase her father would have found to parody the occasion. And of course he at least – Henry Jones, music critic and man of letters – always did have more understanding of what was on display than the throngs of hangers-on in Armani and Missoni, even if his daughters did not.

Henry would have loved this evening, Lou thought. He would have loved his connection to Alice, his family gathered in public, his worlds converging. He'd have been pleased about the baby too, she thought, and tears rose in her eyes which she resisted furiously. Tears for her father were too complicated this evening. Too complicated altogether.

'Hello,' said a voice she didn't recognise, and she looked up to see a face she did, vaguely. A friend of Alice's: a very tall girl in her early twenties, wearing something that looked as though she'd made it herself, and wasn't entirely sure about it now she'd got it on in a public place.

'Hello,' Lou said – and then, because she could see that the girl couldn't remember her name either, and a few words of conversation seemed necessary, 'Lou Jones. Alice's partner.'

'Nerissa Stapleton,' said the girl, and she smiled and twitched at one of the drapes of fabric trailing from her waist.

'Great dress,' Lou said. She glanced down at her own black suit, unadorned by so much as a colourful scarf, and wondered if she should have made more of an effort.

'Alice's collection is fabulous,' Nerissa said. 'I love her work. Do you model for her?'

'No,' said Lou.

It was barely eight o'clock. There was still an hour to go before the results were announced, and whether or not Alice won Lou knew they'd have to stay for a respectable time after that, accepting congratulations or offering them, listening while artists and critics and dealers discussed the judges' decision. Two hours, perhaps. Could she survive that long? Her mind skipped ahead, bargaining with probability. If they left by ten – ten thirty – ten forty-five . . . If the traffic wasn't too bad . . .

The expectant expression on Nerissa's face was beginning to give way to doubt. Even the bare minimum of social interaction was going to be a challenge tonight, Lou realised. It was the strangest sensation, every word and every thought having the same effect as the pitch and yaw of an aeroplane riding through a storm.

'You'll have to excuse me,' she said. 'I'm not feeling very well.'

She managed something she hoped would pass for a smile, and made a dash for the door.

The irony was that for the last few weeks she'd felt so well, so much the same as ever, that she'd wondered, once or twice, if the pregnancy test had been wrong. She'd almost wished for a sign to reassure her. And now she'd got it, she thought, as she slammed the loo door behind her and bent over the bowl with a groan of relief. How on earth did people keep pregnancies hidden?

When the retching finally subsided, Lou was conscious in its wake of a tangled, guilty sort of grief. Pressing her palms against the marble tiles, she wished fervently that she'd told Alice about the pregnancy sooner; certainly before risking exposure on such a public occasion. She should never have gone ahead without her, she thought: she should have waited until Alice's misgivings, whatever they were, had receded.

They'd gone through the preliminaries together, earlier in the year – the strange formality of registering with the clinic and the comedic evenings spent poring over the catalogue of potential donors – but then Alice had got cold feet, hadn't even wanted to talk about it anymore, and between Henry's decline and the build up to the Morris Prize the subject had faded from view. But not from Lou's mind. In the end, almost on the spur of the moment, she'd gone back to the clinic alone. As her father lay dying, the idea of bringing new life into the world had possessed her: no, that wasn't quite true. Nor was it true that her cool legal mind had reckoned up the pros and cons, the chances of success on the first attempt, the likelihood that Alice would see things differently once the deed was done. Lou was by no means sure of that now. It was as if the unquestioning correspondence between the two of them had been unsettled; as if more had changed in Lou herself than that clump of cells deep in her belly.

Hauling herself up at last, Lou stood for a few moments in front of the sink, scrutinising herself in the mirror. She looked pale, her dark hair hanging flat against her face. Not much like a guest of honour at a glamorous reception, she thought, not that she gave a fig about that. There were plenty of people out there to glitter and twitter, glancing over their shoulders to see who was watching, who was listening. Even from her corner, she'd heard the *Art Today* article about the shortlist quoted several times, along with opinions about this being the year for peace not violence, for a return to conventional modes of representation, for work that reflected the global financial crisis. She attempted a smile in the mirror, and heard an echo of her father's voice. Hang in there, it said. Too bad you can't smoke at these things anymore.

Lou made her way back towards the gallery more steadily than she had left it. It seemed vital now to find Alice while the need to confide was still urgent and before nausea overtook her again. As she pushed open the door, the noise of chatter and laughter burst out at her: across the room, she heard a shrill exclamation, and some trick of the mind shaped the words into the sound of her father's name. Lou stopped. So many people, she thought. But as she searched the crowd, there, miraculously, mysteriously, was Alice, coming towards her. Alice unusually elegant in her green silk trousers and long jacket, but still her Alice, solid and comforting, more familiar these days than Lou's own reflection.

For a few seconds Lou's sense of relief was so strong that she didn't register Alice's expression, nor wonder at the coincidence of her approach. She swayed slightly, grasping at the wall again to counter a moment of giddiness, and lifted her eyes to meet Alice's gaze. But before she could speak, before they were close enough to touch, Alice began talking instead.

'My darling,' she said. 'I need to show you something. I should have told you about it, but I didn't. I'm sorry; I was very wrong.'

Someone had found Kitty a chair and a glass of water, while news of her reaction to the Bacchus statue spread in murmured ripples around her. As the first shock receded, Kitty felt several different things at once: embarrassment about the scene she'd made, and grief, and anger too, of course – but it wasn't entirely clear to her who she was angry with, or what about. A feeling that was hard to explain, but which was strangely familiar to Kitty.

She'd thought the Morris Prize show would be a pleasant diversion; that art and sophisticated company and free champagne were just what she needed. The last thing she'd expected was to have her father thrust forcibly back into view, and in a way that managed to capture both his less admirable side – the bit Kitty was trying hard to forget – and his pathetic vulnerability at the end. Surely she should be angry with Alice, then, for doing this without telling them – certainly without telling Kitty?

Alice had talked a lot, for her, about this collection. It had been a welcome distraction during those awful weekends before Henry died, when they'd all drifted around Orchards like ghosts. Henry had been intrigued by Alice's sketches and the photos of sculptures in progress – a special concession, that, because Alice was usually so reticent about her work. They'd all been grateful for the pleasure it had given him.

Kitty had thought she knew what to expect this evening, anyway. The collection was called *Neomythia*. Alice called the pieces exposés of myth, by which she meant exposés of what happened to women in myth. Greek and Roman artists, she said, presented the victims of rape without regard for their suffering. She showed them photographs: Leda resting an arm on the sinuous body of the swan while lifting her cloak compliantly; Danae reclining on a couch with breasts casually bared, gazing up at Zeus's shower of golden confetti; Europa kneeling provocatively on the back of the bull. What message did that send to male aggressors down the centuries, she'd demanded? Henry, frail and shrunken by now, had smiled in a way that conveyed both admiration for Alice's protest and a pang of regret for the passing of his own days as a red-blooded male.

And now here they were, Alice's portrayals of female bodies deformed and degraded by assault: women cowering beneath giant wings, strangled by snakes and stoned by meteorites. Beside the video screens and fussy assemblages of the other finalists, they looked majestic and magnificent. Kitty had wandered from one to the other with a pleasing sense of understanding and of association. She was Alice's sister-in-law, a woman signed up to the fight against oppression. Surely Alice would win, and they would all have something to celebrate at last after the long months of illness and death.

Then she'd come upon Alice's final piece. Audacious, the people around her were saying, to include it. A male figure, withered and alone, rendered with the same sensitivity as the tyrannised women. A defeated Bacchus, his breast ravaged by a pestilence that no intoxication, no wild hope nor creative force could cure. Kitty shuddered, remembering the moment of recognition, the sudden shaft of understanding. A dying roué with the face and hair and thickset torso of her father.

The gaggle of well-wishers around her was drifting away now to other encounters and conversations. Fragments of laughter rose like spray from the sea of chatter, darting briefly towards the high ceiling before falling back to be lost amid the babble. She was all alone, Kitty thought suddenly. Where was Lou? Where was Flora? She looked towards the door, towards the table stacked with bottles and glasses, towards Bacchus on his plinth. And then, as someone shifted in the crowd, she saw Alice leading Lou towards him.

'Oh dear,' she said aloud, although there was no one to hear her. 'I don't think Lou knows. I don't think Alice has told her.'

*

Lou saw her sister's face an instant before her father's. Kitty looked almost as white as the Carrara marble Alice liked best to work with, but Lou had only a fleeting impression of her sister's expression before the statue snatched her attention away.

'I'm sorry,' Alice said – or at least, Lou assumed that was what she was saying. For a few moments, as she stared at the statue, she could hear nothing but the clang of recognition.

'It's a good likeness,' she said eventually. Other words revolved in her mind, lots of different words, but none of them reached her tongue. She looked from the sculpture to Alice, then to Kitty.

'A bit of a shock,' Kitty said. 'Hadn't you seen it?'

Lou shook her head. She wondered how – when – Alice had worked on the piece. Had she studied Henry's features during those weekend visits before he died? Or found some photographs, perhaps?

'Have you seen Flora?' Kitty asked now.

'No.'

Lou put a hand on Kitty's shoulder. She could feel her sister trembling: both of them, she thought, ridiculously undone by the old devil's death – or by his unexpected reappearance. She wondered whether Kitty was thinking, as she was, of that other portrait of Henry, Nicholas Comyn's sketch of him as a young man, which hung in the hall at Orchards. It was partly the resemblance to that which was so disconcerting. The resemblance and the difference – and the uncharacteristic callousness of what Alice had done. Although it was more complicated than that. The tenderness of the portrait hurt almost as much as the criticism implied by representing her father as the libertine Bacchus.

'I'm so sorry,' Alice said again, and it was clear that she was: even sorrier than she needed to be, Lou thought. Henry would have been delighted. He'd have taken the whole thing in his stride in the name of art. He'd always been strangely immune to suffering. But Kitty wasn't; Kitty looked shattered.

As she cast about for something to say, Lou's phone buzzed in her pocket. Kitty reached for hers at the same moment.

'Mum.' Kitty stared at the screen. 'She's not coming. She's staying in France.'

Lou felt something echoing down the years: a particular, guarded kind of disappointment. 'With the cousin?' she asked.

'No – Calais, it says. She must have started for home then changed her mind.'

Lou's eyes rested for a moment on her sister. Kitty was dressed tonight in garishly mismatched layers, her long glass earrings catching the light as she moved. They looked nothing like each other, Kitty's pre-Raphaelite prettiness and peach-skin complexion a stark contrast to Lou's neat features and Italianate colouring – and they were separated, too, by nine years and a whole spectrum of choices and characteristics. But just now, it was the connection between them that struck Lou. Flesh and blood, she thought; and then she thought of the creature inside her, the chain link of generation to generation, and love and grief and distress welled up inside her.

Kitty's eyes were on her too, her expression uncertain. She glanced again at the sculpture. 'I don't . . .' she began – but she was interrupted by an exclamation behind her. A familiar voice, followed almost at once by a familiar face.

'Good Lord,' it said. 'It really is him, isn't it?'

'Landon!'

Kitty's face filled with surprise and pleasure. And relief, Lou thought, feeling, herself, a twist of something more complicated. The present and the absent, she thought. Making do with what you had: that had always been a feature of their lives, hadn't it?

'Hello, dear ladies,' Landon said. His eyes rested on each of them in turn, judging his response. He knew them well enough, Lou thought, to understand that there wasn't to be a scene.

'How are you?' he asked. 'Where's your mother?'

'In France still,' said Kitty. 'She's decided to stay a bit longer. I didn't know you were coming, Landon. Do you know Alice?'

Lou turned, her eyes meeting Alice's briefly. They'd met at Henry's funeral, but . . .

'Alice Zellner,' she said, 'Landon Peverell. Landon is – was – Henry's oldest friend. He's –'

'I know who Landon is,' Alice said. She looked straight at him in the way she did with new people; the way Lou found, at different times, admirable or endearing or a little embarrassing. Not unlike the way a blind person might trace a stranger's features with their fingers, storing them away for future reference. 'I heard you sing at the Proms once,' she said. 'The Mozart Requiem.'

'And of course I can return the compliment.' Landon smiled. 'Congratulations: it's an impressive collection. Very powerful, the Bacchus. The – tumour.'

'Breast cancer,' said Lou. Her voice shook a little, perhaps not enough for anyone else to hear it. 'You know that, of course. Henry died of breast cancer.'

November 1977

Flora stands on the landing, looking down into the hall. She feels nothing like a junior doctor tonight, an aspiring surgeon whom her colleagues are fast learning not to underestimate. She feels like Scarlett O'Hara, like Elizabeth Bennet, like Juliet Capulet. She has always been told she is pretty, even beautiful, and for the first time she's glad of it. She's wearing a new dress and has dried her short hair carefully, so that it looks sleeker and more stylish than usual. When she hears the doorbell she takes a step backward, counting to three before she starts down the stairs.

Henry looks rumpled, as he did the last time she saw him. As he always does, she will soon learn. His clothes are well cut, but casually worn and rarely pressed.

'Hello,' he says, with a smile that seems to convey a multitude of other things – to acknowledge what cannot be said in her parents' house. 'Are you ready?'

Another thing Flora hasn't quite understood yet, but which undoubtedly contributes to her electric state of anticipation: her defences have never been challenged, as far as men are concerned. The men she deals with day by day at the hospital treat her with care, like an unfamiliar and possibly dangerous animal. It's clear to Flora that a certain vigilance is required on both sides to keep at bay the prejudice and fear lurking below the surface of professional courtesy, but she is quite happy with this state of affairs. The men whom her mother invites to parties to tempt her with are a different species, requiring no vigilance of any kind.

Her mother doesn't so much disapprove of Flora's career as ignore it: she treats it as a phase Flora will grow out of. She gets on, undaunted, with finding her a suitable husband, and Flora pays as little attention as she can. But the irony – one of many ironies in their relationship, as she will realise in due course – is that Flora met Henry as a result of her mother's implacable social engineering. Henry was brought to one of Diana Macintyre's famous parties by Landon Peverell. Diana has always regarded Landon – the son of her oldest friend – as a diverting addition to her soirées, and if he isn't quite the pinnacle of her aspirations for her daughter, the fact that they have known each other since babyhood means there's little risk that he'll distract Flora from the reliable young men from Lloyd's and Cazenove and Hoare Govett. Men like Derek Nicolson, whose engagement to her sister Jean – two years younger than Flora, and suitably equipped with a nannying qualification – has just been announced in *The Telegraph*.

Friends of Landon's are usually welcome at Diana's parties, but Flora could tell at once that her mother disapproved of Henry. He seemed to Flora very much like the rest – his clothes and his manner and his accent indistinguishable from those of the favoured candidates for her hand – but some antenna of her mother's was piqued, and it was this (another irony) that made Flora look twice at him.

'This is Henry Jones,' Landon said, 'we were at university together,' and Flora smiled in a way she rarely smiled, especially at men.

'*Enchanté,*' said Henry, perfectly poised between sincerity and self-parody. 'I've heard all about you, of course.'

For the next few hours Flora played along with his flirtation, embroiling herself in a game of tease whose complexity she under-estimated. When he said goodbye at the end of the evening she felt a revelation come over her like a physical change. Lying in bed that night, she traced the outline of his face in her mind's eye, straining her memory for his tone of voice and the twist of his smile. The next day at the hospital she wasn't just distracted, but well-nigh oblivious to the patients in front of her, the bodies laid bare on the operating table. She'd had no practice; built up no immunity. She was like a Pacific island encountering measles for the first time.

'Henry Jones telephoned,' her mother said, when she got home the next evening.

Flora nodded, revealing nothing. Glancing at the hall table, she could see there was no phone number beside Henry's name on the message pad, but she knew he would call again.

'I thought we'd go to Rules,' Henry says, when they are in the taxi.

'Lovely,' says Flora. She has no idea what Rules is, but the name conjures something grown up and expensive. She's conscious of the lingering scent of surgical scrub on her hands, despite the overlay of bath salts. Forever afterwards, anticipation will smell to her of iodine and lavender.

Rules is grown up and expensive, but it's also splendidly old-fashioned, with a menu full of game and potted shrimps. They sit in a corner, beneath a row of hunting prints. Henry orders champagne and oysters, their flesh and serum texture steeped in sexual allusion and giddyingly redolent, too, of the body cavities Flora is familiar with.

'Here's to us,' Henry says, as she lifts the first oyster to her lips, and she smiles at him and swallows, a woman who can handle anything.

3

The sun was sinking as the ferry chuntered south again across the Channel. The clouds sprawled like rumpled bedclothes across the horizon were marbled now with pink and gold: a backdrop, Flora thought, for a scene of high romance. But even as her heart swelled with the exhilaration of escape, misgivings were starting to gather in her mind. The temperature was falling, and she shivered as she stared out at the same stretch of sea she'd crossed once already today.

What had she done? Half an hour ago it had seemed audacious, even admirable, to seize the moment with this grand gesture of liberation. But now, with the light fading and no idea where she was going, it felt more like the wild, futile protest of a child, slipping through the garden gate to run away from home.

In a crowded gallery in London, Lou and Kitty would soon be asking each other where she was. Why hadn't she texted them from Dover? Had she thought, somehow, that her impulsive wish wouldn't come true, and that she'd find herself, after all, heading towards London on the M20? The last of the momentum that had swept her back onto the ferry slid away now with the same disorientating lurch as the boat's swaying movement. In its place there was a glimmer of something cold and unfamiliar that felt uncannily like remorse.

The hotel room was large but plain. white walls, floral curtains in subdued colours, bedspread to match. There was a chest of drawers and a little desk and chair, all made from the same dark, sober wood, and an expanse of polished wooden floor. She'd been lucky to find it, Flora thought. A Google search on her iPhone had spared her the cheerless welcome of the Formule Un or the Ibis. Even so, she felt stranded: cast on her own resources in a way she hadn't faced, quite this starkly, in the weeks since Henry's death. The man on the desk had expressed neither surprise nor pleasure at her late arrival, and she hadn't spoken to anyone else since the ferry docked at Calais. It occurred to her that no one in the world expected anything of her anymore.

She stood for a moment in front of the mirror. Her hair was longer than usual, curling around her ears, and the square jaw, famously pugnacious, was softened by months of strain. So, she asked herself, how is this going to work? Her reflection faced her out, as it had always done, but it didn't offer the reassurance she hoped for. I have no more idea than you, it seemed to say, and its expression alarmed her.

By the time he fell ill, Flora hadn't loved Henry for a long time. At least, that's what she would have said: a convenient gloss. He would have said he loved her, of course. Henry always said he loved her. Not enough, her sister Jean might whisper – Jean who was both more delicate and more ruthless than Flora – but that wasn't the whole story either.

When memory sneaked up on her like this, Flora sometimes thought, with a rush of anguish, of her honeymoon, and sometimes she floundered in search of a name for what she'd lost: something both more complicated and more quotidian than love. It was unfair, she reflected, that life could deliver up an unsatisfactory marriage and then make you regret its ending so keenly – and that the opportunity for reconciliation, near its end, should come at such cost. A cost, indeed, that she was only just beginning to count.

Flora wasn't given to self-pity. Self-pity she saw as the fallback of those without the privilege of free will, or the ability to weigh up side effects and opportunity costs as they exercised it. She had always, she thought now, held herself honestly to account. This thought elicited a draught of reassurance, but it was followed by a flutter of doubt. What exactly could she be held accountable for, among all that had happened in the last sixty years? That was the rub. That was the question staring back at her from the mirror, the reflection she couldn't quite face.

Outside, the sky was dark and starless. It was midnight, although her body clock was so thrown out by travel and emotion that it could have been almost any time at all. Despite her tiredness, Flora wasn't ready to go to bed. She had plenty of books, packed for the trip to Alsace, but she didn't feel like reading. Taking out her phone, she reread her daughters' replies to the text she'd sent from Calais. No reproaches; only a polite curiosity. *Exhibition good* – Lou. *A few surprises* – Kitty. And then, an hour later – *Alice won! All send love* . . . Nothing more.

Flora didn't need reminding that there was precious little waiting for her back in England. Orchards could absorb her energy for a while, despite the improvements she and Henry had made before he died – but interior decoration couldn't replace the operating theatre and the outpatients clinic, the cut and thrust of the conference circuit. And her daughters both had lives of their own: Lou was working towards partnership in a city law firm, and Kitty was doing a postgraduate course in composition at the London College of Music, just as Henry had wanted. She shouldn't forget, Flora thought, how good they'd both been to Henry while he was dying – good to her, too – but certainly they'd be relieved she wasn't coming home yet. They weren't used to taking account of her. She closed her eyes, searching her mind for images of her children. Ordinary moments: little girls in the bath, in the garden. A scattering of memories, she thought. What could she possibly expect of them now, when they'd been raised against the odds, in the interstices of her surgical career?

For the second time that day, an image of Landon came into her head: Landon's address at Henry's funeral, which had succeeded so effortlessly in making her life with Henry – their family life – real and whole, alongside the recitation of Henry's achievements as a public man. Landon who had hardly visited when Henry was ill, but had been such a pillar of strength in the fortnight after his death; whom she had almost allowed herself to rely on for a little while. But she couldn't expect anything of him, either. That was dangerous territory indeed.

Flora moved abruptly away from the window. Her eye fell on the French guide book in her suitcase, and as she picked it up the fold-out map at the back fell open. She tried and failed to concertina it back into place, then carried it over to the desk and spread it out flat. Such a huge country, she thought. She leaned over it, tracing *département* boundaries with her eye; following the Loire and the Rhône, the Seine and the Garonne as they wriggled across the map like coronary arteries; picking out the sharp ridges of the Alps and the Pyrenees. And slowly, slowly, a sort of calm spread through her: something less than happiness, but more than mere resignation. A little like the feeling in theatre when the laparoscope slides into place, offering a first glimpse of the unknown.

It was true, what she'd told the woman on the boat. *I have plenty of time to travel now.* There was no need for a grand plan, no need to make more than one decision at a time. There was more than enough to occupy her here. She'd spent the last week, with Henry's well-meaning cousin, on the eastern side of France: should she head south towards Paris now, or move further west?

4

It was eleven o'clock by the time Lou and Alice left the Taelwyn. Even her gloomiest estimate had been too optimistic, Lou reflected. She wasn't accustomed to being bettered in the game of worst-case scenarios, but she was too tired to care. By the time Alice finally shook the hand of the Chair of Judges and said goodbye, all she could feel was relief.

Alice had driven the minivan to London earlier in the day and left it in an underground car park a few blocks away. They walked along the quiet streets in silence, passing through squares of tall white houses – perfect family houses from some fantasy time in the past, Lou thought, like a set for *The Nutcracker* or *Peter Pan*. The car park was from a different kind of set, dank and dimly lit, ready for an ambush or a shootout. The minivan squawked as they approached, its doors unlocking obediently.

As they drove across Waterloo Bridge and headed down Kennington Road towards the string of long-engulfed villages between central London and the M25, images loomed and faded in Lou's head, a distorted slideshow of the evening behind them. Bacchus, his eyes sharp and knowing, vine leaves wound with terrible delicacy among the strands of his thick hair. Kitty looking at her, oddly blank-faced. Landon, purveying soothing balm. The great swarming sea of people around them all the time.

They had behaved, she thought, as the Joneses did on such occasions: with a kind of equivocation that only partly hid the truth. Not enough had been said, about the sculpture or Flora's absence or anything else; certainly not about Henry, nor how apt the choice of Bacchus was, with its allusions of creativity and joy as well as dissolution and excess. The Joneses had always been expert at reserving their judgement, at preserving a calm exterior. It was, Lou thought, part of the legacy of their childhood.

Lou was accustomed to seeing Kitty as a responsibility – her sometimes wayward, somewhat damaged, little sister. It was hard to believe that Kitty was grown-up now, but there had been a moment this evening when Lou had looked at her and understood that they were feeling the same hotchpotch of conflicting emotions: admiration and affront, pride and embarrassment, affection and antipathy. They'd promised to meet the following week: Bacchus had done that much for them, Lou thought. But she wondered, suddenly, whether Henry's death would bring her closer to Kitty or set them down further apart.

Alice pulled up at a red light, jerking Lou out of her reverie. Lou glanced across at her. Alice's hair was dishevelled, her body tense and upright. Her uncharacteristic tears as she'd accepted the prize medal an hour or two before had owed less to the emotion of winning, Lou understood, than to remorse. She felt a clutch and wriggle in her belly as she remembered that she too had things to explain and to apologise for.

'I'm so sorry,' Alice said again now. 'About Bacchus. About not telling you. I hope I can make amends.'

'There are none to make,' Lou said.

'Well.' Alice kept her eyes on the road. She'd seen how distressed Kitty was; presumably she attributed Lou's silence to the same cause.

'I'm very pleased for you,' Lou said. 'About the prize.'

Where were the words, the courage, to tell Alice about the baby? That would certainly assuage Alice's guilt, and claim it for herself instead. Was that what stopped her? A weary disinclination to be in the wrong for the rest of the journey home? Not just that, Lou knew; nor just the sculpture's confounding of emotions already too complicated to see clearly. No, it was something more primeval. Something about the power the secret knowledge of pregnancy brought: something more familiar to Tudor queens than twenty-first century lawyers, perhaps. This was news for which superstition required the right circumstances, the right reception. She needed to be sure of that before she said anything.

'Remind me how you know Landon Peverell,' Alice asked now.

'He introduced my parents,' Lou said, grateful for the change of subject. 'He and Flora knew each other as children, and he met Henry at Oxford.'

'He doesn't seem very like Henry,' Alice said.

'He's had a sad life,' Lou said. 'His wife's been ill for years; they never had any children.'

She felt a little stab then, a reminder of how the meaning of that phrase had shifted for her. Landon would have made a good father, she thought. Alice glanced at her: there was something softer, easier in her face now.

'I'm glad we didn't go ahead with the baby plan,' she said. 'I hope you don't mind too much.'

Lou opened her mouth, then shut it again. The air around her head seemed to have frozen; for a few moments she could barely breathe. What could she possibly say to Alice now?

She stared through the windscreen at the crisscross of nondescript streets, the shut-up shops, the places still serving pizza and kebabs and curry. The nausea had evaporated, some time when she wasn't paying attention. Perhaps they could stop and eat something. A midnight feast: wasn't that the time for kissing and making up? But the lights had changed, the minivan was accelerating past the garish signs, and the faint waft of garlic and hot meat was gone.

5

Kitty was no stranger to the Piccadilly Line at night. Most evenings the journey home passed almost without her noticing, but occasionally the familiar scene – the echoing ticket hall, the airless tunnels, the lighted train rattling in from the dark – suddenly seemed ominous. Sometimes this happened for no particular reason, but at other times – tonight, for example – it was easier to explain.

She stood near the entrance to the platform, her iPod plugged in and her eyes fixed in an expression of boredom. She'd realised this was one of those off-pitch evenings when she'd noticed a man in a pinstriped suit along the platform and felt a fillip of relief, gone as soon as it was acknowledged. Why shouldn't men in city suits be rapists or murderers? It was the perfect disguise – unless you were a Greek god, and could turn yourself into a shower of gold. Kitty wished suddenly that she'd asked Daniel to come with her this evening. Not for protection, she told herself, but for company.

She looked away, turning her mind deliberately back to the exhibition. Alice was good at suffering, she thought, and impassive cruelty, as well as – but no, she wasn't going to think any more about the figure of Bacchus. Think instead of the agony of Daphne's transformation into a tree: naked arms twisting into stiff twigs, shapely legs taking root. Or Leda, her head pinioned by the swan's sadistic beak. How could you get all that pride and brutality into stone eyes, Kitty wondered, and still make them unmistakably a swan's? How could you show the sweetness of a body so distorted by pain? She knew people asked similar questions about music, but music seemed altogether more straightforward to Kitty. Every detail was coded in the dots on the stave, ready to be recreated each time it was performed – ready to be pored over by students of composition, if they paid proper attention to their studies. But however hard she looked at Alice's sculptures she couldn't fathom how she managed to extract so much emotion from a solid block of stone. Lucky Lou, having someone so talented, so out-of-the-ordinary, to love her.

Kitty had her iPod on shuffle, and as the train approached the soundtrack in her headphones moved from Mia van Arlen to Messiaen. The pin-stripe man sat down opposite her, his attention absorbed by a free paper. As the rich thread of a cello melody filled her ears, Kitty felt her nerves relax at last, absorbing her in the drama of Messiaen's narrative rather than her own.

This was another thing Kitty didn't understand: that people could listen to music as though it was just sound. Sometimes she hated music, wished it didn't exist, but she couldn't ignore it when she heard it; couldn't not feel it. As a little girl she'd understood music better than language for a while. Standing beside her father when she was three or four, listening to a Beethoven quartet, she'd recognised in his face the same emotions she felt, but she couldn't name them. She'd been so overwhelmed by the experience that she'd cried – and then everything had been spoiled, because someone had scooped her up and taken her to bed. After that she'd learned not to betray herself. She'd kept it all inside, her music and what it meant. Even now, alone on the late night tube, she stared ahead as though her attention was focussed on the advertising posters above the pin-stripe man's head, with her mind full of Messiaen.

But when the movement came to an end she turned it off. The events of the evening wouldn't lie quietly, and there were other things on her mind too. It was too much, Kitty thought, to be miserable about her music and her father at the same time. Of course they were connected: it was from Henry that she'd inherited any talent she had, and Henry who'd been responsible for her musical education. But it was tough to find herself wavering in her resolve to abandon the MA course because she'd seen her father's face this evening. It was tough to think that everything she did in the music world would be shaped

41

by him and infused with his memory, but that he'd never again hear anything she heard, or played, or wrote.

And it was just like her mother to disappear just when she could have been – no, it wasn't even that. It would have been worse if Flora had been there to see the statue this evening. She'd disappeared when they were expecting her back, that was all: she'd left them wondering.

It was after midnight when Kitty got out at Wood Green, but the High Road was still busy and brightly lit. When she'd chosen her flat, she'd traded a longer tube journey for a shorter walk to the station, because she liked knowing she could be on the train ten minutes after she woke up, heading anywhere she wanted – but also because she loved the way a tiny bedroom and bathroom and a cupboard-sized kitchen had been carved out of a large Victorian room here, leaving an L-shaped sitting room with a window onto the street. This flat was the first place she'd ever lived alone, and it sometimes felt more like a companion than a home: she was never sure what kind of mood she would find it in. Welcoming tonight, she hoped, starting up the stairs. She could do with –

'Hello,' said a voice from the shadows. A voice she recognised, but even so the shriek of alarm was fully formed before Kitty could stop it.

Daniel had been sitting on the landing with his back against her door: he scrambled to his feet and reached his arms out to hold her.

'Hey – ssh! It's me.'

'I know it's bloody you. What are you doing here? How did you get in?'

'The guy opposite opened the door. He recognised me.'

Kitty was trembling, the pent-up emotion of the evening spilling out now in Daniel's arms. She let him hold her for a moment, paralysed by the familiar push-pull of his presence; the pleasure of remembering his smell, his solidity, the pressure of his hands in the small of her back. Had she really not wanted to see him all this time? Her father's death had been a sea-change, she thought: Life Before had been stopped in its tracks. It had been too hard to start everything up again. Too hard to think about it.

'I haven't seen you for weeks,' Daniel said now, his breath muffling her neck. 'I thought it was about time. I thought . . . I needed to see you, anyway.'

'You scared me.'

'I didn't mean to. I hoped you'd be pleased.'

She and Daniel had met at the auditions for the music college the previous spring. Daniel was nothing like the others – all those musicians who looked as though they'd lived in a dimly-lit practice room for the last decade. Daniel had enough life in him to fuel six people, an electric mix of aloofness and dissatisfaction and vulnerability shimmering through the outward aura of assurance. He'd been given a Rhapsody of Kitty's to play that morning, and she'd been transfixed by his virtuosity, by the way he'd brought her music to life. But she'd felt more than admiration, much more than that. She'd wanted him to look at her, touch her, hold her: she hadn't cared what came of the audition as long as he spoke to her afterwards. Since then there had barely been an hour when she hadn't thought of him, either with longing or with dread.

'So can I come in?' he asked.

Daniel was like a spice whose taste she couldn't remember when it wasn't in her mouth, and longed to recall. Daniel was exhausting.

'Not now,' she said.

He let her go and took a step backward, his eyes on her face. 'It's midnight, Kitty,' he wheedled. 'I've been waiting almost two hours. You're not going to throw me out into the night?'

He sounded almost certain of his chances; there was the slightest undercurrent of a teasing reproof. Was it that, or the small gap of doubt, that triggered something inside her? Kitty looked back at him, at the sweet arch of his cheekbones and the thick curls spilling onto his forehead, and words came out which she seemed to have no hand in.

'You shouldn't have come,' she said. 'It's not fair. You can't . . .'

Even so, she didn't expect him to go. Daniel never gave up without a fight. She turned away from him and put her key in the lock, preparing for the next round.

'All right,' he said. 'If you're sure. I'll see you around.'

Wait, she wanted to say. Or did she? She stood facing the closed door while footsteps shaped themselves on the staircase. In a moment she heard the street door open and close.

Well, that was that, then.

Inside, she turned on the light and stood for a moment looking around, then she kicked off her shoes and threw herself down on the ancient, sagging sofa. Some nights she slept here, like a child in a den, hiding from the grownups and the real world. But tonight, despite her exhaustion, sleep felt a long way away. There was so much she didn't understand, Kitty thought. So much she wanted to say, and ask, and rage against, and she had no idea where to start. Not that it mattered, because there was no one to say any of it to. She hardly knew her sister anymore, her mother was in France, and she'd sent her boyfriend away, cut off everyone else, because her father was dead. Her father whom she had adored and idolised and resented more than anyone in the world.

6

As the days unfolded, Flora's instinct was confirmed: she didn't need an itinerary to explore France. Any road she took was more than satisfactory, leading to a string of interesting towns and villages set in an attractive swathe of countryside. She moved on every day, sometimes following a lead she'd discovered the day before and sometimes picking a direction or a destination at random.

Meanwhile, the story of the tug had been polished for the benefit of her fellow travellers, the Germans and Belgians and Americans she met on the Somme battlefields and at the *chambres d'hôtes* she vastly preferred to hotels. Sometimes she told the tale wryly, implying that it had been a convenient excuse to indulge her whim of turning tail at Dover; sometimes she played up the dramatic intervention of Fate. Either way, having the story to tell meant she didn't have to dwell on Henry's death or her retirement, on anything that had come before the ferry and the vividly recaptured bobbing of the tug. It neatly sidestepped any enquiries about why she was travelling alone or where she was going.

By the end of the week, she had skirted Paris and was heading towards the Loire. The weather had been mixed, the early summer sunshine interspersed with sudden petulant days of rain, as though it were expressing on Flora's behalf the uncertainty and reversals of mood she ought, perhaps, to feel. But as she moved steadily further from home, the sun seemed to have greater conviction each day. Latitude and the advance of the seasons were working together, she thought, to convey her from the temperate English spring towards summer in the heart of France. It was hard to believe so little time had passed since she'd packed her case for that half-forgotten week in Alsace.

'You are making a visit today?' asked Madame over breakfast one day, in a farmhouse south of Blois. Flora's French was progressing slowly, but she was still relieved when her hosts spoke English.

'Maybe,' Flora replied. 'Where would you recommend?'

Madame shrugged; splendidly Gallic, Flora thought.

'There are many famous châteaux nearby. My favourite is Montallon. Not so famous. Not so visited.'

'All right,' Flora said. 'Is it open today?'

'Certainly.'

Madame proffered the coffee pot and Flora accepted a refill. She was growing to like this place. There was nothing especially attractive about the house, but there was something about the way it suited Madame Abelard, a kind of harmony about her occupation of it, that made Flora feel comfortable. Perhaps she would stay a little while, she thought. An idea of how the summer might unfold began to form in her mind: a week here, a week there, a series of stepping stones across France. A journey with a shape to it that she could describe to people. She imagined herself in September, suntanned and fluent in French.

'How long is my room available?' she asked. 'Could I stay a few more days?'

Back in her room, secured now for the rest of the week, Flora took the last few clothes out of her suitcase and hung them in the linseed-scented wardrobe. She thought back to the weeks immediately after Henry's death: the furious spring cleaning, the carloads of junk taken to Oxfam, the guarded expressions of her daughters when they came to visit. All to the good, she thought. What was left was almost anonymous: books stacked neatly in shelves, wardrobes half-empty. No more cupboards full of old china or boxes of ancient magazines. Someone could move in tomorrow, Flora thought, and the idea was strangely pleasing.

Before she could change her mind, she clicked the email icon on her iPhone and looked up the address of a neighbour who ran an estate agency. *Dear Neil,* she typed. *I wonder whether you could find a tenant for Orchards? I am thinking of a summer let, perhaps 3 or 4 months . . .*

*

46

The reason the château of Montallon was not so visited became clear as Flora approached. It was twenty kilometres from the main road along twisting lanes, and the direction signs were half-hidden in the undergrowth. Once or twice Flora had to turn back and hunt down a missed turning. But at last the château came into view, straddling the top of a small hill. Its surroundings must hardly have changed since it was built, Flora thought, the wooded slopes and docile fields of corn and cows. She felt her spirits lift with the sudden exhilaration of the explorer sighting the object of her quest. Round the next corner was a pair of wrought-iron gates, their paintwork gleaming.

Flora parked next to a Volvo with English plates. Through the windscreen she could see a French road map and two child seats. Picturing these parents fretting over sun cream and juice cartons, Flora felt an unexpected failure of will – but she'd come all this way, she told herself firmly. She must go in, now she was here. She locked her car and made her way across the moat (moat!) to the ticket booth.

'*Un, s'il vous plait*,' she said; then, on a questioning rise, '*une?*' and the teenage boy behind the desk grinned as he handed her a leaflet in English.

'It begins there,' he said, pointing. 'You can follow the signs.'

Flora often found the inside of these places less interesting than the outside: something about what was promised by the sweep and curve of ancient stone, and the more mundane reality of the reconstructed interiors. She had limited enthusiasm for kitchens strung with polished brass pans, or four-poster beds with faded hangings. What she liked were the staircases, their steps sculpted by generations of feet, and the fall of light through narrow windows. She also liked seeing these things alone, she'd discovered. Henry had always dawdled or hurried; they had never found a pace to suit them both. She stood for a moment in the château's broad, tiled hall, absorbing both the consolation of this thought and the stab of distress that followed.

She was gazing at the ceiling when the English family appeared – immediately identifiable as the owners of the Volvo. There was an instant of shock when Flora thought she had also recognised the mother as her companion from the ferry, and for that moment the instinct to run away did battle with the desire to greet someone she knew, even slightly, in the middle of a foreign country. But it wasn't the same woman. Of course it wasn't: that family had been on their way back to England. As she had been, Flora reminded herself – another little shock, remembering her audacity that day and how far it had carried her already.

She smiled at the Englishman as he approached, but he didn't notice her. His wife had stopped to point out a suit of armour that stood incongruously against the rococo panelling.

'Come on,' the father said. 'Let's go outside. There's a maze.'

'I'm hungry,' whined the younger boy. 'I want an ice cream.'

'They don't have ice creams,' the mother said. 'I've told you, Joshua. We're here to look at the château.'

'It's so *old* . . .' Flora heard the child say, as he was dragged out through the door. 'Why do we always have to look at *old* things?'

Flora lingered in the château for longer than she might have done. She felt oddly diffident about following the Volvo family outside: she didn't, now, want to be identified as English, certainly not to be suspected of taking an interest in them. Something about the way the man's eyes had swept past her in the hall made her prefer to preserve her anonymity. She hoped they'd have left by the time she emerged, but as she approached the formal gardens she could hear their voices. Apparently they had found a place to buy ice creams after all: the boys brandished the empty sticks like swords while their parents remonstrated fruitlessly.

'Come on,' Flora heard the father say again. 'Let's get going.'

'No no no!' The boys circled, protested, pleaded, all energy and flying limbs. 'Back to the maze! Back to the maze!'

Flora turned right along the terrace as the family headed off in the other direction, then descended the steps to the rose garden. Her mother had loved roses, and Flora could still recite the names of her favourite varieties. Could this pink one be Gertrude Jekyll, or this ivory beauty Glamis Castle? None of them had what her mother would call a proper perfume, though. They were beautiful but scentless – rather like Montallon's carefully preserved interior.

It was almost two o'clock by now, and hotter than she'd bargained for. There was a little café near the entrance, Flora remembered. Madame Abelard's breakfast suddenly seemed a long time ago.

The maze was on the left, halfway to the car park. As she passed it, the sign snagged at Flora's imagination. How often did you find yourself at the entrance to a maze? Why not have a look? Before the impulse faded she turned down a narrow corridor of trees, passing through a welcome band of shade before emerging again into sunlight.

The maze was bigger than she'd imagined, and cleverly positioned so there was no view of the château from inside it: no external landmarks to navigate by. Flora was soon surrounded by high hedges, wandering along blind alleys and facing sudden doublings-back. It was strangely disconcerting, and the heat was stifling now. The sun was directly overhead, and the breeze that brushed the tops of the hedges didn't stir the air beneath. From time to time people passed her, and were lost again. And then she heard familiar voices: the English boys were running along a path not far from her, arguing excitedly about the route.

Flora halted. She felt again an inexplicable reluctance to run into the family – or to be caught wandering alone in the maze. It was as though having to account for herself would spoil everything. She pressed on, hoping that if she put her mind to it she'd find her way swiftly back to the entrance, but it wasn't that easy.

After a few more minutes, triumphant shrieks from the little boys announced their arrival at the centre. Perhaps they would leave now,

Flora thought. But then she heard the mother's voice, drifting through the thick air.

'Joshua! Josh, where are you?'

'You go that way,' Flora heard the father say. 'I'll try down here.'

Despite herself, Flora felt – what? Afraid? Excited? It was as though she was implicated somehow in the family's game of hide and seek – or at least playing out her own subplot, avoiding being seen. Ridiculous, she told herself, but even so, as she wound her way along the narrow passages she scented the thrill of pursuit, the delicious terror of childhood. She was a little girl again, chasing her sister, desperate to catch before she was caught. This way or that? Back to the last turning or round the next corner?

'*Excusez-moi*,' she said, as she squeezed past a gaggle of teenagers.

And then she heard another shout, more urgent than before. 'Joshua? Come back now, Joshua! Where have you got to?'

Staring along an empty alley, Flora felt the beginnings of a sneaking doubt about the situation. There was an echo in the back of her mind of another occasion, another lost child. What had she been thinking of, playing games? She turned abruptly, intent this time on finding the child rather than keeping out of sight.

The convolutions of the maze felt more sinister now. The smell of yew, resinous in the hot sun, reminded Flora of gloomy English churchyards. She stopped for a moment at the next corner, looking about her. She'd been in the maze for long enough now to feel dislocated from the day she'd left behind outside. For an absurd moment she feared that she'd be lost in here forever: she and Joshua, swallowed up by whorls of malevolent evergreen.

'*Avez-vous vu un petit garçon?*' she asked a French couple, the wife puffing along behind her lean-faced husband, and they shook their heads.

After a while Flora found herself at the centre of the maze, but she didn't stop to savour her success. She should go out by a different route, she thought. She blundered along more channels, into more dead ends, round more corners.

Another doubt was rising in her mind now. It was a while since she'd heard the parents calling. Perhaps they'd found the boy and bustled him back to the car park. Perhaps she was being ridiculous, continuing a search that was already over. When she got to the exit, she thought, she'd head for the nearest town and treat herself to a nice lunch, or perhaps . . .

And then there was the exit, and there were the parents and the older boy and, conjured up from somewhere, a gendarme with a pistol holster at his waist.

Flora stared at them. She felt something flood through her, making speech impossible but essential.

'Have you lost your son?' she managed to say. 'Is there anything I can do?'

There was a flicker in the other woman's eyes that Flora recognised, with a shock, as suspicion. She felt her heart thud and tumble. *I'm a doctor*, she wanted to say, as if any of them would care.

And then, before the woman could reply, there was a shout – '*le voilà!*' – and the lean-faced Frenchman lumbered out of the maze, carrying the child in his arms. The look of terror on the boy's face dissolved, the instant he saw his mother, in a torrent of tears.

'*Il est blessé?*' the gendarme asked – 'he's hurt?' – but no one took any notice.

'Why didn't you shout?' the mother was saying, cradling the child in her arms. 'Why didn't you call us, Joshie?'

'*Tout va bien?*' the gendarme tried next, looking at Flora.

'*Je ne sais pas,*' she said. But suddenly she'd had enough. The tableau of the little family had closed in on itself; there was nothing for her here. She was overwhelmed by the sense that she'd made a fool of herself, exposing something she had never meant to reveal. If no one had noticed that only made things worse: it made her invisible as well as absurd.

June 1996

Flora takes a deep breath. She feels her ribcage lift and fall like an unwieldy structure she has no control over, and the terrifying thump of her heart inside it.

'How did it happen?' she asks.

Henry is standing near the window. She recognises his stance almost by instinct. They have played this scene many times before: Henry refusing to commit to conflict, and Flora so paralysed by anger and distress and appalled admiration for his sangfroid that she can hardly speak.

'She just ran away,' he says. He's completely still, not so much as a shrug or the twitch of a frown to give him away. 'I turned my back for a moment, and when I looked for her she'd vanished.'

'Where were you?'

'Clarence Park. Near the pond.'

'She's four.' Flora reaches for the back of a chair, then lets her hand drop. Beside her, on the dressing table, rows of unopened bottles mark the years of Christmas presents, expensive face cream and eau de parfum. She shuts her eyes, trying to imagine herself at the hospital, icy calm, but her voice slips and skids. 'She can't run that fast, Henry. It's open ground. How could she get so far away that you couldn't see her anymore?'

He sighs, and she knows what he's going to say. There's a tiny moment of triumph, just a flicker of it, as he speaks.

'I was with somebody. I was talking to somebody. I took my eyes off her.'

'Who?'

She knows the answer to this question too: not the name, but the meaning of it. This time it's not triumph she feels, but humiliation. She has spent so long not asking, and now she's lost the little piece of dignity that forbearance gave her. And she's risked her child's life, too. It seems clear to her suddenly that this is her fault: she has turned a blind eye, and now Henry has done the same, and Kitty has been put in danger. The beating of her heart is painful; her ribs constrict around it, crushing the turmoil of emotions into a pulp of something so primitive that she can't identify it. My Kitty, she thinks. My precious Kitty. The fact that the child is safe now, sleeping peacefully upstairs, makes little difference to Flora's feelings.

'Her name is Elizabeth,' Henry says. 'She's a cellist.'

He meets her eyes as he speaks, and she can tell there's something for her to read in them. Does he want her to know, or not? But she does know. She knows this woman has been in the shadows for a long time – five or six years now. She knows she's different from the others, the passers-by. For the first time it occurs to her that Henry might leave her; that admitting to Elizabeth's existence might be the first step. Perhaps that might even be the right thing. Perhaps this might be the spur she needs to come to her senses.

A breeze stirs the curtains, and Flora's gaze flicks towards them. Outside the window the light is golden, the promise of a rich sunset foreshadowed in the glow of the terracotta tiles on the barn roof. Something swoops past, close to the sill; a swallow or a bat. At this time of day they are hard to tell apart, similar darting shadows flitting and dipping in pursuit of insects. Other people, she thinks, will be having drinks on the lawn now, entertaining friends, watching their children play.

She nods: the smallest gesture she can manage, and the largest. She says nothing, and Henry says nothing. Then he takes a step towards her, and she can see them both as if from outside the window, lit as clearly in the evening light as the barn and the curtains and the swallows. She starts to cry before he reaches her, because she knows that she won't resist his touch, and that it means nothing will ever change. Even the boiling passion of her love and fear for Kitty isn't enough to alter the terrible, shameful, insoluble tangle of their marriage.

Henry lifts his hand to her face, and kisses her gently.

'Flora,' he says. 'I love you.'

7

It was raining; an unseasonably chilly day. Kitty shivered, wishing she'd worn something warmer. She was early, and she loitered at the spot Lou had suggested, a couple of streets away from Marble Arch in what she thought of as the smart, old-fashioned bit of London. Watching a little girl in a school summer dress being dragged along by an au pair, she longed for a moment for the scratch of gingham seams, the promise of fish fingers for tea.

At last she spotted Lou, hastening towards her under an umbrella. Despite the suit and the briefcase she looked smaller and more inconsequential than Kitty had expected. Kitty hugged her fiercely, as though it was years since they'd seen each other.

'I'm sorry you've been waiting,' Lou said. 'I've got a perfect plan.'

Kitty smiled. That's what Lou used to say when she was little; when their parents were out, or arguing, and Lou had looked after her. Kaftering, Kitty used to call it. *Are you kaftering to me today?*

'Tell me,' she said.

'There's a new Moroccan café on Wigmore Street,' Lou said. 'No one knows about it yet, so it's always quiet. And if you're up for it there's a concert at the Wigmore Hall at 7.30.' Lou looked at her as though sizing something up. 'The Goldberg Variations,' she said. 'Andras Schiff.'

'Will there be any tickets left?' Kitty asked – but she knew the answer already.

'I've bought some,' Lou said. 'Just in case.'

The café was empty apart from a group of men speaking Arabic energetically and with frequent loud laughter. Lou and Kitty sat opposite each other in a booth. Kitty wasn't hungry, but they ordered a couple of *mezze* dishes and some mint tea that arrived almost instantly, hot and sweet and fragrant.

'It's good to see you,' Lou said. 'I'm glad we're doing this.'

'Me too.'

It was odd, Kitty thought, how little they saw of each other. Partly because Lou scuttled home to Alice every night, to what she called their unfashionable corner of Surrey. Partly because while Henry was alive it hadn't seemed right to meet in town rather than at Orchards, and because the whole business of Henry's illness and his rapprochement with Flora had been difficult: because Kitty had been more pleased about that last bit than Lou. But also partly, Kitty thought now, because it still felt as though they belonged to different generations. Lou had been more like an aunt than a sister for most of Kitty's life, and they hadn't yet worked out how to behave with each other as adults.

'So Flora's definitely not coming home,' she said. 'Who'd have guessed that?'

'Have you heard from her?'

'Only an email or two.'

The emails were filled with the names of villages – Quevauvillers, Brueil-en-Vexin, St Rémy-sur-Indre. Kitty supposed these lists were meant to be reassuring, but they felt more like an enigma.

'She's driving down through France, apparently.' She hesitated again. 'It's good, isn't it?' she said. 'I mean, it shows she's enjoying herself. That she's OK.'

'I don't know,' said Lou. 'I honestly don't know what she ...' To Kitty's horror, her sister's face crumpled. 'I'm sorry.' Lou scrubbed at her eyes with her napkin, a rather un-Lou-like gesture 'I'm a bit emotional at the moment.'

'Of course,' said Kitty, but she was surprised, and touched.

'No: there's another reason.' Lou mustered a smile. 'I'm pregnant, actually.'

'Pregnant?' Kitty almost laughed with the shock of it. 'Lou! I'm – I don't know what to say.'

'Congratulations is the usual thing,' said Lou, and Kitty did laugh then, with relief as much as anything. It felt as though she hadn't laughed for weeks.

'How pregnant?' she asked.

'Hardly at all,' said Lou. 'Ten weeks, officially.'

'Alice must be thrilled.'

Lou grimaced: a fleeting twitch, but its meaning was unmistakable. 'I haven't told Alice yet,' she said. 'I haven't told anyone except you.'

'Doesn't she . . .' Kitty stopped, brought up short by a rift opening at her feet; a gap in her understanding. 'But you're going to tell her?'

'I must,' said Lou. 'I know I must. I wanted to – try it out on someone else first.'

'I'm not sure I was the right person,' said Kitty. 'I'm not sure I've said the right things.'

Lou shook her head. 'It was my reaction I was testing, not yours.'

'And?'

A little smile. 'I don't know.' Then a sigh.

Kitty took Lou's hand and stroked it softly. She felt a wash of tenderness for her sister. Lou's skin felt different to hers, as though it was stuck down more firmly over the bones of her hand. As though she'd been put together by a child from felt and pipe cleaners, Kitty thought; a fragile construction. There were so many things she wanted to ask Lou – about Alice and the sculpture and the baby, but about Henry too, and Flora, but she felt . . . reluctant. Embarrassed, almost. She didn't know enough about what Lou thought or felt to be sure of her ground; to know whether they were the right questions. How strange it was that her own sister, her own childhood, should feel, in certain ways, so remote from her – and her sorrow about her father's death was all caught up in the muddle and murk of it. Was it the same for Lou, she wondered? But perhaps this other thing, this baby, had pushed everything else aside in Lou's mind.

The food arrived then, a still life of dishes glistening with olive oil. Lou looked at it without enthusiasm, but she slid the bowls towards them. 'Keep our strength up,' she said. Another childhood phrase, the prelude to a sharing out of illicit sweets. Kitty smiled, acknowledging the allusion.

For a while they said little. Kitty picked the olives out of one dish and a few cubes of chicken from another, and Lou ate even less. Perhaps she had morning sickness, Kitty thought, but she didn't ask. Silence felt easier, as it often did between them. Gradually she felt a fragile sense of wellbeing settle around her, like the tremulous skin on hot milk.

'How's Daniel?' Lou asked.

'I haven't seen him for a while,' Kitty said. That other night didn't count, she told herself: he'd been an apparition then. 'I don't seem to be able to . . .'

She wasn't entirely sure what she meant, but Lou nodded.

'I miss him,' Kitty said then, taking herself by surprise. 'In a way I miss Daniel, but I . . .'

Lou reached across the table and grasped her hand tightly. Kitty waited for her to interpret, to comfort, but instead her sister's lips trembled and her eyes filled with tears again. Kitty looked at her with a pang of distress. She'd been so preoccupied by her own feelings, she thought, that she hadn't taken proper notice of Lou's. Why hadn't she told Alice about the baby? How had Alice not known?

'Oh, Lou,' she said. 'I can see – I can imagine that being pregnant – and the Bacchus thing too . . .'

She stopped. What did she know? But she couldn't bear to think of things going wrong at Veronica Villa. Alice had been so good for Lou, bringing into her life a Midwestern certainty that had always seemed marvellous to Kitty. Henry had said she could carve marble like Donatello, and Kitty had been thrilled by that, too, because

Henry's approbation was something worth having. Or so she'd always assumed. Kitty was beginning to realise that some of the assumptions the Joneses had grown up with, including their assurance of a particular kind of cultural superiority, were rather shameful, except that there had been so little to steer by otherwise that they could be forgiven, perhaps, for clinging to them. And Henry's approval of Alice had been complicated for Lou, Kitty thought now. She'd suspected his motives. But surely the point was that Alice was part of Lou's escape from Henry and his judgements: an alternative compass, as well as an antidote to the hard slog of her career. And Alice loved Lou, that was abundantly clear.

Kitty looked at her sister again, trying to read her expression. Were they both destined to make a mess of their lives, she wondered? Of their relationships, at least? Perhaps that was their inheritance. Perhaps it was the answer to some of those half-formed questions, and the reason they couldn't be spoken.

Lou smiled then, almost convincingly.

'So what do you think about this concert?' she asked.

'Do you want to go?'

'I associate them with you, you know,' Lou said. 'The Goldberg Variations. Dad was sitting at the piano playing them when Mum came home and told us she was pregnant. I've never forgotten that. I tried to learn them later, but they defeated me.'

'Really?' Bach had never been a particular favourite of Kitty's, although Henry had loved Bach, and Kitty's musical tastes often matched his. 'Rather appropriate for our family, I suppose,' she said. 'The Goldberg Variations. All that . . . complexity.'

'The same damn tunes coming back over and over again,' said Lou. 'The Jones Variations, God help us.'

Kitty smiled. That sounded more like Lou, she thought. The Goldberg Variations would always, now, make her think of her family: Flora and

Henry, Lou and Kitty. She liked the idea of them all gathered round the piano, baby Kitty still safe in her mother's womb.

'We'd better go, then,' she said, 'if it's our leitmotif.'

She took her sister's arm as they left the restaurant. The rain had stopped, and they walked up Wigmore Street in watery sunshine.

November 1991

Flora can hear the sound of the piano when she gets out of the car, but it's not until she opens the back door that she realises it's not a record but someone – Henry – playing. As she comes into the house he hesitates over a phrase and stops, then goes back a few bars, repeating the same passage once or twice before playing on.

Flora stands inside the door, listening. There are no lights on at this end of the house, and the darkness of the winter evening enfolds her. She knows this piece: Rachmaninov's Prelude in G minor. It's one of Henry's favourites. He certainly knows it well enough not to stumble, and she assumes it wasn't an error but something more subtle he wanted to correct, a nuance of phrasing or emphasis. She strains her ears, but all she can hear are the notes, the rat-a-tat Russian rhythms and then the melancholy tune: nothing to tell her whether he's playing well or badly, or what mood he's in. She imagines him concentrating, his fingers shaping the arching chords and skittering nimbly over the fast passages, and she yearns for a glimpse, just once, of his insight into music. His pleasure in it, she thinks, is so different from hers.

The piece ends and Flora hesitates, wondering whether to go through to join Henry. But before she can decide, he starts playing again. Something very different this time – Bach, she thinks, pleased that she recognises this too. A lingering, plaintive melody, played so slowly that it almost seems to lay itself bare. To reveal its guts, she thinks: and then she starts, surprised by the surgical image conjured up by some distant part of her mind, and someone turns in response to the slight sound she makes. Lou, standing just inside the sitting room, half-hidden by shadow. Flora's heart skips, partly at the unexpected sight of her daughter, and partly at the notion that they have been listening together, unknowingly complicit.

Lou's movement has caught Henry's attention. He stops playing and calls out.

'Is that Mummy back?'

Lou nods, and Flora comes forward, looking for a smile on her daughter's face. Lou is eight, slight and dark. There's a sharpness about her lately, as her features emerge from babyhood, and a watchfulness that sometimes snags at Flora's notice. She feels a sudden acute desire to be close to Lou, and to be proud of her.

'Is it Mummy?' Henry asks again.

The Mummy comes home to the Daddy and the little girl, Flora thinks, with pleasure and a slight recoil. A familiar feeling; an acknowledgement that nothing is ever that simple. But then she remembers her trump card, and she gathers Lou into her arms.

'That was nice,' she says. 'Play some more.'

She can see the music on the piano now: the Goldberg Variations. Of course. Sitting down in an armchair, she lifts Lou onto her lap. Henry starts playing again, and Flora can feel the music enclosing them all, filling the rich russet and gold space of the room. She has a sudden sense that they are not themselves, but characters in a story; that it's possible for them to be people other than those they have been. She sees them, just for a moment, as other people might. Perhaps as the imagined occupants of the painting of this room that hangs over the mantelpiece, given to them for Christmas last year by Nick Comyn. Given to Henry, really, although Nick always makes a point, in his slightly creepy way, of including them both in the dedication.

The languid theme comes to an end and Henry plunges into the first variation, each hand darting about in different directions and the tune emerging occasionally above the tumult. Flora remembers Henry talking about this piece too, about the difficult beauty of it and the mathematical precision with which it was plotted. She listens to the music rising from the piano and grasps for another parallel from her own world, the flow of blood and the cutting and suturing of tissues. Stitching together happiness, she thinks, and she squeezes Lou tight.

'Enough,' says Henry, after another variation. He turns to them, smiling, almost self-conscious. 'Time for supper, I think. We waited for you.'

Flora hasn't thought about how she'll break her news. She hadn't known for sure that she'd tell them tonight, but it seems inevitable now: the tide has carried them to this moment. She lifts Lou down and stands up, keeping her hand on her daughter's shoulder.

'I've got something to tell you,' she says. 'Something that will please you both very much, I hope.'

Henry's delight is almost too much for her, but she holds her nerve. It's OK, she thinks, to allow him – and herself – this pleasure. And they are both taken up with Lou. Flora realises, with a shot of remorse, that she hadn't really thought about how Lou would feel. She'd imagined her as a big sister, enjoying the responsibility and in due course the company, but not the immediate adjustment. The strength of her reaction is unexpected for a child who guards her emotions so carefully. Flora is touched that Lou is so thrilled by the idea of having a younger sibling, but she can tell there's more to it than that. Henry can tell, too.

'We'll be a proper family, won't we, Looby Lou?' he says, as they sit down to the *salade niçoise* – hopelessly unseasonal – that has been waiting in the fridge.

'Three's a proper family,' Flora objects, her antennae straining to pick up Lou's sensitivities. She doesn't want her daughter to feel that she hasn't been enough, on her own, to hold her parents together. Although isn't that, in a manner of speaking, exactly what Flora has been thinking?

'What will we call the baby?' Lou asks. 'Can we call her Kitty?'

'If she's a girl, of course we can.' Flora smiles. Lou hasn't ever had dolls, and her guinea pigs, Spot and Blot, live a life of neglect in an outhouse. Does she wish maternal instincts on her daughter, she wonders? She catches Henry looking at her across the table – the kind of look she usually, cravenly, yearns for – and feels again that twist of irony that has become so familiar. Henry lifts his glass in a salute.

'Here's to Kitty,' he says, 'and her safe arrival.'

8

Taking refuge in the Ladies at Waterloo station, Lou yielded to the familiar ravages of vomiting. She'd missed the ten fifteen train, and she was almost grateful for the wait for the next one and the opportunity to gather herself.

She'd imagined morning sickness, once upon a time, as a symptom you could take or leave. Not exactly a sign of weakness, but a particular kind of experience one could opt for. But that illusion was long gone. She was besieged by her own body, she thought now; by a constant disquieting awareness of physical frailty.

It had been a mistake to go to the concert this evening: it had made it too late an evening for her. She'd thought of leaving at the interval, but Kitty had been enjoying the music and Lou hadn't wanted to admit how dreadful she felt. She wondered why that was. A kind of shyness, perhaps. A reluctance to show her hand. *I'd never have guessed you wanted a baby*, Kitty had said, and she'd wanted to say, *neither would I, frankly.*

Motherhood certainly wasn't something she'd ever imagined for herself. She'd known early on that she wasn't going to be part of a conventional family when she grew up. Her parents had gay friends, Henry especially, but none of them had children. And when she'd looked at her mother's life, the part of it she'd wanted for herself was the career, the thrill of striving and success. Certainly not the husband – even a better husband than Henry – and not the children either, the complications and compromises they brought. When she'd found Alice, and the two of them found Veronica Villa, that had seemed all she could want, short of partnership at Harvers and Green.

But then . . . but then.

The idea had come upon her gradually. Motherhood shared could be fun; it could be easier than it had been for Flora. Alice had been surprised, perhaps even taken aback, but in the end she'd agreed to come along to the clinic. By then, Lou had a plan. She was older by a couple of years, so it made sense for her to try first for a pregnancy. Alice's work was more flexible, her income less relied-on: she could do the bulk of the childcare once Lou's maternity leave was over.

Lou shivered a little, recalling the cheerful practicality with which she'd thought it all through. The violence of her symptoms felt like a warning: if the first stage was so dramatic in its effects, how would she cope when the baby was a baby, rather than a thing like a seahorse deep inside her belly? Perhaps Alice had understood better the audacity of making a new life and being responsible for it. But then – how could she explain her sudden decision to go it alone at the clinic except as a need to ditch rationality and plunge into the unknown on her own terms, with her own resources? That was where her instincts had led, and she'd believed in them. But now her own resources seemed, for the first time ever, uncertain. Pregnancy was so much more momentous than you would guess from watching other people. There was a terrible hubris about it: the ultimate hubris of mortality, fertility, reproduction: of being merely another living organism, after all. She couldn't do it without Alice.

Alice had grown up in rural Iowa, the daughter of a cattle farmer and a physiotherapist. She had inherited their competence, Lou used to say. She'd learned from them to deliver a calf from a block of stone, and to coax marble limbs to the right angle. Alice had always smiled when Lou said things like that, indulging Lou's fancy-pants notions. Early on, she'd thought a lot of what Lou said was fancy, in one way or another, and Lou had been equally fascinated by her bizarre combination of farming lore and acquaintance with contemporary art. Lou could never decide whether Alice was a wild creative spirit or a conservative farm girl at heart. Her body was all broad arable plains and then that wonderful hair, that sleek copper-coloured skein that she tossed so casually into thick braids or wound up in a loose suffragette knot. Alice had always seemed a little different every time Lou looked at her; there was always a shock of surprise and pleasure when she moved, or spoke, or came into view. I am what I am, Alice said. What you see is what you get. But it was as though Lou looked at Alice, every time, down a kaleidoscope that shifted mysteriously with each glance.

They'd met in a surprising way, stuck on a broken-down train between Glasgow and Carlisle. Alice was heading south from art school and Lou had been visiting a university friend in Skye. Lou remembered Alice clad in the same colours as the fells that day, a marvel of greens and purples and greys, with the palest pink flush in her cheeks and her hair worn long and loose. They'd filled the day with talk, uncovering a mutual fascination that was clearly requited but could never, Lou thought, be sated. She had felt her sharp edges, her secret hiding places, her fearsome bulwarks and barricades soften and yield in a way she had never thought possible. Five years later, it was impossible to imagine life – to imagine anything – without Alice.

Gathering herself now, Lou splashed water on her face. She looked better than she felt; that was a consolation. She tried to imagine Alice coming towards her across the station concourse, just as she'd done at the private view: Alice elegant in that green trouser suit or four-square in her dusty work clothes. The image filled her with doubt as well as longing. In an hour she'd be home, she told herself, and she would find – she would speak – the right words. Everything would be all right.

The train seats felt harder than they did in the mornings, the lights in the carriage brash and unforgiving. As they rolled along the commuter line, Lou imagined the people who got off at each station going back to their homes and families, to lives she couldn't help thinking of as simpler than hers. Simpler than Kitty's, too, she thought, with one of those wrenches of sentiment, unforeseen and disproportionate, that had visited her several times lately.

Was Kitty's heart really in her course, Lou wondered? And could she possibly earn a living from music, however talented she was? Even Henry – hadn't he been able to do what he did, to sustain his patchwork career as critic and compère and *eminence grise*, because of Flora's income? She remembered Henry watching Kitty play the piano when she was a little girl, and the swell of emotion settled into a familiar lapping awareness of sorrow and regret and pity.

Lou herself had been a proficient pianist by the time she left school. She'd sailed through grade after grade of exams, banging out scales and learning pieces with ruthless determination. After Grade 8 she'd worked her way through the preludes and fugues of the *Well Tempered Clavier*, one key after another, but she'd been surprised when people said she must love it, to practise so hard, or that it must be a wonderful gift. She played the piano in the same way as she drove a car, Lou thought now, carefully and without error. It had never occurred to her that music could be the central purpose of her life: she'd always known she'd settle for something that relied on thinking, not feeling. The law suited her perfectly. It made her feel safe.

If either of them had the kind of musical gift Henry recognised it was Kitty, but she hadn't been an obvious prodigy. As a tiny child she would climb onto the piano stool and pick out tunes – carols or pop songs or ditties she made up herself – but if anyone praised her or asked her to do it again, she'd scowl and slam the lid shut. Later, she learned the cello and the flute, then took up percussion, then for a short time the harp: too many instruments to get any good at any of them. She'd landed up at music college this year, Lou assumed, partly to please her parents and partly because it put off the evil hour of deciding what to do with her life, after scraping her way through a degree in English and drama. What came next for Kitty, Lou thought, was almost as big a question as what came next for Flora. Let alone what came next for Lou herself.

When the train finally pulled into Flockhurst, Lou was almost too tired to climb the stairs to the car park. But she couldn't put it off any longer, she told herself. She had to tell Alice about the baby tonight.

Alice was already in bed when she got home; that was the first thing that threw her. Alice usually waited up for her, and that was what Lou had imagined: sitting across the kitchen table, face to face; the kettle boiled, perhaps, for peppermint tea.

'Hi!' Alice had been reading; she sat up when Lou came into the room. 'I wasn't sure when to expect you. Did you have a good time?'

Alice's face was shiny with moisturiser. Lou caught a whiff of its familiar vanilla scent and her stomach clenched.

'I've got something to tell you,' she said. A tiny pause. 'I'm pregnant, actually.' There, those were the words. That was all it took.

'What?'

'I'm pregnant. I did it. The insemination, at the clinic. The donor we chose.'

'When?'

'A couple of weeks before Henry died.' Lou still couldn't read anything in Alice's face. She attempted a smile, but it felt more like a twitch, a nervous tic. 'It worked first time.'

'I see.'

'I know we agreed to wait,' Lou said, a tremor creeping into her voice. She hadn't moved from the end of the bed: there was a two metre stretch of white linen between them. 'I hoped . . .'

'Pregnant,' said Alice, as though she still wasn't sure she'd heard Lou correctly. 'But – my goodness, Lou. I've noticed you've been – off colour, and I wondered . . . but I told myself you couldn't be; that you'd never have done it without me.'

Lou said nothing.

'So when did you find out?' Alice asked. 'That it had – worked?'

'The week before last,' said Lou. 'Just before the Morris Prize show.'

'And you didn't want to tell me while I was caught up in all that?'

This was a lifebelt, Lou recognised that, but somehow it seemed to be just out of her reach. It was over a week since the show, anyway.

'I don't know,' she said. *I haven't really been myself,* she thought. *It's all been a bit overwhelming.* Either of those would do. Or indeed the truth: *I might have told you sooner, but in the car that evening you said . . .*

'I'm telling you now, anyway,' she said. 'I hoped you'd be pleased.'

Alice looked at her for a moment, then raised her eyebrows. Whatever they had been hovering on the brink of, Lou realised, this was the moment when it became impossible to escape it.

'Don't look at me like that,' she said. 'People never used to say anything for three months, not even to their husbands.'

'I'm not your husband,' Alice said.

Lou gave a snort of – what? Disbelief? But she could feel herself trembling, and nausea rising ineluctably. Alice should have got out of bed, she thought. She should have tried harder to understand. She should have been happy, despite everything. Tears pressed infuriatingly in her eyes.

'I guess this is my punishment,' Alice said.

'For what?'

'For the sculpture. The Bacchus.'

'For God's sake.' Lou was suddenly furious. Furious and sorry for herself and horribly, horribly, tired. She swung round and headed for the door. Something resentful and deadly was controlling her now; something she hadn't known she had inside her. Punishment, indeed. How could the baby be a punishment?

'Lou . . .'

Lou didn't turn round. It was too late, she thought, with another stab of anger. Too late for Alice to regret her righteous indignation. She swept out of the door and slammed it shut behind her.

In the bathroom, Lou brushed her teeth and washed her face with exaggerated care, then she took a clean pair of pyjamas out of the airing cupboard. The bedroom door, clearly in view down the corridor, stayed shut. The virago inside her was silent now, watching her.

She'd got it wrong, of course, said the wrong thing just now and done the wrong thing ten weeks ago, but surely . . . Of course it wasn't a question of tit for tat; she hated that concept. But what Alice had done, giving Henry's face to that hateful statue, had been wrong too. She'd accepted Alice's explanations – that she'd been carried away by the idea, that she hadn't wanted to upset Lou by telling her, that she'd hoped the sculpture would be so powerful that Lou would understand. Lou hadn't even pointed out that those three explanations contradicted each other. She'd smiled when everyone agreed Bacchus had swayed the judges' vote in Alice's favour.

The spare room bed was horrible, Lou thought, but more than that she wanted . . .

Alice was sitting exactly as she'd left her. Her hair hung around her shoulders as though it had been poured, molten, over her head. Lou gazed at her, full of fear and desire.

'Hi,' Alice said at last, her voice flat.

Lou waited, but there was nothing more. She felt another prop crumble inside her. Big-hearted, whole-hearted, warm-hearted Alice was supposed to do better than this. For a moment Lou was sure she was going to cry again. She thought of Flora, of all those showdowns with Henry: how had she managed it?

And then she gathered her self-possession.

'I need my pillow,' she said.

9

Flora was grateful to wake to the sound of rain the morning after her visit to Montallon, giving her an excuse to do nothing, go nowhere. She stayed in bed, missing the hour for Madame Abelard's breakfast. A terrible blankness filled her mind this morning, as though the cheerful film she'd been watching for the last week or so – *The New Life of Flora*, or some such catchy feel-good title – had simply cut out. Perhaps if she lay still for long enough, she thought, the next reel might start of its own accord without her having to write the script, arrange the casting, seek out locations. The effort of all that was too much for her: too much to expect, day after day. She'd never had to think of things to do before, and the last six months, six weeks, six days had exhausted her resources. What she needed this morning was for Henry to tempt her out of bed with the suggestion of lunch in the next village: one of those twelve Euro workmen's lunches he loved so much, with four courses and a pichet of wine, a view of the church or the boules court. She felt her throat fill with emotion she didn't have the will to resist.

Her bedroom window looked out on trees and fields, but she didn't open the curtains. Instead she gazed at their *toile de jouy* pattern, watching the little figures come into focus and then fade again as clouds moved across the sky behind them. The yellowed linings gave an impression of high summer that was belied by the steady splash of rain on the glass. The milkmaids and shepherds, busy with their carefree lives, looked incongruously light-hearted, but Flora was past caring. Let the rest of the world be busy and carefree: she would stay here under the covers where nothing would be asked of her; where there were no mazes to lose her way in.

She was half-asleep again when someone knocked at the door. Madame Abelard came into the room, carrying a tray.

'I bring you breakfast,' she said.

Flora looked at her with an unfamiliar feeling: the submissive gratitude of someone at the mercy of other people's kindness.

'Thank you,' she said.

'You are unwell, or tired?' Madame enquired.

'Tired,' Flora said.

Madame nodded. 'So, I bring you breakfast.'

She put the tray down on the bedside table and moved over to the window. Silhouetted against the muffled light she looked like one of the milkmaids, tall and very thin, neither quite as elegant nor quite as well-preserved as one might expect of a Frenchwoman her age. She moved like a puppet, in a sequence of little jolts that gave an impression of impulsiveness.

'You prefer the curtains closed?'

'I don't mind.'

With a shrug, she twitched them open. 'You can see the rain,' she said. 'I think it will stop, but not soon.'

Flora nodded. She looked at the tray beside the bed and felt the choke of tears again.

'Hmm,' said Madame, not looking at her. 'So, I leave you.'

For a minute or two Flora didn't move, waiting for Madame's footsteps to disappear down the staircase. When she sat up and looked properly at the breakfast tray – white china on a crocheted cloth, and two kinds of jam in little dishes – it seemed the nicest thing anyone had done for her for a very long time. The jam was beautiful, like liquid jewels, the croissants golden and crisp. She could hardly bear to disturb the arrangement, but at length she tore the corner off a croissant and dipped it into one of the dishes of jam. She tried one sort and then the other, then both together: the red one was very tart, the amber one sweeter. Both delicious, and – she assumed – home made. Redcurrant, perhaps, and apricot?

For a while she was entirely absorbed by the architecture of taste. There could be a whole spectrum of jam, she thought, with different shades of colour and flavour for every nuance of mood or desire. It reminded her of a picture from an old book showing the arrangement of taste buds on the tongue, bitter and sweet and sour, like the zoning of faculties on a Victorian phrenology head. Nonsense, she knew, but she was strangely charmed by the idea that human sensation could be mapped so tidily.

The coffee was nearly cold by the time she poured it, and stronger than she really liked, but she drank it dutifully, a sip at a time. When she'd finished she climbed out of bed and washed everything up in the tiny hand basin in the corner of the room, then arranged the crockery back on the tray and placed it, after a moment's hesitation, outside her door. She would have liked to let Madame know how much she'd enjoyed it all, how touched she had been by her kindness, but for the moment leaving the dishes neatly stacked was the best she could do.

Now that she was out of bed, Flora pulled on a jumper over her nightdress and inspected the pile of books on the chest of drawers. Several had been given to her after Henry died – a safe gift for the bereaved, she thought wryly. She ought to be amused by the variety of titles chosen for her, from garish chick lit to hefty biographies, respectfully reviewed on the back cover. But she could see that she needed something to read now, if only to satisfy Madame if she should look in again. She picked up *Persuasion* and took it back to bed with her. Good, she thought. This was a perfectly acceptable way to spend the day.

Lunchtime came and went without a sound from elsewhere in the house, and the preoccupations of Anne Elliot held sway in Flora's mind. But as the afternoon wore on, she felt her attention slipping reluctantly away from eighteenth-century Bath and a dilemma sidling into the anaesthetic formlessness of the day. Something – her upbringing, or the work ethic of a lifetime? – told her that however sorry you felt for yourself, staying in bed beyond a certain point was no longer lazy and luxurious but obstinate, perhaps even deliberately nihilistic.

She glanced at the clock. It was a quarter to four, later than she'd thought. Almost too late to go out. She read a few more pages, a seesaw tipping in her head between inertia and restlessness, until the confinement of her room was finally more than she could bear.

Putting on the same clothes she'd worn the day before, Flora went quietly downstairs. Madame was in the hall, a letter in her hand, and for a dizzy moment Flora had the impression she'd been waiting for her to appear, expecting her at just this moment.

'You've been sleeping?' she asked. 'You feel better?'

'Yes,' said Flora. 'Thank you for the breakfast.'

Madame Abelard gave a little smile, as though it was nothing, not a thing worth mentioning.

'The rain is less. I can give you a coat, if you want. It will be pleasant to walk now. There is a nice path to the village.'

'Thank you.'

The village shop would just be reopening for the afternoon, Flora remembered. She felt a surge of relief, as though her behaviour had been given a rational frame: she was emerging in time for something, after all.

Madame's raincoat was too long for her. It swished against the tall grass as she crossed the field, following the shortcut to the village. Only a slight drizzle was falling now, but everything was steeped in water, every leaf and blade coated with a fresh sheen. Flora had never been a child of Nature, but it was hard to resist the imagery of renewal, the tangible sense of the seasons turning, the crops ripening. Perhaps, if she opened her mind to it, the landscape would imprint itself on the blank screen in her head. Perhaps it would start to shape the next reel of the film.

The village shop was tiny, but surprisingly well stocked. As well as tins and packets (three kinds of cassoulet, but no instant coffee) it offered bread baked on the premises and a counter that sold cheese and charcuterie by weight. The young woman behind the till greeted Flora politely. Flora wandered along the shelves, savouring the pleasure of the unfamiliar wares, while an elderly woman completed her purchases at the counter.

She was negotiating for a *petit pain* and a couple of slices of ham when an English voice spoke behind her.

'Hello.'

Flora turned to see a man of about her age, tall and greying and squarely built, wearing Englishman-abroad chinos.

'Hello,' she said, giving the word as little inflection as she could manage. After yesterday, English company really wasn't what she wanted, and the English male aroused a reflex suspicion honed by years of experience. But the man grinned, as though pleased with his find.

'I thought you were English,' he said. 'I saw you in your car the other day. Are you staying in the village?'

'Outside it.'

'Ah, chez Abelard?'

'Yes.' There was a pause. 'You?' Flora asked.

He cocked his head vaguely towards the door of the shop. 'I have a house round the corner. I'm Martin Carver.'

'Flora Macintyre.'

Flora took her parcels from the shopkeeper and handed over a twenty Euro note. She hoped the man would take her place at the counter now and let the conversation lapse, but he didn't move when she stepped aside to make room for him. She felt a flash of annoyance, but she was conscious of something else too. Curiosity, perhaps, or the scent of a challenge.

'Staying long?' he asked.

'I'm not sure yet. A few days.'

'Come and have a drink,' he said. 'It's only two minutes away.'

Flora shook her head with a smile she hoped was polite but firm. 'The *table d'hôte* awaits,' she said.

Martin Carver pulled a face: Flora recognised the amused pout of the middle-aged man flouted in a small and reasonable request.

'Cup of tea?' he said. 'I can run you back to the Abelards' afterwards.'

Flora stared at him. She had no idea, really, whether he was being rude, or whether she was – but what good was forty years in the NHS, she asked herself, if she couldn't refuse a cup of tea? What on earth would Mark Upward think – infamous Mark Upward, whose name, perfect fodder for surgical wit, was never invoked in jest by his juniors, and whom she'd beaten to the clinical directorship of surgery only five years before?

'That's kind,' she said, 'but no, thanks.'

Martin's face cleared. 'Hubby waiting, I expect,' he said. 'Stupid of me. Not that I meant . . .'

'My husband's dead,' said Flora. 'Two months ago.'

She regretted those last three words as soon as they were spoken. They were superfluous, and they changed her reply into one that might be mistaken for *feel sorry for me*. But Martin Carver spared her any compunction on that score.

'No excuse then,' he said, and although the laugh that followed indicated quite clearly that he realised he'd hit the wrong note, it gave Flora an exit she didn't hesitate to take. Slipping her purchases into the capacious pocket of Madame Abelard's coat, she moved decisively towards the door.

'Perhaps we'll run into each other again,' Martin said.

Flora wasn't deceived by the forlorn note in his voice. As she left the shop, she felt a swell of triumph.

She took the longer way back to the Abelards'. The road led past the Mairie, where the Tricolore idled on a flagpole, then circled the church, built of the same white Touraine stone as the rest of St Rémy and boasting a fine altarpiece that Flora hadn't yet seen. She crossed the bridge beneath which a little river flowed quietly, fringed with reeds and an abundance of yellow flowers. Just beyond the last of the houses, she turned off onto the footpath that led through the woods.

The rain had stopped entirely now, and the woods were filled with a lightness and stillness that came as a surprise. Flora's footsteps were muffled by leaf mould and the insulating canopy of trees; there was hardly a bird to break the silence. It was singularly peaceful, but she felt something more than that, something more subtle: a lack of expectation or anticipation. The day was simply being. The world was simply being. The interval of calm after rain could have been provided as an object lesson.

And then it occurred to her that she had made a mistake with Martin Carver.

She stopped, literally brought up short, while the scene in the shop replayed itself in her mind. She was on her own in a foreign country, surely entitled to resist the approaches of strange men, and he had been unduly persistent. But she knew he hadn't meant to offend; his final faux pas had made him, if anything, less unlikeable in her eyes. She knew all about men like him – and there was no need, nowadays, to see them all off as a matter of course. He'd offered her a drink, and she hadn't stopped to consider whether his motives might be straightforward or his company interesting. Perhaps it was her own motives, her own feelings, that she hadn't wanted to scrutinise.

Flora looked up at the fragments of sky between the branches, streaked now with purple and grey. She remembered this feeling from childhood, from the many times she'd ignored her mother's wishes for the sake of it: the empty pleasure of prevailing. She'd felt it since then too, more often than she liked to admit. Well, she thought; spilt milk. Perhaps after all she'd move on somewhere new tomorrow, or the next day. There was plenty more of France to see. There was the whole atlas, pages and pages of villages like this one. But she knew, even as she thought it, that perpetual motion wasn't the answer. She couldn't become a nomad, passing unnoticed through the land and moving on whenever she stopped being a stranger. That was no way to live.

She shook her head a little, a characteristic reflex dismissal of uncomfortable thoughts, and went on up the path until she emerged again into the fields where the Abelards' cows, as pale and creamy as the local stone, grazed quietly in the evening sunshine.

10

The hall was empty when Flora pushed open the heavy front door, but while she was hanging up her borrowed raincoat Madame Abelard appeared from the back of the house. Materialising, Flora thought, like the spirit of the place.

'You had a good walk?' she asked.

'Yes, thank you.'

'The dinner is at eight o'clock. You will join us?'

Flora's spirits rose. Madame Abelard didn't cook for her guests every evening, and despite what she'd said to Martin Carver, Flora hadn't been sure this was a *table d'hôte* night. The roll and ham she'd bought in the shop would keep until tomorrow: she felt suddenly that she'd spent quite enough time alone today.

'Certainly,' she said.

Madame's dining room was furnished with heavy oak pieces that looked as though they had been in the family for generations, but her china was light and delicate and there were always flowers on the table. Flora wondered, as she took her seat, whether she and her husband – who never appeared, never played any part in the *chambres d'hôtes* operation – ate the same delicious food, off the same china, as the guests who passed through their house.

It was fortunate that Flora was disposed to be friendly this evening, since a Swiss-German couple who'd arrived that afternoon were keen to practise their English.

'What region of England are you from?' asked the man, as they ate their soup. Friedrich, he was called. Friedrich and Elisabeth, round-cheeked and well-dressed, leaning forward slightly in their eagerness to communicate.

'Not far from London,' Flora said. 'About an hour away.'

'The Cotswolds?'

'Not quite.'

'We have been to the Cotswolds.' Friedrich beamed. 'It is very beautiful. We like England very much.'

Flora smiled too, spooning up the last of her soup.

'It was raining hard today,' Friedrich ventured next. 'We were in the car all day. *Mais le temps fera mieux demain, n'est-ce pas, Madame?*'

'*Oui, j'espère.*'

Madame Abelard removed the soup bowls efficiently, and reappeared a few moments later with a platter of roast pork, ready sliced and doused in gravy. There were roast potatoes too, smaller and crispier than the floury English type, and a bowl of courgettes cooked to a sweet softness. Flora watched hungrily as Madame dished it up.

'That smells wonderful,' she said. 'What herb is that?'

'*Genévrier,*' Madame said. 'Geniper.'

'Juniper,' offered Friedrich. 'Like for gin.' He smiled again. 'It is very good with pork. It makes it taste like boar.'

The emphasis he placed on the last word made Flora think of someone reading a story to a child and putting too much into the wolf's menacing voice. Madame's eyes met hers as she passed the plates around, and Flora thought she saw a thin smile.

'You have an appetite, after your walk?' Madame asked.

'Yes,' said Flora.

'And you have met Monsieur Carver?'

'Monsieur who?'

'Monsieur Martin.' Madame's pronunciation fell between the English and French forms: it took Flora a moment to understand. 'He telephoned before dinner. To apologise.'

'For what?' Flora could feel her heart accelerating, and she wished it wouldn't.

Madame shrugged. 'He would like you to go to his house on Friday, for lunch. It is a very beautiful house.'

Flora said nothing. Was the beauty of the house Madame's opinion, she wondered, or part of the sales pitch Martin Carver had put her up to?

'We understand you have visited the château of Montallon,' Friedrich said. 'We are planning to go there tomorrow.'

Flora felt a little slump in her stomach. Montallon and Martin Carver, she thought. It seemed impossible to resist associations, however lightly one travelled.

'It's quite a journey from here,' she said – then, with an effort, 'but it's certainly worth a visit. The gardens are lovely.'

'Monsieur Martin is a wine merchant,' said Madame Abelard.

'Is that so?' said Flora. It was the wrong phrase, unnecessarily ungracious, but none of them would understand that. None of them, she thought with a mixture of relief and weariness, understood more than the surface inflection of her language, and she understood even less of theirs.

There was cheese to follow, and a *tarte aux abricots* which would no doubt be delicious, but when Flora had finished her pork she lifted her hands in apology.

'I'm rather tired,' she said. 'I'm going to get an early night, if you'll excuse me.'

There were brief murmurings of concern and regret, then the clatter of plates being cleared. As she slipped out of the door, Flora heard Friedrich switch back into French.

'*C'était délicieux, Madame,*' he said. '*Mes compliments.*'

Persuasion was still sitting on Flora's bedside table: she stood for a moment staring down at it before moving over to the window. The curtains were open and the sky looked very dark after the yellow glow inside. The clock on the dressing table said nine thirty. Flora looked around at the room's modest traces of occupation: the little case, empty now, sitting under a chair; the pile of books; the washbag beside the basin.

What did she think she was doing, escaping from the dinner table like that? They were perfectly pleasant, Friedrich and Elisabeth. The world was full of people like them, and Martin Carver. She might as well get used to them. Why not taste the local cheese, hear about the artisan *fromager* in the next valley, compliment Madame on her *tarte*?

She put her hand on the window frame and pushed it open, letting in a draught of night air, cold and faintly scented by the garden. Without warning the ache of grief for Henry flooded her body: just that, a sudden engorgement, like water soaking through a sponge. Not so much an emotion as a physical sensation, a spreading stain, impossible to resist or to disguise.

This was why, she thought: why she couldn't bear multilingual Friedrich or the cheesemakers' decades of experience. Why the spell cast by the woods could only throw a veil over her situation for a little while. If it were as simple as water, as sorrow, there was some hope that it would diminish over time. But the fury she felt – at Henry, for wasting so much of their happiness on other people, and at herself, of course at herself too – none of that would evaporate so easily. Fury and regret and disappointment. No point denying it: the wrong decisions. The wrong priorities.

Flora collected herself: no, not that. She'd done her best, kept faith with her choices – not quite a pioneer, but a woman who'd forged her own path. She couldn't allow herself to wish she'd done things differently, despite the difficulties and sacrifices and lost opportunities. Not even choosing Henry. Better Henry than a man she was bored by, or had never loved. He'd been right about that.

Outside in the garden the trees shifted slightly in the breeze. The night sky stretched away, no stars visible, no horizon in sight. The familiar refrain returned to her head: a whole world left to her, and what was she to do with it? What more was there to want from life? That was the crux of it. She'd got what she wanted, as far as anyone gets what they want from life, and now it was all gone. The professional acclaim, the intellectual challenge, the satisfaction of keeping everything afloat all those years: what had they left her with? The same blank sheet she'd started out with. Why must everything happen at once in life, and end all at once too? Why hadn't anyone told her to plan for this, investing a little time, year by year; laying down a nest-egg of interest or habit or disposition to keep her comfortable in her retirement?

11

The grand Victorian façade of the music college, its white stucco newly painted, shone in the sunlight. The central panel rose to an arch spanning the full height of the building, with two figures that could be nymphs or angels reclining just below the summit. Heaven might be a bit like this, Kitty thought as she approached the familiar portico: beautiful, but rather intimidating. Somewhere you should be glad to be admitted, but weren't quite sure you wanted to be part of.

She climbed the broad steps, her old school satchel slung over her shoulder. She'd found it at home after Henry died, chucked in a cupboard years before and forgotten, and it had become one of her props this year. One of the details she'd added to the persona of the music student, as much to convince herself as anyone else.

Professor Davidson's room was on the third floor. Kitty knocked and waited. The door opened, as always, on the count of ten, with a flourish that was too business-like to be theatrical. The room was sparsely but elegantly furnished – a wide desk, a piano, several oak chairs. Its tall windows overlooked the busy road, and the college's high spec glazing reduced the scene below to a silent movie, buses and taxis moving noiselessly past.

'How are you, Kitty?'

Janet Davidson looked the part for a professor of composition, Kitty thought, tall and thin, with white hair sweeping past her shoulders. If this was Heaven, she was definitely God. Kitty accepted the chair opposite her and smiled, conscious that she didn't have much else to offer.

'OK,' she said.

Professor Davidson waited for her to say more, then cleared her throat: a familiar tic, enough to strike terror into most of her students, but not Kitty.

'You know it's an honour to be selected for the showcase series, Kitty,' she said – a statement, not a question, Kitty thought. 'And you know the performers will need some time to rehearse before the concert. Shall we say – performance version ready by next Monday?'

'OK,' Kitty said again.

Professor Davidson had been understanding, or perhaps just pragmatic, while her father was dying. They all knew him, of course; it was hard for them to ignore what was happening. But it seemed they weren't quite as ready as Kitty to write off her year here. It was nearly June already: only another month to go, Kitty thought, and what was she going to achieve in that time? It hadn't been a wasted year. She'd got something out of the course, kept herself as busy as she could manage, but they must realise . . . She stared back at the face of God, wondering how to explain herself.

'You have talent,' Professor Davidson said now. 'This is just the beginning, Kitty, but you have to deliver on this piece.'

Kitty nodded. Pointless, she thought, to disagree. It was Prof Davidson's job, after all, to regard an MA in composition as something important and relevant, not just a way for someone to pass a year when they didn't know what to do next, or wanted to please their dying father. All over London there were people who regarded other obscure pursuits as just as important and relevant. She could spend the rest of her life hopping from one course to another if she wanted to, amazed each time by the earnest conviction of her teachers. Ancient Greek, fashion photography, forest management. What fun she could have.

'Have you got the manuscript with you?' Professor Davidson asked. 'Shall we look at it?'

Obediently, Kitty took a plastic wallet out of her satchel. She was working on a song cycle, a setting of poems by Ted Hughes from a book Henry had given her. She'd done nothing to it for weeks, and she was relieved to find that it didn't look quite as sketchy as she'd remembered.

Janet Davidson spread the sheets out carefully, moving her chair round to the side of the desk so that they could both see them. Then she put her hands back into her lap and leaned forward slightly, her eyebrows locking in the frown that indicated full concentration. Kitty had long ago got used to her methods: everything written out by hand until the final performance version, without resorting to the software everyone else used these days, and an overriding belief that music was shaped in the head, not the ears. Beethoven, she had said with devastating finality in their first meeting, hadn't needed his ears to write the *Grosse Fuge* – and that, as far as she was concerned, settled the point.

For a long time there was silence in the room. After a few moments, Kitty's eyes moved from Professor Davidson's face to the manuscript, and began to trace the first few bars of the piece. And then that curious thing happened, something like hearing words in your head when you're reading a book: the music lifted from the page and came alive, the notes she'd written weeks before. The melody flowed tentatively at first and then with greater conviction, finding its feet over the distinct colours of the chords. Kitty followed the staves down the first page, onto the next and the next, bewitched by the mystery of the process. When this happened, she could almost believe there was something to it – to Professor Davidson's belief in composition, and even perhaps her belief in Kitty. She knew it was just a trick, like an optical illusion that seems to mean more than it really is, but it gave her a strange pleasure. A tickling of possibility that she knew wouldn't last beyond the hour she'd spend in this room, but which she felt, nonetheless, a temptation to explore.

And then the music stumbled, somewhere in the middle of page three, losing its balance and setting off again in the wrong direction, and Kitty frowned. Without thinking, she brought her hand down onto the sheet, cutting off the flow of the notes. Professor Davidson turned her head towards her. She said nothing, but raised her eyebrows in query. Kitty could hear the troubled passage in her head, reshaping itself, trying a new tack in a new rhythm – 9/8, Kitty registered – elongating into a change of mood, and then – oh, she could do something different there, a whole new section, which would . . .

She didn't realise she was thinking aloud, humming phrases, shaping chords with her fingers, until Professor Davidson's expression changed again. She picked up a pencil and made a quick addition at the side of the page.

'Oh!' said Kitty. 'You mean . . .'

She was slower with the pencil, the process of transcribing thought into notation still inexpert, but after a moment or two Professor Davidson nodded, took the pencil back, made another amendment. Kitty could see the shape of the piece changing now, becoming tighter and denser than she'd anticipated. Somewhere just beyond her grasp there was a meaning, a feeling, a significance in the patterning of repetition and variation, development and flow.

For almost an hour the two of them worked side by side, turning the pages by mutual assent when they had finished with each one. From time to time one of them moved over to the piano to try out a harmony or a rhythm. Now and then a few words were spoken, but most of the time they worked in silence, the music flowing through their heads and spilling out onto the staves. More and more alterations and revocations; more and more new pages filled with notes like scurrying stick figures. Eventually, sitting back in her chair, Professor Davidson nodded again.

'Yes,' she said. 'You see? It's all there.'

Kitty glanced down at the manuscript, but Janet Davidson shook her head.

'Not there,' she said, 'although that's coming, that'll be fine. It's all in your head. Limitless amounts, Kitty. I don't say what I don't mean. You have talent, if you want to use it.'

Kitty felt jittery now, something like the feeling after a conversation in which you've said more than you intended to. Her head was still ringing with sound, and she shook it gently to settle the fragments of melody back into quiescence.

'I don't know,' she said.

'You don't know if you can do it, or why you might want to?'

'That,' said Kitty. 'What it's for.'

Professor Davidson smiled.

'That's a question for your father,' she said.

Kitty expected tears, or anger, but neither came. Prof Davidson wasn't invoking Henry, allying herself to him as a persuasive tactic. Kitty understood that. Nor was she saying, exactly, that Kitty was on her own now, and must find answers for herself. There was, somewhere, a grain of consolation.

Kitty looked at her for a moment longer, just in case there was more to be said, even though she knew a concluding phrase when she heard it. Then she smiled and stood up. 'Thank you,' she said.

'Try it this once,' Janet Davidson said, as she opened the door. 'You won't regret it. I feel certain you won't.'

PART II

Greville Auctioneers, Friday 12th December 2014

Paintings and drawings by Nicholas Comyn, from the collection of the late Henry Jones

Lot no. 2: View of a garden, 1990

Like several other works in the collection, this painting has a direct connection to Henry Jones: it represents the sitting room at Orchards, the Jones family home, which Comyn visited frequently. Indeed, Comyn's presence is indicated here by his own paintings on the walls of the room – a tribute, perhaps, to Jones' importance to Comyn as both patron and friend. All the paintings shown in this scene are included in the present auction.

The garden of the title is visible through open French windows. It has a dreamlike quality that contrasts sharply with the meticulous rendition of the room from which it is seen. This effect is achieved through the use of a complex tonal palette: the exterior light creates a shimmering ethereality among the greens of trees, lawn and shrubs, whereas the muted light of the interior affirms a more sober reality. Firelight is suggested in the reds and golds of walls and carpets, although there is no fire in the hearth. An acute observation of surface – the deep gloss of mahogany, the sheen of slipware – contrasts with the quotidian clutter of objects, including books piled on top of bookshelves, sheet music on the point of slipping off the piano, wilted flowers in a vase. Several details suggest that someone has recently left the room: a pair of shoes left tidily by the back door; an empty glass on the table.

This work, above all others, demonstrates Comyn's resistance to modernism. The composition, and especially the inclusion of his own paintings, refers clearly to Matisse, whom Comyn much admired. But although it clings to an older, more nostalgic world-view, it is also an uncomfortable portrayal of this domestic scene. In the tension between order and chaos, light and dark, serenity and agitation, this image reveals far more than is immediately apparent. Despite the absence of human figures, Comyn has created a *mise-en-scène* expressive of the lives lived in this room and of the occupants' interior states of mind.

September 1978

The blue TR6 slips along the narrow lanes as smoothly as though it knows its own way. There's certainly no map, and no discussion of the route. Flora tips her head back and shakes out her hair in the wind. It's a beautiful day, and the Triumph's top is folded down, the autumn sun gleaming on the flawless bonnet.

Henry glances across at her and smiles. He smiles easily: it's one of his distinguishing features. He looks relaxed and confident, his honeymoon tan as yet unfaded. As they plunge through tunnels of overarching trees and pass fields bleached to white gold, Flora wonders whether – and how – Henry knows his way through these back roads. Something in her makeup, some predisposition she's a little appalled by, holds fast to practicalities even in the grip of bliss, or its opposite.

The last month has been a switchback ride between those two extremes. The wedding – so fiercely argued over – passed off brilliantly. Flora and her mother shared, for once, a sense of triumph, and almost, almost, at the very end of the day, a moment of solidarity. She'd done what her mother wanted and what she wanted, and they were, they seemed to be, the same thing.

Then there was the honeymoon in Italy: Flora leaning over the hotel balcony with her cropped hair and tailored blouse, the spit of Audrey Hepburn, according to Henry, out of step with the 1970s but in step – oh, how wonderfully in step, at last – with herself, the young doctor-wife-lover-traveller. And the student of culture, following Henry wide-eyed around galleries full of Titians and Caravaggios, into palazzi where husbands had murdered lovers and wives had murdered husbands, and no one slept easy in their beds. Together they gazed at frescoes flung wide across ceilings; touched, furtively, the sleek wood of ancient bedposts; held hands in loggias built for noble families.

On the aeroplane home, with the Italian sun still warming her skin and the memory of long honeymoon nights still perfect in her mind, she thought how easy it would be to do what everyone expected: to give up her job and let Henry provide for her. His career – a ragbag of writing and broadcasting, a little mysterious to Flora – seemed to be flourishing. Was it pure stubbornness to insist on going back to work? Stubbornness and greed: the delicious excess of knowing she had more than other women? Not quite, she thought, glancing down through a gap in the clouds as the plane crested the Alps. Not quite. There was the thrill of surgery too, the pleasure of the physical competence she felt in the operating theatre.

If she'd been born two hundred years earlier, Flora sometimes thought, she might have been one of those young women whose embroidery drew admiration. As it was, she had proved herself adept at another kind of needlework. She hadn't really meant to go into surgery – she'd applied for her first SHO job in the professorial surgical unit simply because it was what would most horrify her mother – but it didn't take long to be sure that she had found her métier. The exhilaration of literally mending people, the risking of knife and needle in human flesh. If she gave all that up now she'd never show the world how good she was. And navigating the political maze of a career in surgery was at least as much of a test as perfecting her craft.

It wouldn't be an easy ride, she thought, reaching across the armrest to take Henry's hand, but she knew she could manage it, and sustain a marriage. Hadn't she married Henry because he wanted her to be her own person? For that reason among others, she reminded herself, letting her hand run up over his wrist and feeling the hairs on the back of her own arm rise in anticipation.

And so, the first day back in London, she kissed him goodbye and set off for the hospital. The luck of the rota meant she was on duty that night, and as she drove through Islington and Clerkenwell, grimmer and grimier than Rome, she felt a pang of regret, stronger than she expected, about sleeping apart from Henry. A premonition, perhaps – but she would never allow superstition to colour her judgement about her marriage. And there was certainly no premonition when she learned that the rota had been changed: there was simply the glory of a stay of execution, and the prospect of surprising Henry that evening.

'Nearly there,' Henry says, and Flora realises she has lost track of time. Has she been asleep, or just daydreaming?

Before she can reply he brakes suddenly, and she sees the house they have come to look at, a glimpse of it through wide gates and the remains of a wooden sign declaring its name: *Orchards*. Long and low beneath a tiled roof whose patchy appearance strikes her only as characterful, its façade is a medley of flint and red brick and its windows all different in shape and size. The garden – still half farmyard – sprawls comfortably around it, enclosing outbuildings in various stages of decay. It couldn't be more unlike the Georgian townhouse she grew up in.

Flora feels something shift inside her – a life settling into place, and a sudden understanding of adulthood. She knows at once that they will live here, she and Henry. She can see exactly how it will be: her new job at the Radcliffe Infirmary, their children growing up in the countryside, Henry travelling to London for concerts and lunches and editorial meetings. Each of them, she thinks, making their way to a kind of prominence. Among the broil of emotions she feels relief, and vindication.

12

The house lay round a curve of the road that concealed it from view until you were almost upon it. Lou's first view of it – now, as always – came almost as a shock: the unruly beech hedge giving way abruptly to the wooden gate, and then the house suddenly before her.

Orchards was beautiful in its way, a brick-and-flint farmhouse shaped into a zigzag by a series of mergers and extensions over the centuries, set in grounds that had always looked neglected: a lawn grown to moss, fringed by half-hearted borders, and a drive made up of equal parts gravel and weeds, though weeds of the kind that stay low and flower often and might almost pass for rockery plants.

Lou stopped her car just inside the gates. The house stood empty now, its squat, rambling form looking strangely defenceless against the blank sky. She was conscious of a familiar curdle of ambivalence. Returning to her childhood home had always been complicated, even when she was young, but that was more true than ever today. She was grateful that the estate agent hadn't arrived yet, so that she had a few moments alone.

She hadn't been back here since Flora went to France – only a matter of weeks, but it seemed much longer. It was more disconcerting than she'd expected to see the house uninhabited. Installing a tenant felt like the baldest acknowledgement of how life had changed: it made sense, of course, if Flora was going to be away all summer, but even so . . . It was a surprise, Lou thought. Another surprise.

There was nothing left of the outbuildings that had once enclosed the farmyard except for a barn which had once housed teenage parties and broken lawnmowers and was now full of things Lou and Kitty had persuaded their mother not to throw on the skip after Henry died: a rocking horse, the cheap kind made from pine planks; chairs with missing spindles; a bedside table that Alice had planned to strip and paint. Perhaps she might take that home today, Lou thought. Would that please Alice, or would it look too much like a petition?

It still made Lou's heart race to remember the night she'd broken the news about her pregnancy. 'Broken' was about right, she'd thought the next morning. She'd felt – she still hoped – that things couldn't help but right themselves in the end. Surely it wasn't possible for two people who loved each other, who were going to be parents together, to fail to rescue themselves from the muddle they'd landed themselves in? Each morning since then, she'd woken hoping to find the air had cleared. But she and Alice still seemed to be marooned on some desert island where communication was all but impossible. Scrupulous politeness was their only tactic – or perhaps, Lou thought sometimes, their weapon of choice.

Was there any part of Alice, Lou wondered now as she gazed up at Orchards' familiar façade, that accepted some of the blame for their predicament? Had she entirely written off her secrecy about the Bacchus sculpture? It seemed to Lou that among the muddle of missed turnings and bad feelings and misunderstandings it was hard to say who was responsible for what. It was like unravelling the threads of a kite, the kind of tangle you could only solve by cutting the threads free. Perhaps the simple truth was that their relationship would never fly again; certainly wouldn't stand the challenge of parenthood.

That thought was especially painful here, thrown into sharp focus by the recollection of her childhood. The years, the memories, could be traced through the mismatched windows in front of her: her bedroom, her parents', Kitty's little attic room. Inside the old kitchen where she'd eaten pizza baked dry by an au pair; from the half-landing she'd watched for car lights up the lane, wondering which of her parents would be home first and whether the evening would be calm or stormy.

But she remembered now, with a gush of relief, the story of her parents' first visit to the house, and how they'd fallen in love with it at once. That had always been one of their favourite tales, a piece of family folklore untainted by anything that came afterwards. *Tell us about buying the house, Daddy,* they'd asked – she and then Kitty – rejoicing in the excitement of that first glimpse and the way their parents had counted out bedrooms for the babies to come, although they'd only been married a few weeks. Odd to think that her mother had been younger than her, then. Twenty-five to her thirty-one: closer to Kitty's age, in fact. Already a doctor but barely more than a girl, in the photographs. When had she – how had it begun, Lou wondered, her father's infidelity? She contemplated for a moment the irony that he had been a good father, a kind man; the central irony of her childhood. Life would have been simpler in many ways if he hadn't.

A crackle of tyres on gravel interrupted her train of thought, and a silver BMW slid into view in the wing mirror. The man who emerged from it was younger than Lou expected.

'Hello, Miss Jones,' he called, hastening towards her.

'Lou.' She held out her hand and he clasped it for a moment.

'Simon Phillips. I'm sorry I'm late.'

'It doesn't matter.'

'I've been doing a valuation up at Woodlands Hill. One of those huge houses, you know?' He pulled a face, at once apologetic and mock-awed. 'Saturdays are always busy, I'm afraid.'

Lou smiled. 'Let's go in,' she said. It had been sunny earlier, but it was cold now she was out of the car. She'd forgotten how the wind barrelled along this valley.

It was very odd, showing the house to a stranger. Lou felt another twinge of treachery as she opened the front door. *My mother's swanning around France*, she wanted to say, to explain herself, but she didn't. He knew that, presumably. It was her mother who'd asked her to show him round.

'The hall,' she said, unnecessarily.

The bulb had gone in the main light and it felt smaller, lower-ceilinged than usual. No pictures on the walls, of course: her father's collection was in a storage vault, waiting for someone to decide what to do with it. All those paintings by Nick Comyn; the ones that were mostly of the house and the family. They'd been amazed by the preliminary valuation when the man from Greville's had come to take them away. Flora clearly hadn't realised how valuable they were, but that begged the question of why she'd been so keen to get them out of Orchards. Looking at the bare walls now, Lou wondered about that. The pastel sketch of Henry had always hung at the bottom of the stairs, and the one of her and Kitty on the beach had been over there on the right. She didn't remember Nick Comyn well – he'd died when she was eleven or twelve, in some vaguely mysterious way – but he'd been a friend of the family. A friend of Henry's, at least, but he'd spent more time with them than most of Henry's friends. He'd come on holiday with them that summer when he'd done the beach scene. The painting was rather gloomy, the sky lowering as it often did over the Welsh coast, but Lou had liked the idea of the two of them crouching there always, building up the defences of their sandcastle against the creep of the tide. The hall looked strange without it, as though they had gone from the house too, she and Kitty.

'Nicely proportioned hall.' Simon glanced upwards, then pulled an electronic measure from his pocket. 'Mind if I . . .?'

'Of course.'

Lou watched, noting the combination of proficiency and clumsiness. He couldn't be more than twenty-two, but he had a professional earnestness that she found rather touching. She turned away, preceding him into the kitchen.

The ground floor had been remodelled in the last few years, partly to accommodate her father's decline and partly, Lou thought, to persuade her parents that it had been a different sort of home all those years. The old kitchen, unchanged since the seventies, had become a den; the long-neglected dining room had been transformed into a state-of-the-art farmhouse kitchen of the Jamie Oliver or Delia Smith variety. Both daughters, with an embarrassing lack of consultation, had bought their mother cookery books the next Christmas.

'Delia's delight,' Lou announced, with a sweep of her arm.

'Delia's your mother?'

'No, no.' Lou laughed. 'Delia's the last person my mother could be taken for. I don't think she's ever actually cooked in here. It's more – oh God, I don't know. It makes her feel she could cook, maybe. If she wanted to.'

Simon gave her an uncertain look. Family business, she could see him thinking. The phrase settled in Lou's mind: surveying the immaculate units, the shiny Rayburn, she wondered whether she and Alice would ever have a kitchen like this. The two of them and their children, being a family. The words caused a lurch of panic deep in her belly.

They moved on to the sitting room, its Liberty curtains faded at the edges.

'The height of chic,' Lou said, as they contemplated the disconsolate trio of sofas in matching fabric. 'Or it was the last time anyone sat in here.' That wasn't strictly true: this had been the music room too, the place where she had played the piano, and Henry, and Kitty. But it was hard not to put a spin on things, somehow.

There had been more Comyns in here, including a painting of the room itself which showed several of the earlier pictures already hanging on the walls. Lou had always been fascinated by that one, the way it showed a version of family life, a moment in history, alongside whatever was going on in the room at any particular time. Henry had pointed out to her once that it showed firelight inside and sunlight outside, and she'd pondered the significance of that for ages. None of them had an eye for art the way Henry did.

'Onwards,' she said. 'This way.'

They viewed the playroom, the utility room, and then she led Simon through to the jumble of back rooms beyond the kitchen. In the old days their guinea pigs had lived out here, and for years her potter's wheel had patterned the walls of the lean-to at the end with splatters of clay, but this part of the house had been smartened up too. The guinea pigs' draughty domain had been converted into a study, used so little that it looked incomplete still, and the lean-to had been replaced by a greenhouse. Neatly stacked gro-bags and packets of seeds testified to her mother's plans to start a vegetable garden. Lou felt another wave of discomfort as they peered through the glass. Those hopeful plans, she thought. Those good intentions they could all see straight through.

'Plenty of scope for the keen horticulturist,' Simon said.

Lou made a strange noise, something aspiring to mirth. 'Plenty of scope for many things here, I can assure you.'

Simon glanced at her and she looked away. She was aware that her commentary, aiming at the tersely witty, had drifted towards self-parody as the visit had progressed. Indeed, the whole occasion had an air of masquerade: moving through the familiar rooms, Lou felt she was looking in from outside, watching herself slip between different incarnations. The lonely child; the teenager with music at full blast to drown the arguments percolating up from below; the student returning reluctantly when her father's cancer was diagnosed. There was hardly room here for a sane, grown-up Lou, let alone one riven with new anxieties: miserable about her own marriage, rather than her parents'. If she had asked, she wondered suddenly, would Alice have come today? Might that have made it easier? She hadn't asked because she'd been afraid of the answer, that was the truth of it. She'd told herself it was simpler to come alone.

'Garden next?' she asked. 'Outbuildings offering the benefit of extensive storage space?'

The open air came as a relief, despite the cold. Lou couldn't remember either of her parents spending much time in the garden, except for the occasional summer barbecue. It had been her territory, then hers and Kitty's: a realm of hideouts and make-believe. Pinning her hair back against the wind, she surveyed the apple trees, bowed and curlicued, which she'd transformed into treasure ships and castles twenty years before.

'Would you be including a gardener in the rent?' Simon asked.

Lou followed his gaze, appraising the overgrown beds running down the side of the lawn, and the area near the house that her parents had replanted last year.

'Whatever you think best,' she said. 'It's been a little neglected, but it could be lovely.'

'Oh, it certainly could.' Simon smiled – with relief, she thought. Poor boy, it couldn't be easy for him, and he'd been very sweet. Very gallant. They stood on the lawn for a few moments, looking back at the house. From this angle it looked even more higgledy-piggledy: a fairytale cottage, the kind that might be held together by icing sugar.

'It's a very special property, Miss Jones,' Simon said. 'It really is.' He hesitated, looking sideways at her. 'Of course you'll have the opportunity to meet any prospective tenants, if you want to.'

'I don't think so.'

Lou shivered; folding her arms, she tucked her elbows close against her. The idea of anyone else living here – boring, happy people – was hard to get her head round, but it was time to hand Orchards over. She felt, then, a wash of relief. She was glad she hadn't said anything too awful, glad she was almost at the point of saying goodbye.

But she'd forgotten the rest of the house, the bedrooms and bathrooms, Kitty's attic.

'Upstairs, now?' Simon asked.

Lou nodded. Ignoring the knot in her stomach, she led him back inside. Nothing had changed up here, and the past lay heavy in the empty rooms. The dusty beams, the smell of old carpets, the air cloistered by the leaded windows were all so pungently evocative that Lou was sure Simon must be able to sense it too.

'My father's dressing room,' she said, as they looked into a room tucked in one of the house's unexpected corners. 'A euphemistic term, of course.' The undressing room, she'd dubbed it, in her see-if-I-care teens. The knocking shop.

'Bedroom four, can we call it?' Simon smiled, not quite meeting her eye.

'We can call it whatever we want.'

Lou moved away down the low corridor.

'Up here,' she said.

They climbed the spiral staircase to Kitty's room. Lou pulled back the curtains and looked out at the garden and the woods beyond. Kitty used to have a doll's house under the eaves. Where had that gone, she wondered? Surely not into the skip?

'Lovely view,' Simon said.

'Down again,' said Lou, and he followed her without a word.

Her old bedroom led off the spare room; there was no passageway between them.

'Where have we got to?' she asked. 'Bedroom three and three and a half? I expect you could find a way to make that work. We always did.'

'Miss Jones,' said Simon.

'Lou,' she said. She turned in the doorway and found herself right up against his face. He looked stricken, as though he'd seen something he wished he hadn't.

'I'm so sorry,' he said.

'It doesn't matter.' Lou attempted a smile.

'I mean to say, I'm sorry about your father. And about the house. I can see you're very attached to it.'

Lou looked at him for a few seconds longer, and for one or two of them she thought he might be going to kiss her. His face was so close to hers, and so anxious to please. For a moment it seemed inevitable, even desirable; and then, her heart beating fast with confusion and chagrin, she turned away.

13

Flora woke early on Friday morning, conscious almost at once of a sense of lightness and ease. The *toile* milkmaids were almost invisible today, bleached by sunshine. Outside, dew gleamed on the grass, and the distant hills were sharply defined against the blue sky.

Standing at the window, Flora felt, like a child, the excitement of a new day. Like the acute misery of other mornings this sudden joy was unexpected, even disconcerting – but if she was to survive, she told herself, she must be glad of mornings like this one. This wouldn't be the last reversal of the rollercoaster, but for now it was real enough, and she should embrace it.

Her clothes made a pitiful showing in the wardrobe. She must go shopping, she thought. She couldn't keeping wearing the same few things she'd taken to Cousin Hettie's in Colmar. She chose a pair of linen trousers and a blue batik top, then she opened the jewellery box that had sat untouched by her bed since she arrived and took out a pair of earrings. Catching sight of her reflection in the mirror on the dressing table she was pleased – not so much with the result as with the effort, she thought.

No one else was in the breakfast room when she came downstairs.

'You are well this morning?' Madame asked, bringing out a pot of coffee. She didn't wait for a reply; apparently she had faith in her judgement on the matter. 'Monsieur Carver is delivering some wine this morning.'

'Oh.' Flora had forgotten about Martin Carver. Forgotten it was Friday, too. She caught Madame's eye, and felt herself blushing at the assumption that the batik and the earrings were intended for him.

'Shall I tell him you look forward to lunch?'

'All right,' Flora heard herself saying. 'Thank you.'

What else was she to do with the day, after all? She had dressed herself up for it now; she couldn't retreat again.

Madame nodded. 'It is a beautiful house,' she said again.

And it was. Les Violettes was a neat eighteenth-century townhouse, surrounded by a walled garden and bordered at the front by pollarded trees. The glass in the tall windows was textured with age; the paint-work, a delicate shade of yellow, had been recently renewed.

Martin Carver opened the door almost as soon as she touched the bell.

'I'm so glad,' he said. 'I'm afraid I was terribly rude the other day.'

'I rather thought I was,' said Flora, and she laughed a little. Part of her wondered what on earth she was doing here, but another part was content to see where the day might lead. Martin seemed, on second encounter, less sure of himself than she'd imagined. If she was less sure of herself too, that at least put them on an equal footing.

'Well, then: let's start again. Welcome.'

He stood back to let her pass. The hall ran the depth of the house, a staircase ascending to the left. The interior was dark and cool, but a French window opposite the front door admitted a draught of sun-shine from the garden. Flora, not a connoisseur of furnishings, noticed a chandelier and some attractive prints, a delicate inlaid chest.

'What a lovely house,' she said.

'It was my mother's,' said Martin. 'Her family's.'

'She was French?'

'Yes. I spent most of my childhood here. Only sound British.'

'That must be an advantage, with business in France. Madame Abelard tells me you're a wine merchant.'

He laughed. 'More of an advantage speaking English, since that's where I flog most of the stuff. Come on through. Too nice a day to be inside, don't you think?'

A table was laid in the garden, on a terrace perfectly placed to catch the midday sun. It was an entrancing garden, reminiscent somehow of the *toile* milkmaids' pastoral idyll. Pink rose bushes flanked the lawn down one side, and on the other box hedges were planted in an intricate pattern. There were several places to sit: a wrought-iron bench under the high wall; a round table beneath a willow bower; an old millstone resting in the middle of the lawn. They seemed to Flora like the settings for different acts of a play, one she wouldn't be here long enough to see all the way through.

'I've dug out a bottle of '59 Vouvray,' said Martin. 'I hope you don't object to *demi-sec*.'

'Not in the least.'

This, Flora thought, as she took a seat beneath the vine that ran rampant across the back of the house, was going to be a pleasurable occasion. Lucky it had come on the right day; that she was in the right frame of mind to enjoy it. The felicity of that was worth savouring, too. She arranged her chair so she could see the tiny fountain at the far end of the terrace, a chubby boy holding a pitcher from which water trickled lazily.

'*Santé.*' Martin handed her a glass. He paused for a moment to register the flavours of the wine. 'Mmm,' he said. 'Good. Peaches. Very ripe peaches, don't you think?'

Flora took a tentative sip. She had rarely tasted anything so delicious. 1959, had he said? She didn't even want to think about what it might be worth.

She couldn't understand, now, why she'd reacted so strongly to him in the shop. She knew exactly who Martin was: she'd grown up among men like this, worked with them all her life. He had a hint of Mark Upward's bluff arrogance – that fleeting thought had been apposite – but also something of Landon's civility. Now that she had nothing to prove, what could be simpler than enjoying his company – and his wine?

'Yes, peaches,' she said – then, entering into the spirit, 'and pears, perhaps?'

'Dessert pears,' Martin agreed. 'Excellent. It's a pleasure to have someone to share it with.'

Flora raised her eyebrows. 'But you must know everyone around here, if you grew up in the village.'

'More or less. All the oldies, anyway.'

'Like the Abelards?'

'Formidable Francine.' Martin grinned. 'I was a mate of her brother's when we were kids. He died young.'

'She's been very kind to me,' said Flora.

'Oh, she has a heart of gold. Only a dash of witchcraft, and she needs it with that useless husband of hers.'

Flora swilled the wine in her glass. 'I do sometimes have the feeling she can read minds,' she said, 'but she cooks like a dream.'

'Well, that's something to live up to.' Martin got to his feet. 'No, stay there. It's all ready.'

Flora wasn't sure whether Martin had cooked the meal himself, but he talked knowledgeably, interestingly, about the ingredients: the tomatoes that were among the last of an early variety he particularly liked, and the *confit de canard* that had been left to steep in its herbs overnight. He told her, too, about the village and the expat community in the *département*, amusing her with anecdote and intrigue and minor tragedy. He'd had, it seemed to her, the benefit of living two different lives: he was countless steps ahead of her in appreciating the delights of France.

It wasn't until the duck was finished, and most of the Vouvray, that conversation began to dwindle. Flora felt full and rather sleepy, lulled by the shush of insects and warmed by the June sunshine. She'd enjoyed herself – was still enjoying herself – but she had a sense that a watershed was approaching.

'I should be going soon,' she said.

'Going?' Martin looked perturbed. 'Why on earth, halfway through lunch?'

'Oh.' Flora flushed. Stupid, she thought. This was France, after all.

'I've made a *tarte aux abricots*. My mother's recipe.' Martin leaned across the table and poured the last of the wine into her glass.

Another *tarte aux abricots*. She'd better not run away from this one. But even if her instincts on etiquette were unreliable, Flora told herself, dredging up the thought from beneath the pleasant carapace the wine had laid over her mind, her antennae were well tuned for certain other inflections of social intercourse.

'Is your wife English or French?' she asked.

Martin lifted an eyebrow.

'English,' he said. 'Ex-wife now. Happily ensconced in the family pile in Berkshire.'

Flora flushed again. She realised, too late, that he'd misinterpreted her question. So much for her surgical precision, her famous bluntness. She looked away, towards the fountain where the boy stood patiently with his never-emptying jug.

'I suppose I was a difficult bugger to live with, always flitting hither and thither,' Martin said. 'I spend most of my time here these days. I like it here. I bought my brother out when my mother died.'

'That seems a happy solution,' Flora said. Safe ground, she thought. She could do imperturbable too.

'I've been thinking I ought to find a base in England, though,' he said. 'I'm sick of hotels.'

'Do you go over often?'

'My eldest's getting married this summer,' Martin said, 'which requires my presence for a month or two. I thought I'd rent somewhere.'

'There must be agencies who specialise in summer lets,' said Flora.

But a thought was taking shape, an audacious and unlikely thought that she wouldn't have entertained without the wine, the lunch, the haloes of ripening grapes. Perhaps not even without the conversational slips and misapprehensions that had left her feeling strangely heady.

'Whereabouts would you want to be?' she asked.

'Within reach of London. Within reach of the family.'

'You could rent my house,' Flora said. 'I'm looking for a tenant. Just for the summer, while I'm here.'

Martin stared at her. 'Where's your house?'

'In Oxfordshire. Not far from Didcot.'

'That would do,' he said. 'What're you asking? Rent, I mean?'

Flora looked around at the gravel paths, the box hedges and lavender and the decorously pruned shrubs. Something rose in her chest, carrying the words out on a little eddy.

'How about a swap?' she said. 'I'll stay here, you go there.'

She half expected to regret the proposal at once, but she didn't. In fact once it was voiced, the idea seemed to her quite deliciously pleasing. Not simply the elegance of it, the avoidance of management fees and legal agreements (although she spared a thought for the estate agent's dutiful emails); not simply the sudden allure of staying here, right here, for a month or two, trying out the nooks and corners of the garden and finding the perfect moment to sit in each of them. There was something more elusive, more rarefied, too. Something about a particular kind of intimacy: having free rein in someone else's house, among their possessions. Something about the curious blend of safety and risk involved in trying out someone else's life, and letting them loose in yours.

'Well,' said Martin, 'I'm not a man to shilly-shally. I'm heading back to London on Monday, so if you're serious, I can take a look at the place then.'

August 1978

Above the heavy front door there's a half moon of glass, patterned with art deco swirls, which Flora already associates with the pleasure of coming home. There's no light shining through it yet on this summer evening, and her heart skips at the thought of Henry sitting at his desk as the house settles to dusk. This, she thinks, is the first of thousands of homecomings: the first thread in the weft of married life.

'Henry?' she calls, as the door shuts behind her. There's no response. Can he be out? Damn: she should have rung from the hospital, as soon as she knew she wasn't on duty tonight after all. She puts down her bag and starts up the stairs. 'Henry? I'm back.'

On the landing she hesitates. The bedroom door is shut, but now she can hear – imagines she can hear – muffled voices. A radio? Burglars?

'Henry?' she calls again, loud enough to be sure an intruder would hear. A tingle of fear, only half-credible, flickers through her chest. She keeps one hand on the newel post, ready to sprint back down the stairs and out of the house.

There's silence, and then – thank God! – a voice she recognises. 'Flora?'

Chiding herself, she runs along the landing and throws open the bedroom door – then stops short. Henry is in bed, and beside him, taking no trouble to conceal herself, is a woman with a lot of blonde hair and an expression of unabashed amusement.

As the sound of the front door slamming shut echoes in the narrow hallway, Henry faces Flora, his back to the front door. Along with an eddy of perfume there is something less tangible in the air: the ghostly remains of Flora's joy at returning to her husband after her

111

first day back at work as a married woman. That, more than the perfume, causes the constriction in her throat and the throb of distress in her chest.

'Why?' she manages to say.

Henry looks at her and she looks straight back: this is important, some unfamiliar part of her brain tells her. It's no good avoiding his eyes, or his expression. She remembers his kisses this morning, his sweet words, and she feels as though she's falling, as though they are both plummeting downwards in a lift.

'I don't expect you to understand,' he says.

Flora shakes her head. For the first time she feels a bite of anger, clean and sharp and almost welcome, cutting through the disbelief and confusion.

'I mean, why did you marry me?'

'Because I love you,' he says. 'Because you love me.'

'For God's sake.' Flora can feel her shoulders trembling. 'For Christ's sake, Henry, don't demean me any further.'

'My darling . . .'

He takes a step towards her, then stops. Flora can see the door handle now, and for a second, a long, considering second, she wills herself to push past him. She isn't a runner-away, a giver-up, but she can see that it might be the best and the bravest thing to do, after two weeks of marriage. She could run to Landon, perhaps. She remembers his reaction when she told him about her engagement and it strikes her suddenly, sharply, that she might have made a terrible mistake, overlooking the boy-next-door.

For a long time neither of them says anything more, although the buzz of thought is almost audible, the things each of them knows the other is thinking. Flora hasn't had much experience of men, and she can't flatter herself that she suspected Henry's weakness before this evening, but she understands the situation very clearly now. Henry hasn't apologised, and she knows that's not an oversight. Should he at least be sorry that he's been found out so soon, she wonders, or is it better this way?

She looks up at the semi-circle of light above the door, the pale gold of a late summer sunset. She can see what lies ahead: or at least, she can see that her marriage is going to be entirely different from what she expected. She feels, just now, very young and very innocent. Despite her medical training, her headstrong independence, she is the product of a sheltered upbringing. The honeymoon is over, she tells herself, and she has to shut her eyes to keep the tears in.

'Flora,' Henry says. The tremor has spread through her body now, and she doesn't resist when he puts his arms around her. 'I'm telling you the truth,' he says. 'I love you, and I want to be married to you. If you change your mind I'll understand, but if you stay with me I can give you everything you want. I'll always support you. I'll always love you.'

Even as she stands there Flora can feel the moment slipping past, the moment when she can say, *that's not everything I want.* Her career for his infidelity: does he really expect her to accept that bargain? But she doesn't reject it. She doesn't escape through the door; she doesn't pull away from him; she doesn't find the words to put her case.

While he holds her – while she stands stiffly encircled in his arms, resisting the pulse of desire that feels undignified, even vulgar, in the circumstances – she opens her eyes again, and gazes into the rooms on either side of them, filled with the heavy curtains and dark furniture she didn't choose. Henry's heirlooms, inherited along with the money that persuaded her mother he was a suitable husband.

'We can move out of London,' he says, as though he's read her mind. 'We'll find a house in the country, wherever there's a job for you. I can do my work anywhere.'

Henry hesitates for a moment, and Flora thinks he's going to say, *we can be happy*. But he doesn't. He doesn't say anything else, and perhaps it's this restraint that tips the balance. She lets him take her hands and lead her into the kitchen, and she accepts the glass of wine he pours for her. Just one glass: there's an operating list tomorrow, and she needs a steady hand.

14

A couple of years ago, when her father's cancer first came back, Kitty went to see a counsellor. It was her mother's idea – and the woman reminded her of Flora, in a way. Kitty didn't go back after the first session, but some of the things the counsellor said stuck in her mind.

How would you describe yourself in one sentence?

Kitty still played that game sometimes. Sum yourself up in ten words, or six, or two. She never quite hit the right note: always too morbid or too flippant. She wasn't suited to introspection, she decided. She couldn't keep enough of a distance to see herself squarely.

Then there was another question: *What obstacles have you encountered in your closest relationships?*

Kitty didn't need a counsellor to answer that one. Not so much Henry's cancer as his affairs. Answer that, she'd wanted to ask: how could she love someone who'd caused them all such hurt? How could she love him so much and – not hate him; it wasn't that simple. Fear the power he had over her. Resent her susceptibility to him. Much the same as her feelings about Daniel, she thought now.

She hadn't seen Daniel since that evening when he'd turned up on her doorstep. It was true, what she'd said to Lou: she missed him. She missed the sex, and the reassurance of having someone close, and being wanted by him. But the longer she didn't see him, the more she felt it was right to stay away, not to answer his calls or his texts or his emails even though it pleased her that he kept sending them. The obstacles to her relationship with Daniel, she thought, were too deeply entangled with him, with the two of them, to count as something separate. The reasons for wanting him were also warning signs: the way her feelings engulfed her as soon as she was near him; the fascination, complication, of sharing music; the fact that he had no parents and hers were . . . Oh, and anyway, how could you explain, how could you analyse – whatever it was they had? Sometimes the whole thing felt like a figment of her imagination, a mirage that would disappear if she opened her eyes or clicked her fingers, and at other times it felt so real and so essential that – like her own psyche – she couldn't stand far enough back to see it clearly, and couldn't be complete without it. Was that love, or self-delusion? How could she tell?

After their first encounter at the music college auditions, that moment of *coup de foudre*, they hadn't seen each other until the autumn. Daniel had spent six months as an intern with an opera company in Melbourne, and although her father would have paid for a plane ticket if Kitty had asked, it would have been impossible, ridiculous, to follow him across the world after such a brief meeting. Nothing had happened by then, nothing substantial or definite that she could rely on in the intervening months, and although she'd been quite certain, after that first day, of the understanding between them, it hadn't been enough to save her from agonies of doubt and speculation. She'd read and reread Daniel's blog, and occasionally allowed herself to post a response. When October arrived, she knew that he knew who she was, but nothing else was clear anymore: even her own feelings had been tortured out of recognition over the summer. And Henry's health had gone downhill, too. Nothing was quite as it had been.

Daniel was the first person she saw when she walked into the auditorium that September morning, eight months ago now. Back from his Australian winter, he was smaller than she remembered and his hair had grown. And he was looking out for her: that was instantly clear. His smile of recognition came as a shock, as did the tumble of doubt in her stomach, the unsettling sense that she had been deluding herself (and even, somehow, Daniel) all summer.

Whether it was down to chance or the staff's recollection of their collaboration at the auditions, Kitty never found out, but they were thrown together for the three-day exercise designed as an ice-breaker and introduction to the course. The two of them and a hapless cellist whom Kitty hadn't seen again after the end-of-week performance, and for whom she'd written a painfully derivative Elgaresque *Romance* which entirely failed to disguise the romance already consuming Kitty and Daniel. For three days they were barely apart. At night they confessed that they'd thought of nothing but each other during the months of separation, and by day they played, planned, experimented, revelled in the extraordinary harmony between them. Every time Daniel left a room or entered it, Kitty felt again that tumult that she assumed was love.

And then the week ended, the whole group came back together to play to each other, and Kitty saw that others had bonded just as they had, and had produced performances just as interesting as theirs. She saw, too, that Daniel was certain of his claim on her. The floundering inside her had turned by now into something that was conspicuously closer to dread than to love.

Looking back, it felt as if there had been a showdown, perhaps more than one, but in fact there had simply been the slither and soar of a relationship that no sooner got on its feet than she wanted it to stop, and that was no sooner dismantled than she wanted it back. Some-times it seemed that the difficulty was entirely on her side, but she had just enough self-knowledge to recognise that what she was being offered wasn't entirely straightforward.

And then Henry's death had provided a watershed, and Kitty had seized it. Was this what she wanted, she wondered again now? It seemed to her sometimes that she was cutting off her nose to spite her face – but there was another reason to stay away from Daniel just now, a good reason to put him out of her mind. Since her tutorial with Prof Davidson she was writing, composing, in a different way from before: she was deeply absorbed by her song cycle. She didn't want to let Janet Davidson down, but that wasn't the only thing driving her. She under-stood what that word meant now: a driving force. It wasn't pleasure but compulsion, urging her onwards. She'd found a public library not far from the college where she could concentrate, certain she wouldn't be disturbed. Every day now the hours slipped smoothly past, and Kitty worked.

On Fridays the library stayed open until half past seven. At seven fifteen, the librarian started moving quietly among the tables, shutting down the computers. Kitty was the last person left. The elderly man with the ancient tweed jacket had left half an hour ago, and the tall black woman who'd been typing noisily for a couple of hours had gone too. Kitty sat back in her chair and stared up at the blank ceiling. Had she really been here all day? Worse, had she been here all day and not finished yet?

The deadline for the song cycle was in three days, the concert performance only a week away, and something wasn't right with the last song. The poem was difficult for her: *An October Salmon*, one of Henry's favourites. The dying salmon whose glory days are still a vivid memory was painfully poignant. Sometimes, instead of the torn and damaged fish, Kitty saw Alice's Bacchus, his sharp eyes watching her while she worked. Perhaps she shouldn't have chosen that poem, but it hadn't been a choice, exactly. It was more as if the poem had insisted on its inclusion. Kitty stared at the words again, each of them completely familiar by now, their pitch and tone engraved in her head. How could she do justice to their bitterness – death's clownish ceremonials – and to the dignity of the ending? How could her music convey the stillness, the stopped-ness of the old salmon, as well as the perpetual motion of the ocean? She had never felt before this overwhelming desire to identify what was missing from a piece, or the desolating sense that it was beyond her grasp.

When she was a small child, Kitty had taken for granted the soundtrack that played in her head. She'd assumed that places and scenes had their own melody, and that everyone heard them in the same key, just as they saw the world in the same colours. When she understood that this musical accompaniment wasn't something other people had, it had made her feel special. Her experience of life, and her memories, had an extra layer of pleasure or suspense or fear, almost as if she was living in a movie: a special gift bestowed on her by some benevolent deity. But after Henry's death, the world had fallen silent: a devastating change. It was only recently that she'd realised how helpful the stream of music in her mind was for a composer – a kind of sixth sense, like the special way a painter might see the world in terms of shape and texture – and now it had gone. She couldn't have explained this to anyone else. She'd hardly been able to acknowledge it to herself as part of what she'd lost. It was too private, too peculiar a thing to put into words – a sign of madness, even – but she'd thought life would never be the same again.

These last few days, though, she had found another way to access the music in her head. It was harder this way, but more satisfying. In the past it had always been there, waiting, whenever she'd cared to listen in: she'd been able to draw out whichever strand of melody presented itself for a particular mood or occasion, or release a jack-in-the-box fragment of orchestral colour. But she'd never felt in control of it, and it had seemed almost a cheat to write it down, as though she was poaching something that didn't really belong to her – like the shoemaker and the elves.

Since her meeting with Janet Davidson, the process had been entirely different. Perhaps it was merely a question of focus and intention, but she'd found herself striving to find the building blocks, to select and shape what she wrote, not simply transcribing something ready-made. Her automatic soundtrack was still muted: the music only flowed when she sought it out, but it brought an exhilaration she'd never experienced before. This felt like honest toil, like proper creativity. Sometimes she'd had to feel her way in the dark, agonising over one tonality or another, but the material hadn't let her down – until just now. Now, she saw that she'd been deceiving herself into believing she was honing a craft rather than mining a natural resource. She had absolutely no idea what to do when she was stuck: she had no other tools at her disposal beyond the dry technicalities of chords and progressions.

She felt a burst of anger, now, towards Janet Davidson. Surely this is what she should have been taught, over the course of the MA? Surely it shouldn't be a case of waiting blindly for inspiration? And if it was, then clearly Prof Davidson was wrong, and what Kitty had written so far had been a flash in the pan, not something she could go on doing. That thought made her feel worse than she had since Henry died. No, worse than she'd ever felt: as though the whole of her, everything that mattered, had been sucked into a whirlpool. Things she hadn't even known were important until they were being snatched away.

And now, she thought with another stab of frustration, she had to stop anyway. The librarian was watching her, and the clock was ticking towards seven thirty. Kitty could feel the song slipping away, the thread of it escaping like the lifeblood of the salmon. God, she hated music. Hated Janet Davidson, and hated herself for being lured into such a ludicrous pursuit. See what she'd been driven to now: a dead end.

She stuffed the sheets of music into her satchel, frightened by the strength of her feelings. She'd been working too hard, she told herself. She needed a drink, an evening off.

It was a surprise to come out into the sunshine. The days were getting longer: it would be light for another hour or two still, and the London streets were full of bustle and optimism. But Kitty felt flat and tired now that the first rush of anger had cooled. She wished there were something happening this evening, something in her diary, but there wasn't. That was her own fault, of course. It wasn't just Daniel she'd pushed aside when her father was dying. She'd been living a strange, isolated sort of life these last few months, and she couldn't face explaining herself to any of the school friends or fellow students she

120

could possibly call. Instead she walked to the tube station and made her way down to the northbound platform.

The flat looked bored, almost hostile, when she opened her front door. *Not you again*, it seemed to say. Kitty dropped her bag on the floor and went through to the tiny kitchen. There was a bottle of wine in the fridge and a plastic tub of olives, sell-by yesterday. She opened the wine and poured herself a glass, then ripped the plastic film off the olives and dug a half-finished packet of digestive biscuits out of the cupboard.

She'd just got up to pour a second glass of wine when the doorbell rang. She didn't answer it the first time: no one ever came to the door. But it rang again, for longer this time, and she thought with a surge of almost-pleasure of a neighbour in trouble, needing her help. She had an entryphone, but instead of pressing the button she went to the window and looked out. Standing outside on the pavement, just far enough from the building for her to see him, was Daniel.

For a long moment Kitty stared down at him. He looked strange from this angle, just a tangle of dark hair and that long coat of his, but unmistakably familiar too, as though her brain had scanned his appearance so minutely that she would recognise any part of him now, from any angle. He stood on one leg, the other cocked behind him, attentive and impatient. The temptation to let him in, to let him fill up her evening and her weekend, was powerful.

But she didn't. She stood completely still by the window, watching, until Daniel gave up and went away. She saw him pull his phone from his pocket, and heard hers vibrating on the other side of the room a moment later, and then he turned abruptly and headed off up the road. He didn't look up at the window, and he didn't look back once he'd started walking. For a moment Kitty fought an urge to rush for the entryphone, for the stairs, to pursue him into the street, but it evaporated sooner than she expected.

Her satchel was lying where she'd dropped it, just inside the door. She took out the sheets of manuscript and smoothed them flat. She could hear the salmon's song in her head, his terrible resignation to his fate. She could hear how the words would be sung: the baritone voice straining for the top notes, the melody unsupported by the rushing semiquavers on the piano. Perhaps there wasn't so much missing after all. Perhaps it was right that the piece barely held together. But she sat down at the little table in the corner and let it fill her mind again, let it carry her along, show her its nooks and crannies and eddies and crevices. These were her tools, she thought: time and thought, and the willingness to expend them.

15

It was late afternoon by the time Flora left Les Violettes. The path through the woods was sharply streaked with shadows, and the glimpses of countryside between the trees, snatches of green and blue, made Flora think of jewels, and of the cornflower and forget-me-not dyes of her batik blouse.

It struck her then how little colour there was in her memories of the last few weeks. The grey-scale shades of her room in the evening and the close-weave text of her book; the darkness of the yew hedges in the maze, intercut with chalk-white paths. Even the monochrome patterning of sea and sky from the ferry, divided by a thread of land. How strange it would be, she thought, to live without colour.

That evening at dinner she behaved beautifully. She listened sympathetically while Friedrich explained the difficulty of finding one's way to Montallon. ('There are signs,' his wife interjected, 'but not easy to see.') She sampled the goat's cheese Madame offered, appreciating not just the variety of tastes but the names – the sharp *Sainte Maure de Touraine*, with its distinctive stalk of straw; the soft, sour *Pouligny Saint Pierre*; the nutty *Crottin de Chavignol*. She enjoyed the *tarte tatin*, and the glass of sweet *Coteaux de l'Aubance* Madame Abelard served with it, but she did not share with her fellow guests the delicious memory of the 1959 Vouvray. Something about Madame's expression, the way her eyes dwelled on Flora, stopped her from mentioning Martin, or Les Violettes. Something that gave her, despite herself, a tantalising glimpse of intrigue.

She woke the next morning with the pleasant feeling that a responsibility had been lifted from her shoulders. She didn't have to entertain herself today: Martin was collecting her at ten. A tour of essential sites, he'd said. She could hardly accept the loan of his house and not allow him to introduce her to its surroundings. She wore her linen trousers again, and a cheesecloth blouse that had seemed improbably skimpy when she'd packed it three weeks ago.

'First stop,' Martin said, as they turned out of the Abelards' gate in his *sportif* Citroën, 'the best producer in Vouvray. No point living here if you don't know where to go for wine. Sauvignon you can get anywhere, but there's more of a knack to Vouvray.'

The Brouillard *cave* was literally a cave. Martin was pleased by Flora's surprise as they pulled off the steep road and into an unkempt driveway where a series of doors led directly into the rock face.

'Rather charming, isn't it?' he said. 'Perfect conditions for the wine, of course.'

'Where do they grow the grapes?' Flora asked. There was no room here for vineyards, nothing but a few children's toys scattered around and a stack of empty wine bottles.

'Just up the road.' Martin gestured vaguely. 'Acres of vines up there.'

As he spoke, the largest door opened and a plump woman emerged.

'Madame Brouillard, Madame Macintyre,' Martin said.

The woman shook Flora's hand, then she and Martin plunged into a conversation Flora could only half-understand. She followed them into the darkness, the cold a shock even though she'd antici-pated it. The cave ran deep into the rock, filled with neat piles of boxed bottles, wooden casks of maturing wine, great steel drums for the maceration. The smell – yeasty and sweet and damp, with an edge of rot – was pungent but oddly pleasant. This was like an elves' workshop, Flora thought, or a moonshine still. Martin broke off now and then to explain something to her, or to ask her a question, but otherwise she was content to listen to the rapid-fire French, picking up an occasional word and marvelling at the strange circumstances in which things were made.

They left with two dozen bottles for Flora. She could hardly remem-ber what she had chosen, after the little ceremony of the tasting: which *année* and *cuvée*, whether *sec* or *moelleux*, *tranquil* or *mousseux*. A whole poetry of wine, she thought; and something recalled her train of thought from her walk home the previous evening.

'What do you suppose it would be like if we could only see in black and white?' she asked, as they pulled onto the main road along the banks of the Loire.

Martin glanced at her, then after a moment he laughed, as though he'd realised belatedly that she was making a joke. 'You ought to know,' he said, 'with your scientific education.'

Flora felt a little abashed now – mostly at the uncharacteristic flippancy of the question, but also at the way the admission of ignorance diminished her in his eyes.

'My expertise is embarrassingly narrow,' she said.

'What is your expertise?'

'The place where the oesophagus joins the stomach.'

Martin looked at her again, and this time Flora laughed.

'That's what happens to surgeons. The focus narrows and narrows. Orthopods close in on the ankle or the elbow; I started with the whole bowel and finished up as an expert on the gastro-oesophageal junction.'

It sounded absurd, put like that. Almost as though she'd made it up, Flora thought, although no one outside the medical profession would ever think of inventing anything so preposterous: a whole career devoted to one obscure corner of the body, and a book's worth of scientific papers on surgical techniques for the different cancers that attacked it. It had fascinated her, of course, the crucial distinction between malignancies that spread from above or below the junction and those that started at the knuckle itself, but it seemed suddenly extraordinary that it had occupied so much of her life.

'Impressive,' Martin said. 'And fascinating, I should think.'

Flora shook her head with a smile. Another problem with a career in surgery – who wants to hear about it, unless they're after your professional assistance?

The Loire drifted along beside them, a great wide streak of water broken up by narrow islands and lazy side-streams. What was required now, Flora wondered? Some intelligent questions about winemaking? An observation about the river? The trouble was that she and Martin had moved too swiftly from being complete strangers to an assumption of familiarity that had little basis in fact – and neither of them, apparently, was much good at small talk. That was par for the course among surgeons, but surely wine merchants were supposed to have the gift of the gab?

'Where are we going now?' she asked eventually, as they swooped over the river and down into the flat plain below.

Martin perked up. He grinned suddenly, like a little boy up to mischief.

'It's a surprise,' he said.

The surprise was a zoo. A wonderful zoo, in a landscaped park with abundant space for the animals. A sign at the entrance announced the birth of a baby koala a couple of weeks before; another encouraged visitors to visit the manatees, the white tigers, the birds of prey that flew free in the amphitheatre three times a day.

'We used to bring the children here,' Martin said, as they watched the antics of the penguins. Flora examined his tone for unease, but found none. The penguins' tank was bounded on one side by a glass wall so that visitors could watch them swimming underwater. Flora was sorry she had let the battery run down on her iPhone. It occurred to her that this was the first time for a long time that she'd wanted to take a photograph. She wanted to remember the neat black bodies of the penguins skimming and dipping and twisting, and Martin standing in front of them, his hands in the pockets of his trademark chinos: a stranger who had brought her to the zoo.

Flora wasn't sure when she realised how the day was going to end. It crept up on her, an understanding that these last couple of days had a shape and a pattern to them that she couldn't resist. As they walked around the park, observing elephants and orangutans, watching a troupe of chimpanzees play, she was increasingly conscious of a tingle of anticipation that she hadn't felt for forty years; a teasing mishmash of uncertainty and inevitability, and of trepidation and desire.

They didn't leave the zoo until six o'clock. There was no discussion about what happened next. The journey home was short and somehow dreamlike: the straight roads, the late sun colouring the flat landscape, and then the tall gates of Les Violettes. Dreamlike, Flora thought, in the sense of things being known that you have no reason to know; things being understood without explanation. An acceptance of a different order, different rules, a different world.

Martin carried her boxes of wine into the house and put them in a corner of the cellar. He came back up with a bottle of his own, a sparkling Vouvray this time. He poured them each a glass, and lifted his in a toast.

'Good,' he said, 'good day,' and he looked at her for a moment in a way that made her tremble a little.

His kitchen was perfectly ordered, the tiled surfaces free of clutter and a slice of the garden, the beautiful garden, visible through the back window. Flora thought with pleasure of cooking in here and carrying food outside onto the terrace every day; then she thought of doing so without Martin and the pleasure ebbed away. Stop, stop, she told herself, but she knew she couldn't. The delicate flavour of the wine was already infusing into her bloodstream, and her brain, and her heart. The world wasn't black and white, she thought; and colours might look different at different times, but it was no use waiting until the light changed, the moment passed, to make a sober judgement.

Martin opened the fridge and Flora saw a little array of dishes and pots, a supper for two left ready. He took out a jar of *foie gras* and a small casserole dish which he slid into the oven. Then he put plates and cutlery on a tray, and found a candle in a drawer. Flora watched him, learning his movements, telling herself she was learning the way around his kitchen.

'Outside?' he said, and Flora nodded.

This evening they sat on the lawn, looking back at the house. This was a view Flora hadn't seen, a different perspective on the garden with the rear of the house as backdrop. She counted three floors, three symmetrical sets of windows, tall and graceful.

'I'll show you the rest of the house later,' Martin said, following her gaze.

He cut some bread and passed Flora the jar of *foie gras*.

'You do like it?' he asked, as she hesitated.

'Yes, of course. Of course I like it.'

He smiled. 'What, then?'

She shook her head. Ridiculous, impossible, to explain the pleasure of the moment. He was different from yesterday lunchtime; but everything had changed since then. She looked back on that time already with nostalgia, even though she knew, hoped she knew, that what was to come was even more delightful.

The casserole contained *coq au vin*, which they ate, after the *foie gras*, with bread and salad. There were figs and cheese waiting too, but Flora declined both and Martin didn't press her. It was dark by now, the night air cool and soft, the candle casting a little pool of light into which bugs glided now and then. Flora didn't want to move, to spoil the moment, but the ache of anticipation had grown almost unbearable.

'Let me show you around, then,' Martin said, and he took her hand as she got up from the table.

He didn't take her to his bedroom, but to a room overlooking the garden which he had prepared – had he? – for her. A guest room, she assumed, with songbirds on the walls and lace on the bed. She realised when he put his hands on her shoulders that she'd had no idea, until that moment, whether her instincts were right. The flood of relief and surprise and gratitude was greater even than she'd expected. This felt an extraordinary thing to happen to her, to anyone. She couldn't remember kissing someone like this before, or the acute pleasure of being touched, undressed, with such gentleness and lack of reserve. She was both sharply aware of her body and unembarrassed by it, as though she had been returned to her essential self: almost a spiritual sense of purification and remaking, a shedding of the weary depreciation of long life.

'Flora,' he said, and her name sounded like a mantra, a spell, an affirmation.

May 1990

The house is completely still when Flora gets home. It's four o'clock in the morning and everyone is asleep. Even the embers of the fire Henry was lighting when she left eight hours ago lie silent in the grate, although she can smell the wood smoke still, the flavour of it colouring the cold air in the hall.

Returning from the hospital after operating at night, Flora finds it hard to go straight to bed. She needs to sleep for an hour or two before she has to get up again, but first she can take a little time, at this dead hour, for herself.

She flicks a switch, and the kitchen fills with fluorescent light, illuminating the chipped yellow Formica they've never changed. Opening the fridge, Flora reaches for a small jar and a half-bottle of wine near the back. She takes them out carefully, so the chink of glass doesn't wake her husband or her daughter, puts everything she needs on a tray and carries it up to the bathroom at the far end of the house.

This is a ritual she keeps to herself: a set piece that signifies pleasure of a particular, private kind. She can feel a sense of calm creeping up on her as she shuts the bathroom door; the high-tensile, euphoric calm that is familiar after fifteen years of surgical on-call. Her mind replays the complicated procedure that filled five of the hours she's been away: the child who almost died, the moments when they thought she would, the drawn look on the usually devil-may-care face of the anaesthetist. Blood and stench and steel tools too large for that narrow little body.

She ought to dread the intrusion of such drama and near-tragedy into the texture of family life, but she doesn't. She loves the thrill of the operating theatre, especially when she's summoned like the cavalry to a case where the odds look grim. This is what she went into surgery for: the years of diligence and drudgery have given her what seems to some an almost superhuman power. Day by day she forgets it, taking her skill and deftness for granted, but in the middle of the night, caught in the blaze of the theatre lights, the magic of it comes back to her. She can still feel the strain in the muscles of her arms, still hear the thump of her heartbeat as the monitors raced and plummeted, and she feels vividly, ecstatically alive.

She turns on the hot tap and scoops a handful of jasmine bath salts – prohibitively expensive – from the jar she keeps on top of the bathroom cabinet. The noise in the old pipes as the water starts to flow causes her a moment's worry, but the house is full of shudderings and squeaks; they sleep with its sounds every night. Flora imagines Henry turning over in his sleep, the twitch of Lou's hand on the pillow, as she watches the bath fill.

With a sigh, she slips into the water, holding her breath for a moment as her lungs fill with scented steam and her skin tingles with heat. Bliss, she thinks. Absolute bliss. She lies back, the glass of Sauternes in her hand. Henry doesn't like sweet wine: she buys this for herself, a case of half-bottles at a time. Savouring the taste of honey on her tongue, she thinks again of the child with the perforated bowel, and a swell of triumph rises in her chest. The little girl is out of danger, safely asleep in the paediatric intensive care unit, and Flora is cocooned by Sauternes and *foie gras* and the ambrosial scent of jasmine.

16

Flora knew at once where she was. Years of waking for surgical emergencies had instilled the habit of instant alertness, but this morning there was no need to follow it with instant action.

The other side of the bed was still warm, the faint smell of another body lingering between the sheets, and a streak of golden light between the curtains suggested the sun had risen several hours ago. The morning after the night before, she thought. It was a long time since she'd been in this position, facing the consequences of sexual recklessness – except perhaps after certain reconciliations with Henry which she'd later thought ill-considered. And on those occasions, she'd woken to a sinking awareness of weakness, or wishful thinking, that was conspicuously absent this time.

She shut her eyes again, remembering the way night had fallen more suddenly than she was used to, and Martin had been more diffident than she expected. The birds on the wallpaper, the slight smell of lavender in the room, the luxury of being held in his arms until she fell asleep. There was nothing to qualify the pleasure of the memory except a slight fearfulness that she had no wish to address now.

She listened for signs of movement below, imagining Martin preparing breakfast in the kitchen – perhaps even setting a tray. But that thought reminded her of Francine Abelard, and Flora didn't want to think about Madame Abelard: about her kindness, her long friendship with Martin, her reaction to Flora's absence last night. There was a dressing gown on the back of the door; slipping it on, Flora opened the curtains, and her heart bloomed at the sight of the garden laid out beneath her. Whatever else happened, she thought, Les Violettes was hers for the summer.

Just then, she heard the front door open. Another dip and flutter, recollecting what lay immediately in store. She came downstairs quietly, but Martin heard her before she reached the kitchen.

'Morning,' he said. 'Perfect timing. Just back from the village.'

He made a show of holding out a plate of croissants, as though pleased to have a prop to hand.

'Delicious,' said Flora.

For a few seconds they stood looking at each other – not awkwardly, Flora thought; more as though to savour the moment before anything else was said or done – and then Martin came towards her and kissed her on the forehead, one hand still balancing the plate.

'I promise this isn't what happens every time I meet someone in the village shop,' he said.

'I'm glad to hear it.'

It occurred to her that she might have expected to see him differently this morning – to realise that he was older or fatter or less well-kempt than she had remembered – but she didn't. It was remarkable how straight-forward the situation felt: no betrayal, no guilt, no dismaying reality to face up to. Perhaps this was what the next twenty-five years were for, she thought impishly, as she watched Martin spoon coffee into the cafetière.

'I Googled you this morning,' he said, when they were sitting on the terrace.

'How very modern.'

'You're a distinguished woman: I didn't realise. You've been very modest.'

'You didn't ask for a CV.'

Martin tore a piece off his croissant and spread jam on it with the care Flora had begun to associate with his approach to food. The right amount of jam, she thought. The right kind too, no doubt. She remembered again her morning in bed, sampling Madame Abelard's jam: an age ago.

'I wouldn't have dared to speak to you if I'd known,' Martin said.
She smiled. 'Well, then, I'm glad you didn't.'

Martin offered to drive her back to the farm, but Flora preferred to walk. She needed the exercise, but more than that she dreaded the idea of reappearing on the Abelards' doorstep, at midday, with Martin. She rather dreaded the idea of returning at all, in fact. Quite apart from a natural fastidiousness about hospitality and the dignity of appearances, if she was going to be living in the village for the rest of the summer, the Abelards' opinion was of more than passing importance.

She had half-imagined Madame waiting in the hall for her, but she needn't have worried. Only the skinny farmyard cat witnessed her arrival, slinking out of the barn to mew at her in hope of a titbit. Flora shut the heavy front door behind her and climbed the stairs. The silence was strange. She had always felt, before, the presence of people here – of Madame, at least; her husband was rarely to be seen, either in the house or about the farm – but today she was sure the house was empty. There were no cars outside, no faint clatter of dishes from the kitchen, no whisper of a voice or a radio. It was dark inside – darker than Les Violettes, with its white paint and large windows. The landing, laid with threadbare rugs, was longer than she'd noticed before, with more doors leading off it. Flora had to resist an impulse to explore, now she had the house to herself. Which of these rooms were occupied by the Abelards, she wondered, and which by guests? Had new visitors arrived yesterday? Had there been a jolly party around the *table d'hôte* last night, conversing in some polyglot combination of languages?

When she opened her own door, the barrenness of the room came as a shock. The milkmaids looked forlorn this morning, pushed clumsily back from the window: Flora straightened the folds of material, glancing down at the view that had kept her company these last few days. She couldn't put her finger on what she was feeling. Anticlimax, she supposed, but it felt more complicated than that. Not a sense of flatness, but of restlessness, impatience, hunger. And of doubt: suddenly, like a change of light, a different view of her situation. She was sixty, a widow, wholly out of practice in the matter of pleasure-seeking. Did she have any right to this – to any of this?

She rested her hands on the windowsill and stared out at the apple trees, the woods beyond, the distant spire. And then her sister Jean's face rose in her mind's eye, wearing an expression Flora had seen many times: not just disapproval, but the expectation of disaster to follow. Come-uppance, Jean would say. And perhaps she was right, Flora thought. Would the joy she had felt this morning tarnish more quickly than she could have imagined possible?

She pushed open the window and leaned out a little way to feel the sun on her face. No, she wouldn't give it up just yet. Wasn't this exactly what she'd felt all those years ago, waiting for someone to call – waiting for Henry, probably? She might be older and wiser, but the uncertainty, the doubt, was surely the same; the sense that happiness was more than she deserved. At least she wouldn't be left in limbo this time, anyway. Martin was coming to take her out for dinner this evening, before he left for England tomorrow. That much she could count on. As for his departure, she knew that was one reason things had followed the course they had with so little hesitation – so there was, she told herself firmly, no cause for regret.

She turned away from the window now and considered the afternoon ahead. A walk, she thought. A long walk, and then a bath. Perhaps she should email Lou and Kitty too, not to tell them about Martin, certainly not that, but to mention the possibility of the house swap. Perhaps one of them might come and visit her, this summer. The thought of her daughters at Les Violettes, admiring the garden in the full heat of August, was both complicated and delightful.

17

Sitting rigid in her seat in the concert hall, Kitty was back in primary school, waiting her turn to show a painting or recite a poem in assembly. She remembered vividly the weight of expectation, and the intensity of feelings running so close to the surface that she was sure they must be visible: dread and longing steeping her skin.

The hall could hold two hundred, and already half the seats were full. Kitty gazed at the white walls, the blue upholstered chairs, the gold lilies at the side of the stage. The shush of conversation swelled and receded around her, echoing up to the steepled roof. The acoustics were taunting her, she thought, showing off the refinement that would ensure every note was heard, every trill and slur and discord.

It wasn't the first time Kitty had heard her music performed, but this felt like a new experience. The lunchtime series at St Mark's, Marlborough Square: Kitty Jones juxtaposed with Schumann and Brahms, performed by the young Czech baritone who'd won the college Lieder Prize earlier in the year. And, God help her, by Daniel. Daniel who was already sitting at the piano, his pale hands arranging the pages of manuscript on the scrolled stand. Daniel who knew every inch of Kitty from the texture of her skin to her harmonic fingerprint; whose interpretation of her music mattered more than anything, just now. She'd wondered if Daniel might be asked to play her piece, though she'd been glad not to know in advance, more than happy that the College never involved composers in rehearsal for the showcase, insisting that their music stood alone.

Kitty felt sick now. She could see Janet Davidson on the far side of the hall, but she didn't want to speak to her. As the clock at the back of the hall ticked silently past 12:55, Kitty shut her eyes, pretending, like a child, that she was alone and could hear nothing.

*

The opening notes lifted from the piano as slowly and carefully as if they were being thought of for the first time. Lifted and then lingered in the air, languorous but persuasive, perfectly placed. Kitty opened her eyes again, and her mouth opened too, as though she needed to see and breathe and taste the sound as well as hear it. It felt as though the song needed her complete attention to will it on – although the extraordinary truth was that Andrej and Daniel were making the sounds she could hear, evoking so precisely the music in her head. This must be like giving birth, seeing what was inside you take shape in the world.

The rest of the audience had vanished now. There was only Kitty and the performers and the space above them in which the sound waves hovered and spread. Not even Kitty, perhaps; all that mattered of her was in the music. Andrej's voice held a long G, closed it on a careful, not quite English diphthong, then slid gracefully onto a high E and unfurled the plaintive phrase that signified to Kitty something more than the words of the setting: something that Andrej's impeccable breath control seemed to yield up between the notes. Kitty's heartbeat accelerated with them, drawing out a pure thread of emotion from the interplay of words and melody. This was something she had never known before, a surge of feeling she couldn't explain or control, bringing recognition beyond rational meaning: something that felt very much like love.

Afterwards Kitty smiled or frowned; she couldn't have said which. She stood among the hubbub of comment and congratulation (they were assiduous, her fellow students: they couldn't be thought offhand on such an occasion) but it swirled round her, past her. And then Daniel was there, and Andrej, who had sung Schumann with less verve than Kitty's songs, and who looked disheartened now it was over.

'What did you think?' Daniel asked, and Kitty could see that people were listening, waiting to see how the tortuous relationship between composer and performer would play out.

'Good,' Kitty said. Not enough, not the right word at all.

'It's a great piece,' he said. 'Great music.'

'Thank you.'

Daniel looked at her for a moment longer, then he smiled in a way Kitty recognised – B minor, she thought; a B minor cadence of a smile – and moved away.

Kitty looked after him for a moment, then her eyes moved to Andrej. 'Thank you,' she said. 'Your voice is beautiful.'

Outside, the crowd was rapidly reabsorbed into the bustle of the London afternoon. Kitty walked towards the tube station, her head lifted towards the invisible sun. The sky was the neutral grey of winter today, but the branches of the apple trees in the square were sprigged with blossom, late this year but proof, nonetheless, of the inevitable momentum of the seasons.

Kitty felt an intoxicating sense of limbo and of promise. She could feel the air against her cheeks, the scent of earth and tarmac filling her lungs, things sharply defined all around her. Unfamiliar emotions swilled in her head, but there was something delicious in the knowledge that she didn't need to seize them at once: that they would be there when she was ready for them, like a strange city waiting to be mapped.

'Kitty!'

Daniel's voice, not far behind. Kitty's heart slipped and caught itself. She clutched her coat across her chest, burying her knuckles in the velvet of the collar. She knew he would follow her, catch her up. Could she – did she want to – escape him? She took another step, and another. She could feel the street sliding out of view now, and the pull of Daniel's advance.

'Kitty!' he called again. 'Kitty, please!'

Kitty stopped. Daniel drew level, close enough now for her to feel the glow of heat from his short sprint.

'This is silly,' he said. 'I don't understand.'

For a moment Kitty held on to the sense of clarity she'd had, the spring of possibility within her. Then she turned to look at Daniel and felt other things, the familiar temptation of yielding to his conviction.

She couldn't think of herself alone when Daniel was there; that must mean something.

'I'm sorry about your father,' Daniel said. Her head was cradled against his chest. He lifted her hair out of the nape of her neck slowly, one strand at a time.

'You said.'

Kitty could feel Daniel's fingers brushing her shoulder, and the slow rise and fall of his ribcage. The concert, the apple blossom, the quality of the air in the street had all merged and settled into a particular kind of memory, like a day recalled from a photograph.

'I didn't think you'd noticed.'

'I did.'

He moved slightly, craning his head to glimpse her face. 'You've been avoiding me.'

'I'm here now,' Kitty said.

'Yes.'

She was here, and it had been nice, this last hour; it had been lovely. Soothed by the pressure of skin against skin and the soporific half-light of late afternoon, it was hard to understand her reluctance to see him. He played her music beautifully; that was important. He had the same infallible instincts as Henry, the same innate understanding. She'd never met anyone else who'd been born with the entire musical canon apparently hard-wired into their brain, and that was something to admire – to be thrilled by, even. And she liked him holding her like this.

She made a little noise of remorse and confusion, burrowing her head further into the crook of his arm, and he kissed her forehead.

'Tell me about your father,' he said.

'What about him?'

'Anything. Tell me about a time you remember with him, when you were little.'

Kitty waited for the shudder of grief, but it didn't come. Instead there was a wash of something lighter and sweeter, and a picture of herself in a red dress made of some thin, cool material, standing beside a duck pond.

'He used to take me out at the weekends,' she said. 'When my mother was at the hospital. We'd go on expeditions.'

'With your sister?'

'Not always. She was much older. But there were other people, sometimes.'

Quite often, in fact. Certainly on the duck pond day. She could see the surface of the pond now, filled with the reflection of the sky, through a fringe of reeds as tall as her. The ducks were silent, gliding like ghosts over the grey water.

'So where did you go?' Daniel asked.

'Sometimes to the zoo, or the cinema. Usually just to the park.' Kitty paused. 'I got lost, once. I ran away. I'd never seen my father so angry.'

Round to the far side of the pond she had run, on and on, down a long avenue of trees that sheltered her from the sun. Past a kiosk she thought she recognised, and people picnicking and playing football, until her legs hurt and there was nothing familiar in sight. And then a blank, a blur, until her father was there again, and the woman and the child who had been there before had gone. He was crying, her father. She knew he was only pretending to be angry and that he was sorry, and she let him gather her up and carry her home. She remembered that vividly, a journey that went on and on like a dream. *My darling,* he'd said, his voice filling the whole space inside her. *My precious girl.*

For a while neither of them spoke. The light had ebbed further, and the shadows filling the room were growing darker and softer.

'I never knew my father,' Daniel said.

Kitty twisted towards him, and her stomach twisted too. She had forgotten Daniel's situation, carried away by her own story.

'I thought they died when you were five?' she said.

'My mother did. I didn't know my father. He wasn't on the scene.'

She ought to have known that, Kitty thought. Daniel rarely talked about his family, but she could have asked him more questions.

'Have you tried to find him?'

'I've never felt the lack of him. I had my grandparents.'

Kitty's stomach pitched again: the grandparents were dead too now, she knew that much. She couldn't imagine what it must feel like to be entirely alone in the world.

'Poor Daniel,' she said, stretching her hand up to touch his face.

'Why poor me? You can't lose something if you've never had it.'

Kitty squeezed her eyes shut. Sometimes she knew what Daniel was feeling without looking at him, and at other times the expression on his face almost overpowered her. He had a way of mixing emotions like cocktails, with a kick she didn't expect. She felt herself suddenly on the verge of tears that weren't hers to shed.

'I suppose not,' she said; then, 'I love you, Daniel,' although in fact what she was thinking was that all this was too much for her, just at the moment. Her neck hurt from lying curled against him, and the light had gone from the day, and she wanted to go home now and spend the evening on her own. She wanted to find that city, the one her music had opened up for her, and she didn't want to hear Daniel's reply.

18

Flora climbed gratefully into the bath when she got back from her walk. The abbey she could see from her bedroom window was further than it looked, and her legs ached, but the exercise had done her good. There was nothing like walking to bring things back into perspective, she thought. No surprise that it had spawned so many metaphors. They rolled through her head as she lay in the hot water, a comforting liturgy of common sense: putting your best foot forward; getting your feet back on the ground; reminding you where you stood.

She'd thought about Montallon this afternoon, about the English family and the lost child and the way she'd been drawn into their drama. She hadn't made a fool of herself, she thought, not then and not over Martin, but she'd touched a boundary she'd never had to be aware of before. She couldn't rely on the instincts she'd honed in her previous life to guide her in every circumstance now: the world was less well-known than it had always seemed, and her place in it less assured.

She dipped her head under the surface, letting the meniscus close over her face, then shook her hair out in the way she used to as a child, sending a spray of droplets over the side of the bath. Fresh air and water: a ritual of purification for a new life. She felt a surge of contentment that reminded her of those late-night baths she used to take after operating; those sweet moments of solitude and self-reliance.

But she was aware – how could she not be? – that she was in a delicate position. Delicate in many ways: not simply the fragile heart of the widow, although that wasn't the least of it. Henry was dead, and she'd endured years of his infidelity, but he was too recently dead for her emotions to be straightforward. But what she felt on Henry's account wasn't so much guilt as pity: the compassion of the living for the dead, a phenomenon she'd observed many times in her professional life. *A decent interval*, she thought. Should she mind that two months wasn't a decent interval? And then there were her decades of distinguished service to the feminist cause, and the lessons she ought to have learned last time she'd fallen for a romantic ideal. Part of her was astonished to catch herself succumbing with just as little caution as she'd done four decades before, and that part of her was determined to protect her dignity more effectively this time.

By the time she finally climbed out of the bath it was ten to eight. She got dressed in a hurry then, stopping only briefly to glance at the mirror. Her cheeks were flushed with heat; she looked healthy and happy. She smiled, pursed her lips, gathered herself.

Martin was already here. She heard his voice as she reached the bottom of the stairs, speaking French of the rapid, animated kind he'd used with the wine-maker yesterday. Flora followed the sound to the kitchen door. She hadn't seen Francine Abelard all day, and her scruples on that score competed now with a twinge of what might pass for jealousy. It must be Francine that Martin was speaking to so fervently – and speaking about what, she wondered? About her? Or about something else entirely?

Madame Abelard saw her first.

'*Et voilà*,' she said. 'Good evening, Madame.'

Martin turned and smiled at her. He said something too, something simple and polite which Flora didn't hear because her head was filled suddenly with white noise, as though she was changing channel on an old-fashioned television set. There was nothing unexpected about him, about what he said or how he looked, but she had a sudden, powerful sense of misapprehension. She'd tuned into the wrong channel, she thought, allowed the wrong picture to take shape in her mind. The wrong idea of herself, as much as anything. She remembered vividly at that moment his hands on her body, his arms around her, images distilling disconcertingly from the fog in her head.

Francine took a step back, as though reading something in Flora's expression.

'*Alors*,' she said, '*allez-vous-en*.'

It seemed to Flora then that this outing was a terrible mistake. She had no idea whether it was meant to paper over what had happened last night or to cement it, but she sincerely wished that neither was necessary: that they could simply forget it. But Martin was looking at her expectantly, and Madame too. There was no choice, Flora could see that. She was dressed to go out for dinner, and she couldn't possibly explain – certainly not in front of Madame Abelard – that in some obscure way this wasn't at all what she'd expected. She followed Martin out to the car and let him whisk her away through the dusk.

The restaurant Martin had chosen looked unprepossessing – a single-storey building at the side of the road. The interior was similarly drab: a lot of pale wood, and plain tables arranged in rows. More like a classroom than a restaurant, Flora thought. This was not, surely, the place a man of Martin's discernment would bring someone he wanted to impress. She felt a pricking of disappointment, and then of impatience. How perverse she was. Hadn't she wanted to abandon the evening altogether, ten minutes ago? How could she want the situation further distorted by romantic flummery?

'You're quiet this evening,' Martin said, when the waitress left them at their table.

'I'm rather tired,' Flora said. 'I went for a long walk this afternoon.'

'Working up an appetite?' Martin smiled. 'That's good. You'll need one.'

As soon as she opened the menu Flora understood. Romantic flummery might not be Martin's line, but food certainly was. Neither her French nor her culinary discernment was as expert as his, but the quality of the cuisine was immediately apparent, even to her, from the descriptions of the food.

'They'll have a Michelin star by next year,' Martin said, with satisfaction. 'Worked bloody hard for it, too.' He shut the menu and smiled at her. He was wearing a tie, Flora noticed belatedly, and a shirt that looked brand new. 'Let's leave it to Pascal,' he said. 'Nothing you don't eat, is there?'

Flora shook her head. After the tumult of the last hour she felt a blessed sense of relief. She had never been to a Michelin starred restaurant before, or even one on the verge of such distinction, but just now it seemed the perfect answer. They could spend the evening eating their way through a sequence of delights that neither of them would have to choose.

After that, conversation flowed quite easily, although it covered ground Flora hadn't anticipated.

'Was your husband a doctor too?' Martin asked, as the *amuses bouches* arrived.

'Heavens, no,' said Flora. 'Nothing like that. He was a music critic. He wrote reviews and introduced concerts, that sort of thing. The Proms, for years and years. He had a chat show, too.'

'On the radio?'

'Henry Jones' Musical World. It had quite a following, for Radio Three.'

'Henry Jones?' Martin looked incredulous. 'How extraordinary. We're connected, then. My wife's a cousin of his – a distant cousin of some kind.'

'Really?'

Flora felt the ground between them shifting, making their meeting both less simple and less unexpected. His wife and her husband: well, well. Not after all two strangers, but threads twining within a social pattern. Signs and coincidence, she thought, remembering that moment on the ferry, aeons ago now. She was still suspicious of their intrusion into her life, although the last few weeks had revealed them everywhere.

'They met, I think, a while back,' Martin said. 'Their paths crossed. Some family business.'

Flora shrugged. It wasn't likely she would remember a family matter of Henry's. Henry's family hadn't featured much in their life. It wasn't the kind that went in for gatherings or genealogy.

'Some financial arrangement, I think.' Martin looked at Flora as though something had occurred to him, but after a moment, a tiny moment, he shook his head. 'Miranda used to listen to his show. She has the musical gene too. Friday afternoon, wasn't it?'

'Two o'clock.'

Flora had never listened to Henry's programme: she'd always had an outpatients clinic on Friday afternoons. Towards the end, when she was at home with him, Radio Three had played some repeats, but he hadn't wanted to listen to them. Especially not the older ones, with guests who'd died since the programme was made. Harold Pinter, Ted Heath, Muriel Spark.

'Quite the power couple,' said Martin.

'Hardly.' Flora felt a familiar twist of regret, the kind that shades into irony, for the gap between the glamorous image Martin's phrase conjured up and the shabbier reality of her marriage.

The waiter appeared, carrying two more plates.

'*Terrine de canard aux noix,*' he said, bowing as he backed away again.

'How beautiful,' Flora said. 'Too pretty to eat, almost.'

The décor might be plain here, she thought, but the dishes were not. The terrine was served with a fan of perfect French toast, fringed by redcurrants and little fronds of some herb she didn't recognise. She smiled at Martin. She didn't mean to talk about Henry anymore. This was a nice occasion: she wouldn't let it be spoiled by shadows.

'Tell me about Madame Abelard,' she said instead. 'Tell me about her family.'

'Dear Francine,' said Martin. 'Oh, that's a long, sad story.'

'We've got all evening.'

'So we have.' Martin hesitated, though; Flora could sense his reluctance.

'Not if you don't –' she started to say, and at the same time Martin said, 'I suppose you've guessed we were lovers.'

Flora's heart jumped a little; but only a little, she was pleased about that. More at the unexpectedness of the words than at what they conveyed, she thought.

'Not anymore,' Martin said. 'Not for a long time. We were childhood sweethearts, donkeys years ago. We were practically engaged when we were seventeen. Then her brother died while I was away at university in England, and when I came back the next summer she was married to that oaf Claude Abelard.'

'Why?' Flora asked.

'I've never understood. For the farm, I suppose: it was a prosperous concern back then. Francine's family fell apart when Jean-Pierre died, that was the thing. The whole village was rocked by it.'

'And he was a friend of yours?'

'They both were. He was a year older than me, Francine a year younger. He was a terrific chap. Generous, capable, turned his hand to anything. The father was a lawyer, but he was an invalid. They were all waiting for Jean-Pierre to take up the reins, keep the family on the road.'

'How did he die?'

'Meningitis. Went off to university in Paris, and he was dead within a month. Just a small outbreak, but he copped it. Terrible luck.'

'Awful,' Flora agreed. 'Poor Francine. So she married Monsieur Abelard, and that was it for the two of you?'

'Not quite.' Martin made a rueful gesture.

'I'm sorry,' Flora said. 'It's none of my business.'

Martin looked at her for a moment or two. 'Not for a long time now,' he said. 'Just friends, or – just friends now.'

He took a piece of bread from the basket and tore it apart. Flora ate the last morsel of her terrine with a delicacy that felt unfamiliar; the tang of the redcurrants reminded her uncomfortably of Francine Abelard.

The next few courses passed with small talk about Martin's business and his daughter's wedding. A different sort of dialogue, Flora thought, as though they'd remembered that they hardly knew each other. They ate fish and then lamb, and then a cheese trolley appeared beside the table and a recitation of their names and provenances was given, which reminded Flora of a party game she'd played as a child. She was very full already, and still unaccustomed to the French habit of eating cheese before dessert, but she chose a couple, and slivers were cut and placed in front of her.

'I should have introduced you to the neighbours,' Martin said. 'Some you can give a wide berth to, but there are a few you might like to meet.'

'You haven't seen my house yet,' Flora said. 'You might not like it.'

He smiled at her. 'Ah, but you like Les Violettes, don't you? I'm not sure I have a choice in the matter.'

And now there was just the dessert to come. What happened next, Flora wondered, as the waiter set before her a confection that looked more like modern art than food? Had she forgotten, somehow, that this genteel social dance would end very soon with the two of them on opposite sides of the Channel?

Martin hadn't tasted his *gourmandise de chocolat* either. Flora caught his eye, and he reached a hand across the table to take hers. She felt a charge of pleasure run up her arm and down towards her belly. It seemed to her now that she'd been waiting for this all evening; that she'd wanted to touch him since that first moment in Francine Abelard's kitchen. But it felt enough, this clasping of hands. As much as she could manage, just now.

'I've got to be off early tomorrow,' he said. 'It's too late to . . . I have to go, I'm afraid. But if you like we could –'

'No,' Flora said, although her heart beat painfully. Better, she thought, to be the one to assert common sense. So much better than waiting for him to do it. 'I'll go home. Back to the Abelards.'

He said nothing for a few moments; she thought she could read relief in his face. 'I'll give you a set of keys,' he said. 'You can move in whenever you like. Marie-José comes on Monday mornings. She'll show you everything you need.'

Flora nodded. She reached into her bag and took out her keys – the only set of keys for Orchards she'd brought with her. 'You've got the address?' she said. 'I'll let the agents know. And my daughters.'

'Of course if they want to come home – or you do . . .'

He looked troubled, Flora thought. An unfamiliar phenomenon: a man with scruples. Or was that wishful thinking? He'd got exactly what he wanted, she thought suddenly. A clean exit. She felt sure, all at once, that he had never lost sight of that fact; that despite her best efforts she had been naïve. Life had prepared her well enough for this sort of scene, though. She mustered her self-possession, and the requisite degree of briskness.

'I don't expect they will,' she said. 'But thank you, anyway.'

'I'll be back,' he said. 'Some time in the summer, I'll be back.'

'As you like,' said Flora.

'Of course if you'd rather I stayed elsewhere . . .'

'Don't be ridiculous.' Flora almost managed a laugh. But Martin was still frowning, and she felt a quiver of irritation now. They understood each other perfectly: what more, exactly, could he want from her?

'It's been a very pleasurable few days, Flora,' he said.

'Yes.' She smiled, and looked him straight in the eye. 'Yes, it has.'

November 2004

They are in bed, awake, naked. This is not something to be taken for granted; not so much a part of the normal run of things that it should pass without notice.

Flora has just got back from a conference in Geneva, where she's been awarded a medal by the European Surgical Society, and she and Henry have been celebrating with a bottle of Chassagne-Montrachet. She feels happy, and tender: she's at the pinnacle of her career, and her marriage has settled. Her patience and her judgement have been rewarded at last. She leans across to kiss Henry, and feels a quiver in her belly.

The workings of her body please Flora more and more as she gets older. There's one thing to be said for the vicissitudes of her marriage: sex has never been dull. Passion could have declined slowly into companionship, for them as for others, but instead an exhilarating spectrum of emotions has been brought to their bed over the last twenty-five years – rage, remorse, regret and even, sometimes, retaliation. Imagine how things might have been if she'd accepted one of those men her mother intended for her, stalwarts of the Tory party and the City Livery Companies for a quarter of a century now. She laughs at the thought, and Henry raises an eyebrow.

'What's funny?'

'Tony Glover.'

'Who's he?'

'My mother wanted me to marry him,' Flora says. 'A suitable beau.'

'I thought she wanted you to marry Landon?'

'Only as a last resort. Tony Glover was the apogee of her hopes.'

Henry frowns, miming offence.

'I've kept you in the manner to which she was accustomed, haven't I?'

'Well,' Flora says. 'On and off.'

His chest jerks up and down as he laughs. 'I've never regretted it for a moment,' he says. 'Marrying you.'

'I should hope not.'

'Have you?'

Flora's heart bobs, riding out a ripple on the water, but it passes.

'No,' she says. 'At times, maybe, but – no.'

She kisses him again, then runs her hand down over his chest, its familiar lines softened by the years. The triangle of hair below his throat is greying faster than the thick curls on his head, she notices.

'There's a bump there,' he says. 'A cyst, or something.'

'Where?'

'In my tit,' he says, 'or near it. Male menopause, maybe. Growing boobs in my old age. I'll be impotent before you know it.'

Flora smiles, sliding her hand round the contour of his ribcage. 'Not yet,' she says. 'Not just yet.'

Something rings: her hand halts, tightens, relaxes again. The house phone, not her mobile.

'Leave it,' she says. 'It won't be for me. Not on duty this weekend.'

The phone stops, then rings again.

'Better get it,' Henry says. 'Could be one of the girls.'

'Unlikely.' Kitty's staying the night with a friend; Lou is at university and has better things to do on Saturday nights than ring her parents.

The phone rings on. Henry leans towards it without a word.

'Hello?' he says. 'No. Yes. Maybe tomorrow. OK.'

'Who was it?' Flora asks. Her voice is gentle, unthreatening, but her eyes are wide open.

'No one.' Henry pats her on the shoulder; a tell-tale gesture. She smiles and says nothing, and he looms above her, the swing of his penis ungainly as a shipyard crane.

Afterwards Flora lies still and silent, listening to Henry's breathing slowing, deepening; to the sudden catch and gurgle in his throat as he

151

slides into sleep. She feels the warmth of him, his weight in the bed, the comfort of having her husband beside her. For a long while she doesn't move: she should savour this moment, she thinks. This might be the last time for a long time – perhaps for ever – that she lies beside him, naked, awake.

When she's sure he's asleep she rolls gently out of bed. In the dark, she tiptoes round to Henry's side and lifts the phone from its cradle. Cradle, she thinks; there's an irony. Another irony to add to the list. Slowly, deliberately, she presses 1471, then the redial key, and after two rings the phone is answered.

'Darling,' says a woman's voice. 'I thought you'd manage to slip away.'

19

In the days after Martin's departure Flora felt weightless. Drifting around the house, trying out the smell of the empty rooms, she felt as though gravity operated differently in this new life of hers, attaching her less firmly to the ground. Perhaps because this was really someone else's life – a life whose trappings she had taken on like a disguise to conceal the fact that Flora herself, the essence of her, was hardly here at all? Or because, like an astronaut floating above the earth's atmosphere, she could look back at her old life now from a distance that made everything look strange and unfamiliar?

There was also, sometimes, the peculiar sense that she had landed at Les Violettes all at once, as though she'd been borne through the summer in the eye of a small tornado that had whisked her blindly across uncertain stretches of time and space before depositing her quite suddenly in this unknown house. And although she'd reached a still point now, time merged and flowed alarmingly in her mind, recent events jostling for position with memories from years before. She caught herself thinking of Kitty in pigtails plaited by the au pair, or planning operating lists in her head, her brain busy with the careful balancing of challenge and routine that had characterised her years as a Consultant. Was it possible that her daughters were grown up and her husband dead? Impossible, surely, that the fleeting romance of the last couple of weeks was more than a figment of her imagination.

She did her best to live in the present, and to take pleasure in her sole occupation of Les Violettes. She paid the house close attention, noticing things she would never have seen as a casual visitor: the intricate beading along the skirting boards; the desk drawer that gave a little squawk of protest as it opened. She took books off shelves and kept them by her bed, scanned guidebooks for outings she might undertake at some point in the future, gazed at the photographs of

Martin's family, his wife and suntanned children smiling in a faded, long-ago summer. She imagined Martin doing similar things at Orchards, conjuring glimpses of him so vivid that she thought they must be telepathy. Once she woke in the night, certain she'd made a terrible mistake staying on here, and then she lay still, imagining herself as a *toile* shepherdess, oblivious to everything except the joys of the garden. By the morning she was content again; content enough to get up and begin another day.

There was a supermarket five miles away, but Flora bought most of her food in the village shop. Not just, she told herself, because it was where she'd first seen Martin; where her path had branched that day. She liked the daily ritual of calling in for bread and milk, the *Bonjour, Madame* and the counting out of foreign coins. Rituals had become important: she spent an hour or two in the garden every afternoon, weeding and dead-heading – tasks she'd never attempted before but which she found fulfilling and pleasingly tiring – and she took to walking into the village in the evenings as well as the mornings, passing the water tower and the row of cypresses by the river, the houses topped by steep slate roofs like lids you might lift off. She'd always been good with faces, and before long she was nodding and smiling at the people she passed every day. The small satisfaction of this social contact made her feel both a degree less isolated, and a degree more. It put the little life she was building for herself here into perspective.

She'd been relieved at first not to run into Francine Abelard, but when she saw her coming out of the shop one morning, almost a week after Martin's departure, Flora's spirits lifted unexpectedly. Madame Abelard was wearing the same kind of clothes as always – a skirt of some indeterminate dark material, a pale blouse and a long cardigan – and she had several bags of shopping in her hands. She stopped when she saw Flora.

'*Bonjour*, Madame,' she said. 'Do you enjoy Les Violettes?'

'Very much.' Flora remembered Francine's commendation of the house, that first time.

'You are not lonely?'

'No.' Flora hesitated. 'I'm not used to having nothing to do, though. I'm getting used to it slowly.'

Francine gave her the appraising, percipient look Flora remembered so well. She wished she knew whether it signified sympathy or criticism: there were so few people left to have an opinion of her that it rather mattered what Francine thought. For a moment she considered asking her to lunch, but then she remembered how busy she was, how the running of the farm as well as the *chambres d'hôtes* fell largely to her, and blushed at her presumption.

'You like music, I think?' Francine said, her words taking Flora by surprise. 'There is a concert next week in Tours. Every year they have a performance in the church. Will you come with me? Claude prefers to stay at home, and you would enjoy it, I hope.'

Flora recalled fleetingly her frivolous suggestion that Francine could read her mind, and then, more pertinently, the kindness she had been shown during her stay at the *chambres d'hôtes*.

'Thank you,' she said, 'that would be lovely.'

'Then I will arrange it. I will telephone to Les Violettes.'

'Good,' said Flora. 'I look forward to it.'

Francine nodded a farewell as she turned back up the road, and Flora went on into the shop. Music might not be her first choice of entertainment, but she was cheered by the prospect of an evening out. And she would like to get to know Francine Abelard better, too. Friendship, she thought, was something she'd never really mastered. There hadn't been many women to befriend in her old life: there had been so little time for anything beyond her work and her family, and alliances with other doctors were always uneasy. The possibility of friendship with Francine lit like a bulb inside her now, illuminating the loneliness of recent days.

When she'd finished her shopping, Flora walked slowly back through the village. It was only ten o'clock, but already the sun was burning through the early haze. Flora could feel the advance of summer, especially when she was in the garden: not just the heat on her back, but the plants responding to the call of the sun, unfurling their last leaves and surging into bloom. Today was going to be the hottest day yet, she thought. The pale stone of the village already had a bleached look, and the air was scented with dust and pollen. The smell of holidays.

She thought of Les Violettes waiting quietly for her: the garden, and the grandfather clock needing winding, and the cheese and ham she could eat for lunch. The future, she thought, not the past. The life she was making here that belonged entirely to her. Deep inside her something stirred: a thread of optimism, taking her by surprise.

20

Lou stood at the junction of two paths with shops and houses running in both directions, none of them taller than her waist. This little world was strangely charming, caught in a 1930's glow of leisurely English life. Castles, zoos, mazes and funfairs were surrounded by fields and trees, linked by roads and rivers and bridges and by a network of tiny, busy trains. On her right, a football pitch was dotted with players engaged in an everlasting friendly fixture. As she looked down, trying to identify the colours of each team's strip, it seemed to Lou for a moment that she could hear the shouts of the crowd, urging them on – and then the sounds resolved into the voice of her god-daughter Maebh, calling her to come and look at something, and she turned and smiled and allowed herself to be led off to inspect a miniature wedding party, arranged for the photographer in front of a pretty church.

She'd promised herself to Maebh and Dearbhla several weeks ago, one of the twice- or thrice-yearly outings that Dearbhla regarded as part of a godmother's duties, but the timing couldn't have been better, Lou thought, and nor could the location. Maebh's delight was irresistible, and a morning spent wandering in her wake, sharing her joy, was just what Lou needed.

'Alice didn't fancy this, then?' Dearbhla asked, as Maebh ran off to find something else to marvel at.

'She's been very busy,' Lou said.

She knew this was a nicety on Dearbhla's part, as well as a half-truth on hers. Dearbhla always made a point of asking Alice, but Lou suspected she was always relieved when the invitation wasn't taken up. Not that – she couldn't accuse Dearbhla of prejudice, despite her forthright Catholicism. It was more that Dearbhla enjoyed her company too much to share her.

Their friendship had been forged on their first day at university, and it had survived the vicissitudes of student life and the divergence of their paths thereafter. Dearbhla's Sligo accent had kindled Lou's interest when they'd said their first diffident 'hellos' outside the ungraceful concrete hall of residence, and she'd never regretted the impulse to befriend this odd-looking, straight-talking, fire-filled Irishwoman. Dearbhla was brilliant: she'd got a First and a place on a sought-after MA course, but halfway through her PhD she'd married a Biology teacher from County Cork, and Maebh had been born a year later. Since then her thesis hadn't been mentioned. She'd been the first of Lou's friends to have a baby, and was still the only one to succumb to that particular brand of motherhood that felt to outsiders as much of a holy mystery as her religion had been when they were students together.

Lou was surprised that no more babies had appeared in the four years since Maebh's birth, but over Dearbhla's marriage a discreet veil had always been drawn. Meanwhile, Maebh was unquestionably bonny and absorbing. She had her father's ginger hair but Dearbhla's milky skin and rosy cheeks, and in her flowery dress she looked absolutely the part for the model village's once-upon-a-time ambience. Lou felt a tug of emotion – affection for this sweet child, to whom she had devoted less attention than a godmother perhaps should (and Lou was ever-mindful of the honour of the appointment, as a non-Catholic), but also one of those disbelieving lurches of wonder at the thought that she too would be the mother of a child like this in a very few years. She could just about imagine a baby by now, but a walking, talking, laughing being like Maebh – could that possibly come true? Watching Maebh skip clumsily along the path between an aerodrome and a boating lake, Lou caught a glimpse, just the tiniest glimpse, of a miraculous future, like a door opening a crack onto a world too dazzlingly bright to look at full on. A world that still filled her with as much fear as delight.

She turned slightly, and caught Dearbhla's eyes on her.

'Penny?' Dearbhla asked.

'I was thinking how delightful she is.'

'You could have babies,' said Dearbhla. 'There are ways.' She grinned, the old wicked Dearbhla grin, and Lou felt herself flush from the feet up, a billow of heat that swept right to the crown of her head.

'Oh, I see.' Dearbhla raised an eyebrow. 'When were you going to tell me, then?'

'Right now,' said Lou, and she laughed. 'I'd forgotten your sixth sense.'

'My Irish witchcraft,' said Dearbhla. 'No, it was you who gave it away. You never could keep a secret. How many weeks, then?'

'Only twelve,' said Lou.

'And you're not retching?'

'Not today.' Lou felt a little breathless. This business of telling people was still new, and still fraught with the memory of telling Alice. And she'd anticipated Dearbhla's reaction being more complicated than it seemed to be – though why, she wasn't sure, since Dearbhla had taken so much else in her stride. *I'm the Catholic, not you,* she'd said, years ago, when another university friend had moved into a flat with her divorcé boyfriend.

'Is Alice pleased?' Dearbhla asked.

Lou hesitated. She wanted to answer the question properly; wanted it quite badly, in fact, since Dearbhla seemed suddenly the very person to offer the kind of sane advice she needed, but they had never – there had always been a no-go area in their friendship, she thought. She floundered for a moment, weighing up one uncertainty against another, and then Maebh came rushing towards them again, her stubby plaits bouncing.

'There's ice creams, Mummy. Can I have an ice cream?'

'Ooh, I think we could all manage an ice cream,' said Dearbhla. 'Couldn't we, Lou?'

They sat at a wooden picnic table in the play area. The little girl chattered away about the delights of the village, and Lou was struck by how much she'd noticed – the sheepdog herding his flock, and the fireman up a ladder. She ought to remember Kitty at this age, Lou thought, but memories of Kitty's childhood eluded her just now.

'You're very observant, Maebh,' she said.

'What's azervant?' asked Maebh.

'It means you're good at looking,' said her mother. 'And you're good at eating ice cream, too. That hasn't taken you long, has it?'

'It's delicious,' said Maebh, producing the word carefully, and offering it to Lou with a heart-stopping smile before handing her empty cone to Dearbhla. 'Can I go on the slide now?'

'Let me just wipe your face, then.'

When she had run off again, Dearbhla turned back to Lou.

'So, then?' she said. 'Who's the lucky man? Is there one?'

'A donor,' said Lou. 'Anathema to you, I'm sure, a father picked out of a catalogue.'

Dearbhla shrugged. 'We all get to pick,' she said. 'Does that make Alice the Daddy, then?'

'That's rather a moot point,' said Lou. 'The whole thing is – oh, I don't know. Everything feels so complicated.'

'No one said motherhood was an easy option, did they?'

'They certainly didn't.'

Dearbhla looked at her for a moment.

'Funny – I always thought it would have been easier with another woman.'

Lou gave her a rueful smile. 'Not so far.'

She waited for Dearbhla to speak again, but when she did it was to say, 'You know, it's funny you having babies just when I'm thinking of going back to work.'

'Are you?'

'Well, going to work, I suppose. I've never really done anything that counts as a job. But Maebh'll be starting school in September, you know.'

So perhaps there weren't going to be any more babies, Lou thought. And no more talk of her own, or at least of her present circumstances. From the top of the slide Maebh yelled, 'Look at me! Look at me!' and they both turned to wave as she slithered down and ran back to the bottom of the ladder.

'I'll tell you the truth, Lou: I love Maebh to bits, but I need something for myself, now. Marriage isn't all it's cracked up to be, to be honest. Your mother would agree, I know that.' She made a face. 'How is your mother, by the way? What does she think about this baby lark?'

'I haven't told her yet,' said Lou. 'She's off travelling in France. You're only the third person I've told.'

'Well, I'm flattered. But you should, you know. Think how you'd feel if your baby didn't tell you that you were going to be a granny.'

That was a situation as yet beyond Lou's imagination, but even so she felt a little prick of pain at the thought of it; a pain that brought with it a paradoxical flush of reassurance.

'I'm sorry things have been –' She stopped, realising that her sympathy, like Dearbhla's, was best left unspoken. 'Have you got anything in mind, work-wise?'

'I was wondering about your line, actually.' Dearbhla crushed the remains of her ice cream cone into the waterlogged ashtray on the table. 'I could see myself as a local solicitor. There's one here, even: did you see it? Crook and Swindler. Next to Mr Chop the Butcher.'

'So you're thinking of doing the CPE?' Lou said. 'A law conversion course?'

'Do you think I'm mad? I was dreading telling you, to be honest. I thought you'd laugh.'

'Why? You can even do it part-time.'

'We could afford a childminder.' Dearbhla's eyes flicked to Maebh again, and in her glance Lou caught a hint of suffering and sacrifice not to be declared.

'Let me know if I can do anything,' said Lou. 'I could write you a reference.'

Dearbhla looked straight at her then, and for a moment Lou thought she might be going to cry.

'I could have Maebh some time,' Lou said. 'I'd like that. If you'd like some time to – I don't know.'

'That's very kind of you,' Dearbhla said, her voice melodiously even. 'She'd like it too.' She glanced towards the slide again, and then down at her watch.

'One more go, Maebh, or we won't have time to go round the rest,' she called, and then she looked at Lou again. 'My prescription for you, Louisa, is a weekend away with that Alice of yours. By the seaside, perhaps. It's a well-known cure for morning sickness.'

March 1984

Flora has never liked Gillian Sutherland, but even so her news is unwelcome; a shifting of ground Flora thought she could rely on. She and Gillian have paced each other – at arm's length – through the procession of Fellowship exams and promotion. They have carefully avoided pitting themselves against each other in the scramble for jobs, but been pleased (Flora assumes) to find themselves ascending from SHO to Registrar to Senior Registrar at the same time. The existence of another woman on the surgical ladder has been enough to reassure Flora that she's not an anomaly – and Gillian has been, if anything, more single-minded than Flora, shameless in her employment of feminine wiles in the cause of advancement. She is all set, everyone can see, to be the first female surgical Consultant since the legendary Barbara Benjamin.

But apparently not. Flora stares at Gillian across the Formica table while words jostle in her head, reshaping themselves like dominoes into a succession of slightly different questions.

'Why?' is all she asks in the end.

Gillian laughs, and her face reminds Flora of a prefect at her school, a leggy, handsome girl who flunked her A levels after falling flamboyantly for the captain of rugby at the boys' school. The same mix of certainty and doubt at the corners of her mouth, willing you to agree with her even though she's decided your opinion isn't one she wants.

'Why stop?' Gillian asks. 'Heavens, Flora, we can't all be like you. Things change, you know. I'm not interested in martyrdom.'

'Nor am I,' says Flora, stung, but she can see there's no point pursuing the conversation. She thinks, waspishly, of a more pertinent analogy: a patient who's given up on life, despite the heroic hours on the operating table devoted to their rescue.

'I want to look after this baby,' Gillian says, her gaze dipping downwards; and then, after a tiny hesitation, 'Bob wants me to. We always said if we had children . . .'

RACHEL CROWTHER

For a moment there's a look of appeal in her eyes.

'Well,' Flora says. 'Each to her own. Congratulations.'

She picks up her tray and makes for the door, hating herself a little, but only enough to kindle an answering spark of self-righteousness.

'Would you have liked me to give up work when Lou was born?' she asks Henry that night, as they clear the table after their late supper. Omelette; a loyal standby.

Henry looks at her, a quizzical note in his face that could mean anything.

'Why?' he asks. 'Are you thinking . . .?'

'Gillian Sutherland's throwing in the towel,' she says. 'I saw her today, at the conference. She's pregnant, and she's stopping at twenty-eight weeks and not coming back.'

'She might change her mind. People do.'

Flora shakes her head. 'Not a chance. Lose your handhold for a moment and you've had it. No one would employ her after she's made a song and dance about motherhood. She'll set the rest of us back too – it'll confirm their belief that it's what we all want, deep down. You should see them, fawning over her like a disarmed warhead.'

Henry laughs. 'What a turn of phrase you have,' he says. 'You make them sound like Soviet salvage experts.'

'Not so far from the truth.'

Henry puts the last of the glasses into the dishwasher and straightens up.

'No one's going to disarm you, my love,' he says. 'Not a chance.'

This, Flora tells herself, is what other people envy: Henry's support, and his belief in her. The fact that he doesn't tell her what to think, but reassures her that what she thinks is right. Whatever she thinks, presumably. She could always change her mind, and . . .

Henry puts a hand on her shoulder, his grip firm enough to be more than a casual gesture.

164

'Do you want to stop?' he asks. 'Has she made you wonder . . .?'

Flora thinks of Lou's first birthday party two weeks ago, of the tottering steps she's taking now, and she squeezes her fists tight.

'No,' she says. 'It's just a surprise to find that she's – different from me.'

'You were never much like her,' says Henry. 'She doesn't, for example, have nearly as nice a bottom as yours.'

'Shut up.'

Flora knows what's coming – Henry's way of making things better – and she's grateful, but part of her would rather continue the conversation. There's another step, she thinks now, and another, that they never take. The deal. The balance. The upsides and the downsides.

But what's the point, really? Most women in her position would give their eye teeth for Henry and the life they have. The baby, the twin careers, the perfect understanding. If it suits Henry to have a wife who spends so much time at work, can she really complain? It suits him to have a wife he's proud of, too; she knows that. Not just a wife with enough self-esteem to carry herself with dignity, but one who brings something, a big something, to the party. It would be impossible to explain the intricacies of it to anyone else.

'Come on,' Henry says, 'it's late. The great surgeon needs her rest.'

'I'll look in on Lou on the way up,' Flora says.

She climbs the stairs slowly, the sight and smell and feel of her daughter filling her head. She can conjure the child so vividly, that distinct, solid, not-quite-baby, not-quite-toddler weight when you pick her up, and her jerky, purposeful movements. As she leans over the cot Lou sighs and murmurs in her sleep, rolling onto her back so that her small face looks up at her mother. Her eyes are tightly shut, her dark hair lying in wisps across her forehead. Not a care in the world, Flora thinks. Not a single care.

21

Flora took a cup of coffee into the sitting room and sat down to check her email. This too had become part of her routine, something she only allowed herself to do once a day. There were often no new messages, but for some reason she'd expected more today, and rather than closing the screen, she scrolled back instead through the correspondence of the last few weeks.

Martin's email reporting that he was settled at Orchards had been several stilted paragraphs long. *I am very comfortable here,* he'd written, *and I hope St Rémy is suiting you just as well,* before moving on with evident relief to the weather. Reading it, she'd been reminded of her first impression of him that afternoon in the shop: an Englishman of an entirely recognisable type. Nothing, she told herself, to justify the quiver of anticipation his name evoked, nor to warrant re-reading his words. But she skimmed through her reply again now, wondering whether it had been too brusque, whether she should have asked another question or two; and then, chiding herself, she closed it. Remember that last night, she thought. Remember the pain she might have avoided if she'd been more careful.

Both Kitty and Lou had been in touch intermittently, but it was clear that they didn't always know what to say to her. Kitty asked the same questions each time: *How are you enjoying France? Is it hot there?* She'd mentioned a song cycle she'd been writing for her MA course, but otherwise said little about herself. Was she all right, Flora wondered? Kitty had taken Henry's death badly. Had she been upset by that business of the sculpture? Wished her mother were there, even?

Frowning, Flora leaned back in her chair. Lou had told her about Alice's statue of Bacchus in her first email, soon after the private view. Flora could tell that Lou expected her to be shocked, but instead she'd found the story oddly amusing. Perhaps it was the effect of distance, or of Lou's rather legalistic prose. But if it was true that Bacchus had tipped the balance in Alice's favour with the Morris Prize judges, wasn't there a certain justice in the notion of Henry, rendered in marble by his lesbian daughter-in-law, adding lustre to her career after his death? And of Henry showcased (although Lou tactfully did not remind her of this) in a collection that represented male oppression.

Flora skipped on to Lou's emails. *I've been to Orchards with the agent,* she'd written. *He says it will let quite easily.* And then, a week later: *I've heard from your Frenchman. He seems delighted with Orchards.*

Was she wrong, Flora wondered, to detect a note of reproach in this message – for wasting Lou's time, or for acting irrationally? She and Lou often failed to hit the right note with each other, she thought. She'd imagined them being friends as Lou grew up, but perhaps that wasn't how it worked. Had they missed a turning somewhere? Was that her fault?

Sitting at Madame Carver's pretty desk, she felt a sudden tension in the invisible thread that linked her to her daughters. For the first time she felt trapped here, enclosed by the high walls that bounded the house and garden and by the decorum that held her to the plans she'd made.

An image came into her mind of Lou as a baby: her preternatural composure, accepting the embrace of whoever held her in their arms, and the swiftness with which she'd settled into a routine that meant she was asleep by the time Flora got home from work. She felt again her pent-up desire as she'd lifted Lou from her cot every evening, willing her to cry to show that she'd noticed her mother's absence, as well as her return. Of course she'd never expected the path she'd chosen to be easy, but those few minutes every evening had threatened her confidence in the balance she'd achieved, and her fitness as a mother. Amid the tangle of emotions that accompanied her second pregnancy, Flora had rejoiced, guiltily, at the chance to start afresh – and things had been different that time. The infant Kitty had woken every night for several years. Flora's concentration in the operating theatre had suffered, but she'd been happier. This baby needed her mother; she claimed her fair share of Flora's energies.

Flora sighed. It was Lou, of course, who'd grown up more sure of herself, but Flora had always believed that had happened despite her neglect, not because of her example. Perhaps, she thought now, she'd been wrong, all these years, to read rejection into Lou's competence. She ought to talk to her daughters, rather than waiting for emails to flit to and fro. Why didn't she do that? Why didn't they?

She shut her eyes for a moment, imagining the day stretching ahead of her, and the next day, and the next. She wondered what Lou and Kitty would be doing at this moment: whether they too were eking out the summer. Whether they were happy.

PART III

Greville Auctioneers, Friday 12th December 2014

Paintings and drawings by Nicholas Comyn, from the collection of the late Henry Jones

Lot no. 3: Beach scene, 1994

This painting was among the last Comyn produced before his death the following year. Although he often sketched outside, this is one of only a few outdoor scenes he completed. It depicts the two Jones children, Louisa and Kitty, on holiday in North Wales, and the unusually free and rapid brush strokes represent a significant departure for Comyn: there is a spontaneity in this piece which is absent from his earlier work. The children are a prominent part of the composition, but not central to it; they are, in effect, part of the landscape, a landscape which is both faithful to the topography of the coastline and yet expressive.

Given the short time left to Comyn at this point, it is perhaps tempting to read more into the image of dark clouds hanging over the beach than was intended. It would be typical of Comyn's faithfulness to his subject matter, and his insistence on painting what was before him, not to portray this family holiday scene in imaginary sunshine.

The image of children playing as storm clouds gather will be familiar to most aficionados of British beach holidays, and in the hands of an artist of Comyn's calibre it makes for a powerfully evocative painting. The quality of light Comyn captures just above the horizon, and the colour the weather lends to the beach and the figures playing on it, is masterly.

22

Alice had been enthusiastic about going away for the weekend. Alice ever-practical, Lou thought, jubilant at this evidence that she too was keen to find a remedy for their impasse. Fresh air and a clear horizon, and salt spray to temper the morning sickness. Surely that recipe couldn't fail?

Neither of them knew the south coast: that, as well as its proximity, made it the right place to go. Not Brighton or Bognor but Seaford, a modest little town that made no special claims apart from its beach and the English Channel laid out beyond. They rented a white clapperboard house on Marine Parade where they could sit and look out at the pleasing striation of sky and sea and stones.

At breakfast on Saturday morning, Alice glanced at Lou's untouched plate.

'Not feeling so good?' she asked.

Lou made a gesture of resignation. The smell of toast, usually redolent of cosiness and comfort, was perilous this morning.

'Isn't it better if you eat?'

'Not today, I don't think.'

Lou's nausea still ebbed and flowed. The midwife who'd conducted her booking visit had told her it usually began to let up by this stage, but the online forum she'd found had been less reassuring.

Across the table, Alice pushed back her chair and stood up.

'No point sitting staring at it,' she said, gathering up their plates.

Watching her, Lou was conscious of how familiar Alice's movements were. She never did anything impulsively. There was a sense of purpose and balance about her that reminded Lou of her handling of her tools, mindful that any ill-considered gesture might dislodge a fragment of stone that would have been better left where it was, but that hesitation could be just as disastrous, once you'd made up your mind.

Noticing Lou's eyes on her, Alice smiled: a smile that seemed to Lou, like so many recently, to have nothing behind it. The glimmer of pleasure it kindled in Lou's mind melted away before it flowered into hope.

'How about a walk on the beach?' Alice said. 'It's a lovely morning.'

What Lou really wanted was to go back to sleep, but there was no point being at the seaside if you spent the day in bed. No point coming away unless she made an effort.

'OK,' she said. 'Good idea.'

The tide was low, exposing the beach. To the right, it ran in a sharp curve towards Newhaven, and to the left in an extended crescent of sand and shingle towards Seaford Head. It was a fine morning, the sky blue inland and opalescent ahead, as though the sea was lighting it from beneath. Apart from the occasional deckchair or kite, everything was grey, blue, brown, calm. Lou and Alice crunched over the ridge of stones and down towards the sea, their footing growing firmer as they reached the damp sand below the tide line, then turned towards the sharp white outline of the cliffs.

Distance had an elastic quality on the beach, Lou thought, especially one like this with so few landmarks. It was hard to tell how far you'd gone, or how long you'd been walking. That was good: a blessed antidote to her professional life where time was monitored minute by minute, allotted and billed and accounted for. A trail of footsteps spooled slowly out behind them, cutting through the collage of pebbles and slipper limpets that were scattered sparsely in some areas and strewn more thickly where the tide had gathered and paused.

'It's beautiful here,' Alice said, after a while. 'I'm glad we've come.'

'It reminds me of Wales,' Lou said. 'Being on the beach like this.'

'When was that?'

'When Kitty was little. We went to Wales every August for a while. There were pebble beaches there too: I remember Henry skimming stones. I could never get the hang of it.'

Alice picked up a flat stone. 'I'll teach you,' she said.

She turned, and Lou watched her walk a few steps towards the sea and then stop, twist round, and send the stone out low over the water so that it bounced once, twice, three times, before it hit a wave on the rise and disappeared from view.

Lou felt a surge of joy, a sudden clearing of the air.

'Bet you can't do it again!' she called.

Alice grinned. She bent to pick up a second stone and flicked it out across the incoming tide. It bounced twice, a flicker of black against the glimmering surface, before dropping into the water.

'Where did you learn to do that, in the Midwestern plains?' Lou asked.

'You haven't heard of the Iowa Great Lakes?' Alice lifted her eyebrows, play-acting disbelief. 'While you were vacationing in Wales, we were taking trips to Spirit Lake. There's enough water there to skim a few pebbles.' She selected another stone and held it out to Lou. 'You have a go.'

Lou remembered well the frustration of failure, all those years ago, but also the thrill with which she'd weighed each new stone in her hand, sure that its contours were perfect for skimming. She remembered Henry on the beach, too. Henry in his element as the hearty father on holiday, and Nick Comyn mooning after him.

'Don't think I haven't tried,' she said.

'Try it my way.'

Alice put the stone into her hand and held her arm to show her the technique, the cocking of the wrist and the right moment for release. Another in the repertoire of deft movements that conveyed her smoothly through life, Lou thought, filled with longing and with a sudden, fearful optimism.

'It's all right for you,' she said. 'Stone's your thing. You can make it do whatever you want.'

'Just flick it,' Alice said. 'Send it on its way.'

Lou crouched a little, angled her arm, and spun the stone straight into the spume at the edge of the sea. The next one Alice handed her went higher, looping upwards before it dropped down into the water.

'Keep focussed on the horizon,' Alice said. 'You need enough spin to lift it off the surface.'

Lou frowned, cocked her wrist and tried again. This time the stone sped towards the sea in a straight line and bounced, just once, a tiny hop from one ripple to the next.

'See?'

Alice touched her shoulder, a fleeting gesture altogether different from the purposeful way she'd held Lou's hand a moment before. Lou felt a shiver run through her, leaving a sort of numbness in its wake.

'Your go,' she said.

Alice picked up a tiny flat pebble and whipped it out across the water. It bounced four or five times, but Lou hardly saw it. She could feel Alice's fingers still, the ghost of their presence, and her flesh goosepimpled beneath them.

Alice didn't move away from the sea this time; didn't bend to pick up another stone. Had she felt her flinch, Lou wondered? Her heart was beating furiously. She'd wanted Alice to touch her so badly: what had made her recoil? Her mind raced now, chasing her heartbeat, unsettling the stack of assumptions and defences she had built up.

In the last week or two she'd felt self-conscious with Alice in a way she never had before, but she'd assumed that was the result of the froideur between them, not a contributory cause. When she took off her clothes she was aware of difference, imbalance, vulnerability: emotions that made her think of a woman baring herself for a man. She'd even taken to wearing the dressing gown Aunt Jean had given her for Christmas, pulling the wings of it around her to cover the tiny prominence at the base of her belly. Could it be, she wondered now, that she was deceiving herself: that her feelings for Alice had changed? Could the ambiguity she had been attributing to Alice emanate from her instead?

For a few moments they stood a little way apart, watching the roll and suck of the sea, and then Alice turned.

'Home?' she said, 'or on?'

'Your call,' said Lou – conscious, as she so often was these days, of the exact timbre and pitch of her voice.

'Let's go on, if you're not too tired,' said Alice, and she turned towards the cliffs again.

Deliberately, calmly, Lou fell into step beside her, waiting for the minutes to pass and her heart to subside. The pebbles were layered more thickly now, and by mutual assent they scrambled back to the concrete promenade. Before long it ended in a railed platform from which the next, wilder bit of coastline could be admired, and a path running up towards the grassy clifftop.

'Shall we go up?' Lou suggested.

The path was steeper than it looked, but within a few minutes the reward was delivered: an aerial view of Seaford and the Downs in one direction, and in the other a panorama of sea and sky. A fringe of purple flowers ran along the cliff edge, separating the green of the grass from the stark white of the chalk, and in the distance a ferry chugged slowly past, making its way from Newhaven towards the shadow of France on the horizon. Wonderful, Lou thought. Wonderful to be on higher ground, to look down on the town and the beach and the creeping tide. From here, things looked tidy, ordered, explicable, and her misgivings a few minutes before felt unaccountable.

'I need to say something,' she said, almost without knowing she was going to speak. 'You may not want to hear it, but . . .'

Alice turned. 'Say what?'

'Sorry,' said Lou. 'About the baby. About doing it without you.'

For a long time Alice didn't answer. The sky was very blue behind her, like a backcloth cut from satin. Her hair, caught up in its habitual loose knot, glinted as though seamed with gold. As Lou stared at her, she was conscious of the tumbling, insistent song of a lark high above, drawing her up and away, and it was as if all the happy memories they had amassed together flowed through her mind, and through Alice's too, and she stood quite still, daring Alice to throw them away – to cast them over the edge of the cliff and never see them again.

'Everything's fine,' Alice said in the end, her voice rougher than usual, blasé in the wrong way.

'It's quite clearly not,' said Lou, and the words were clear too, clear and hard as beach pebbles. She moved, half-involuntarily, closer to the edge of the cliff.

Alice sighed. 'Well, then,' she said. 'What you said just now: *Stone's your thing. You can make it do whatever you want.* Don't tell me that wasn't a reference to Bacchus.'

'It wasn't,' Lou protested. 'It was just something to say.'

For several moments Alice looked at her, and then she gave another of those empty smiles.

'Everything's fine, then,' she said.

'You know I love you,' Lou said – but even as the words came out there were those doubts again, those awful possibilities. Alice seemed to be looking at her from a great distance: the space between them, barely a metre, was like a chasm neither of them could cross. She was pregnant and Alice was not, whispered a voice in her head – the same voice that had held sway that fateful night at Veronica Villa. It wasn't even Alice's child she was carrying, so what business was it of hers? Shameful thoughts, her conscience protested: why was she listening to them? They reminded her of the trolling a gay woman had been subjected to on the pregnancy forum: *What do you expect, going against nature? You're an aberration and I hope you suffer for it.* She'd never taken any notice of crap like that; never thought of the prejudice against lesbians having babies as any different to the prejudice against lesbians doing anything else. But what if some of the doubt and discomfort and distress was down to her, not Alice? What if it was the effect of the hormones, making her . . . more like any other pregnant woman? Driving a wedge between her and Alice? Maybe everyone went through this; maybe straight women had the same feelings about their partners. But she could see that if it was your husband's child in your belly that would, that must, be a powerful bond, a biological imperative that would . . .

And then, quite suddenly, she saw herself as a child, white with fury, ripping the hair from a doll Henry had given her; as an adolescent, testing the bite of a blade against her wrist. She remembered the frantic desire to be rescued, the terror of not knowing her way back. This, she thought, was what those experiences had been leading up to. This was the moment when she had to hold tight, to stay away from the cliff. Her head was filled again by the skylark, frenetic with song.

'I want to do this with you,' she said. 'I can't go back now. Can't we try?'

For a moment it felt as though she was speaking to a stranger; as though the Alice she'd known had vanished. And then at last, at last, she sensed something loosen in Alice's body.

Lou took her hand, and Alice let herself be pulled in close. Lou shut her eyes, cherishing the warmth of Alice's body against hers. She felt Alice draw in a deep breath and let it out in a long, settling sigh.

When Lou opened her eyes again she could see the scattered holidaymakers on the beach below them, families and teenage boys and older couples, sitting or walking or kicking balls. All of human life, Lou thought – every stage of it, here by the seaside – and her eyes blurred with tears.

August 1997

By the third day, they have established a routine. After breakfast they go down to the beach, provisioned with swimsuits and buckets and sun cream, and they stay there until lunchtime. Back at the house – only a ten minute walk, but uphill, with espadrilles full of sand, so that Kitty invariably pleads to be carried – they make sandwiches for lunch, followed by the expensive Belgian biscuits Henry bought from Fortnum's as a holiday treat.

The afternoons are less prescribed, their obligations to the beach having been satisfied. Flora occupies herself with small tasks of the kind she saves up for holidays: copying entries from an old address book to a new one, hesitating over the names of acquaintances she hasn't seen for years. Henry reads fat volumes of Dickens and Henry James; the same ones, it seems to Flora, that he brings on holiday every year. Lou has brought a pile of books too, this year. She's starting her GCSE courses next term, and has bought everything on the reading list supplied by her English teacher. Then after an hour or two, Kitty begs Lou to walk to the sweet shop with her, or Henry suggests an outing.

Yesterday they visited a castle planted squarely on the jut of a cliff top, part of Edward the First's fortifications against Llywelyn ap Gruffydd, and ate ice creams on a bench looking down from the battlements into the Irish Sea. On the way home they bought fish and chips, and the authentic seaside smell of vinegar and oil and damp newspaper was still lingering in the kitchen when they came down for breakfast this morning.

Henry is good at family holidays. This morning he's teaching the girls to skim stones, holding Lou's hand and demonstrating the angle of the wrist, the knack of the flicking motion. Standing a little way off, Flora can see Lou taking pleasure in the lesson, although she hasn't managed to get a single stone to bounce yet. Lou's hair, cut very short at the beginning of the summer, has grown out a little. It suits her like this, Flora thinks. Ruffled by the wind, it looks like the carefully tousled locks of a Greek statue. She's wearing an old T-shirt, a favourite from last summer, washed out and shapeless but it, too, suits her, the colour like the milky sky of these late summer mornings.

Flora feels a sudden sense of relief that she can't, at first, understand. She stares at her daughter for a few moments, letting the emotion take shape in her mind, placing it against the background of the wide beach, the lap of the waves, the cloudless sky. And then it comes to her: Lou is growing up. They have completed almost enough summers, survived almost enough years, to bring her safely to the threshold of adulthood, and she's becoming the person she is meant to be. A different person from any they could have imagined fourteen years ago, but the right person, the real Lou, emerging from the jostles and knocks of the childhood they've provided for her. Looking at the way she stands, the smile she turns to Henry now, her jaunty shrug as he hands her another stone, Flora is filled with a pride she knows she doesn't deserve, a feeling so strong that it stops her breath in her throat for a moment. She wants to freeze this scene, keeping everything just as it is, but at the same time she's impatient to rush time onwards so that she can see what becomes of this miraculous daughter. Will she, too, stand on the beach and watch her children? What will she make of that abrasive intelligence, or the sharp beauty Flora can see she's poised to claim?

A shout disturbs her reverie, and she turns to see Kitty, ten yards away, holding a stone of her own.

'Look!' she's shouting. 'Look at me, Daddy!' – and she lobs the stone so high in the air that it loops up over her head and falls behind her, plopping silently onto the damp sand. Kitty twists wildly, trying to see where it's gone, and Lou and Henry bend over with laughter – all of them, Flora thinks, like characters from a cartoon, their movements comically exaggerated. Caught between gratification and chagrin, Kitty picks up another stone and throws it towards the sea. Her aim is better this time, and it falls just at the water's edge, raising a tiny splash.

'Good shot,' says Henry. 'We'll make a bowler of you yet.'

He hands a pebble to Kitty, but she shakes her head. 'Find a bigger one, Daddy,' she says. 'Show how far you can throw it.'

Henry grins. He scans the ground, then picks up a stone the size of a cricket ball and weighs it in his hand.

'Like this?' he asks. 'This would do for a cannon ball, wouldn't it? We could fire it at Llywelyn ap Gruffydd.'

He turns, hooking his arm behind his shoulder and bringing it back up with a showy display of masculine skill. Watching him, Flora can see everything happen in slow motion: the uncurling of his arm, the slight twist of his body at the last minute so that the stone flies off in a different direction from the one they expect – not towards the sea but parallel to the tide line, heading towards the small figures they didn't realise were there: the two boys squatting over a sandcastle in the distance. There is a long moment of suspense in which the stone describes an arc through the air; a long moment of silence in which any of them might scream but no one does; and then the cannon ball stone – a fleck now against the grey-blue sky – drops back down towards the sand. Before it hits the ground Flora can feel the shock of it reverberating through her body, and can taste the sour tang of tragedy. There is a catapulting of time, forward and backward between the moment before and the moment after – and then nothing.

Flora shuts her eyes for a second, barely a second, and when she opens them again she wonders if she's imagined it – the throwing of the stone, or the preternatural calm that followed it – and she strains her eyes towards the boys. They haven't moved; they're quite still, crouched low on the sand, and in that moment she can't tell whether they're dead, or whether the stone merited no more than a glance as it landed, surely only inches away from them. She starts shouting now – she who is famously calm in the face of calamity – and the girls turn towards her, the same bewildered expression on both their faces. And then Henry, who has been frozen in the position of the thrower since the stone left his hand, starts running across the sand.

'Frankly,' Henry says as he comes back towards them, his face stupid with relief, 'it would have been more miraculous if I had hit them, the only people on this huge empty beach. A chance in a million – you could work out the odds, Lou, given the radius of the throw and –'

'I don't give a damn about the maths, Henry,' Flora snaps, her heart still throbbing with fury and disbelief. 'The point is that you threw that stone knowing you might hit someone. Might kill them.'

'That thought wasn't exactly in my mind,' Henry says. He dares a wink at Kitty, and Flora almost spits at him.

'Well, it should have been. God, think of the consequences, if you'd . . . What on earth possessed you? With the children around and –'

'There's no need to be melodramatic,' Henry says. 'No harm done.'

Flora stares at him. The wind has picked up: it scoops eddies of sand and cold air against their bare legs as they stand among the debris of their morning at the seaside. 'That's not worthy even of you,' she says. '*I got away with it, so who cares?* I suppose that's been your motto all along, you – fuckwit.'

Lou's eyes widen, and Flora feels herself trembling.

'If you say so.'

'Don't be so bloody glib. Can't you just admit – can't you for once take responsibility for . . .'

'I'll admit to whatever you like, Flora.' He meets her eyes, a questioning look on his face. *Are we really going to do this?* it says. *On the beach, in front of the children?* The girls' eyes are on her too. She's the one misbehaving, Flora thinks, looking at their tense faces. She's the one making a scene. She wants to weep, suddenly. She shuts her mouth tight and bends to gather up towels and buckets, cramming them back into the flowery beach bag while her family stands and watches her.

As they make their way back to the house they are silent, all of them, but the echo of their voices hangs in the air, and distilling from them the unavoidable fact that the day, the whole holiday, has been tainted.

Flora realises, as they approach the straggle of shops, that she's still shaking, and she knows it's from the shock of her own over-reaction as much as the knowledge – still sharp and clear in her mind's eye – of what might have been; what nearly was. She has spent years ignoring what might have been, and even what might be, what's out of sight, but she's been tripped up this morning. Her daughters have seen more than she wanted them to.

She makes an effort to gather herself, preparing to meet the eyes of the cluster of people standing outside the post office with a smile. But as they come nearer she can hear the hushed voices, feel the sense of shock in the air, and her blood runs cold. No, no, she thinks – she wants to tell them they've made a mistake, heard the wrong story – the boys are fine, it was a close shave but nothing more – unless – a terrible thought now – perhaps it was Henry who was mistaken? Perhaps he couldn't face up to what had happened?

'What?' she says, involuntarily. The man nearest her looks up from the newspaper they have all been studying, and she realises there's a radio on, a tinny voice coming out of the centre of the huddle.

He gives her a look of sympathy, or something like it. Fellow feeling.

'Terrible, isn't it?' he says.

'What?' Flora says again, her voice shrill now, ready to defend her family.

The man frowns slightly, as though he can't believe she doesn't know. 'Princess Diana,' he says. 'Dead, isn't she? In Paris, with Dodi.'

'Princess Diana?' Flora echoes.

'A car crash,' says an older woman Flora recognises from one of the shops. 'Terrible. Such a waste.'

Flora glances at Henry and sees, behind his expression of concern, the shadow of a grin.

'What's happened?' Kitty asks. 'Is Princess Diana really dead?'

'Apparently, my precious.' Henry puts a hand on her head.

And that, Flora sees, is that. The non-event of the stone that hit no one has been dwarfed by a public tragedy. The moral of their story has been drowned by the myriad voices of mourning and speculation that will fill the world's airspace for days, weeks, months to come. As the tide turns, preparing to fill the moat dug by the small boys on the beach – as Lou turns another infinitesimal degree towards adulthood, and Kitty glimpses the unpredictability of the world – a life is snuffed out far away, on the television, and its reverberations overrun everything else. Flora is grateful that the hand of Fate didn't fall differently that morning, of course she is, but she feels something unfamiliar stirring inside her. She feels sorry for Princess Diana, but even sorrier for herself.

23

'Julia Hoxton?' said Alice. 'Isn't she an opera singer?'

'A conductor.' Lou read the letter again. Why her, she was wondering? Had this woman written to Flora and Kitty as well? 'Quite a famous conductor,' she said. 'I didn't realise she knew Henry.'

Her father's musical friends had come to Orchards occasionally, but Lou couldn't remember Julia Hoxton being among them. There was, of course, one obvious explanation for that. She thought of the women lurking at the fringes of Henry's funeral, women wearing too much makeup or too little, defiantly unaccompanied.

'Are you upset?' Alice asked. 'It sounds like a nice thing to do, organising a concert for him.'

'Yes,' said Lou. 'I suppose it is.'

'You must be proud,' said Alice.

Lou considered this. She'd never been proud of Henry in the same way she'd been proud of Flora, despite the glamour of his work – being on the radio, even the television sometimes. But he'd been a staunch supporter of musical education, too, and presumably that was why he was remembered fondly by people like Julia Hoxton.

'She wants to raise money for a prize in his memory,' she said, reading the letter again.

Alice yawned. In her pyjamas, with her hair loose and wild, she looked every inch the dishevelled sculptor. Six forty-five was too early for her, but she got up each morning now to see Lou off. Part of a compact, Lou thought, that neither of them had voiced and both were trying hard to stick to.

'Would your father have liked that?'

'I'm sure he would.' Lou smiled; a rare occurrence this early in the day. 'Posthumous fame was just his kind of thing. I'd better go.'

She got to her feet, and Alice came round the table to kiss her goodbye. A chaste, wifely kiss, Lou thought. It might feel as though they were both acting parts, but the daily round had been easier since Seaford, and she was grateful for that.

The drive to the station was beautiful at this time of year, the woods speckled with the crimson of rhododendrons, but Lou thought of Alice trudging out to the studio, perhaps even back to bed, with envy. She'd considered changing her season ticket to first class when she got pregnant, but she hadn't. It wasn't the money so much as the principle, the idea of trading on weakness, but she looked at the spacious carriages each morning with longing. Today there was only one seat left in standard, next to a large man whose coat gave off a powerful scent of mothballs.

She had papers to read, but she didn't get them out straightaway. Instead she shut her eyes and thought of the rhododendrons, of Alice's hair tangled with sleep, of the cool morning air on her cheeks as she waited on the platform. And of Julia Hoxton. Perhaps her name was too familiar now for Lou to remember it being spoken in a private context. Had she had a fling with Henry? Would she, if so, really have the gall to organise a public event in his memory?

She had always, Lou thought now, been more sanguine than Kitty about her father's infidelity, but more resolutely disapproving. She remembered Kitty white with anxiety when another crisis broke, desperate to heal the breach. Kitty had been younger, of course, and wired to make the best of things. Her father had held sway in her heart in a way Lou had found hard to accept. And in Flora's, too. That was something she had never come to terms with.

Of course Flora had raged sometimes, even thrown Henry out once or twice; and of course Lou understood that her dignity was important, and her loyalty to the family that was bound together with such a strange and makeshift assortment of knots. But surely her endurance had cost her more than she had shown? Surely her marriage had eroded something inside her, over time? That, Lou assumed, was why she'd given up work to nurse Henry at the last – because in the end, it mattered more to her to prove that her marriage had come right than that her career had been a blazing success.

And that, Lou realised, was why Julia Hoxton's letter troubled her. Flora had reclaimed Henry, and now someone else wanted to assert some kind of public right over him. As the train rolled through the familiar railway landscape of fields and factories and back gardens, Lou pondered. Families, she thought, rarely left you in peace for long. The other week there had been Flora's disconcerting announcement that she'd arranged to swap houses for the summer with a wine merchant she'd met in France, and now there was this dilemma to address.

Lou sighed. She needed to speak to her mother. She needed to tell her about the baby, for one thing. It was high time that Flora heard that news.

24

After the Wigmore Hall encounter Lou and Kitty had promised they'd meet more often, and Kitty had really meant to stick to that resolution. She'd been too absorbed by her song cycle, she thought now, and then by Daniel. Neither of those preoccupations was very willing to share her attention. It felt, walking through the London streets this morning, as though it was weeks since she'd been out and about on her own. Weeks since she'd seen Lou, certainly.

They'd arranged to meet in the same Moroccan café: it was convenient for Lou's office, and there was something in the Jones genes that liked establishing traditions. The good old same old, Henry used to call it. Lou looked better than she had the last time. When Kitty said so, she gave a characteristic sideways smile.

'We had a weekend away,' she said. 'A bit of sea air. How about you, Kits?'

'Well, I had a little success, actually,' Kitty admitted. 'My song cycle was in a lunchtime concert last week.'

'Oh, I would have come! You should have told me.'

'I know,' Kitty said. 'I know I should. The thing is that until it happened, I didn't really believe in it. But actually – well, it was quite good. The college is pleased, anyway.'

More than that: Janet Davidson had actually beamed, the next time they met. She was talking about Kitty doing a PhD. Apparently that was what composers did these days, now there weren't any Grand Dukes to fund you while you wrote your early symphonies.

'Will it be performed again?' Lou asked. 'I'd love to hear it.'

'There might be a recording. I'll see if I can get hold of it, if you like.'

'I would like. Don't you want to hear it yourself?'

'I heard it. And it's in here, anyway.' Kitty tapped her head. 'I can hear it whenever I want.'

Lou looked at her for a moment, a new expression on her face. 'Have you found your métier, little sister?'

'Maybe.' Kitty gave a small shrug, attempting something between nonchalance and take-it-in-your-stride sincerity. She felt rather shy about discussing her music with Lou. The idea that Lou would take it seriously wasn't something she felt sure of. She'd never known quite what Lou thought about music and musicians.

Their food arrived then, a similar selection of *mezze* dishes to last time. The good old same old, Kitty thought. But they both looked at them with more enthusiasm this time. Kitty, at least, was famished.

'And dare I ask how Daniel is?' Lou asked, spooning green beans onto her plate.

'He is,' said Kitty.

'Meaning . . .?'

Another little shrug, with a different inflection. 'Meaning I've been seeing a lot of him.'

'Good,' said Lou – and then, after a hesitation, 'is it good?'

Kitty helped herself to a piece of skewered chicken while she contemplated the answer. 'This is the first time for days I've been away from him for long enough to think about that.'

Lou said nothing; just raised her eyebrows in another question.

'I feel . . .' Kitty said, 'oh, I don't know. Life feels very – vivid, when I'm with Daniel. As though any other kind of life is second rate.'

'But?'

'I don't know if there is a but. I haven't written anything since the concert, but I can't really blame Daniel for that.'

Although she could, of course. It was hard, somehow, to call up her own musical language when Daniel was around. She craved his affirmation almost as much as she had once craved Henry's, but she dreaded his judgement. She had thought once her piece was finished, performed – now she could think of herself as a proper composer, almost . . . but it wasn't that simple. She couldn't explain any of that to Lou, though. And it wasn't the whole truth, anyway: surely no one could think about work when they were spending so much time in bed.

Kitty sighed. 'I think – I sort of feel it ought to be clearer, but I think I'm in love with him.'

Lou made a sceptical face, peering over imaginary glasses: an old gag, designed to make Kitty laugh. Instead, Kitty found herself suddenly on the brink of tears.

'Oh, Kits,' said Lou, taking her hand, 'I'm sorry. I didn't mean to upset you.'

'I know,' said Kitty, 'I know. It's – nothing, really.'

She stopped, biting her lip. Why was it that the moment she spoke the word *love* a kind of dread overtook her? Why was it so much harder to know what she felt when she was away from Daniel? He was so sure about everything, that was the thing. Unnaturally sure, she sometimes thought, for someone of their age, but that was supposed to be a good thing, in this commitment-phobic world. When she was with him, his certainty soothed her. But when she wasn't, when that blanket was lifted. . .

Sometimes she almost felt as if she and Daniel had known each other in a previous life, and things had ended badly for them then, but she knew that was nonsense. Perhaps it was her mother's life that haunted her, she thought now; the echo of her father's behaviour. Sometimes she looked at Daniel in her mind's eye and saw Henry instead.

'Let's talk about something else,' she said. 'How are you? How's Alice?'

She leaned forward to take a piece of pickled beetroot from a bowl, and Lou frowned, as though trying to recall their last conversation. Kitty remembered it well enough: she remembered the ambivalence in Lou's voice.

'Things have been a bit difficult,' Lou said. 'They're better now, I think. Not – perfect, but better.'

Kitty waited, but that seemed to be the end of it. 'And the baby?' she asked.

'Growing. In fact I've got . . .' Lou reached into her bag and produced a black and white image that bore an uncanny resemblance to a cave painting.

'Gosh,' said Kitty. 'Is that . . .?'

'It's an ultrasound scan,' Lou said. 'That's the head, look, and the body.'

Kitty hardly dared to look at Lou's face. The picture didn't look much like a baby, but it was proof, even so. And Lou showing it to her was a different kind of proof. Goodness, she thought, Lou really is going to be a mother. She was going to have to get used to that idea.

'Have you told Flora yet?' she asked.

'No, but I need to. I've been meaning to.'

'It feels odd, doesn't it, having her so far away?' Kitty said. She had been thinking about Flora on the tube this morning: thinking that she missed her, a more straightforward feeling than she'd expected. 'Odd having someone else living at Orchards, too.'

'Yes, that's definitely odd.' Lou hesitated. 'I went there, you know. To show the agent round, before Flora came up with the house swap plan.'

'How was that?'

'I'm afraid I scared the life out of the poor estate agent with my insinuations about family life chez Jones.'

'Really?'

'Oh, I'm sure he's heard worse,' said Lou. 'But I've – felt the after-shocks a bit, lately.'

Kitty's heart beat a little faster. Now was the moment to ask, she thought – but what? Was it really worth digging it all up?

'I was planning to go some time,' she said instead. 'To collect some stuff from the barn.'

'Don't be put off by me,' Lou said. Her face had composed itself again. 'Or the tenant. He seems nice. Perhaps you could find out what Flora's up to in France.'

'Life after Henry,' said Kitty, and she felt a rush of sadness. Not so much for her mother or her father, she thought, as for the missed opportunity to talk to Lou about them. For her lack of courage.

'That reminds me,' Lou said. 'Have you heard from someone called Julia Hoxton?'

'The conductor?' asked Kitty.

'Yes. She wants to do a memorial concert for Henry. Did she write to you?'

'How would she find me?' Kitty asked. 'How would she even know I existed?'

'I could ask the same thing,' said Lou. 'But she found me somehow. She's proposing something on a pretty grand scale.'

'Oh.'

'That was rather my feeling. Should we say no?'

'She ought to ask Flora,' said Kitty. 'But can we stop her, if she wants to do it?'

'Maybe Landon could be an intermediary,' said Lou.

'That's a good idea,' said Kitty. 'Dear Landon. I keep thinking about his eulogy at Henry's funeral. He found such nice things to say.'

'Admirable chap,' Lou said.

Kitty smiled at her imitation of Henry, but she felt a dart of grief too. There was such a resemblance in Lou's face, suddenly – an unmistakable imprint of Henry. Perhaps now, she thought; another chance. But just then there was a sound like a subdued fire alarm.

'Damn,' Lou said, frowning at her phone. 'I'm so sorry, Kits, but I'm going to have to go. A client has arrived early. Look, have this – lunch is on me.'

She handed Kitty two twenty pound notes. Kitty demurred briefly; then, when it was clear that Lou wouldn't be refused, she stood up to embrace her.

'Sorry,' Lou said again. 'I wouldn't usually – but it's a big case.'

'Go,' said Kitty. 'Don't worry.'

Lou put a hand on Kitty's shoulder. 'Look after yourself, little sister,' she said.

25

At first, Flora didn't recognise the voice that answered the phone.

'Alice?' she said.

'No, it's Lou. Alice isn't here. Can I take a message?'

Flora felt a strange frisson. Like a glimpse of a stranger, she thought, catching her daughter unawares.

'It's me,' she said. 'Flora.'

'Ma?' There was a tiny pause. 'How are you? Is everything OK?'

Ma – when had Lou last called her that?

'Everything's fine,' Flora said. 'I just thought . . . It seemed a long time since we'd spoken. I wondered how you were.'

'I was going to ring you, actually,' Lou said. 'I've got some news.'

'About Orchards?'

'No.' Lou laughed at the other end of the line; a little laugh, very characteristic, that made Flora's heart ache suddenly. 'About me. I'm pregnant.'

'Oh, Lou!' Blood thudded in Flora's ears: of all the things Lou might have said, this was possibly the least expected. 'Congratulations,' she said. 'How wonderful. How many weeks?'

Lou hesitated. 'I'm just about through the first trimester,' she said. When she went on there was something in her tone of voice that Flora couldn't decipher. 'We've talked about it for a while, but it happened very quickly once . . .'

Flora could feel the prick of tears now, and she wasn't sure whether she was glad or sorry that Lou wasn't there to see them. Would she feel the same if Lou wasn't gay; if this news was less of a surprise? She so rarely thought in those terms, but it seemed impossible not to, on this occasion. Impossible, either, not to think of the moment when she'd found out she was pregnant herself.

'I had some difficulty conceiving you,' she said.

'Really?'

'It took over a year,' Flora said. 'We almost gave up hope.'

It had been Henry's problem, not hers. A low sperm count: nicely ironic, Flora had thought at the time. And perhaps just as well. Who knew what sordid consequences had been averted by that quirk of reproductive physiology?

'I didn't know that,' Lou said. 'I should count my blessings, then.'

About her baby's conception, Flora wondered, or her own? She couldn't think why they'd never told her. Lou would have liked to know that she'd been wanted and planned and waited for.

'How are you feeling?' she asked. 'Are you through the morning sickness?'

'It's been pretty bad, but it's beginning to ease off. I feel fine, otherwise. Fine.'

'I'm very pleased, Lou,' Flora said. There was another silence then, and in the middle of it she said, 'your father would have been pleased too.'

Lou's announcement reverberated in Flora's mind after she'd put the phone down, leaving her feeling unexpectedly shaky. She carried a glass of wine outside, and sat on the bench at the end of the garden from which she could see the blazing finale of the sunset reflected in the tall windows of the house: a treat regularly bestowed at the end of these late June days. The chirp of cicadas filled the air, adding to a sense of the exotic and far-from-home; the far-fetched, even. *Lou pregnant?* she could hear Henry saying. *What were the odds on that, then?*

But as well as surprise she felt an extravagant sense of joy. She'd never thought about being a grandmother, but the allure of it was a powerful thing. A deep-rooted desire to see the line continued, perhaps; a primal pleasure in the prospect of new life. Flora had never set much store by primitive emotions, but this one had caught her full on.

She was also aware, though, of a more complicated reaction. Things were different for working mothers these days, of course. Doctors could take career breaks with impunity, and presumably lawyers could too. And this child would have two mothers to share its care. But even so, having a baby was, for Lou, a more deliberate, more audacious decision. It made Flora feel proud, and a little humble. For her, motherhood had been the natural corollary to marrying Henry. He'd longed to be a father: even in the face of scientific evidence Flora had felt responsible for their failure to conceive. Lou had come, finally, as the consummation of a grand rapprochement, after a row that had raged for weeks. She and Henry had made their baby in the way that medieval monarchs made marriages: to seal the peace and cement their allegiance, overcoming the odds at last in an outpouring of hope. Misguided hope, Lou might have said, with her clear-eyed vision.

The sunset had drained from the windows now, leaving behind the heavy grey of dusk. Flora sat on, watching the tiny bats loop and dart over the garden, their suddenness and silence another part of the spell of evening here. Had it been fair to make her children the glue for her marriage, she wondered – especially Kitty? Would it have been better for them if she'd left Henry – perhaps accepted one of those glamorous research chairs in Sweden or America she'd been offered in the nineties?

She should have been braver about facing those questions in her full-throttle forties, she thought, when other dice could still be cast. But perhaps she needed to find the courage now to face regret square on, if it was there: regret about marrying Henry, or about pursuing her career so doggedly, or about giving it up to nurse him at the end. Regret about missed opportunities and futile guilt: oh, that was dangerous ground. The secrets she'd kept for so long, the scruples and taboos she'd allowed to enclose her like Sleeping Beauty's briars. Did she dare to hack them down?

February 2001

Standing in front of the stove, Flora fights off a familiar feeling of frustration. It should not, she thinks, be so difficult to produce, just for once, a meal which doesn't make her family laugh or squirm. She is a competent person, and she has done everything in the order specified by the recipe book, but the cake in the oven is defiantly refusing to rise and the consistency of the mixture in the pan in front of her is quite wrong. It irritates her to fall prey to the cliché of the working mother who can't cook. She's never set her mind against it; never taken pride, as some women do, in being domestically incompetent. Why shouldn't she be able to make a proper cake, and a passable version of beef bourguignon, for Lou's eighteenth birthday?

'Can I help?' asks Kitty, and Flora turns to see her watching from the kitchen doorway. Kitty is hardly the delivering angel she needs, but Flora recognises an opportunity of a different kind: cooking with her eight-year-old. Like many other forms of maternal virtue, it's one she has exercised less often than she might have done.

'Of course,' she says. Kitty's wearing the new dress her aunt Jean sent for Christmas: it's a little small, but very pretty, with smocking and lace – not the kind of thing Flora would think of buying her. She looks sweet in it, something about her bare knees appealingly old-fashioned.

'What do you think?' Flora asks, tilting the casserole so that Kitty can see the contents.

'Is it meant to be that watery?' Kitty asks.

'I'm not sure. Probably not.'

'Did you put flour on the meat? Sylvie always put flour on, to thicken it.'

Sylvie is the French au pair, now departed, whose culinary skills remain legendary in the family.

'Shall we add some flour, then?' Flora asks.

Kitty climbs onto a chair to get a packet down from the cupboard.

'It's brown,' she says. 'Is that OK?'

'I'm sure it is. Very healthy.'

Flora adds a spoonful or two to the pan with a Galloping Gourmet flourish.

'Sylvie always mixed it with the juice if she added more,' Kitty says doubtfully, as Flora prods at the pearls of flour floating now among the meat and the onions.

'Oh well.'

'I don't think it matters.' Kitty, peering at the bourguignon from her vantage point on the teetering chair, puts a reassuring hand on Flora's shoulder. 'Lou won't mind the lumps.'

'Let's hope not.'

Why, Flora wonders, didn't Lou want to go out for her birthday? Does she too have a misguided vision of a cosy family gathering at home? She searches in vain for a whisk in the cutlery drawer, then puts the lid on the casserole and shoves it in the oven.

Henry is in ebullient mode. Her incompetence in the kitchen has cheered him, Flora thinks, although not in an unkind way. He is sweetly affectionate in the face of her discombobulation, smiling as if he has just recalled a particular charm of hers, then kissing her forehead and apologising for not being back in time to help. His goodwill, though, makes Flora perversely cross.

'Champagne,' he says, while the girls lay the table and Flora frets over the potatoes. 'Rodier's your favourite, isn't it, my love?'

'I really don't mind,' Flora says. 'It should be Lou's choice, anyway.'

'I don't exactly have a favourite champagne yet,' says Lou. She looks pale, Flora thinks. She's been working very hard for her mocks, and she's lost some weight: not much, but enough to be noticeable.

'We had Rodier for your christening,' Henry says, and Lou gives a half-smile that is meant, Flora surmises, to remind him that she isn't especially pleased to have been christened without consent. Henry takes it for approval, however, and disappears to the cellar.

'Can I have champagne?' Kitty asks, and then she glances after her father, as though wondering whether she might have been more likely to get a favourable answer from him.

'Of course,' says Flora. She smiles, reminding Kitty that she has been her mother's ally in the kitchen.

Henry comes back holding a bottle, and tests the temperature against the inside of his wrist, as he always does.

'Cellar chilled,' he says. 'Perfect.'

He tears the foil off with a practised gesture, then thumbs out the cork before any of them are expecting it. It flies across the room, making Kitty jump. She laughs, and Lou grabs a glass from the table to catch the first spurt of champagne.

'Wait,' says Henry. 'My party trick. Wait.'

He leaps onto a chair, brandishing the bottle in one hand and the glass in the other, holds both high above his head and pours. A trickle of champagne spills onto his head, but the rest goes into the glass, and Kitty claps.

'Don't try this at home,' says Henry, grinning at her. 'I make it look easy, but it takes years of practice.'

'I don't understand why these potatoes aren't done,' Flora says. 'They've been on for hours.' She's exhausted, she realises. Her operating list started at seven thirty this morning to accommodate a series of tricky cases, including a Roux-en-Y reconstruction that didn't go entirely smoothly. She turns the gas right up and bangs the lid back on the saucepan, and the girls turn to look at her.

'Never mind,' Lou says, 'we're not in any hurry. Have a glass of champagne, Ma.'

Flora takes the glass she's offered and manages a smile. Ma, she thinks. Lou has never really settled on a name for her. It's a long time since she called her Mummy, and she seems to find Mum uncomfortable too. Flora's happy to be called Flora, but Ma feels like a special effort. An endearment.

'Happy birthday, my love,' she says. 'I can hardly believe you're eighteen.'

'I can hardly believe you're spending your birthday with your devoted family,' says Henry, handing half a glass to Kitty and pouring one for himself, 'not being whisked off somewhere by a terrifying boyfriend.'

There's a short silence – like a tiny black hole, Flora thinks, that they might all fall into. In that instant something occurs to her. Perhaps, she thinks, Lou is never going to be whisked off by a terrifying boyfriend, or even a dull one. She looks at Lou, and an aura of transformation glimmers around her for a moment, like a halo in a medieval painting.

'Well, aren't we lucky she wants to be with us?' Flora says.

'Won't be long, though,' says Henry, with an air of satisfaction. 'Beautiful girl like you.'

He lifts his glass to Lou. The black hole hovers, still, at the centre of the kitchen. Kitty giggles.

'What?' says Henry. 'She is beautiful, you scallywag. We'll have dozens of young men calling for her soon, you wait and see. I shall have to get my protective patriarch speech up to scratch.'

'Don't, Henry,' says Flora. 'Shush, Kitty.'

Kitty has lost control of herself now, speechless with silent giggles that don't seem to Flora to have much to do with mirth.

'Oh, come on.' Henry has finished one glass of champagne already. He pours himself another, and bestows his warmest, crinkliest smile on Lou. 'I'm not embarrassing her, am I, Lou? Since when has she been a shrinking violet? I'm allowed to toast my lovely daughter on her eighteenth birthday.'

'Dad,' says Lou, 'enough.'

He puts out a hand to touch her shoulder, and she flinches – just the tiniest movement, but none of them miss it.

'Please, Henry,' says Flora, and at the same time Henry says, 'Louisa Grace, don't be like that with your old Dad,' and Kitty makes a small shrieking noise that turns out to be a reaction to the potatoes boiling over spectacularly on the stove.

After that, by mutual assent, they lapse into the kind of conversation that has seen them through any number of tight spots, exchanging the familiar jokes and anecdotes that represent their folklore. The *good old same old*, Henry calls them, this stock of stories that are produced whenever there's a need for them, and the little traditions they have built up over the years. Perhaps every family has the same staples to fall back on.

The bourguignon isn't bad. Using fillet steak, and a whole bottle of red Burgundy, was a good idea. The flour pearls are barely discernible. It strikes Flora that this is a nice thing to do, sitting around the table *en famille*, and that they don't do it often enough. She draws breath to say this, then stops. It will seem like a request for reassurance, or even forgiveness, from the girls, and that's not fair. Certainly not tonight.

Kitty is telling a complicated joke they have all heard many times before. They listen patiently, even when Kitty loses track of the narrative halfway through, but the punchline, when it comes, doesn't raise enough of a laugh, and she looks disappointed.

'I know a joke,' says Henry. 'It's about a wide-mouthed frog.'

Another of his party pieces: the girls both smile in anticipation. There is something about Henry's face that lends itself to the comedy of the wide mouth. He has never minded making himself ridiculous.

'Once upon a time there was a wide-mouthed frog who lived in a deep, dark jungle. . .' Henry begins.

Flora listens – half-listens – thinking about Lou and that glimpse she had of her a few minutes ago; that shaft of insight. It would make sense, she thinks, of a quality she has recognised in Lou, something she finds herself identifying as a particular kind of integrity. The lack, at least, of the conformity and the knowing self-consciousness common among her peers. The lack, presumably, of the need or desire to please men.

She watches Lou now, the lines of her face sleeker and finer than they were, no longer girlish. If her insight is right, Flora wonders, does she mind? Does she, as mothers are supposed to, wish a husband and children for her daughter? Having paid such a high price herself, could she, of all people, really be sorry to see Lou spared the mixed blessings of marriage? Oh, but children, she thinks, with a dart of emotion that takes her quite by surprise. That would be a loss. Could she imagine Lou happy without children?

Henry has nearly reached the end of the joke.

'. . . and then the wide-mouthed frog meets a tiger, and he says, "Hello, what kind of animal are you?"'

Flora remembers the occasion when a much smaller Kitty told this joke and – misunderstanding the point – delivered the last line with the frog's wide mouth unchanged. That, she thinks, is partly why they all laugh at it still. The memory of that moment of unintentional hilarity makes it funnier for them than it really is. She looks at Kitty now, her face absorbed and intent, then back at Lou. Lou has drunk a couple of glasses of champagne and she looks more relaxed, but Flora notices, again, that slightly detached poise she has acquired.

Did she intend to make some kind of announcement tonight, Flora wonders? Is that why she wanted them all gathered? It seems unlikely – too melodramatic for Lou, and for the Joneses. And Henry's reaction couldn't have been counted on: if Lou was in any doubt about that, she can't be any longer. Flora sighs, briefly, while the others laugh at the punchline, and Henry roars like a tiger devouring a wide-mouthed frog. All she wants for Lou, she thinks, is happiness.

'Cake,' she says. 'Not the world's best cake, but it's amazing what you can do with chocolate fudge icing, isn't it, Kitty?'

26

Lou didn't move for a while after her mother had rung off. It was a long time since they'd spoken to each other, and it felt even longer. Did Flora sound different, she wondered, or was it she who'd changed over the course of the summer?

The house seemed very quiet now, as though there had been a party in full swing before the phone rang and everyone had vanished now: echoes of conversation seemed to linger, half-finished, in the corners of the room. In fact the house had been quiet all evening – Alice was out, teaching a class – and Lou had been quite content, earlier, with her own company. But now she glanced at the clock, wondering how long it would be until Alice came back.

She'd been finishing supper when Flora rang, and she got up now to clear the table, making a deliberate clatter as though to demonstrate her equanimity. Flora had sounded pleased about the baby; Lou was glad about that. But it was hard not to analyse her mother's tone of voice, or to wonder about that out-of-the-blue reference to her difficulty in conceiving – indeed, to dwell on any number of things that had been said or not said. There was often a sense, with Flora, that they were trying to communicate through an invisible barrier which made it hard to be sure precisely what the other person was saying, or hearing. Would it be the same with her child? Would they ever be as close again as in these few months when their circulations mingled across the placenta?

She turned on the tap to rinse the pan she'd cooked her pasta in and sluiced it too vigorously, splashing hot water over herself.

'Damn,' she said, out loud – and she felt tears welling up and a tight band of little-girl distress at her throat. What on earth was this for? Her emotions had been under better control lately; it made her feel foolish and fragile to cry without warning.

She put the saucepan down on the draining board and stood looking out at the garden, green and lush in the late evening light. Alice
had transformed the overgrown yard they'd inherited into a pretty little bower: her farming background gave her a feel for soil and roots
and light and shade, and her artist's sensibility for the colours and tex-
tures of the end result. The climbing rose she'd trained up the side of
her studio was thick, now, with creamy flowers, and the first scattering
of petals lay beneath it, pale and unbruised, lining the path to Alice's
door. It struck Lou, as her eyes followed the trail of rose petals, that she
had been more conscious recently of Alice's presence around Veronica
Villa: of discarded teacups and jumpers, sketches and scribbled notes.
Had there been an increase in this flotsam lately, or had she simply
been more aware of it – searching for clues to what Alice was thinking,
perhaps, as they battled on with a shared life that still felt unnaturally
effortful?

God, how she wished things were easier. No doubt she was as much
to blame as Alice; she knew she was at the mercy of a giddying swirl
of hormones that made her reactions, her feelings, mysterious to her.
She wondered suddenly what it had been like for her mother, sharing
a house which was so full of Henry: surrounded by Henry's pictures
and books and music, when she must often have wished all signs of
him away. For her and for Kitty, the effects of growing up in that house
were almost impossible to throw off, however hard they worked at creating new habitats for themselves. Would their performance as parents
inevitably be shaped by their childhood too?

Lou turned away from the window, fighting down a surge of
resentment. That wasn't how she thought about life, she told herself.
It was hateful, defeatist, to believe you were limited by the circumstances of the past. If there was no way to rise above all that then she
might as well . . .

But then she checked herself. She heard again her mother's voice
on the phone, the hesitancy that could easily be misunderstood. And

then a challenging thought: that the past wasn't just something to be beaten down, any more than it was something to submit to. That you had obligations to it, as well as the right to judge it. For the moment she couldn't go any further than that, but she had the painful feeling that she had got more things wrong than she had counted before – and that Flora had ridden out the storms of the last thirty years with more wisdom and grace than she had given her credit for.

Lou was lying in the bath when Alice came home. She listened to her footsteps pausing in the kitchen, then coming up the stairs and along the landing.

'Hello.' Alice halted, framed in the doorway.

'Hello.'

Lou lay still. It was the first time for weeks that she hadn't shut the bathroom door; Alice would realise that. Alice stood perfectly still too. Her face looked opaque, the way it did sometimes when a piece of sculpture resisted her approaches.

After a few moments Lou lifted herself out of the tub and stood on the bathmat, naked. Alice said nothing, but still she didn't move away. When Lou reached for a towel and began to dry herself Alice stayed in the doorway. Like a statue, Lou thought. Like one of her own statues – a Madonna without child. She felt something turn in her belly: not the baby, but something harder and fiercer asserting itself or – perhaps – preparing to yield.

'Come to bed,' Alice said. 'Come to bed, my love.'

In the half-dark Lou could see the whole of Alice's body, from the cramped curl of her toes to the tender space behind her ears, and all the astonishing pale spread of her skin between, the dips and surges and corners of her like symbols in a language no one spoke but them: a syntax of signs and directions that led her eyes onwards and downwards and inwards, hesitating over the pink line of the scar near her hip bone, a little emphasis of vulnerability. She knew that Alice was thinking what she was: that this was how they were meant to be, their bodies opened wide to each other, expecting nothing and everything. It seemed to her that she could feel her gaze caressing Alice's body, and that Alice was a different reflection of herself: the softness of Alice's belly and the tight curve of her own. As her hand traced Alice's skin she could feel its touch herself; the tingle of fingertips, the brush of tiny hairs, the slight resistance of sweat and flesh. She was filled with impatience and with a desire to hold this moment forever, the tremulous calm of it like the surface of a pond before the pebble drops into it.

She felt Alice move slightly, bringing her body closer, and she thought, this is the end as well as the beginning. But in the drowsiness of Alice's embrace she couldn't think what was ending and what was beginning, whether there was any sense in that, only that she was full of sadness and pleasure. And then she felt, or perhaps imagined, a flicker of feet treading their soft footprints inside her – and she felt tears rising in her throat; tears for herself, and for her child, and for Alice, too. For what must surely be love.

27

As they got closer to Orchards, Kitty began to wonder whether it was a mistake to have come, and especially to have brought Daniel. He was driving, and something about the set of his features increased her misgivings: he was anticipating a glimpse of her past, she thought, an insight into the Jones clan. She knew he'd longed to be introduced to Henry before he died, and she couldn't help being glad she hadn't indulged him. Everyone wanted a piece of Henry. They always had.

'OK?' Daniel asked, as he slowed at a crossroads.

'Yes. Not far now.'

They lapsed back into silence, and Kitty gazed out of the window at the Oxfordshire landscape, the fertile fields and prettified villages where no one ordinary could afford to buy a house anymore. A thread of music rose in her head, something very English, in the way Elgar was, or Britten, but –

'What's he like, the man who's living there?' Daniel asked.

Kitty stared at him: for a moment she had no idea what he meant. The tune was fading now, and she was irritated to lose her grasp on it. It'd had a pentatonic tonality that interested her; sad but somehow resolute. Moving forward, like the seasons, the ploughing and harvesting, the new roads carving through the landscape . . . She sighed.

'He sounded nice,' she said.

Daniel looked at her again, and Kitty felt a twist of that particular, painful emotion his smile evoked. Did he realise he'd interrupted something? No, how could he. He was just making conversation. That was what people did, in the car.

There were still moments when she wished she'd held her nerve after the concert and not allowed him to reel her in again: moments when the dread she'd felt, talking to Lou the other day, almost overcame her. Was it like this for other people, she wondered? Perhaps it was just her; perhaps she would only ever be able to love anyone in this exhausting, hopeful, contrary way. Perhaps nothing would ever transform her view of life in the way love was supposed to.

She smiled at herself then. That was a proper emo music student thought. 'Left here,' she said. 'We're nearly there.'

The car swung into the lane, passing the pub and the church and the row of cottages opposite the green. After another minute, Orchards came into view.

'Here,' Kitty said, and Daniel braked hard.

'Wow,' he said. 'It's nothing like I expected.'

The place looked different, Kitty thought, as she got out to open the gate, but it was hard to say how. The lawn had been mown and the hedges clipped: was that all? A silver Range Rover and a Citroen with French plates were parked at the side of the house where her parents used to leave their cars, Henry's string of vintage Triumphs and Flora's steadfast Saab. The Saab, she supposed, was in France. Lou had wanted the last Triumph, but it had rusted so much over the winter that they'd ended up selling it for scrap.

Daniel parked next to the Range Rover. Turning towards the house, Kitty felt a sudden tremor as the past surged up in her mind: like slipping into a parallel universe, she thought. There was a moment of dizziness, but then Daniel was out of the car, putting a hand on her arm, and the front door was opened by a tall man wearing a tweed jacket.

'You must be Kitty,' he said. 'I'm Martin Carver. I'm Flora's – your mother's – well, I suppose I'm the tenant.'

Kitty held out her hand, like a child remembering her manners. 'This is my friend Daniel,' she said.

Martin shook Daniel's hand too, then stood back, deferring to Kitty's superior claim on the house. 'I've just made coffee,' he said. 'But please make yourselves at home. If you want to go over to the barn first . . .'

'Coffee would be lovely,' said Daniel. 'Thanks.'

Kitty followed them into the hall. The inside looked both the same and different too: some of the furniture had gone, and lots of pictures – all those pictures by Henry's school friend who'd turned out to be famous. The family album, Henry had called them, though never in Flora's presence. Some of them Kitty had liked better than others, but the gaps on the walls where they'd hung were more obvious than Kitty had expected, making the house look somehow only half-alive. But what was left was utterly familiar – the pale yellow wallpaper, the hall table with the round mirror – too familiar, Kitty thought, for someone else to be in occupation.

'My ex-wife is here this morning,' Martin said, and on cue a woman came out of the kitchen. She was short and plump and smiling, but her smile changed the instant she saw Kitty and Daniel.

'Daniel!' she said. 'Good Lord. Are you . . .?'

And then her expression changed again. It was curious, Kitty thought, how some people could hide so much, and others couldn't help revealing every nuance of feeling. Friendliness, surprise and something that looked very much like dismay had flitted across this woman's face in the last few seconds. Kitty looked at Daniel. His expression gave no hint that anything was amiss – but Daniel was good at presenting a blank face when he wanted to.

'Miranda,' he said. 'How weird.'

The woman was staring at them both still. 'I had no idea,' she said. She turned to Martin, a look of appeal.

'What?' Kitty said. 'What's weird?'

'Miranda's my – sort of my godmother,' Daniel said. 'She was a friend of my mother's. We haven't seen much of each other lately, though.'

Kitty frowned. The expression on Miranda's face didn't quite fit that story, but Miranda was smiling again now, giving herself a little shake as though things were settling back into place now the surprise had worn off.

'Let's have that coffee,' said Martin, and he turned away before Kitty could ask any more.

Kitty had imagined Martin following them around the house, asking polite questions and saying flattering things about Orchards, but he and Miranda stayed where they were when she put down her coffee cup.

'Please help yourself,' he said. 'Let me know if you need a hand moving anything.'

'There's not much,' Kitty said. 'Just a few boxes.' She looked at Daniel. She could see she wasn't going to get away with not showing him round, now they were here. 'But perhaps we could . . .'

'Of course. Whatever. Take as long as you like.' Martin gestured at Miranda with a hint of jolly resignation. 'We're talking weddings – our daughter's about to tie the knot.' Then he hesitated for a moment, looking at Kitty. 'You're very like your mother.'

'Am I?'

'You have her eyes,' said Martin.

An odd expression flitted across his face then. Embarrassment, possibly? Kitty's interest was piqued.

'How do you know my mother?' she asked. 'I mean, how did you meet her? I ought to know, but I . . .'

'We met in the village,' said Martin. 'In St Rémy. My house is there, and your mother was staying nearby. We ran into each other in the village shop.'

'Really?' said Kitty. It sounded spectacularly unlike Flora to strike up conversation with a stranger, but who knew. Life after Henry, she thought.

'She's staying in my house, you know.'

'Yes.' Kitty hesitated. 'Yes, I know.' She wanted to ask how Flora was, how he'd found her, but she was conscious of Daniel beside her and Miranda across the table, both of them listening in. 'She says it's a lovely house.'

'And so is Orchards,' said Martin. She thought he was going to say something else, but then he seemed to think better of it. Instead he smiled, and lifted a hand as if to dismiss them. 'Make yourselves at home,' he said.

'That was a bit awkward,' Kitty said, as Daniel shut the kitchen door behind them.

'Tricky divorce,' Daniel said, 'but I suppose divorce always is. She's remarried, I think.'

'She looks the marrying kind,' said Kitty, with an edge of malice. She hadn't forgiven Miranda for that disconcerting moment in the hall: it had left a kind of mist in the air that made it even harder to see things straight.

'I wonder what his house is like?' Daniel said. 'Where your mother's staying?'

Kitty didn't answer. She wondered whether Flora had talked to Martin about her and Lou. About Henry.

'This is the snug,' she said, pushing open a door.

The room smelled stale, as though no one had been in it since Flora left. It had been a kitchen for most of Kitty's life, and she wondered whether it looked as strange to outsiders in its new guise as it still did to her. The pristine carpet and sofas and the flat screen television looked implausible, like props brought in to camouflage a crime scene. Kitty could feel Daniel's eyes on her, trying to read her reactions.

'Did you see a lot of Miranda, when you were younger?' she asked. 'Did you know the family?'

'Not really. My grandparents didn't like them: they were suspicious of posh people. Girls with ponies and all that. But Miranda – I think she must have known my father too, unless my mother arranged things before she died. Every year, until I was twenty-one, she gave me some money from him. She used to take me out for tea. I liked that: it was our little ritual.'

'But it stopped when you were twenty-one?'

'I got the money then. The capital. Fifty grand.'

Kitty raised her eyebrows. 'He'd left it to you?'

'I guess. I never knew whether he was alive or dead.'

'He must have been dead,' said Kitty. 'He must have died before your mother.' He must have been married, she was thinking. Perhaps he was a famous musician, and that was where Daniel got his talent from. She glanced at Daniel, but there was no sign of curiosity in his face.

'It must have been fun growing up here,' he said.

'Not really,' said Kitty, but she felt a squeeze of guilt as she said it. There were happy memories, too: where were they today?

They went on into the sitting room – and then suddenly there it was, the joyous side of her childhood. Henry singing *Ich Grolle Nicht* at the top of his voice: their bedtime treat when Flora was out, or even when she wasn't. Schumann lieder delivered at full histrionic volume, Henry banging out the piano accompaniment with great flourishes of his arms while she and Lou capered about in pyjamas. Them being a family, and Orchards a home. A sadness that felt almost like anger filled Kitty's chest, and when she spoke again her voice sounded tight.

'Do you want to see upstairs?'

'Not if you don't want me to,' Daniel said.

It had definitely been a mistake to bring him, Kitty thought. A mistake to come at all. What had made her think she needed those boxes, anyway? She'd have taken them away sooner if she really needed them.

'Let's go over to the barn,' she said.

Miranda appeared in the kitchen doorway as they passed again, and smiled in a way that looked like a prelude to conversation.

'So are you two . . .' she began, and then she gave a little laugh. 'I've got weddings on the brain,' she said. 'You're not on the verge of that, I suppose, with your father just . . .'

'No,' said Kitty.

Miranda laughed again. 'Just checking up on my godson,' she said. 'Taking a belated interest.' Her eyes lingered on Kitty as though appraising her, then swerved away. 'I'll leave you to it, then.'

'Was she always like that?' Kitty asked, as they crossed the yard.

'Like what?'

'A bit peculiar.'

'She's just being friendly,' Daniel said. 'She's always been nice to me.'

'Hmm.'

Kitty looked up towards the roof where the swallows nested. The sky was full of them today, circling and diving, and she could hear the chatter of chicks under the eaves as they approached the heavy double doors. The barn was dark inside, the smell of it deeply embedded in her memory, cold stone and creosote and dust.

Her belongings were stashed in the far corner. All Kitty really wanted now was to leave, but it seemed important to take something with them. An alibi, she thought. The boxes were labelled *sheet music, photographs, diaries* in big bold letters, as though the contents were ordinary objects that could be sorted and classified, not things that snagged at her memory, unravelling bits of the past the moment she looked at them.

As she stood staring at them, Daniel took her arm.

'Kitty,' he said. 'I know it's hard coming back here. I'm sorry about the Miranda thing too, but it's really not important. None of that matters to me – my mother or my father, none of it. God, I hardly remember my mother, even. I'm not hung up about my past, I promise.'

Kitty pulled her arm away.

'And I am?'

'I didn't say that. It's different for you. I know you think I don't understand, because I don't have a home like this or a father to mourn, but I do.'

Kitty brushed angrily at her eyes. This wasn't fair, she thought. Taking advantage of her distress to press his suit. 'I'm fine,' she said. 'I'm just a bit . . .'

In the darkness she could feel the air trembling, the present and the past and the future wavering between doubt and certainty like a flickering picture, a hologram you could look at in several different ways.

'I want to be with you, Kitty,' Daniel said, his voice gentler now. 'Ever since I met you I've known that's what I wanted. It's like – I know it's a cliché, but it feels like chemistry. Like we're meant to be together.'

'Chemistry,' said Kitty. 'Maybe. But I . . .' The magnetic attraction between atoms, she was thinking. The exchange of electrons in an ionic bond. Perhaps that was what it was like between them, but did that mean they were supposed to be together, or that they were elements that should be kept apart so they didn't react? It seemed to her suddenly that being with Daniel made her into part of a compound that had more of his characteristics than hers. 'I don't know if chemistry's a good thing,' she said. 'I don't know if it's good for me.'

'I know you think –' he began, but she interrupted him.

'You don't know what I think,' she said. 'That's the thing.'

Her voice was sharper than she meant, and she saw his reaction to it very clearly: the surprise, and the sudden dejection. Oh, she was silly, and perverse, and cruel. She must . . . But everything was more complicated here. Even Daniel could see that.

'Give me a chance, Kitty,' he said. 'These last few months have been horrible. The last week or two we've – but we need more time. We need to be together, do things together.'

He put his arms around her, and Kitty stood very still, letting him hold her. It was the same old story, she thought – not knowing whether her misgivings were reasonable or whether she was conjuring them out of nothing. She wasn't even sure, just now, whether she believed in Daniel's certainty. Why would he want her, anyway? She was a mess. She wasn't very nice to him, and she was a mess. But it was comforting to feel the roughness of his cheek against hers, the beat of his heart and the fierce strength of his arms.

She felt a deep sigh heaving up from her belly, the shudder of her ribcage as it passed. Perhaps it was better not to think so much. She heard an echo of that melody again, the measured melancholy of the pentatonic scale.

'OK,' she said. 'OK.'

'Good.' Daniel held her tight for a moment longer, and Kitty shut her eyes, letting a feeling of calm settle inside her like a cadence resolving gently, softly. Above her a single swallow swooped through the shadows, the flutter of its wings disturbing the air for a moment before it was gone.

'Come on,' Daniel said, giving her a little shake. 'Let's get the things we came for, then get out of here.'

28

In the excitement over Lou and the baby, Flora had forgotten about Francine Abelard's invitation. When the front doorbell rang one evening she assumed it must be someone looking for Martin, and as she went to answer it she corralled phrases of explanation in her head. *Il passe l'été en Angleterre,* she muttered to herself. *Je reste dans sa maison.*

But when she opened the door, there was Francine, her coat drawn up around her neck as though the night were ten degrees colder.

'Hello,' Flora said.

'I have come to talk with you about the concert,' said Francine.

There was a moment's pause, during which Flora wondered why Francine had come in person rather than phoning, and Francine – or so it seemed to Flora – maintained a serene indifference to that question.

'Do come in,' Flora said. 'Or would you rather . . .'

'I am not in a hurry.' Francine smiled.

'Would you like coffee?' Flora asked, stepping back from the doorway. 'Or perhaps a glass of wine?'

Francine cocked her head suggestively. 'Monsieur Carver has some very good cognac in his cupboard,' she said. 'I think maybe he could spare a little.'

'*Santé.*'

Lifting her glass towards the dark sky, Francine smiled at Flora, a different smile from any she'd seen before. This one was definitely conspiratorial. Flora, who had suspected until that moment that she was to be cross-questioned about her relationship with Martin, or her custodianship of Les Violettes, felt a flush of relief.

'Cheers,' she said. She wasn't a brandy drinker, but the taste of this venerable cognac seemed to fill her whole head. It made the night air feel warm on her skin, a strange but pleasing sensation.

'It's good,' Francine said. 'Don't you think?'

'I don't know much about brandy,' Flora said. 'I wouldn't have dared to drink it without you.' Despite the smiles of collusion, this felt rather like a game of draughts: if she made one careless move, Francine might take all her pieces.

'It is – what's the word in English? – *médicinal*. And good for talking.'

'And for celebrating,' Flora said. She hadn't had a chance to tell anyone else yet, she realised. 'My daughter's pregnant.'

'Congratulations,' said Francine. 'Does she have a nice husband?'

'A nice wife,' Flora said, and Francine laughed suddenly, loudly, unexpectedly.

'Even better,' she said. 'We all need that, *n'est-ce pas?* A nice wife.' She chuckled again. 'I have no children,' she said. 'But I would like grandchildren.'

'I never thought I'd have any,' Flora said. There were so many things she'd never thought about, she realised, and so many others to which she'd devoted hours of thought that were of absolutely no consequence in the end. 'Did you want children?' she asked.

She heard the question a fraction before Francine, and wished she could snatch it back. Stupid, stupid, she thought, but it was too late to unsay it.

'Of course. Did I feel sad, yes. But there are many things in life to make us sad. I have my house, my friends. I like my visitors, some more than the others.'

Flora acknowledged the compliment with a little dip of her head. Her view of Francine was shifting with each turn of the conversation. This, she supposed, was how friendship worked. You met, you talked, you found out more about each other. This was what other people learned in primary school; what she had somehow ignored in her haste to master maths and biology.

'It's worse to be made unhappy by children,' Francine said. 'This is true for some people, I think.'

'Is it?' Another thing Flora had never considered.

'Some of my guests are unhappy. The women. The mothers.'

'With their children, or their husbands?' Flora asked.

'That is a question, of course. But if you have no children, you can lose the husband, if you want to. Isn't that so?'

Could Francine lose her husband, then, if she wanted to? Was this, possibly, what Francine had come to tell her: that she intended to exchange her husband for another whom she'd foolishly passed over years before? Flora felt a blush creep round from her ears.

'Things change,' she said. 'Sometimes people find a way to be happier than they have been.'

'Like you,' said Francine, without a blink.

Flora laughed then, and drained the last of her cognac. That was enough of a lesson in friendship for one evening, she thought. Perhaps it wasn't so much draughts as monopoly, and Francine, she could see, owned most of the board.

'Tell me about the concert,' she said. 'When is it?'

September 1989

The performance is electrifying. They should come to the theatre more often, Flora thinks. She says so, in the interval – and Henry, pouring Sémillon Blanc into two glasses, raises an eyebrow. She knows what he means: that she's too busy to go out in the evenings. That's true, but it's not the whole truth. She could make the time, as she has done tonight. He rarely suggests outings to the theatre. It was the novelty of this production, the great opera singer trying his hand at a spoken role as Othello, that Henry couldn't resist.

'We only came to see this because of Willard White,' she says.

Henry lifts his glass. 'And the rest of them,' he says. 'Imogen Stubbs, Zoe Wanamaker, Ian McKellen. Stellar cast. Especially for the Young Vic.'

The Young Vic is one of Henry's favourite theatres, Flora knows; an opportunity for him to use words like accessible and immediate and experimental.

'It would be quite different in a bigger theatre,' she says, determined to voice an opinion, even if it's not an original one.

'It would have made more money in a bigger theatre,' Henry says, 'but it's good to see artistic integrity's alive and kicking. That's a lovely dress, by the way.'

Flora glances down. 'Thank you,' she says. It was expensive, the dress, bought on a whim she can't account for. It's short, fitted, made of raw silk, and she can see that the Young Vic isn't quite the right arena for it. But even so, she thinks.

'It's a horrid play,' Henry says. 'I've always thought so.'

He smiles again, and for a moment they look straight at each other. Flora has a sense, not unfamiliar, of conversation leapfrogging; of not being sure where it might find itself, a sentence or two hence. She's irked, too: it goes without saying, surely, that they are both aware of the irony of the plot, the husband deceived into believing in his wife's infidelity.

'Brilliant, though,' she says, as breezily as she can manage. 'And Willard can certainly act, can't he?'

The bell rings. Henry, more accustomed to performances and to being, in his way, important to them, ignores it, but Flora empties her glass and gets up.

'We're in the middle of the row,' she reminds him. 'I don't want to climb over everyone in this dress.'

As the second half progresses, Flora finds her mind – loosened by the interval wine – sliding between fact and fiction, sometimes completely immersed in the play, at others watching from a hovering distance. Sitting in the dark, her own emotions reverberate in the small space between audience and actors. Othello, she thinks with mounting frustration, has none of her grounds for jealousy – and as the last act approaches she feels an almost irresistible desire to do something, to shout out loud that he's got it wrong. Of course she knows you can't do that, she's not a lunatic, but she can feel the tussle inside her between temptation and restraint, like standing at the edge of a cliff and knowing you could jump off. Her hands grip the edge of her seat as she watches Othello's terrible descent towards murder.

And then there's a noise close to them, a sound she assumes at first is coming from someone else who has been pushed beyond endurance by the tension on stage. She glances round. In the row behind them a man is having a grand mal fit, his arms and legs writhing, and choked, gurgling sounds coming from his mouth.

Flora clicks instantly into professional mode. They are sitting on benches arranged in a horseshoe around the stage, an arrangement which has its downsides but which makes it easy to manoeuvre herself into a position where she can help. Whispering reassurances to the people nearby, she kneels down in the cramped space beside the man's head. Behind her, she can hear Willard White's voice, increasingly impassioned. Flora turns the man onto his side, sliding her coat alongside him to protect his limbs from the wooden bench. It's years since she managed an epileptic fit, but she knows that the drama on stage is more important, in its way, than this; or at least, that it's not necessary to interrupt it.

And so Flora crouches, with her back to the stage, while Henry and several hundred other people watch Othello smother his wife. She listens to the tragic consequence of reason overcome by deceiving rhetoric, to the once-adoring husband ignoring the desperate pleas and protestations of love that continue, pathetically, until Desdemona's last breath. Her hands resting on the wrenching, contorted body of a stranger, Flora feels a potent mix of sadness and of peace.

By some odd synchronicity, the fit ends at almost exactly the same moment as the play. By the time the standing ovations are over and the audience is beginning to filter reluctantly out of the auditorium, the man is lying still, his wife leaning over him and murmuring quietly.

'All OK?' Flora asks. 'Can I do anything more?'

The woman shakes her head. 'Thank you,' she says. 'We'll be fine.'

'If you're sure.' Flora hesitates for a moment, and then she turns to Henry, and they both stand up.

As they shuffle their way along the row to join the press of people making for the door, Flora feels Henry's hand in the small of her back. She waits for him to move it, but he doesn't; there it is, a slight but definite pressure, as they edge forward in the middle of the crowd, and a tingle of pleasure radiates up her spine. These exits would be no good in a fire, she thinks, but she doesn't care. She'd be happy never to reach the door, never even to turn and look at Henry, just to stand here and feel the warmth of his hand through the expensive, crumpled stuff of her dress. The strange submersion of belief and disbelief she felt earlier swirls in her head again, the mingling of fact and fantasy, and for a moment she thinks she might faint with the excess of it all – but then there's someone speaking, a man who was sitting in the same row as them.

'So lucky your wife's a nurse,' he says.

'Oh, she's not,' Henry says. There's a jaunty edge to his voice; the man looks at them both, his face foolish. 'She's an undertaker, actually,' Henry says.

The man keeps smiling, bound by some code of decorum, and Henry slides his hand further down Flora's back, its intention clear now.

Flora doesn't get the joke until they're in the taxi.

'Idiot,' Henry says, amicably. 'Nurse, indeed.'

His arm is around her shoulder, and he pulls her towards him. 'A lovely dress,' he says, into her hair, 'for the sexiest surgeon in London.'

Flora shuts her eyes, feeling the jolt and rumble of the taxi as it weaves its way across the city towards Paddington. Here they are, she thinks, Othello and Desdemona, transposed and delivered by the suspension of disbelief.

29

Flora came in from the garden earlier than usual on Saturday afternoon. The evening had lain enticingly ahead of her as she toiled in the flowerbeds. It was a marker of how life had changed, she thought, that she'd spent some time calculating how long she might need to get ready.

The beautiful bathroom, with its blue panelled walls and its state-of-the-art shower, was one of the great joys of Les Violettes. Standing under the powerful jets felt like something from a myth: like being transformed into a water nymph. Flora remembered lying in the bath the night Martin had taken her out for dinner, and how the water had felt magical then too. Could that really be only three weeks ago?

Perhaps it was the effect of her exertions in the garden, or the veil of water that surrounded her, but she found she could look back on that brief dalliance now with a calmness different from the flat rationality she was expert at applying to life. She'd been wrong to regret it: she could see now that it had served an important purpose. It had provided some punctuation in the blank sprawl of her new existence. The film she'd imagined living through during those dark days at the Abelards' had moved on through several reels now, and that was a good thing. Simply living was a good thing, passing the days, seeing that you could survive.

Turning off the water, she wrapped herself in one of Martin's enormous towels and took out the black dress she had bought in a boutique (the only boutique) in St Rémy. No harm in dressing up for the occasion, she'd thought – this was France, and women of her age were expected to make an effort – but the result made her feel a little self-conscious. Looking in the mirror, it struck her that the years of benign neglect had left her skin remarkably smooth, and the streaking of grey through her hair could almost be mistaken for expensive highlighting. Not convincing in Paris or London, perhaps, but enough for here. Enough for her.

While she waited for Francine, Flora stood on the terrace, admiring the vibrancy of the roses, the dusty shimmer of purple over the lavender bushes. The sun was descending slowly, and the garden was filled with a beautiful light: a reward for a cloudy day, this intensity of colour before dusk. Francine's company wasn't the least of the pleasures in store this evening, despite – or perhaps because of – the twists and turns of their last meeting. Flora was curious to see what was round the next corner. About the concert itself she had mixed feelings. It was a performance of Purcell's *Dido and Aeneas*, which Francine – who had formed from somewhere a high opinion of Flora's cultural fluency – clearly assumed she was familiar with. Purcell, Flora thought, was not especially dangerous territory. Henry had had a brief fling with baroque opera at one stage, perhaps coinciding with a brief fling with a mezzo-soprano who specialised in trouser roles – but Flora had never, in any case, gone with him to many concerts. She'd decided early on that it was easier to leave his world well alone.

The church of St Julien was set back a little from a square in the *centre historique* of Tours, its antiquity clear even to the casual observer. Inside it was strikingly beautiful, the familiar pale Touraine stone spun and stretched into marvellous arches and pillars and windows. But before Flora had time to take in the details of the architecture, her attention was caught by a poster advertising the concert. Halfway down, in plain view, she read: *Aeneas – Landon Peverell*.

Flora stared, certain at first that she'd made a mistake.

Francine was at her shoulder.

'It is a good choir,' she said. 'I am sure you will enjoy it.'

They had expensive seats, in the middle of the second row. Her father had been the treasurer of the choir, Francine had explained. Two tickets were still sent every year, with the compliments of the committee. Looking at the chairs set out for the soloists, Flora wished the committee's gratitude had waned a little by now. Did performers look closely enough at the audience, she wondered, to recognise acquaintances they weren't expecting to see? She couldn't account for her agitation about seeing Landon: or at least, she could have offered two or three explanations, but none of them was adequate. Being in France was part of it, though; it would seem somehow less like chance, her being at the concert.

The choir was filing onto the stage now, and the orchestra filling the space in front. The soloists followed shortly, and Flora's question was answered almost at once. Landon was right in the middle, only a few feet away from her, and before he'd taken his seat – before the singers had made their bow – his eyes had fallen on her and he had smiled, and raised his eyebrows, and smiled again. While the conductor made his own sweeping bow and turned to open his score, Francine looked quizzically at Flora.

'An old friend,' Flora whispered. 'I had no idea he was singing.' But she could tell from the way Francine's eyes dwelled for a moment on her dress, then flicked back to Landon, that she didn't believe her.

The concert began, the orchestra setting the scene before one of the sopranos led the choir into the first chorus. It was a dramatic piece, even in a concert version. The lack of staging and gesture made it harder to follow the story, but Flora was happy to let the music wash over her. It had been a very long time since she'd heard Landon perform live, and she'd forgotten how imposing he looked on stage and how convincingly he communicated. He might be the wrong side of sixty, but his voice was still wonderful. The choir and orchestra were good too, but it was Landon's face that her eyes kept stealing back to, hoping that his weren't on her.

Flora had entertained a wild hope that she might be able to slip incognito into the throng of the audience during the interval, but even if she'd dipped her eyes in time to miss the look Landon gave her before leaving the stage, there was no avoiding Francine's determination to assist. She knew the layout of the church, and she steered Flora firmly towards the door to the vestry.

Landon appeared almost at once, and his face spread into a smile when he saw that she was already there, waiting for him.

'Well,' he said, 'what a lovely surprise.'

30

Alice's career had ticked along modestly for the first few years Lou had known her, her creative work vying for time with the mixed bag of teaching that provided most of her income. But her success in the Morris Prize had triggered a flood of enquiries from different quarters: there had been a feature in *Art Today*, an invitation to teach on a prestigious American summer school. Alice regarded most of this attention as a curious phenomenon that had touched her by chance and would pass soon enough. But there was one project that excited her: an outdoor sculpture for a children's adventure centre near Birmingham. Parnells was funded by a local tycoon, and – according to its glossy brochure – aimed to provide an environment that children with and without disabilities could explore together.

The brief, Alice reported after a meeting with the trustees, was for art that inspired without patronising.

'We have to think as much about equal access as aesthetics,' she said, over supper.

It was hard to tell from her tone whether she was excited or bemused. It all sounded terrifying to Lou: the kind of place where she might be exposed as a capitalist with the wrong principles. She felt more comfortable defending her own ideological corner than minding her Ps and Qs in other people's.

'It sounds great,' she said. 'We should go and visit.'

It threatened rain on the day of the Parnells trip. Heavy skies followed them up the M40, and they passed through several miles of featureless countryside before spotting a jaunty sign for the centre. But the site itself was breathtaking. Inside and out, there were colourful areas, noisy areas and scented areas; exhibits to touch and press; playground equipment to swing on and slide down and slither over.

The woman who showed them round radiated enthusiasm and good-heartedness, and Lou was ashamed of her earlier misgivings. As they circled the lake (a homage to Monet, with its bridges and water lilies), she reflected that she'd never been much good with children, but now she was pregnant she felt an instant affinity was expected. Even passing a pram in the street she had the sense that she was being tested. She'd expected to find the children at Parnells an even greater challenge, and in some ways they were, but not in the way she'd anticipated. Watching a group with cerebral palsy romping in the rainforest-themed soft play area, she felt profoundly moved. She didn't think Alice had noticed, but as they moved away Alice slipped a hand through her arm.

'We'd better see the site we have in mind for you,' said their guide – Parnells' Head of Education, Lou had gathered. 'It doesn't look like much yet, but that's because we wanted to give you a blank canvas.' She smiled, pleased with her turn of phrase. 'We want your piece to be very much at the centre of it, conceptually.'

She led them out through the back of the main building and round to the far side of the administration block, where an area about the size of a squash court was roughly fenced off. Patches of concrete testified to the recent demolition of three or four small out-buildings. It looked unprepossessing to Lou: she couldn't help feeling disappointed.

Alice stood very still – a stance which might suggest misgiving, but which Lou knew was simply a sign of concentration. Her eyes moved slowly from one side to the other, then upwards. Lou followed them to the skyline, where a low hill broke the horizon, scrubby woodland tumbling down it towards the perimeter of the site.

'It's perfect,' she said. 'There's space to breathe here. Space to think.'

Alice was quiet on the way home. Lou imagined her head filled with whatever language she used to think about her work: strings of shapes and angles, perhaps, rather than words. But when she did speak, what she said was entirely unexpected.

'What would we do if there was a problem with our baby?' she asked.

She hadn't referred to it before as 'our baby', but Lou felt no pleasure at the words. Instead she felt a flash of dread, sharp as a gunshot. 'What kind of problem?'

'Any kind of problem,' Alice said. 'Any of those problems the Parnells' children have.'

'Oh!' Lou's heart thumped a few times in her chest. She called up the scan picture, a curled-up homunculus with tiny splayed fingers. It had never occurred to her that the baby wouldn't be perfect. All those tests and scans had seemed proof against flaws.

'We'd cope, I'm sure,' Alice said. She smiled at Lou: a smile intended, presumably, to show solidarity. 'We could take it to Parnells. We could be a Parnells family.'

And then Lou felt a surge of anger stronger than anything she'd ever known before, a flare of hatred and repulsion that burst like a firework in her head. Trapped in the seat beside Alice she couldn't run away, but that was her instinct: to take her baby and run. She shut her eyes, blood rushing in her head, her chest, her belly – racing to the rescue of the baby in a great gush of maternal reassurance. All this time she'd longed for Alice to take an interest in it, but now . . .

She could feel words swarming in the space around their heads: words that might bruise and scar, on the brink of being said. I'm the mother, she wanted to shout. It's my baby, not ours. How dare you claim it now? How dare you blight it with your wicked thoughts? But the urge to say them did battle, furiously, with the urge to keep quiet. Some instinct was telling her – as it must have told Flora all those years ago – that her baby needed a protector; that she needed Alice. Oh, but she was so tired of all this compromise and effort. Tired of everything being so hard.

'That's a terrible thing to say,' she said, hardly believing that she was speaking aloud; hardly knowing whether she was.

Alice turned to look at her. 'I'm sorry?'

'How dare you tempt Fate like that?' Lou said.

'I'm sorry,' Alice said again, her tone of voice different this time – but still wrong, Lou thought, fury rising inside her again. Still self-righteous and sure of herself; pleased with her magnanimity.

'It's not your fucking baby,' Lou shouted. The words glittered and fizzed, filling her with terror and exhilaration. 'We're not a fucking family. We'll never be a family. I never want to be like –'

'Don't tar me with the brush of your family,' said Alice. 'Don't blame me for that.'

Alice's eyes were fixed on the road, her shoulders set firm, her chin up to face what was coming. She looked magnificent, Lou couldn't help thinking, although she banished the thought angrily.

'This has nothing to do with my family,' she said.

'Everything has to do with your family,' said Alice. 'Every damn thing.'

'How dare you?' said Lou again. The anger was boiling up into grief now; into passionate, agonising self-pity. 'You have no idea about my family. Just because you come from a line of fucking boring blameless Middle Americans.'

'Oh, so it's my family's fault now?'

'They made you,' said Lou. 'They made you so self-satisfied and thick-skinned and . . .'

'Well, at least I know now,' Alice said. 'Thank you for your honesty.'

Lou was silent then. The firework had fizzled out in her head, leaving behind a buzzing numbness. She shouldn't have said those things. She could hear her voice still, the echo of her words thrown back in mockery. A boil had been growing inside them both these last few weeks, she thought, and they hadn't managed to lance it. Mistrust had festered below the surface, feeding on half-truths and hurt feelings. She could feel the poison draining now, the proper shape of their feelings being restored. But still those lacerating words hung in the air, and she couldn't take them back. She could hear Alice's words too – *At least I know now*.

Alice's hair was held up in a knot that exposed the fine sweep of her neck, the silhouette of a Greek amphora, and Lou longed to reach out her hand, to offer a benediction they would both understand without recourse to more clumsy words. But it was as if a magnetic field had sprung up between them, making touch impossible. She felt so horribly, wretchedly tired. If she closed her eyes, she thought, the tumult in her head would settle and she would be able to see a way forward. There was nothing to be done for now, while the car was bowling along, but let the echoes subside into the rumble of the engine, and . . .

She must have gone to sleep, Lou realised. When she woke, the car had stopped and Alice had got out. She sat for a while sleepily piecing together the day she'd slipped out of. She remembered children's faces, radiantly happy, and Alice looking at a blank plot of land and seeing something wonderful – and then an explosion of rage and bile.

They were at a motorway service station. Through the windscreen Lou could see Alice standing on a grass verge, talking into her mobile phone. Had she stopped for this call, Lou wondered, or for some other reason? She realised with a plummet of fear that she had absolutely no idea what Alice might be saying. Would she turn in a moment and smile to show that everything was all right, or was she was even now arranging to move out of Veronica Villa? She should get out of the car, Lou thought, and rush over to Alice and pour apologies into her arms – but she didn't move.

The dashboard clock read 4.55. She must have slept for a couple of hours. She felt better for it: better for her outburst, too. Ready to make amends. She would explain herself, put things in context, plead the turmoil of pregnancy. Surely it was only a matter of degrees of apology and restitution. She remembered that she'd booked some annual leave next week; the two of them could go up to London to see an exhibition, have lunch somewhere nice.

And then Alice turned and that cosy image evaporated. Her expression made Lou's heart thud: in the seconds it took Alice to walk back to the car Lou flailed in search of something to say; some way in.

'Alice?' she said, as the car door opened. 'Has something happened?'

'It's my Mom,' Alice said. 'She's been in an accident.'

Relief suffused Lou's whole body, followed by a backlash of guilt.

'I'm so sorry,' she said. 'What kind of accident? Is she OK?'

Alice's mother was only fifty and looked younger; she was the strongest woman Lou had ever met. Lou heard her voice saying *fucking boring blameless Middle Americans*. Jesus Christ.

'She's in hospital,' Alice said. 'It was a truck, it hit her head on.' She plunged a hand into her hair, a gesture Lou had never seen before. 'I need to get on a flight,' she said. 'We're not far from Heathrow.'

'What about – don't you need to book?' Lou asked. 'Don't you need to pack?' Her mind felt muddy and jumbled: the only thing she could see clearly was Alice flying away from her.

'I guess you're right.' Alice's face was taut.

Lou unbuckled her seatbelt. 'I'll drive,' she said. 'Then you can use your phone.'

Alice was still standing with her hand on the driver's door when Lou got there. She looked like a hovercraft that had slumped back to the ground, heavier and more ungainly than usual. Lou put a hand on her shoulder, wishing passionately that she could gather her in her arms and make her feel loved.

'I'm sorry,' she said. 'I'm sorry for everything.'

Alice said nothing, but she stumped away round the car and climbed in.

'Home,' said Lou. 'Full speed home.'

Inside, she felt like a young wife being left for the war.

31

Kitty was fast asleep when the doorbell rang, and it took her a while to come to. She reached for her phone to check the time: not quite ten. Perhaps it was a parcel. Or Daniel had lost the key she'd given him. By the time she'd hauled herself out of bed she feared whoever it was might have gone away, but they hadn't. Through the intercom she heard a voice she didn't expect.

'Kitty? It's Martin Carver. Did I wake you?'

'Yes,' said Kitty, 'but it doesn't matter.' She hesitated. 'Do you want to come up?'

She pressed the buzzer and sloped back to the bedroom to pull on a jumper and a pair of jeans over her T-shirt. It was Sunday. What on earth was Martin Carver doing here on a Sunday morning?

By the time he reached the second floor Kitty was waiting, holding the door open for him.

'You're just in time for breakfast,' she said, in what she hoped was a capable tone. If there was a problem at Orchards, she ought to seem competent.

'I've brought supplies,' Martin said, holding up a paper bag.

Looking properly at his face for the first time, Kitty saw that he looked troubled; not the kind of troubled that went with a tenant's complaint. Not, surely, the kind that went with an intention to seduce his landlady's daughter, either, though?

'I'll put the kettle on,' she said. 'Tea or coffee? I only have instant, I'm afraid.'

'Instant's fine,' he said, though Kitty suspected it was a long time since he'd drunk Nescafé.

She could feel Martin watching her while she cleared the little table that doubled as desk and dumping space, and the impression of father-liness was somehow more worrying than the possibility of seduction.

'Sorry about the mess,' she said, covering her awkwardness with bustle. 'I'll open the curtains. Have a seat. That chair's broken – try this one.'

Martin sat down obediently. 'You're really very like your mother,' he said.

'People don't usually say that.'

'Don't they?' He took two Danish pastries out of his bag. A thought occurred to Kitty then, but even if – surely that couldn't be the reason for his visit?

She fetched their coffee from the kitchen and sat down carefully on the broken chair. Martin passed her a pastry, but she wasn't really hungry.

'I assume,' she said, 'that if you'd just been passing, you'd have said so by now.'

'It's a bit out of the way for "just passing",' he agreed.

'So . . .?' Kitty looked at him expectantly.

Martin said nothing for a few moments. Kitty had the impression that he'd prepared a speech, then lost confidence in it.

'It's about Daniel,' he said at last.

So she hadn't imagined those strange vibes at Orchards. 'Is he the rightful property of one of your daughters?' she asked. 'Betrothed from the cradle, or something?'

'No, no. I'm afraid . . .' He sighed. 'Miranda should have come,' he said. 'She would have been much better at this than me. I'm afraid it's worse than that.'

'Has something happened to him?' Drenched suddenly with cold, Kitty's mind flitted back: she'd last seen Daniel at – what, midnight? Why hadn't she made him come home with her?

But Martin was shaking his head.

'Not as far as I know,' he said, 'although I haven't spoken to him since you came to Orchards. We don't have any way of getting hold of him, since . . .' He held up a hand, halting himself. 'Back a bit,' he said.

'Back a bit.' He stopped, brushed his cheek with his hand. 'Miranda knew Daniel's mother,' he said.

Kitty nodded. 'Daniel told me.' Her hands were shaking a little. At least she knew now that she loved Daniel, she told herself. Whatever Martin had come to say, it would be OK. She watched his face, another explanation taking shape in her mind: Daniel was the heir to something, and she wasn't deemed suitable.

'She knew his father, too,' Martin went on. 'Miranda acted as trustee, until Daniel was twenty-one, for the money his father settled on him.'

'I know that too,' Kitty said. Or maybe his father was a ne'er-do-well, and they thought they should warn her. A sort of Magwitch scenario. That wouldn't be so bad. It wasn't as though she had any illusions about Daniel's family.

Martin still had his pastry in one hand; his plate was covered with flakes, as though he'd clenched it too tightly in his fist.

'Bloody hell,' he said. 'It shouldn't be me telling you this. Maybe it's not you I should be telling, either, but you're an adult, we thought . . .'

'For fuck's sake,' said Kitty, 'just tell me, will you? You're scaring the pants off me.'

'Daniel's father was Henry Jones,' Martin said. 'He didn't want Daniel to know. He didn't want –'

'Wait,' said Kitty. 'You mean my Henry Jones? My father?'

Martin nodded. 'It's the most appalling coincidence,' he said. 'If Daniel had known . . .'

'Christ.' Kitty lifted both hands to cover her head. Just for a moment she felt nothing except surprise and disbelief and even – possibly – a shred of amusement, but she knew that something appalling was about to come crashing down on her. What were the chances, she thought? Was that why – that awful sense of magnetism, of ambivalence – should she have guessed? Should she have recognised him? Now she knew, she could see Henry in him quite clearly. And then, in an instant, she felt violently sick. Her chair clattered to the floor as she pushed herself away from the table and ran to the bathroom – conscious, all the while, of how miserably small the flat was, how there was no getting away, no hiding anything.

She had no idea how long she was gone – maybe only a few minutes, though it felt much longer, a horrible timeless interval of throwing up until she thought her guts must have turned inside out, of trying and failing not to think, of splashing water on her face so fiercely it soaked the whole tiny room. Martin was still sitting there when she came out.

'I'm so sorry,' he said, and she could see that he was; a little sorry for himself, too, but that was understandable. The worst thing was, Kitty thought now, in a moment of perfect lucidity, that there wasn't any aspect of this that wasn't Henry's fault.

'Do you know,' she said, her voice sounding bizarrely composed, 'my sister told me the other day that my parents had trouble getting pregnant. That's why she and I were born nine years apart. She thought she thought it was Henry who . . .' She broke off.

'Come and sit down,' said Martin. 'Just come and sit here for a little while, unless – would you rather I went?'

'No.' That, oddly, was the last thing Kitty wanted. She almost wished he'd touch her, hug her, but she couldn't ask him that. She stared at the massacred remains of breakfast on his plate. 'We always thought,' she began, 'whatever he got up to, we were his children. We thought everything else –'

Martin reached across the table and put his hand over hers.

'For my mother's sake, too,' Kitty went on, struggling to get the words around the bolus of unwept tears in her throat. 'That was the deal, we thought. We were his family.'

'I suppose that's why he didn't want you to know,' said Martin, his voice very gentle. 'I suppose he thought you'd never need to. He never saw Daniel – not after his mother died.'

'He saw him before that, though,' Kitty said, suddenly vehement as something slotted into place in her mind. That day at the pond, she thought. The woman and the child: she must have known what it meant all along. That was why she'd run away. 'He saw him with me, when I was very little. I'm sure he did.'

Martin nodded slightly, as though he was thinking, computing. After a moment he said, 'Even Daniel's grandparents had no idea who Henry was. No one did, except Miranda.'

He stopped again. Kitty wanted him to go on, but she couldn't ask him to. It was awful, she thought, to want to know more: as though the bombshell he'd just handed her could somehow be defused with talk. As though knowing every detail of Henry's deception and desertion could take away some of the pain. The instinct to hide under the bed-clothes was surely more natural. But she had the feeling this was her only chance to hear the whole story – and she had to do something, just now, to fill the time before she faced up to what happened next. She looked back at him, hoping he understood.

'Miranda introduced them, Henry and Elizabeth,' Martin said eventually. 'They met through her. Miranda was a cousin of Henry's: second cousin, or even third. They didn't know each other growing up, but they met at a family funeral – oh, in their twenties, I suppose. They were both musicians; they stayed in touch, saw each other from time to time. And Elizabeth and Miranda had been at music college together. She –' he hesitated '– she'd always been a little unstable, Elizabeth. I think Miranda was horrified, frankly, when she fell in love with Henry, because she could see . . .'

'Poor Elizabeth,' said Kitty. The emotion was unexpected, but she understood exactly how it would have been; that it wasn't Elizabeth's fault. She could fill in the rest of the details: an affair that lasted longer than the others; a child whose existence no one ever suspected. 'And she died –'

'It was a car crash,' Martin said. 'She was travelling back from a concert. She played the cello in a chamber orchestra.'

'Did he love her?' Kitty asked, before she could bite the words back.

Martin made a little gesture of uncertainty, or perhaps resistance. 'I never met him,' he said. 'I couldn't –'

'No,' said Kitty. 'Of course not.'

She'd heard enough now. Suddenly enough: she needed to keep something of her father back. Something for herself. She could feel nausea gathering again in her belly, a slow, chronic weight, this time, that she knew would stay with her. But there was something else; something she needed to ask.

'Will you tell Daniel?' she said. 'I can't . . .'

'Of course. Miranda should do that.'

'And would you tell him,' Kitty said, blundering on, not really sure whether she meant it or whether she just wished she meant it, 'would you tell him I'm sorry he never met Henry.'

Henry would, she thought, have been just the father Daniel needed – and that was finally one thought too many for her.

PART IV

Paintings and drawings by Nicholas Comyn, from the collection of the late Henry Jones

Lot no. 4: Cellist, 1993

This is one of several portraits Comyn painted of musicians. The face of the young female cellist is hardly glimpsed: she is shown side on, her body wrapped around the cello and her head bent to hear the resonances of the strings. Her hair – similar in tone to the cello – falls forward in a skein of bronze, introducing a sense of movement that brings this portrait vividly alive.

The setting is a small room rather than a concert hall, which contributes to the sense of intimacy – but even the painter is excluded from the world the cellist inhabits. One could argue that this is a depiction of music itself as much as a portrait, although the sensuality of the figure makes it impossible to disregard her as a presence. The fluid, organic rendering of the cellist is foregrounded by a rigid metal music stand, but it is not possible to decipher the music that sits on it.

Although there are strong similarities with the famous series Comyn painted of members of the Capella string quartet, this portrait is exceptional in its expression of musicality. Comyn was himself a competent cellist, and it is possible that he knew the subject of this portrait personally. The inclusion of certain objects in the composition – a letter thrust back into an envelope, a teacup on the floor – suggests a specific setting. In the mirror on the far left, a shadowy figure is just visible, hinting at the presence of another person in the room.

This painting was damaged at some point and subsequently restored. The site of the tear is just discernible as a straight line across the body of the cello and the cellist.

32

'What a beautiful garden,' Landon said, as Flora emerged from the back door with a tray. 'I can imagine sitting just here all summer.'

It was a flawless day. Flora was pleased that Les Violettes was looking its best for him – and still more than a little amazed that he'd had time to come and visit her before flying home. She recalled their conversation in the interval of the concert, the way things had been simpler than she'd anticipated, almost as if this meeting had been planned.

'I had no idea you were singing,' she had said.

'I had no idea you were in France,' he'd replied. 'I rang you last week, actually. At Orchards. I left a message.'

'I've been here for six weeks now. I'm becoming quite the ex-pat.'

'How delightful. Staying with friends?'

'No, I –' Flora had hesitated. The speed with which things had happened, plans had formed, had seemed indecorous once she had to explain it. 'I've done a house swap,' she'd said. 'Just for the summer.'

People were moving back towards their seats by then. Flora had glanced over her shoulder, conscious of Francine hovering discreetly a few feet away.

'Can we meet afterwards?' Landon had asked.

'Don't you have to see the organisers? The other singers?'

'Only for a drink.' Landon had smiled. 'Let's make a plan.'

She'd rarely known him to be so impulsive: the version of Landon that had always – almost always – been just out of her grasp. He'd been playing a part that evening, of course – but then so had she, and in a strange way that had made things easier. They were Landon Peverell the celebrated baritone and Flora Macintyre the retired surgeon meeting on a public occasion, and those were roles they could carry off without a blink.

The odd thing was, she thought now, that although they'd known each other since childhood, they'd seen rather little of each other over the years: Landon had never been at anyone's beck and call, except of course Rosanna's. He was always dutiful on that front, Flora was sure of that, but loyalty to his friends had never been expressed through the frequency of his visits. But he had always made things better between her and Henry when he did come; that was an irony. He'd been common ground for them. Looking at him now, sitting in the garden she had got to know so well in so short a time, she felt a stab of grief for the years that had passed when she might have known him better.

'I only have Vouvray,' she said, setting the tray down on the stone table. 'I hope that'll do.'

'My dear!' Landon laughed, making a little parodic moue. 'You are funny.'

'It's true,' said Flora. 'My landlord took me to buy some, and I've been drinking my way through it. Rather slowly, I might say.'

'In that case I shall feel duty bound to assist.'

He smiled in the way he always had, lifting his head a little. Like a tortoise raising itself into the sunlight, Flora thought, though nothing else about Landon was remotely tortoise-like. He looked, just then, like the youthful Landon in the portrait by Nick Comyn, wearing a fur cape and a garish waistcoat to play Leporello. She imagined his face in a then-and-now photograph, his square cheekbones and his long nose unchanged, his eyes more serious. That much must be true of them all: the sobering effect of everything they'd seen. Everything they'd done, or not quite managed to do.

She hadn't followed Landon's career in detail, but she'd been aware of a few highlights, and then of the lack of them. There had been that ENO production, years back – Falstaff, was it? – that had been so hideously panned. Not Landon's fault, but he'd caught the fallout, as Henry put it. Though of course that wasn't the whole story.

She handed him a glass, and he tilted it towards her.

'Well,' he said, 'I'm very glad to see you comfortably settled here. I worried about you, you know. What you'd do. This I wouldn't have guessed.'

'Life is full of surprises.'

'I'm not surprised you nosed out this little gem,' Landon said. 'But I'm intrigued by your host. A man of impeccable taste, clearly.'

'I could introduce you,' said Flora. 'But he's at Orchards and I'm here, and then he'll be here and I'll be there.'

Landon looked at her for a moment.

'But you hit it off,' he said. 'You must have hit it off rather well, to come up with this arrangement.'

'It was my idea,' said Flora. 'I thought how much I'd like to spend more time here.'

'I don't blame you. If your landlord is as charming as his house you could do worse than install yourself permanently.'

Flora must have looked distressed, because Landon was suddenly contrite. 'My dear Flora, I apologise. That was in bad taste.'

'Yes,' said Flora. And then, before she had time to think better of it, 'How's Rosanna?'

'She's well, thank you.'

'Good.'

Landon hesitated for a moment, then he said, 'Better these days, generally speaking. She's painting a little.'

'Good,' said Flora again.

Flora had only met Landon's wife a handful of times. She rarely accompanied him, either to concerts or to visit friends. But she knew Rosanna's story – the stillbirths, the long course of depression. She'd had terrible luck, Flora thought, in everything except her husband. For twenty years now she'd lived in the cocoon she'd retreated to within a few years of their marriage: a life lived truly on the timescale of an exotic butterfly, born to flourish, to dazzle, for a day and a night.

At least, Flora thought, there had been something solid about Henry, and their marriage, even at its most chaotic and difficult. Their lives had been fully lived. She was glad of that; glad she hadn't traded in her own tokens for so little return.

'I saw the girls at the Morris Prize show,' Landon said.

'How was it?' she asked. 'Tell me about the Bacchus.'

'Quite startling.' Landon raised his eyebrows. 'She's very good, you know. Alice. It's very like him. Moving, too. And the cancer, of course.'

'What?'

'The cancer, on his chest.' He looked at her. 'You didn't know about that bit?'

'No.'

It was odd, Flora thought: it wasn't that she'd stopped thinking about Henry over the last few weeks, but the pattern of memories had changed. She hadn't thought about his illness for a while; it caught her off guard.

'I'm sorry,' Landon said. 'That was clumsy, too. More clumsiness.'

Flora shook her head, but she didn't ask any more. Of course Henry's cancer hadn't been visible, it wasn't something you could sculpt, but she supposed that was a question of artistic licence. She of all people shouldn't feel squeamish about representations of human flesh.

Landon put a hand on her knee. That was nice of him, Flora thought, but even so, some of the pleasure had gone out of the evening. She put down her wine glass, feeling a little wave of self-pity rising inside her.

'I missed it, you know,' she said.

'Missed what?'

'The cancer. He'd noticed a lump. I would have looked at it, but we . . .' She laughed abruptly. 'His mistress rang,' she said, 'at just the wrong moment. God knows which one, but I'd thought there wasn't one anymore. I forgot about the lump. I didn't – there was a froideur, after that. I didn't see him undressed for quite some time. The next I heard it was invading the chest wall. There's an irony for you.'

'Several, I should say.' Landon didn't move, but she felt him come closer; felt a door opening between them. 'Poor Flora,' he said.

'Life with Henry was all ironies,' Flora said, 'some more painful than others.'

'You could have left him.'

'For you?' She hadn't meant to say that: it felt as though the words had been sprung on her. And then she heard her voice again: 'You know, for years I thought you were in love with me. It meant quite a lot, believing that. It wasn't until –'

'I was, in a way,' he said.

She stared at him, astonished and angry and jubilant all at the same time.

'What the hell does that mean?'

'You chose Henry,' he said. 'I'm not a great romantic. You were both my friends; I put it aside.'

Flora was silent for a moment. The years seemed to swim in her head, that great stretch of years, and all the threads of emotion and experience they had contained. She could hardly tell, in the confusion of them, which thread she would pull out.

'Your dedication to Rosanna has been pretty romantic,' she said eventually.

Her heart fluttered in her chest. This was a forbidden subject: the extraordinary sacrifices Landon had made for Rosanna. She waited for him to react, but his expression didn't change.

'I'm glad you see it that way,' he said.

'I thought of you when Henry was dying,' Flora said. 'When I was looking after him. I thought of you and Rosanna.'

She felt shaky now, as though the last of the scaffolding that held her in place, held them both in place, had come away.

'I'm glad I did it,' she said. 'Took early retirement, and had that time with him. It was – I loved him, you know. I really did.'

'I never doubted it,' Landon said.

'I did. I doubted it all the time.' Flora made a sound that was half laughter, half a groaning, animal noise of pain. 'Those last few months were some of the best we had together. I had him all to myself. I used to think about that too: how shameful it was that I should triumph in my sole possession when he was dying.'

'Hardly shameful to want to have the nursing of your husband to yourself. Lots of women wouldn't have done what you did. He knew you did it for love.'

'God, he was a swine,' said Flora. 'Why the hell did I have to fall for such a swine?'

Landon came and knelt beside her then and put his arms around her. She could imagine him speaking, saying things that were comforting or platitudinous or intended to make her laugh, but he said nothing more, and nor did she. Even though this was the moment, she thought. This was the opportunity to tell him. There was no doubt that was the generous thing to do – but it was more complicated than that, and she owed less to him than to others. She shut her eyes, keeping the words back and wondering how this moment would resolve, how they'd get back to normality from here, take up their wine glasses again and find something else to talk about. And then suddenly he was speaking.

'It would be the easiest thing in the world to go upstairs now,' he said, 'and find our way into bed together. Twice in a lifetime would be forgivable, I think. But I don't think we should do that, Flora.'

Flora opened her eyes in astonishment. It hadn't occurred to her for a moment that they would end up in bed, but now he'd mentioned the possibility it seemed the right way, absolutely the right way, for the evening to end. Wasn't that what he meant, in his roundabout way? Wasn't it a proposition?

She would never have believed, either, that desire could be kindled so rapidly, from such an unlikely start. Not so much the prospect of pleasure as the identification of unmet need, she thought – but she was hardly thinking at all; there was hardly time to think.

'Why not?' she said. 'Why on earth not?'

April 2014

'Not *God be in my Head*,' Henry says.

'What?'

It's a little while since he last spoke; Flora realises she must have dozed off. It's very hot: she turned the heating right up this morning, and the sun is streaming through the windows now.

'For the funeral. Not *God be in my Head*. Appalling piece.'

'Well,' says Flora, struggling to settle on the right tone, 'I'm relieved you told me. It was right at the top of my list.'

Henry manages a smile. 'You're supposed to take me seriously. Prerogative of the dying.'

'Take you seriously?' Perhaps not the right tone; the navigable waters between the over-hearty and the sentimental or the querulous seem narrower than usual this morning. 'Good Lord, Henry, where would we be if I started taking you seriously?'

'That's very unfair. I've always taken you deadly seriously.'

He coughs; not a violent cough, but it's painful to watch, as though it might easily tear a hole in him. Flora wonders whether the heat is drying his throat. Perhaps she should turn the thermostat down. She stirs herself, preparing to get up.

'Do you want anything?' she asks. 'Cup of tea?'

'I mean it,' he says.

'I've got it.' Flora smiles, patting his hand. 'Not *God be in my Head*.'

Henry moves his head on the pillow. 'Not that,' he says. 'I mean that I've always taken you seriously. Been your greatest admirer. I hope you know that.'

Flora looks at him, his face altered almost beyond recognition but those eyes, when he's fully alert, still very much his.

'I know,' she says. 'You've told me. You've often told me.'

'No,' he says.

He looks cross: he wants her to do more of the work in this conversation, Flora understands. He wants her to give him a break – to forgive him, even. She feels a prick of annoyance, a feeling she hasn't had for some time. Isn't she doing enough? Hasn't she made enough sacrifices to be sitting here with him? It's not like Henry to want to gloss things over. They've survived, all these years, on the finest of nuances, on tacit acceptance rather than pretence.

'Flora,' he says, 'I've been very fortunate.'

Flora hesitates. In what way, precisely? she wants to ask. Fortunate in having me, or in having all the others as well? But he's dying; she can't say any of that. Or doesn't want to.

'Good,' she says. 'I'm glad. Let me make you a cup of tea.'

Before he can speak again she sweeps out of the room, the stiflingly hot room, and through to the kitchen. She finds, as she fills the kettle, that she's trembling. It distresses her that she doesn't know why: whether it's the mention of Henry's funeral, or his sudden desire to make amends, or to justify himself; whatever he hoped to do just now. That's not the deal, she thinks. That sort of conversation has always been ... And haven't these last months been proof enough, anyway? Can't that happiness be allowed to stand for – whatever it is that he wants to say?

As the kettle comes to the boil she stares out of the window. The piece of garden outside the kitchen is better tended than any they have ever had, this little area that was replanted after the building work turned it into a mud bath. The shrubs whose names sound to her oddly like diseases (*hydrangea macrophylla*, *viburnum rigidum*, *rosa rugosa*) are about to flower. Their foliage is thick with buds, waiting to reveal the colours neither she nor Henry have yet seen.

Godammit, Flora thinks. God bloody dammit. The thought of Henry speaking from the maw of death frightens her, but so does the idea of cheapening what they've been through by tying it up in a trite little parcel at the last, as if to prepare it for burial. So does the feeling that she's expected to humour Henry, now, in a different sort of game.

She takes a teapot and cups out of the cupboard and puts them on a tray. Niceties she wouldn't have bothered with before, she thinks, but there is so little left that she can do.

Henry's eyes are shut when she goes back into the bedroom. Flora feels that icy plunge that has become familiar these last few days – although she knows about death, she reminds herself; she would recognise it – and then she puts the tea tray down and leans over to check the morphine pump. They have the minimum of medical paraphernalia, but its presence consoles her. Not just because it keeps Henry comfortable, she knows that.

'Kitty's coming later,' she says, and Henry's eyes flutter open.

Oh, there's no hiding his preference now, Flora thinks. Poor Lou; Henry will never know that he should feel more for her, by rights. Rights never got much of a look in, though, in this family. No point in weighing her own part in that against . . . But she stops herself. God be in my head and in my understanding. No wonder Henry doesn't want that sung at his funeral.

She sits down beside the bed and touches his hand. She forgot to turn down the thermostat, but just as well: his hands are cold. Old man's hands, these days; those square pianist's fingers, sprigged with dark hair, have shrivelled like something left in the oven for too long. She smiles, and takes both his hands in hers, and he smiles too.

'Thank you,' he says.

33

It took Kitty some time to make herself understood. Lou didn't react to her anguish as she'd expected: the ever-competent big sister sounded distracted, almost violently distracted, as though Kitty had rung in the middle of a hurricane and she was struggling to hang onto pieces of furniture that might fly away.

'For God's sake, Lou,' Kitty shouted in the end, 'please listen. Daniel is Henry's son. Henry was his father. What the fuck am I going to do?'

There was a long silence then, and eventually Lou said, 'I'll meet you in London. Can you hang on until 2?'

'Where?' Kitty said. 'Here?'

'Wigmore Street,' Lou said. 'Is Wigmore Street OK?'

And so here Kitty was, and here was Lou coming through the door, looking every bit as miserable as Kitty felt.

'My poor Kitty,' she began, leaning across to enfold Kitty in her arms. 'I haven't digested it yet. Are you sure it's true?'

'It's not the kind of thing anyone would make up, is it?'

'I meant more . . .' Lou straightened up, her face soft with anguish. 'Could it be – mistaken identity? It's a common enough name, Henry Jones.'

'He's living at Orchards,' Kitty reminded her. 'They know exactly which Henry Jones they're talking about.'

Lou nodded, hesitated a moment longer, then slid onto the seat opposite Kitty.

'And is there proof?' she asked. 'Did he offer you any evidence?'

Kitty gave a wan smile. 'It isn't a legal case, Lou. They're not asking for anything. They just felt I ought to know. We ought to know, so we'd –' She bit her lip, stopping tears. She'd kept thinking, these last few hours, that she should have guessed; that maybe she had known, at

254

some level, and had chosen to ignore it. The violence of her feelings, the dread and the uncertainty and the temptation: she must have understood, deep down, that there was a reason for it all. 'I thought things were bad enough when Henry died,' she said. 'I thought that was a pretty shitty deal.'

'Listen,' said Lou, 'it'll be OK. I don't underestimate – but you will get over it, you know. Maybe it would help if we found someone for you to talk to.'

Kitty waved a hand irritably. 'Lots of fun for them, an inadvertent victim of incest.'

'You can choose not to be a victim,' Lou said.

'Oh, shut up.' Kitty scowled at her. 'God, Lou, you're not that wise and well-balanced, even you. I can't . . . It's just so horrible. How the hell are we going to tell Flora? And you know, he's our half-brother. He doesn't have any family. He's never had a family, except his grandparents, and they're both dead.'

Lou made a face. 'You're right, that's all very tricky.'

'The thing is . . .' Kitty felt herself crumple. 'Oh God, I can't . . .'

Lou reached across the table and put her hands on Kitty's hunched shoulders, enclosing them both for a moment in a little private space of their own. 'Poor baby,' she whispered. 'I'm so sorry. I'm so sorry to do the lawyer bit, and the therapist bit. I'm on your side, you know.'

Kitty nodded; a tiny movement. Now there were tears she couldn't hold back, spilling through her fingers as though something had burst in the fierceness of her grasp. If only she'd found out a few days earlier, while her feelings for Daniel were still unsettled. If only the visit to Orchards had ended differently. That was the final piece of cruelty: that she'd yielded at last to Daniel's blandishments that afternoon, when inside the house Martin and Miranda had already known the truth. 'The thing is,' she began, 'he's like the other half of me, and now I know why, and I know it's a terrible thing, but I'm in love with him, and if I have to see him . . .'

Lou's grip on her shoulders tightened. 'Poor baby,' she crooned again. 'Poor, poor Kits. And Henry just dead, too. I can see –'

Kitty pulled back sharply. 'If you think I've fallen in love with Daniel because I've lost Dad, that's fucking rubbish,' she said. 'That's like me saying you fell in love with Alice because you didn't want to end up like Mum, being betrayed by a man.'

'That's not what I meant,' Lou said. 'I meant –'

'It's all right for you, Ms Smuggo Life-all-sorted-out Lesbian,' Kitty said. 'Life isn't that fucking simple for all of us.'

'Stop swearing,' said Lou. 'Alice is leaving me.'

Kitty stared. 'What?'

Lou took a deep breath. 'She's going to America. I've just taken her to the airport.'

'For ever?'

'Her mother's had an accident,' Lou said. 'She's flying home.'

'That doesn't sound –'

Lou shook her head. 'It's all a terrible cock-up,' she said. 'I lost my temper, and said things I . . .'

It was her turn to weep now: Kitty gazed at her helplessly.

'Poor Lou,' she said. 'What a sorry pair we are. Bloody hell.'

The café was almost full today: all around them people were eating and laughing. What would all these good Muslims say, Kitty wondered, to one sister inadvertently sleeping with her half-brother, and the other deserted by her lesbian lover?

'I've been thinking,' Lou said, 'perhaps we should go and see Flora.'

'In France?' Kitty said. 'You mean – now?'

'It's just – I've booked some holiday, and I thought we . . . I thought you might like to . . .'

Kitty stared at her. Oh, to disappear like that, she thought: to slip away to some quiet French village a million miles from Daniel. To see her mother, too – although that thought caused a flutter of apprehension as well as pleasure.

'Would Flora want us?' she asked.

'Why not? She's got a whole house.'

'But isn't she . . . Hasn't she gone there to get away from everything?'

'I think she'd be pleased,' said Lou. She managed a smile – and if she was persuading herself that things were simpler than they really were, Kitty thought, she was making a pretty convincing job of it.

'The mothership,' Lou said. 'Two drifting satellites returning to the mothership.'

34

The truth was that such a precipitate departure presented Lou with several difficulties, all of which she decided to ignore until the flights were booked and the plan was irrevocable. That, she told herself as she and Kitty made their way back to Waterloo, was something she was good at – dealing calmly with let and hindrance.

She was glad Kitty was coming home with her for the night: she'd been dreading returning alone to Veronica Villa. The previous evening had been horrible, with Alice shut up in the studio for hours, talking to her family, then emerging at last to sit and pick at the salad Lou had made. Lou had longed for the evening to end. She'd wanted so badly to undo what she'd said in the car, but her words had hung in the air, too monstrous to deny. They would still be there, she thought, lying in wait for her in the familiar, deserted rooms.

But Kitty's presence made a difference. It felt almost like being children together again in some comforting, uncomplicated place in the past. They stopped to buy fish and chips, and when they had stuffed the greasy remains in the bin they curled up on the sofa to search the web for cheap flights.

'France is an hour ahead,' Lou said. 'That makes it eleven thirty. Is that too late to call?'

Who knew, she was thinking, what Flora's routine was these days? She felt a spring of doubt, suddenly, about landing themselves on their mother out of the blue.

Kitty yawned. 'The flights won't sell out overnight,' she said. 'Let's go to bed. We can ring her first thing.'

They were both up early in the morning, shivering a little in the kitchen while the kettle boiled. Looking out at the garden, damp and disconsolate after a night of heavy rain, Lou felt a surge of yearning at the prospect of abandoning the disappointing English summer for sunnier climes, and an equal and opposite surge of desolation at the thought of turning her back on Veronica Villa. Not that there was any point in keeping a vigil here all summer, but even so . . .

'It's eight in France now,' she said. 'What do you think?'

'She was always up early,' Kitty said. 'But she's on holiday, I suppose. She might . . .'

'Let's try her,' said Lou. 'We need to book the flights.'

Scrolling through her contacts list, she found the landline number for Les Violettes first. The phone rang twice, three times, four, and then a male voice answered.

'*Bonjour?*'

'Oh!' Lou's French deserted her in her surprise, as did her tact. 'Who's that?'

'This is Landon Peverell. Is that – Lou?'

'Landon! Are you staying with Flora?' Lou raised her eyebrows at Kitty. Landon, she was thinking, would be a welcome addition to the house party.

'I had a concert nearby, by happy chance.'

'How is she?'

There was a hesitation at the other end which gave Lou a moment's uncertainty, but Landon's voice was unchanged when he spoke again.

'She's very well. She's found herself a beautiful house to stay in. She's right here, if you want to speak to her.'

'Thank you. It's very nice to hear you, Landon.'

'Goodbye, Lou dear,' he said, and then there was Flora's voice, exactly as Lou had imagined it.

'Lou?' she said. 'Is everything all right?'

Half an hour later, her chest tight with the knowledge that she was committed to being at Gatwick by four thirty, Lou was shepherding Kitty out of the house.

'Do you always leave this early?' Kitty asked, as they drove through woodlands dark with summer rain.

'Earlier, most days. It's a hard life, being a grown up.'

'I don't think I'll be one, then,' said Kitty, and she laughed, almost her familiar little-girl chuckle.

The 8.11 was packed. They stood in the corridor, saying little, and parted on the platform at the other end with a brief hug.

'Will you be OK?' Lou asked. 'Hand luggage only, remember? I'll see you at the airport.'

Kitty nodded, waved, and disappeared towards the escalators.

All right, Lou thought. Seven hours to extricate herself from work, home and the promise to take Maebh to the zoo on Saturday. If she had a camera crew on hand she could be a one-woman reality TV show. She set off on foot towards Waterloo Bridge: a brisk walk, she thought, would help her think.

Work should have been the biggest problem. Lou only had three days of annual leave left, and she was determined to be away longer than that – but a plan had lodged in her mind last night. The firm had settled an embarrassing and expensive discrimination suit last year, and the partner concerned happened to be Lou's boss. By the time she reached the office, Lou had prepared her request with careful attention to phrasing and nuance. It fell, strictly speaking, between the rules for sick leave, maternity leave and compassionate leave, but as she'd hoped Clive Fletcher almost fell over himself in his eagerness to approve it.

'Not a problem,' he said, trying hard to introduce an expression of sympathetic consideration into his bluff face. 'Speak to HR, but tell them it's absolutely not a problem from my side. Important to, er – at this sort of time, I know.'

'Thank you,' said Lou. She felt a small qualm at what was, in its way, as ruthless an exploitation of a weak spot as the behaviour that had got Clive into trouble, but only a small qualm. Ruthlessness was a quality much admired at Harvers and Green. 'I'll make sure everything's straightened out before I go.'

She glanced around his office – filing cabinets, sleek desk, glimpse of sky through the window – and resisted the fleeting suspicion that she was making a mistake. It was only a holiday, after all. She smiled at Clive and shut the door quietly behind her.

Lou had finished two significant pieces of work the week before, and she despatched various loose ends in the next couple of hours, leaving her desk clear and her inbox empty. Just as she was leaving, Phil Zadig sidled up to her.

'Everything OK?' he asked.

'Fine,' Lou said. 'I'm just taking some leave.'

Phil glanced, not very covertly, at her belly. He wasn't the only one of Lou's male colleagues to hope that her pregnancy, announced the week before, might hamper her in the race for partnership, but Lou had to admire his gall.

'Happy to cover anything that comes up,' he said; and Lou, who hadn't the least intention of giving him any ground, smiled graciously.

By midday she was on her way again. The next thing on her conscience was Maebh and Dearbhla. Lou felt queasier about letting them down than she did about tying her boss into such an elegant knot, but she was let off this commitment, too, more lightly than she'd feared.

'I've been trying to get hold of you,' Dearbhla said, when she picked up the phone. 'Maebh's got slapped cheek.'

'She's what?'

'She's got slapped cheek disease. I couldn't let you have her just now. I know the risk's small, but I'd never forgive myself.'

There was a brief silence while Lou processed this information. Dearbhla clearly still assumed everyone had read the parenting manuals as carefully as she had: or did she just assume it of Lou, these days?

'It's most dangerous in the first trimester, of course,' Dearbhla went on, her tone that of someone used to husbanding her patience carefully, meting it out without a flicker, 'but you never know, with these teratogenic viruses. I'm sure there'll be another chance before you're – you know, busy with your own.'

'That's very thoughtful of you,' Lou said. 'I suppose it would be safer.'

She should admit the truth, she thought; she didn't like to be in a false position with Dearbhla. But the whole truth was more than she could bear to acknowledge.

'Let's fix another date,' she said. 'Send Maebh my love.'

Well, Lou thought, she'd successfully negotiated Mumsnet and the legal establishment. But there was still a proper parting to be taken from Veronica Villa.

As she made her way through Lincoln's Inn Fields and down towards Aldwych, Lou's mind followed a trail like an Escher print, circling from one premise to another. It was odd that something inanimate should present the greatest obstacle to her departure; ironic that something inanimate should be the principal thing she and Alice shared; poignant that what they shared made it hardest for her to go away. A kind of logical entrapment that made her feel both sad and helpless, like the impossibility of arguing or negotiating or brazening her way out of the impasse she had found herself in with Alice.

The commuter line was deserted at this time of day, its dirt and drabness more obvious without the usual density of passengers. Her only companion was an elderly woman who checked her handbag compulsively every few minutes as though fearful that invisible hands might have rifled through it while she wasn't looking. It seemed to Lou that she had already left her normal life, slipping into a realm full-time workers never saw.

Over the next few hours Lou tackled the domestic problems raised by her departure one by one. A neighbour agreed to feed the fish; the car's MOT was deferred; bills were paid and the fridge cleared. The emotional effort involved in all this felt disproportionate to the time it took, but Lou had expected that. All afternoon she was conscious of how little sign of Alice there was in the house. She thought back to the evening, not so long ago, when Alice's belongings had seemed to be everywhere. Now it was as if – like a prudent burglar careful to leave the crime scene cleansed of incriminating DNA – Alice had deliberately removed all traces of her personality from the house before she left. *Tell me what's going on,* Lou kept wanting to say, as she wandered from room to room. *However did things go so wrong?*

Thank God, she thought often and vehemently, for Kitty and her distracting drama, and for Flora's uncharacteristic acquisition of a bolthole in deepest France. Thank God for the ease with which a temporary escape had presented itself.

35

Flora heard Landon before she saw him, the next morning. He was talking – perhaps in his sleep, she thought at first, half-asleep herself still. It took her a few moments to realise that he was on the telephone, and a few more to understand to whom he was speaking.

'Your mother's right here,' he said, when he saw that she was awake. 'Goodbye, Lou dear.'

'Lou?' Flora was abruptly alert, and horrified by the thought that her daughter might guess she was lying in bed, and with Landon. 'Is everything all right?'

'Well,' said Lou, 'not entirely. But I'm not ill; nothing like that.'

'What's the matter?'

'Never mind now,' said Lou. 'Listen: how would it be if we came to visit you?'

'You and Alice?'

'Me and Kitty.'

'It would be lovely.' Flora pushed her hair behind her ear with her free hand. 'Can you spare the time?'

Lou laughed briefly. 'We both find ourselves in need of a holiday,' she said. 'There's a flight to Tours this evening. Is that within reach?'

'This evening?' Flora felt a lurch of shock and surprise that registered partly in her mind and partly in her belly. 'Yes, I could come and meet you. But Lou –'

'Are you sure? That would be wonderful. The plane lands at nine.'

'All right,' said Flora. 'I'll be there.

'Wonderful,' Lou said again. 'Will Landon still be there? How long is he staying?'

Flora glanced across at him. 'I'm not sure,' she said. 'It was a surprise visit. Rather like yours.'

'Your lucky week, then,' said Lou. 'Looking forward to seeing you, Mum.'

Flora put the phone down slowly. My goodness, she thought. Weeks of nothing, and then all this. And meanwhile, she still hadn't exchanged a word with Landon. He was looking at her, his face somehow terribly familiar.

'They're coming to stay,' she said.

'An unexpected pleasure.' Landon reached out a finger and touched her cheek. 'Like you.'

Flora smiled, but her face wouldn't hold it for long. It wasn't that she regretted what had happened, or that anything was spoiled by it. It wasn't even that her sense of herself was altered by this second sexual adventure of the summer, although God knows she hadn't expected either of them. That might come, of course, a belated feeling of bashfulness (or even, possibly, of liberation) but for now there was simply a sense of facing up to reality – an understanding that neither she nor Landon would pretend, and nothing had changed. They were old; he was still married; they'd never really loved each other – not enough, anyway, to overturn a lifetime of dedication to the status quo. *Tristesse*, she thought. That was precisely the term for it.

'I'm glad,' Landon said, after a moment.

'Glad the girls are coming?'

'No, glad we did that. We both deserved it.'

No one but Landon could have made those words sound tender, Flora thought. But without raising expectations; without allowing himself the indulgence of extending unfounded hope. What a perplexing man he was. She called up her memories of him: a little boy on the beach, a highwayman at that fateful New Year's Eve party, a noble William Tell in a small opera festival in Somerset. For a moment she was seduced by the idea that they were both still waiting for their real lives to begin, the lives they'd put aside to concentrate on other things – but then, with a smile, she dismissed it.

'Can you stay to see them?' she asked. 'Lou's pregnant, you know. Isn't that a thought?'

'Lou?' His eyes opened wide, the weariness lifting for a moment. 'How lovely. How – unexpected.'

Flora laughed, and he joined in.

'I haven't asked,' she said. 'A donor, I expect. I'm very pleased for her. And for me, of course.'

Landon nodded. 'You'll be a good granny,' he said. 'You'll have time for it, now.'

'I suppose I will.'

'Tell me,' Landon said then. 'What do you tend to do about breakfast?'

'I tend to go out and buy bread, but not –' she glanced at the clock on the chest of drawers. 'Good Lord, is it really only eight o'clock?'

'It is. But I agree about going out for bread. Too Peter Mayle for words. Can we improvise?'

'Probably. I think there's milk, and some porridge in the cupboard. Will that do?'

'I'll make it,' said Landon. 'It's one of my unsuspected talents, cooking porridge.'

He hadn't given an answer, Flora realised, about staying to see Lou and Kitty. Perhaps it was better not to ask again.

The summer had reached the point when the sun shone every day, and the creep of light around the curtains this morning signified the start of the slow, delicious warming up of another day. That much could be relied on, Flora thought. That and the charms of Les Violettes, the bees among the lavender and the aromatic scents of eucalyptus and juniper. She lay back against the pillows, pleased by the thought that the situation called for nothing more than this, on her part. The summer, she felt suddenly, had taken on its own momentum.

While Flora was still weighing up how long it might take Landon to make porridge, he appeared at the door with a tray.

'Goodness,' she said. 'Room service.'

'My mother took trouble over my upbringing,' he said. 'As did yours.'

'Over my upbringing, or yours?' Flora asked, and he smiled. The right note, she thought. Their slick one-liners should be allowed to stand, just for the moment.

She smoothed the duvet to make a level platform for the tray, and Landon set it down in front of her.

'Thank you,' she said. 'What a treat.'

'He's got a very well-stocked kitchen, your friend. Beautiful pans.'

'Has he?' Flora laughed, conscious of giving herself away. 'You know how it is in France,' she said. 'You hardly have to cook at all.'

'You might, if you're going to have houseguests.' He put on a mock-grave face. 'Perhaps I shall have to stay, after all. I could earn my keep as house boy.'

'Can you?' Flora couldn't keep the pleasure from her voice. 'Aren't you expected home?'

'Rosanna's sister is staying this week. There was to be another concert next weekend.'

'Was?'

'Cancelled,' he said. 'A problem with the church. Apparently the roof's in danger of falling in.'

'Well, if it means you can stay and see the girls . . .'

Flora risked a direct look at him then, and a smile that wasn't tied to a witticism. He looked a little ragged this morning; she was touched by this glimpse of a Landon with his defences down. It wasn't just on stage that he made an effort, she thought. He kept up a performance more or less all the time. As if he'd noticed her scrutiny, he touched his fingertips to his cheek, and the unguarded expression vanished.

'By the way, have you had a communication from Julia Hoxton?' he asked.

Flora shook her head.

'Covent Garden Julia Hoxton?' Landon prompted. 'She wants to put on a memorial concert.'

'For Henry?'

'In aid of a scholarship fund. It's a generous thought, but it's your call. I'm surprised she hasn't been in touch.'

'Perhaps she wrote to Orchards. Martin's supposed to send on the post.' Flora hesitated. 'Was she . . .?'

'No,' Landon said. 'No, no. Just a friend. An admirer in the professional sense.' He curled his fingers delicately, as though assessing the ripeness of a peach. 'But if you'd prefer, I'll see her off. I can say –'

'No,' said Flora. 'She should do it, if the girls agree. Henry ought to have – we've done nothing about his professional life.'

'Good,' said Landon. 'Good.'

'Will you sing?'

He made a self-deprecating gesture. 'She did mention . . . And Kitty should write a piece.'

'I don't suppose she'd want to do that, even for Henry. She's not exactly . . .'

'Oh, but she is,' Landon said. 'She is, you know. She had a triumph, a couple of weeks ago: a song cycle performed at St Mark's, Marlborough Square. I'm told it was quite something.'

'She mentioned it,' Flora said. Ah, if he'd wanted to pique her . . . 'She didn't tell me how it had gone,' she admitted.

Landon looked at her carefully. 'There will be other occasions, I'm quite sure,' he said. 'But if the Hoxton affair goes ahead, Kitty should certainly write something.'

The porridge was overcooked: that was something. Flora inspected a large lump of it on her spoon, and Landon laughed suddenly.

'My cover's blown,' he said. 'Breakfast in bed is not my forte. Please forgive me.'

After breakfast they both bathed, and Flora moved Landon's few things into another bedroom. Neither of them said anything about that, but once it was done things seemed easier again.

There was, suddenly, plenty to do. They drove to the supermarket in Champigny to stock up for Lou and Kitty's arrival; they made up two beds on the top floor. Landon found a pair of secateurs and cut some roses, while Flora – resisting the urge to prove something – produced bread and cheese and a salad for lunch. A late lunch: it was two o'clock by then, the garden limp and breathless in the heat.

'There's something else I ought to tell you,' Flora said, as they ate. 'I'm thinking of selling the Comyns.'

Landon said nothing for a moment. Flora had known he'd disapprove: if their paths hadn't crossed, she thought, she wouldn't have felt it necessary to say anything, but since he was here it seemed wrong not to mention it. He'd been just as much Nick Comyn's friend as Henry had. They'd made that famous trip through Europe together, while they were all at Oxford.

'Not for the money, I take it.'

'No. But we were surprised, when they were valued for probate.'

Landon made his tortoise movement again, that elder-statesman-like lifting of the head. Was she required to give a reason, Flora wondered? Could she produce one?

'All of them?' Landon asked. 'The ones of the family?'

Flora spread her hands impatiently. 'I haven't decided,' she said. 'I just thought you'd like to know. Goodness, I might sell Orchards too. I might sell anything.'

'Of course. Of course you might.'

'I was fond of Nick,' Flora said, although she hadn't been, really. Less and less, as the paintings accumulated on the walls at Orchards, and he was there more and more often. As he claimed more and more of Henry's attention, she admitted: although she'd known he was no threat, she'd resented his adoration of Henry even so. But that wasn't really why she wanted the paintings gone, was it?

'Forgive me,' Landon said. 'It's entirely your affair. It seems a shame to – but there's no need for sentimentality. The whole episode was painful, but it's a long time ago.'

'His death, you mean?' For a moment Flora wasn't sure what he was talking about. Had there been another twist, something she hadn't . . .?

'It was just after Rosanna was diagnosed,' Landon said. 'I was pre-occupied. And Henry was – well, Kitty was very young. You were both busy.'

Ah, thought Flora: so it was his death. That mysterious car accident.

'We took him on holiday that last summer, you know. He came to Wales with us.' She'd felt Nick's eyes on them all week, she remembered. Watching, weighing. She'd wondered whether Henry had asked Nick to paint him, but it was the girls he'd painted that time. On the beach, under a black cloud. She glanced at Landon, and made an effort. 'He was very kind to the girls. Lou spent the whole holiday drawing, although she's never had an artistic bone in her body.'

'That's rather a harsh judgement of someone who's married to a sculptor.'

Married, Flora understood, was a peace offering. Perhaps she shouldn't say any more. But the implication of neglect itched at her.

'Henry didn't believe the suicide theory,' she said.

He hadn't wanted to, certainly. But he'd been deeply upset; rattled by the idea that someone under his patronage – someone he'd loved – could die. Perhaps that was what had made him cleave to Elizabeth in a way he hadn't to her predecessors. There was another irony, if so. Flora sighed, and Landon's eyes rested on her again.

'Water under the bridge, anyway,' he said.

She suspected he hadn't said all he wanted to on the subject, but that he'd decided this wasn't the moment. Well, they were her paintings now. It was her decision. *No need for sentimentality*, indeed. Whoever said women were the mawkish ones?

After a moment Landon smiled. 'It's a long time ago,' he said again. 'Let's take these things inside before they melt. Do we have time for a walk before we go and meet the young ladies?'

36

'Don't tell Mum,' Kitty said, as the 'Fasten Seatbelts' sign came on for the descent into Tours. 'You won't tell her, will you, unless I do?'

Lou looked at her sister. They had barely spoken since the plane took off. Kitty had been absorbed by a book, and Lou – too tired for reading – had stared out of the window, allowing the white hum of the engines to fill her ears and the empty expanse of sky to carry her far away from Veronica Villa and Seaford and Orchards. It felt very strange to think that it was only thirty-six hours since she'd taken Alice to Heathrow; to think how many miles there were between them now.

'About Daniel?' she asked.

Kitty nodded. 'Just – you know.'

She looked exhausted, Lou thought. Her skin was almost transparent, her eyes over-bright. Lou hoped it was the right thing for Kitty, fleeing to France like this. The book Kitty had been reading slipped off her table and Lou bent to retrieve it. Not a novel, she saw, but a score: Stravinsky's *Rite of Spring*.

'For Flora's sake, too,' Kitty said, slipping the score back into her bag. 'I mean, she'll have to know eventually, but . . .'

Somehow, in the press of other concerns, Lou had lost sight of what the news about Daniel meant for Flora. Considering it now, she felt a rush of adrenaline. Who could possibly guess how she'd react? Quite apart from the usual caveats, it was months since they'd seen Flora. So many things had changed since then. She put her hand in Kitty's. Perhaps after all this wasn't so much an escape as a leap from one patch of emotional turmoil into another, she thought, as the plane bumped and lurched its way down through the technicolour clouds, and the green and gold landscape of France came into view, softened by twilight.

*

Flora was in the arrivals hall to meet them, and Landon was there too, tall and spare beside her. Lou registered, in his stance, an unexpected glimpse of the gawky teenager he must once have been, and then her gaze shifted to her mother.

That moment of recognition, shot through with pleasure and – yes, definitely surprise – could only have lasted a second or two, but it seemed to Lou to spool out in slow motion. Flora had changed, certainly. This woman with a tan and soft linen clothes looked like a Flora who'd taken another path, some time in the past. It wasn't just her appearance: there was something entirely unfamiliar in the way she came forward to greet them both.

'Mum,' Lou said. 'It's lovely to see you.'

Kitty was caught up in the embrace too; a most un-Jones-like hug that sealed the three of them together for a few seconds. Lou felt something flowing through her, a swift current of alteration, and then they were all stepping back, smiling, recovering themselves.

'Hello, Landon,' Kitty said. 'How nice that you're here.'

'The temptation of seeing you both proved too great to resist,' he said, 'and your mother's cooking, of course, is always a lure.'

They laughed; an old joke. Trust Landon, Lou thought, to help them back to familiar ground.

The car journey was duller than Lou had expected: a series of long straight roads through a no-man's-land of strung-out villages hanging from the coat tails of Tours, and then an expanse of flat farmland. It was quite dark by now, a large moon and a scatter of stars hanging palely over the horizon. Conversation was desultory, as though none of them knew how to recapture, or to follow, the ease and warmth of their airport welcome.

'How was the flight?' Flora asked.

'Ryanair,' said Kitty. 'Still, we were lucky to get seats.'

'A last minute whim, I gather?' said Landon.

Lou felt Kitty stiffen beside her. 'Call us impetuous,' she said. 'Once we had the idea, there was no stopping us, was there, Kits?'

Flora drove as she always had, her elbows cocked, level with her hands. A surgical posture, Lou though suddenly. Wasn't that how you saw surgeons' arms, when they showed operations on the television? For better control of the instruments, presumably. She'd never seen her mother operate, though. All those thousands of operations Flora must have done, and her daughters had never been there to admire her skill.

'What have you been doing with yourself, Ma?' she asked.

'Less than you might think.' Flora half-turned. 'Tending the garden. Reading. Getting to know the locals.'

'Preparing to run off with a swarthy Frenchman?' offered Kitty.

'That too,' Flora agreed. 'Just wait until you see the choice on offer.'

Lou chuckled, but after that the conversation lapsed. This was unknown terrain. Better to say nothing than to find themselves heading up a no through road.

37

Lying in bed, Kitty could hear the rhythmic chant of insects that identified this as a foreign night. The sound was insistent, but she found the monotony soothing in the same way as the swish and lull of the sea. The smell of the room was foreign too, a dusty lavender and hot linen smell that evoked something she couldn't pin down. Comfort, perhaps? No, not as comfortable as comfort: somewhere she wasn't quite at home, but would like to be.

That was certainly an apt description of Les Violettes. It seemed to her a house of dreams, with its sighing interior spaces and its walled garden full of scent and shadow. That was the reason Flora looked so different, surely. A few weeks here would be enough to mend anyone. But even so, as the cicadas kept up their incantation Kitty wondered about her mother, and about what the summer had done for her.

There was a sound outside her door, a footfall rather than a knock.

'Lou?'

The door opened. 'Still awake? Can I come in?'

Kitty moved over and Lou climbed in beside her. This was nice, Kitty thought: curling up with her sister, feeling the warmth of the bed around them. They hadn't done this for years.

'You know what this reminds me of?' Lou asked.

'Hot chocolate,' said Kitty. 'Muse and Nirvana.'

'Whatever happened to Muse and Nirvana?'

'I've got them on my iPod still. No shouting to drown out here, though.'

'No.'

'Is that –' Kitty began, and then she stopped. Her view of the past had shifted, these last few days. Her view of Henry, above all. The loss of her illusions was part of the pain she'd felt since Martin Carver's visit: thinking about it put her in a rage. 'Was Flora miserable all that time?' she asked.

Lou stroked her hand. 'We'll never know,' she said. 'I'm not sure she knows, anymore. I don't suppose you can sum up forty years like that.'

'I guess not.'

'She seems happy now, though.'

Lou looked sideways at her, and Kitty nodded.

'Is it Landon, do you think?' Lou asked.

'Landon what?'

'Landon who's making her happy.'

'He's only been here a couple of days.'

'True.'

'And there's Rosanna,' Kitty added. There was silence for a moment, and in it the cicadas beat seemed to swell until it filled the room. 'Unless it's just that she seems happy because we're both . . .'

Kitty felt her sister's neck tense beneath her. Stupid, she thought. Stupid, stupid. Better to pretend they were back in Nirvana-land. But it was too late.

'We do have to tell her,' Lou said.

'About Daniel?'

'Yes. She'll find out in the end, and she won't understand why we didn't say anything.'

Kitty shut her eyes for a moment. Speaking Daniel's name aloud gave her a sick feeling that reminded her of the first weeks after Henry died – but this was worse, she thought now. That loss had been expected; part of the natural order. She hadn't known at the time that that was something to be grateful for, but she did now.

'Have you heard from him?' Lou asked.

'A couple of texts,' Kitty said. 'He tried to call me after Martin had been to see him, but not again.'

There was a pause. Lou didn't ask any more, but Kitty could feel words bubbling up now. She needed to say some of this, she thought, and Lou was the best, the only, person to talk to.

'The irony is,' she said, 'that he's been nicer about it than I could have believed. Kinder, when he . . . When you'd expect . . .' She plucked at the edge of the sheet with her fingers.

'Poor Kits,' said Lou. 'It's really horrid. Really not what you deserve.'

'You don't feel as if it should be possible,' Kitty said. 'You feel as if there must be something wrong with you, some missing instinct.'

'He's only a half-brother,' Lou said. 'Genetically, I suppose, it's more like a cousin, and that's . . .' But even Lou could see genetics wasn't the point.

'None of this would have happened if Henry had told the truth,' Kitty said. 'He lied to us right up until he died.'

'Not explicitly,' Lou said. She pulled Kitty closer, an arm around her shoulders. This was a reversal, Kitty thought: for Lou to defend Henry. 'We *were* his only family,' Lou went on. 'Daniel had a raw deal on that front, didn't he? Daniel never even knew who he was.'

'That makes it worse,' said Kitty staunchly. 'He deprived Daniel of a father, and now Daniel's lost me too. We could have been – if we'd known, he could have been – part of the family.'

'He still could,' Lou said. 'I know it doesn't feel possible now, but maybe . . .'

'Sssh,' said Kitty. 'Enough.'

The whole thing was like a great boulder, she thought. It was such an effort to force herself to think about it, and then a relief to be doing it, to shift the weight of it just a tiny bit, but it was too exhausting to keep it up for very long.

'Will you stay here with me?' she asked.

'All night?' said Lou. 'Of course, if you want.'

She ought to ask Lou about Alice, Kitty thought, but she was so tired now; too tired to work out whether Lou wanted to talk about it, whether there was anything to say. And so they lay in silence, Lou's arm around her shoulder and Kitty's hand resting on Lou's pregnant belly. It was surprising, Kitty thought, what you could bear. How much disillusion and disappointment and humiliation and anger. And it was surprising how soothing it was to be held in her sister's arms, the warmth of her like an anaesthetic, shushing the pain, making it matter less. She could feel her mind racing, slowing, slipping towards sleep now.

'Will you love the baby more than me?' she asked.

'You goose,' said Lou. 'You've got a long head start, you know. And you know all the words to *Time is Running Out*.'

'There aren't very many,' Kitty said. And after that she shut her eyes and let the cicadas fade out, and her grip on the world slacken and fall away.

January 2009

On the first of January, Flora wakes to a feeling of weariness. Christmas has been accomplished, ensemble, with some panache, which is something to congratulate themselves on. Henry is in remission and the family is together, and the fatted calf has not been spared. Flora and Lou have both been back at work these last few days, but now the four of them have another long weekend together – which might be gilding the lily, she thinks, or over-egging the pudding. Whatever the right phrase is.

Hearing the creak of the attic stairs, she throws back the duvet in sudden haste, fearful that Kitty might appear in their doorway. It isn't so much that Kitty is too old to come into her parents' bed as that Flora is self-conscious about the notion of the parental bed these days. Sharing Henry's bed again – or letting him share hers – feels like a provisional arrangement still. There are delicacies about the situation which have not been resolved, and Flora cavils at the idea of their sixteen-year-old daughter (already, who knows, old enough to share someone else's bed) visiting them there.

Instead, she meets Kitty on the landing, wearing her Christmas pyjamas and an expression of animation which is unusual this early in the day.

'Isn't it the fair?' Kitty asks. 'I've just been thinking – it'll be this weekend, won't it?'

The fair in Great Barworth used to be an annual family fixture. *Back in the day*, as Henry says, resolutely à la mode, when the matter is discussed over breakfast. According to local mythology it has taken place on the first weekend of January since the Middle Ages – although what there would have been to sell in the depths of winter back then God knows, as Henry also says.

'Maybe it was a pagan festival,' Kitty says, irrepressibly cheerful. 'Village wenches dancing themselves to death to appease the Sun god.'

Flora loathes the fair. The rides alarm her, and she is firmly in the camp that finds the ambience threatening rather than thrilling.

Lou, who might be an ally, hasn't emerged from her room yet. She returned to Orchards last night a degree or two more agitated than she was over Christmas. Flora suspects a romance, as yet undeclared and presumably not wholly satisfactory.

'It's definitely on,' says Henry. 'I drove past yesterday, on the way to the garage.'

'Hurrah!' says Kitty. 'We can go tonight.'

The rain has stopped, but the fairground field is already thick with mud. What will it be like by Monday, Flora wonders? She's amazed by people's footwear – there's hardly a wellington boot in sight among the designer trainers and suede ankle boots. The smell of hot sugar pervades the air: candy floss, toffee apples, popcorn, doughnuts. There is surely something misanthropic about her that she can't enjoy this.

'They're about to get on,' says Lou, and Flora turns to see Kitty and Henry climbing aboard the big wheel. Kitty is wearing the garish scarf Jean and Derek sent her for Christmas. She looks, for a moment, ten years younger; an excited child.

'D'you remember when she was sick?' Lou says, and Flora nods.

'All over Henry's shoes,' Lou says, and Flora nods again, and smiles.

They crane their necks to watch Kitty and Henry being lifted into the air, then accelerating, whisking around faster and faster, down and up and over.

'Sure you didn't want a go?' Flora asks, and Lou shakes her head.

'Dodgems?' Flora asks.

'Maybe,' says Lou. 'Let's see what Kitty wants to do next.'

'OK,' Flora says; and then, feeling a sudden pressure of expectation in her chest, 'Are you all right, Lou? You've seemed a bit . . .'

Lou turns, her face both guarded and eager.

'I wondered if it might be – an affair of the heart,' Flora says, seizing a passing current of boldness. Lou's love life has been kept almost entirely from view, so far.

Lou smiles, just. Flora expects a shrug, a dismissive syllable, but instead Lou says, 'She's American, and she's gone home for the holidays. It's felt like a long time.'

'When's she coming back?' Flora asks. 'Can we meet her?'

There is a long pause then, and Flora begins to think she's said the wrong thing.

'I wasn't sure . . .' Lou says at last. 'What about Dad?'

Ah, Flora thinks: that's her fault. She's said too little, not too much, these last few years. It's a long time since that other Christmas, that awful Christmas when she and Lou . . .

'Dad knows,' she says.

Lou doesn't look at her. 'Since when?'

'I can't remember exactly. I'm sorry; I should have – I thought he might say something.' Lou must have noticed that the teasing about boyfriends has stopped, at least? But perhaps not. 'He's a musician,' she says, in what's meant to be a reassuring tone. 'Half his friends are gay.'

'Not quite the same thing as his daughter,' Lou says. It's hard to tell from her voice whether she's upset or relieved.

'He loves you very much,' Flora says.

The phrase has a false ring in her ears: those words cover a multitude of sins in this family, and Lou knows it. Flora lifts her eyes to the wheel, the whirl of faces and flying hair, the collective whoop and whinny of congenial fear. Kitty's scarf whips out as the wind catches it, covering her face for a moment as she and Henry rise up into the air again.

'I know he was hoping for a string of grandchildren,' Lou says. 'Choristers in ruffs and cassocks.'

Flora doesn't say that Henry might not live long enough, anyway, to see his grandchildren in ruffs and cassocks.

'Kitty might turn out maternal,' she says instead. 'She used to love the doll's house.'

Then she wonders whether this is evidence of stereotyping, or simply of not understanding her daughters as she should. She tries to laugh, but produces only a huffing sound that might be mistaken for contempt.

To her relief, the wheel is slowing down now. There's Kitty again, poised in mid-air, her head tipped back as though she's laughing at something Henry has said. Kitty has always found it easy to enjoy things, Flora thinks, but the insight makes her obscurely sad. Laughing on a big wheel is the easy part, she thinks. It's not the same thing as being happy. It just means you have further to fall, back to earth.

38

Coming downstairs at the start of another day, it felt strange to Flora to know that Les Violettes was full of people: most of the people left in the world who mattered to her, she thought. Outside, the sun was filtering through the garden in the way it did every morning, a low glancing dazzle to wake the plants and drive out the last remnants of the night. She filled the kettle and set it to boil, then went outside to savour the coolness that would be gone in half an hour.

She still wasn't sure how long Landon was planning to stay. They hadn't spoken any more about it during the course of the day before: a day that seemed blissfully happy in retrospect, although at the time it had been laced with trepidation. She was surprised how much it meant to have Landon here just now, and how much she didn't want him to leave. It was partly the relief of having an old friend around, after several weeks among strangers. Partly, too, that she felt easier with him than she had for years, and wanted to savour that felicity. But that wasn't all. His presence had aroused certain expectations, she acknowledged – of herself, and of the occasion, if not of him.

Flora picked a eucalyptus leaf and rubbed it between her fingers, releasing its clean medicinal smell. It wasn't only Landon, of course, who'd caused the flutter in her chest yesterday. There had been just as much apprehension about her daughters' arrival: she hadn't been sure why Lou and Kitty were coming, or how they would find her, or she them, after what felt like an interval of months rather than weeks. And then there had been that surprising burst of emotion in the under-whelming setting of Tours airport, like a scene marked by balloons and confetti, and the drive home by moonlight with everyone tongue-tied, it seemed, by tiredness and other things. Kitty washed out, and Lou certainly not blooming in pregnancy. Perhaps she was out of touch with the effects of working life and the English summer, but they'd both looked so pale and drawn, and she'd felt like a proper mother for once, sweeping them up into the welcoming embrace of Les Violettes and putting them to bed.

And now, standing in the garden, she could feel anticipation flowering inside her: an expansive, heart-racing thrill of pleasure and fear. The stage was set, not just for a few days together as an almost-family on holiday, but for what she must do while Landon and the girls were here. She shut her eyes, wishing suddenly that Henry were here, ready with a joke and a sliver of wise advice, but Henry was no good because he was implicated in all this – and because he was dead, dammit. That awful, immutable fact, waiting for her around every corner still. There was no way she could make things all right with Henry now, she thought – but no way, either, that anything she said or did could hurt him. That was something, at least. One less person to figure into the reckoning.

The doorbell jolted her out of her train of thought. The postman, presumably. Flora turned and went back inside. But instead she found Francine Abelard on the doorstep, with a basket over her arm of the type French farmers' wives carry in black and white films.

'Do you like rhubarb?' she asked. 'We have so much.'

'That's very kind,' said Flora.

'Take it, then. You have guests to feed, I think.'

Flora smiled, understanding suddenly what this early morning visit was about. Francine had found out, somehow, that Landon was staying at Les Violettes.

'Come in,' she said. 'No one's up yet, but I'm making coffee.'

She laid the fat pink stalks out on the table while the coffee brewed. She did like rhubarb, but she had never cooked it. Could she ask Francine what to do? Would Francine tell her without being asked?

'How is your visitor?' asked Francine. She didn't sit down – she rarely did, Flora had noticed – but she gave no impression that she was in a hurry to leave.

'It's nice to see him,' Flora said, with a touch of prudishness which would not, she knew, deceive canny Francine. 'And my daughters are here too. Another unexpected visit.'

'So it pours with rain,' said Francine. 'Is that the right expression?'

'Something like that.' Flora plunged the coffee and poured them each a cup.

Francine moved towards the garden and Flora followed obediently.

'And with me, the Swiss couple are returning.' Francine looked up at the vine-covered trellis and then down at the roses, the box hedges, as if assessing Flora's care of them. 'I am honoured,' she said, in a passable imitation of Friedrich's accent. 'They have changed their plans so they will return to us.'

'They enjoyed your cooking so much,' Flora said, attempting to echo Francine's parody, but she felt a flicker of discomfort, remembering that she too had been a paying guest *chez Abelard*, even if she had crossed a boundary since then into a different category of acquaintance.

'The grapes are growing well this year,' Francine said. 'Soon you will be able to eat them.'

'I didn't realise they were edible,' Flora said. 'I thought French grapes were all for wine.'

Francine made a *hmph* sound, conveying amused disbelief, and the two of them stood together on the terrace for a few minutes in what could pass for companionable silence. This was friendship again, Flora thought: another step on the path. How long would it be a question of filling up time, finding things to say, until one day, like a fire catching light, you didn't have to make an effort to feed it anymore? She was torn between hoping Lou or Kitty would appear, and hoping they would sleep for long enough to avoid witnessing this encounter.

There was a noise from inside the house. Francine looked at her, pursing her lips in the way she did; in the way she had that morning of the jam.

285

'I will go home now,' she said, draining her cup. 'Come to the farm if you want more rhubarb.'

'Thank you.'

Following her back into the house, Flora wondered for the first time whether Francine Abelard's interest in her life was entirely what she wanted.

39

Kitty was still sound asleep when Lou woke, her limbs cast recklessly akimbo and her face blank and sweet in repose. Lou's back was horribly stiff, but despite the discomfort of being squeezed into half a single bed it had been consoling, when she woke in the night, to find Kitty beside her. To be needed, and not alone.

She slipped quietly out of the room, imagining herself the first person up and feeling a tingle of anticipation about the day ahead. But as she entered the kitchen she heard voices in the garden, and after a moment Flora appeared with another woman, tall and dark and unfamiliar.

'Lou!' said Flora. 'You're up early. This is my friend Francine Abelard.'

'*Bonjour.*' Lou held out her hand, glad that she was wearing her most decorous pyjamas.

'*Vous parlez Français?*'

'I learned it at school,' Lou said. '*Je parle un petit peu.*'

'The same as your mother.' Francine smiled. 'I must go home now. We have guests this evening and I have to prepare.'

'Your English is excellent,' Lou said. 'I can see why my mother hasn't learned any French.'

Francine shrugged, and Lou thought how unexpected it was that Flora had befriended a real Frenchwoman, shrugs and all. How unexpected all of this was, really.

'Good morning,' her mother said, as the front door shut behind Francine. They hugged awkwardly – a more familiar embrace than last night's. 'There's coffee in the pot, if you . . .'

'I'll make some tea, if that's OK,' Lou said.

Flora opened a cupboard. 'Take your pick,' she said. 'I never thought the French were interested in tea, but there are lots of different kinds in the shops.'

Flora had probably spent more time shopping in the last few weeks than she had for years in England, Lou thought. She chose an Earl Grey bag and put it in a mug.

'How are you, Lou?' Flora asked.

Lou didn't answer at once, but as her mother passed her the kettle their fingers brushed against each other, and deep in her chest Lou was conscious of a quiet surge of release.

'Shall we go outside?' she said. 'Is it warm enough?'

The garden was even more beautiful than Lou had surmised from the glimpse she'd had in the dark the previous night.

'This could be a painting,' she said, 'or a stage set. Alice would love it.'

The words came out without her thinking, and in their wake she felt the quickening of grief. The thought of this beautiful garden without Alice in it – of anything beautiful and perfect without Alice in it – was suddenly unbearable.

'Oh, Lou,' said Flora. 'Oh dear, what's happened? Come and sit – please, come and sit down.'

Lou allowed herself to be led to a little table on the terrace, near a fountain which burbled heedlessly while she held her face in her hands and wept.

'My darling,' said Flora, sitting down beside her. 'I'm so sorry. Is it the baby?'

'No, the baby's fine.'

'Alice, then?'

Lou nodded. 'Alice has gone home,' she managed to say – not very audibly, but Flora seemed to understand.

'To America?'

'Her mother's in hospital. She had an accident. But . . .'

Flora's hand rested on Lou's shoulder, still and heavy. For a few moments they sat in silence in the gathering heat of the sun.

'I'm sorry,' Lou said eventually. 'I'm sorry. I'm so afraid she won't come back.'

'Why?' Flora asked.

'I haven't –' Lou began. 'I mean, things have been – complicated. We had a row.' She stopped again, choking back another lump of emotion. 'I'm afraid I've spoiled everything. I said terrible things, just before she . . . just before the phone call came.'

'So there wasn't time to put things right?'

'No.'

Lou thought again about that last evening, when time and courage had slipped away from her in the face of Alice's implacable coolness and the imperative of her family tragedy. She thought beyond that too, to the weeks of awkwardness and uncertainty, remembering not just Alice's remoteness but her own passivity – and that terrible moment on the beach when she'd shrunk from Alice's touch.

'Have you spoken to her since she left?' her mother asked.

'No,' said Lou. 'It's – her mobile doesn't work over there, and I assume – they'll be at the hospital most of the day.'

She couldn't bear to ring at the wrong time, she meant to say, and hear Alice sounding irritable or cross. But it wasn't really a question of timing. Presumably Flora knew that too.

Flora said nothing for a few more moments, and then she sighed.

'I'm out of my depth, I'm afraid,' she said. 'My own experience is very limited. Very – specialised.'

Lou felt a spasm in her throat which she recognised as laughter of the darkest kind. Within a moment it had been commuted into sorrow, and a clutch of other emotions. Regret, painfully raw. Chagrin. Frustration. Alice appeared in her mind's eye then, like an image flashed from a slide projector: Alice naked, marble-white and smooth, the curve of her hips a perfect arc. Alice's russet hair shining, out of reach.

'I can't tell you,' Flora said, her voice tight, 'how glad I am that you came here. That you felt you could.'

'I'm glad too,' said Lou. 'I'm glad to be here. We can all . . .' She turned herself a little, lifting an arm around her mother's neck.

Flora held her tight, her hair tickling Lou's shoulder and her breath warm on Lou's face. Lou could tell she was searching for things to say, and she wanted to tell her it wasn't necessary, that this was enough – all she could manage for now, anyway. But perhaps Flora understood that. They sat, with Lou squeezing out, now and then, a shuddering sob or sigh, and Flora quite still, quite unlike the bustling, perpetual motion mother of Lou's childhood.

After a while Lou was conscious of the hum of insects, as though someone was gradually turning up the volume of the background scene, drawing it slowly into focus.

'It's so pretty here,' she said. 'I can see why you chose to stay. It's done you good, hasn't it?'

'Yes,' said Flora. 'Yes, I think it has.' She stroked the back of Lou's neck delicately, tenderly. 'I hope . . .'

Lou's hand pressed tighter on her mother's back.

'What do you want to do today?' she asked. 'Have you got something in mind?'

November 1997

On the plane back from Belfast, Flora is in a good mood. Many of her colleagues find examining tedious, but she has always enjoyed it. There were more women than usual among the candidates for Fellowship this time, one or two of them among the best of the batch. Flora finds herself speculating about their futures, wondering how much the world has changed in twenty years, and how far their ambition will carry them.

There is some turbulence over the Irish Sea, and the plane lands a few minutes late at Heathrow. As she waits for her baggage, Flora checks her pager and finds the number for Orchards. She hesitates – her flight has come up on the board above the carousels, but the first bags have yet to appear – then dips across the hall to a payphone. The line is engaged. She lets the answering service pick up and leaves a brief message: *Hello, it's me, the plane's landed, I should be home in an hour or so.*

It's just after nine when she drives up the lane, and she can see the lights on in the house. But when she pulls into the drive there's a surprise. It's not Henry's car parked in front, but her sister's, bearing the personalised number plate Derek bought her a few birthdays ago. It's clear to Flora in an instant that there is no explanation for Jean's presence which isn't bad news. During the couple of seconds it takes her to stop the car and wrench the door open, she flounders desperately in search of bad news that might have spared her children – and then (an act of consideration that will temper her view of her sister for ever) Jean opens the front door, flanked by Lou and Kitty.

'What's happened?' Flora demands. 'My darlings, what's happened?'

'It's all right, Mummy,' says Lou – the unfamiliar appellation called up for her aunt, Flora realises. 'Daddy's had to go out. A friend of his has had an accident.'

Flora's gaze flicks from Lou to Kitty, who is wearing a nightie Flora has never seen before, and then to Jean. Disapproval has set like wax over her sister's face.

'Auntie Jean came to look after us,' says Kitty. 'Daddy rang her up.'

'That's very kind of her,' says Flora. She manages a smile. The girls are all right, that's all that matters. The girls are all right, and she can afford to be nice to Jean. They exchange a look now, and Flora reads the 'don't ask' signs. Her curiosity is piqued, but so are her defences, which were briefly submerged by shock and relief.

'Let's get inside,' she says. 'It's chilly out here. Do we all need some hot chocolate?'

'Kitty has brushed her teeth,' says Jean.

Flora is ready to overrule her, but Kitty speaks first. 'I don't want any hot chocolate,' she says. 'Will you put me to bed, Mummy?'

Climbing the stairs with Kitty's hand in hers, Flora feels a powerful wash of emotion. She can't, for the moment, sort out the different elements of it – the feelings about Jean, and Henry, and her late return – but the presence of her child beside her, the warmth of those soft fingers, is a comfort beyond the reach of her calm analytical brain. Up in Kitty's room, she lies down on the narrow bed beside her daughter. The smell of shampoo and talcum powder surrounds her, evidence of proper preparation for bedtime. She imagines Jean wrapping Kitty's head in a towel, rubbing it too vigorously, just like their mother used to.

'When will Daddy be back?' Kitty asks.

'I don't know, darling,' says Flora. 'I don't know where he's gone.'

'I think he's at a hospital,' says Kitty. 'Maybe it's your hospital, Mummy.'

'Maybe.' Flora kisses her on the forehead. 'I expect he'll be back in the morning. Go to sleep now, Kitty. Everything's all right.'

She feels suddenly very tired. It's been a long day, and she still has to face Jean, and who knows what after that. She'd like to stay longer with Kitty, but she wants to get the next bit over with. She levers herself off the bed and stands for a moment looking down. Kitty is lying with her head right in the middle of the pillow, like a child in a story book. More often than not, when she comes home from a trip, Kitty throws a tantrum. Flora knows this quiescence is an indication that Kitty knows everything is not all right, but she's grateful, nonetheless.

'Go to sleep now,' she says again, as she shuts the door. 'I love you, Kitty.'

At the bottom of Kitty's staircase Lou is hovering, waiting for her. Her expression is hard to read, and she doesn't quite meet Flora's eyes.

'OK?' says Flora.

Lou nods.

Flora hesitates. Better to quiz Lou than Jean, she thinks.

'How long has Dad been gone?' she asks.

'A few hours,' says Lou. 'He didn't say much, but he seemed pretty upset.'

'I'm sorry I wasn't here,' Flora says.

'It's OK. We were fine with Jean.'

Flora grins at the dropping of 'Auntie', but she knows Jean is down below, that she might be listening. 'It was very kind of her to come,' she says, and Lou nods again.

'I'm going to bed now,' Lou says, and Flora lifts a hand to touch her cheek. Sometimes, these days, there's something about Lou that makes Flora feel she doesn't need mothering anymore – but she knows that's not true, and that she should resist the temptation to feel either exonerated or pushed away. Lou is only fourteen, after all.

'Thanks for looking after Kitty,' she says, and Lou offers her cheek for a kiss.

Down in the kitchen, Jean is standing over the kettle.

'I didn't know if you'd have eaten,' she says.

'You don't have to feed me,' says Flora. 'You've done quite enough.'

'It was a pleasure,' says Jean, in a tone that implies it was anything but.

'I'm very grateful,' Flora says, hating herself for not managing more. Things haven't changed between them since they were children. To give her sister proper satisfaction she would have to admit to things her pride won't allow her to acknowledge: they've never been able to agree to differ. 'The new au pair's coming next week. It's typical that –' she hesitates over the phrasing '– something like this should happen right now.'

'I didn't ask any questions,' says Jean. Her implication isn't lost on Flora: she read the suggestion of impropriety in Jean's face on the door-step, and she knows quite well there may be more for Jean to accuse her of than reckless absence. Strangely, she doesn't resent being lumped together with Henry, or being held to account for his behaviour, what-ever it may prove to have been. Given the choice of siding with Jean or with Henry, she has no hesitation in allying herself with her husband. They are, for better or worse, a team. Looking at her sister, she is con-scious of all this flowing through her head: a perverse loyalty to Henry and, above all, a wish to get Jean out of her house as fast as possible.

'Have *you* eaten?' she asks.

'I had something with the children. Macaroni cheese.'

The kettle is boiling now, and Jean has taken a box of tea bags out of a cupboard. That means she intends to stay long enough to drink it, Flora thinks. She's not hungry, but she feels an impulse to cook her-self something homely and comforting, something to disprove Jean's impression of her as a fly-by-night career woman who pooh-poohs domestic labour. She's not very good at spontaneous culinary creation, though. She opens the fridge with a sinking expectation of failure. But there's a packet of smoked salmon and some eggs: Henry's staples, she thinks, with a rush of affection.

'I'm going to knock up scrambled egg and smoked salmon,' she says. 'Sure you wouldn't like some?'

Jean frowns, as though such frivolity is surprising even in Flora. Gruel, Flora thinks wickedly, is more the kind of thing Jean would prescribe for her. Poor Jean, whose life has been devoted to making a home for the children who never arrived. She can see things from Jean's point of view, of course. She can even see that Jean would be a better mother than her, in certain respects. But the longer Jean stays the less she likes her – and the less she likes herself, too. She simply doesn't have the energy, she tells herself, to engage with her sister.

Before she has finished scrambling the eggs, Jean has given up hope of – whatever she hoped for. Capitulation, Flora thinks. Jean picks up her bag, which has been hanging over the back of a chair, and sighs.

'I'd better be getting back to Derek,' she says. 'It'll take me the best part of an hour.'

Flora glances at the clock: it's almost ten now. At the last minute she feels a surge of guilt, and of sisterly warmth.

'Thank you for coming to hold the fort,' she says, turning from the hob with a smile. 'I'm sorry Henry had to call you. I'm sure he wouldn't have done unless . . .'

'Well,' says Jean, slipping an arm into her coat, 'I hope everything's all right in the end. Tell him I said so.'

'I will. We must . . .' The sentence fades away.

Jean has only been gone five minutes when the lights of Henry's car sweep across the drive. Thank goodness, Flora thinks – but when Henry comes through the door her heart jolts violently. She has never seen him looking like this before, not even when Nick Comyn died. He's been crying, and has taken no trouble to conceal it: she imagines him driving with tears streaming down his cheeks. Despite herself, she rushes to console him.

'Oh, Henry,' she croons. 'What's happened?'

She can see herself, all this time: part of her is watching, surprised and even – yes – a little disapproving. But it's the memory of Jean's disapproval that spurs her on; the reminder that she and Henry are on the same side – that they have to be. And Henry doesn't resist: he takes her in his arms and holds her against him. She can smell whisky on his breath, and tobacco too, for the first time in years.

She doesn't have to ask him what's happened. There's no keeping it in; neither shame nor embarrassment seems to play any part. While the scrambled egg sets hard in the pan, Henry clings to Flora and pours out his heartbreak.

'It's Elizabeth,' he says. 'She's dead. A car crash.'

Flora says nothing for a long while. What is there to say? What is there to feel, even? She holds this man in her arms, her husband of almost twenty years, and wonders where her anger has gone.

40

It was hotter than Kitty had expected. She had long ago taken off the skimpy cardigan she'd been wearing over her cotton dress. She was afraid the air conditioning in Flora's Saab wasn't going to be much good on the way home: Kitty liked the heat, but she didn't like sweaty cars, their smell redolent of long, car-sick journeys as a child. Landon would let her sit in the front if she asked, but she was trying not to draw attention to herself. For one thing, it was Lou's turn to have people thinking about her, and for another, Kitty wasn't sure she wanted to be noticed today.

They were at a château, not one of the famous ones like Chenonceau or Amboise but a little one not far from St Rémy. Kitty hadn't been enthusiastic when Flora suggested it: all she'd really wanted was to stay at Les Violettes all day. But she was glad they'd come, even if there was something rather surreal about the outing. It reminded her of holidays from her childhood, all those castles and cathedrals Henry had taken them to, but Henry wasn't here now and Landon was, and she and Lou weren't children anymore. It was like a where-are-they-now sequel, reassembling the cast of a soap opera years later for a single, oddly unsettling episode – but families, she thought, were soap operas that went on and on whether you liked it or not, and the emotions inside them were always more complicated than you could possibly imagine from the outside.

She had come down that morning to find Lou and Flora sitting together in the garden. Lou had been crying, and Kitty's first reaction had been relief, because if Flora was occupied with Lou's misery, she was less likely to notice Kitty's. But then she'd envied Lou a little – because she had unburdened herself to Flora, but also because her own situation felt so much – messier. After all, Alice would surely come back sooner or later, and at least Lou knew what she felt. She was married and pregnant and had a proper job that everyone knew she was good at: the future was clear to her.

Kitty was completely torn, now, between wanting to explain herself and wanting not to at any price, and the shabby confusion of her feelings, the shame and fury and disappointment, made her feel unworthy of her mother's consolation. Whenever someone's glance flicked towards her, her heart would gallop as she wondered whether this was it, whether in a moment she'd have tipped over into telling and wouldn't be able to stop – and the relief she knew she'd feel then was almost enough to overcome the desperate urge to hold back.

She kicked at the ground with the open toe of her sandal, distracting herself with the dry, cool feel of the grass. They'd been wandering in the gardens for a while, admiring the formal arrangement of little hedges and flowers Landon called a parterre and smelling the herbs in the vegetable garden, and now they were skirting the strip of meadow, filled with long grass and wildflowers, that ran beside the river. They hadn't been into the house yet – the château. Kitty was impatient now to get out of the heat, and she never felt you got a proper sense of these places, anyway, until you'd been inside and seen what it was like to look out through the windows. As they reached a gravel path that wound back through the formal gardens, Lou halted.

'Inside now?'

'Inside,' agreed Landon. 'Hot out here, isn't it? Sweltering.'

'We could go for a swim this afternoon,' said Flora. 'There's a lake the other side of the village with a *plan d'eau*, a little man-made beach. They're good at all that, the French.'

Lou was right, Kitty thought: Flora did look happy. Sort of simply happy, as though the sunshine and the gardens and all of them being there was enough to make everything all right. She watched Flora take Lou's arm, as they turned towards the château, and felt a pang of jealousy.

Kitty was no good at describing buildings, but this castle looked just like a castle in a child's drawing, waiting to be populated by ladies in flowing dresses and cone-shaped hats. It was built from grey stone with a slight sheen to it, and the entrance was flanked by two towers. As they approached, the walls rose above them, one of those surprises of perspective that look like tricksy camerawork.

And then, as they approached the big wooden door, a faint strain of muted strings drifted into Kitty's head. She recognised it instantly as G sharp minor – a key with a lot of black notes, marshalled here into a doleful pavane with a rumble of drums behind it. Kitty felt a shiver run down the full length of her back, from the top of her head to the base of her spine, like a glissando on a xylophone. The tone of the music was sombre, even portentous, but the fact that it was there at all – that was an immeasurable, an overwhelming thing. Since Martin had broken the news about Daniel the stream of music in her head had been turned off. Although she'd thought that was the least of her worries she understood, now, that the silence had been a terrible thing to bear.

She stopped a few yards before the huge front door and let the notes filter through her, grasping at the glimmer of insight they brought, the layer of meaning, the draught of solace. The sense that there were resources she could call on; that however bad things felt she was, would be, could be, in control of her own destiny. Was that folly? Delusion? Just for a moment, she felt the presence of her father in the thread of melody in her head, and her eyes filled with tears.

41

It was late afternoon, but the sun was still full in the sky. Lou lay on the sweating grass, letting the last vestiges of the dream that had jolted her awake fall away. She'd been in the shadow of a big oak tree when she fell asleep, but the sun had moved and she was hot now. Flora and Kitty had disappeared, leaving their towels laid out beside her. Shading her eyes, Lou thought she could see them down in the water, thirty yards away. The scene made her think of Seurat, something very typically French. There was a little beach beside the lake, a sandy strip created to encourage bathers, and a scattering of families and teenagers and older couples sat along the length of it or on the grassy slope above. Twenty or thirty people were swimming in an area roped off with floats, and beyond them the water stretched away, ringed by dark trees.

'Ah, you're awake.'

Lou turned her head: she'd forgotten for a moment that Landon was with them.

'Hello,' she said. 'Are the others swimming?'

'Yes.'

'You didn't fancy it?'

'I was concerned about the sun,' he said. 'I thought I'd stay and keep an eye.'

'On me?' Lou was touched. 'That's sweet of you. Is there any water left?'

She levered herself upright as Landon passed her a bottle and a plastic cup.

'I might have a dip,' she said. 'Do you want to come?'

'No.' He smiled. 'You go. I'm happy to watch.'

The lake was warmer than she'd expected, though bracing enough after lying in the sun for so long. She stood in the shallows for a few minutes with children paddling around her, feeling the small weight of her own child in her belly, the muggy warmth of the day on her skin.

'Lou!' Kitty waved and splashed towards her. 'Isn't this perfect? Mum's gone off across the lake.'

Sure enough, there was the back of Flora's head, ducking under the rope and striking off towards the far bank.

'Not you?' Lou asked.

'There might be eels.' Kitty laughed, and Lou thought how different she looked already, after less than twenty-four hours here. Was that evidence of the resilience of youth, or the restorative powers of the French countryside? Simply, perhaps, the plain fact that no misery could keep up its grip on you every moment of the day.

'Time to swim,' she said, 'here I come,' and she waded swiftly into deeper water and ducked forward to launch herself. Kitty was right: it felt glorious, water all around her and the wide sky above. 'Oh,' she said, 'that's blissful. I could float here forever.'

'We can,' said Kitty. 'Why not? We can stay here all summer. Come and swim every day.'

'I think Harvers and Green might be expecting me back at some point, unfortunately.'

'Oh, bother them. Look at Flora – she escaped.'

'Flora's sixty.'

Kitty laughed again; she was in that sort of mood, Lou thought. Well, she certainly deserved a little *joie de vivre*.

For some time the two of them swam and talked and drifted, reminding each other how they used to do star floats, somersaults, handstands; watching children ducking each other and old ladies in black rubber swimming hats executing stately circuits in breaststroke. Not Seurat but Monsieur Hulot, Lou thought.

When something splattered into the water beside her she turned, looking for a child who might have thrown a pebble, but then there was another splash, and another.

'It's raining,' Kitty said. 'How funny, the sky was completely blue a minute ago.'

But now, when they looked up, they could see a mass of dark clouds. The surface of the lake was soon pitted by heavy drops, falling more and more rapidly. The other bathers were squealing and splashing their way to the bank, rushing for their towels and whatever shelter they could find.

'Silly,' Kitty said, 'we're much better off in the water,' but then there was a roll of thunder and – only a second or two later – a flash of lightning.

'I'm not so sure,' Lou said. 'Maybe we should get out.'

Landon was coming towards them across the strip of sand, holding towels. 'That took me by surprise,' he said. 'Where's your mother?'

'Coming back, I hope,' said Lou, wrapping a towel around her shoulders, but when they turned to look there was no sign of Flora.

'Oh God,' said Kitty, 'where is she? She set off across the lake, but . . .'

Lou felt a rush of fear, the colourless kind that accompanies a completely unexpected threat. The three of them stood at the edge of the lake, Landon barely less wet than they were by now. Another crash of thunder and an answering bolt of lightning elicited screams from the children further up the bank.

'I'll speak to the lifeguard,' Landon said, and he turned towards the wooden hut in front of which, not so long ago, a posse of athletic young men had lounged, but it was deserted and padlocked.

'They've taken the flag down,' said Lou. 'That was quick.'

'Perhaps she's sheltering somewhere,' said Kitty. 'She must be. She couldn't have been struck by lightning, could she?'

'I doubt it,' said Landon. He wasn't, Lou thought, one of those men who plunge heedlessly into action in a crisis, but she could see he was troubled by his failure to seize on a solution.

'Shall I go back in?' Kitty suggested. 'I could swim across the way she went, and –'

'We're better placed to see her from here,' Landon said. 'There's no point putting you in danger too.'

The locals had all fled to their cars by now. The rain streamed down, and so much light had gone from the sky that it felt like late evening. Possibilities bobbed in Lou's mind: could the shock of the storm's sudden onset have brought on a seizure of some kind? A cardiac arrest, an asthma attack, an epileptic fit? None of them could take their eyes off the lake, and she told herself that sooner or later they'd spot Flora, making her way back towards the beach. But her head would be almost invisible against the stormy surface of the water, and the thunder was coming more frequently now. The latest jag of lightning cracked over the lake, shattering the sky like a sheet of glass. She wouldn't like to be in there now, Lou thought. What the hell had happened?

'We can't do nothing,' Kitty said. 'We can't just stand here. What about walking round the lake? Maybe she made for the edge somewhere else?'

'You can't,' said Lou. She'd already looked: a high fence blocked the way in one direction, and a bank rose steeply from the water in the other. 'The only way round is by that road we came along, and that loops right away from the lake. We'd be better to stay here and ring the emergency services.'

But she was thinking that it was all too late, too slow, too cumbersome. The lake that had seemed so benign and inviting looked to her now like a death trap, a bottomless body of water in which any number of people could have drowned in the time Flora had been missing. What they would need, she was beginning to fear, were police divers and dredging equipment, not an air ambulance to winch her mother's gasping form from the water.

'How long has she been gone?' Landon asked, as though his mind was working along the same lines as Lou's.

Lou shook her head. 'I really have no idea,' she said. 'She was setting off just as I went into the water.'

Landon looked at his watch, its surface bleary with rain. 'I didn't look at the time,' he said. 'When did you last see her?'

Lou and Kitty shook their heads, silent as schoolchildren caught in a sin of omission. They'd been playing, enjoying themselves, not thinking of their mother. On the grass behind them, their belongings would be drenched by now, the sodden heaps of clothes unwearable. She had never, Lou thought, felt quite so helpless, quite so much at a loss.

They had almost decided the best thing would be for Landon to go and find a *gendarmerie* when a jeep pulled into the car park. Lou glanced towards it, wondering whether this might be someone in authority, coming to check on the *plan d'eau*. The rear door opened, and a figure got out with a shawl draped around them.

Lou thought at first that the resemblance to Flora was mere wishful thinking. The light was bad, and the car was partly obscured by the branches of the oak tree. But then the figure was waving and making its way towards them, and Kitty and Landon had spotted it too, and Kitty was turning and running up the slope.

For the second time that day, Lou felt tears welling up without warning.

'Mummy!' she heard Kitty shouting. 'Oh God, Mummy, we were so worried!'

PART V

Greville Auctioneers, Friday 12th December 2014

Paintings and drawings by Nicholas Comyn, from the collection of the late Henry Jones

Lot no. 5: Landon Peverell as Leporello, 1974

The opera singer Landon Peverell was, like Henry Jones, a life-long friend of Nicholas Comyn. The three were contemporaries at university and remained close until Comyn's death, sharing an interest in both visual art and music.

This portrait commemorates an early triumph for Peverell, when, aged 23, he understudied the part of Leporello in Mozart's *Don Giovanni* at Glyndebourne – and took over the role for the last three performances, to overwhelmingly positive reviews. Peverell is shown here in costume, wearing a fur-edged cloak over a dark suit and Harlequin-style waistcoat. A Homburg hat is held loosely in his left hand, and in the right he holds the battered leather notebook in which his master's conquests are detailed.

Like many of its productions, Glyndebourne's 1974 *Don Giovanni* also exemplified the connections between the arts, with a memorable set designed by John Piper. Piper's atmospheric evocation of ruined buildings and overgrown gardens, which appears in the background of Comyn's painting, intensified the strains of subterfuge, concealment and deception in the production – and Peverell gave a consummate account of the half-apologetic, half-complicit servant of the seducer Don Giovanni.

The evocation of personality in this painting, as well as physical likeness, is exceptionally skilful. Both wry humour and affection are evident in a deeply personal rendition of a public figure.

42

The storm had altered the texture of the day, Flora thought, leaving a crackle of electricity in the air. When they had finally got back to Les Violettes, everyone had busied themselves with separate tasks, as though each of them was too highly charged to be in the same room as the others. Kitty had run her mother a bath, Landon had lit a fire and Lou had searched out a laundry rack to set in front of it. When Flora came downstairs again, the house smelled of wood smoke and wet clothes, like an indoor campfire. The rain had subsided at last and the thunder had burned itself out, leaving behind a conspicuous hush. Coming into the sitting room, Flora found the other three scattered in its corners.

'What time is it?' she asked.

'Seven o'clock,' said Lou.

It felt much later, Flora thought, looking out at the scoured sky. It felt as though the year had moved on a few turns: a strange feeling. She went from window to window, drawing the curtains.

'Food,' said Landon. 'What shall we do about food? We need a faithful retainer to produce a raised pie and some pickles.'

'Very *Railway Children*,' said Lou, with a little smile.

Flora thought with misgiving of the shelves in the larder, which were almost empty again. The road to St Rémy was blocked by a fallen branch; coming home, they'd had to follow a long diversion which involved traversing a flood. No one would feel like going out again.

'There's not much in the house,' she said.

'I saw some tomato soup this morning when I was looking for jam,' Lou said.

'There are eggs,' said Kitty, 'and some bread left.'

In the end a meal was constructed more, Flora thought, through force of will than hard ingredients, as if this were a party game or a survival challenge. But filling the table with food – a large omelette, small bowls of soup, a salad resurrected from a stray lettuce left in the bottom of the fridge – drew the little party back together again. There were smiles, the clink of wine glasses, a pair of candles discovered by Kitty in a drawer.

'Here's to happy endings,' said Landon, lifting his glass in a gesture that saluted Flora then circled in a little flourish to include her daughters.

'I'm sorry to have alarmed you all,' Flora said, not for the first time. She wouldn't explain herself again. The story was straightforward enough: the scramble onto the bank when the first lightning struck; the path that led eventually, as she'd hoped, to the road; the passing car that stopped to pick up a bedraggled stray. She'd known they would worry, but not how much. Both sides were still a little embarrassed by that excess – a little annoyed, even – which was perhaps not, Flora thought, the reaction any of them would have expected.

'Never mind.' Landon put his glass down. He'd cast himself as Master of Ceremonies, Flora saw. 'We've had culture, adventure and now culinary contrivance today, not to mention meteorological extravagance. When I think that I almost left this morning . . .'

'Have some omelette,' said Lou. 'It's nicer warm.'

'Elizabeth David, eat your heart out,' said Landon, his tone still theatrical, as though he wasn't ready to relinquish the spotlight yet.

'Shut up and eat, she means,' said Kitty, her smile conveying her assurance that she'd get away with a little cheeky familiarity. To everyone's surprise, though, she almost didn't. Landon's expression changed, and Flora recognised the *amour propre* of the public man he'd become, and the chain of association around the table that didn't include him: the difficulty of being an outsider, even in this loosely bound family. And then Landon laughed, and Kitty blushed with relief, and they concentrated, for a few minutes, on eating.

43

The whole evening had been very peculiar. It was hard, Kitty thought, to say how, exactly, or even why – except that it was to do with the storm and Flora getting lost and being found again, and the four of them being together through what felt now like a very long day.

As they sat in the sitting room waiting for Flora to come downstairs, then fussed around in the kitchen looking for tin openers and matches and chopping boards, she could feel the criss-crossing threads that joined them all together, even Landon. It was as though they were caught in a web that held them just a little apart from each other, and every time one of them moved or spoke or even thought something, the others all felt it: all evening the threads tweaked and stretched and tugged at them. From the outside they might look like people with separate lives and free wills, but any of them could have told you it didn't feel like that.

'Have you done much opera lately, Landon?' Lou asked, as they sat around the dining room table.

'No, not for years,' he said, with a brisk gesture that seemed to Kitty to reveal the depths of his disappointment, even though it was presumably intended to convey a breezy nonchalance. 'Apart from the odd concert performance, like the one your mother saw last weekend. Staged productions – oh, you know. One gets too . . .'

Too old, Kitty wondered? Or too weary of the rehearsal, and the commitment so far in advance? He'd never been able to leave Rosanna, that was the story. How had he managed to leave her for so long now, then? What had made him stay on here?

'It's lovely to have everyone here,' Flora said then, picking up – of course – Kitty's train of thought. Feeling it down the lines of the web, and saying things she wouldn't usually say. 'Being on your own for a few weeks makes you appreciate company. Family. Old friends.'

'For the sake of auld lang syne,' said Lou, and then she blushed, as though realising that the phrase had sounded more sarcastic than she'd intended. Like the kind of snippy thing she'd have said at sixteen, Kitty thought. 'It's great to be here, Mum,' she said then. 'I'm not sure I can cope with many more days as action-packed as this one, but . . .'

'A quiet day tomorrow,' agreed Flora. 'It'll take them a while to clear up the mess from the storm, anyway. We can lie low.'

She looked at Landon, just a quick glance, but Kitty knew she was hoping he'd stay longer, and hoping they wouldn't notice her wishing it.

But then it was Landon's turn to feel the tug on the thread, to react, to deflect the conversation onwards. His eyes passed over Lou, and Kitty guessed that he'd been told about Alice and wouldn't raise the subject in public. She knew before his gaze reached her that it was her he'd light on, and that he was going to quiz her in the way older men thought was acceptable, flattering even, to young women. She felt a flush rising in her cheeks, fuelled by emotions she hadn't had time to prepare for. She hadn't thought about Daniel all afternoon, that was the irony. The lake and the storm had occupied her fully enough to keep him at bay, and her defences were down.

In the second before Landon spoke she looked up at the botanical prints that hung on the wall behind him, hoping they might steady her nerve, but the delicate realism of stems and petals and furled leaves offered no protection. Suddenly the room was full of Daniel, his face and smell and voice, a distorted mass of sensations that reminded Kitty of the teratomas in Flora's pathology book, those tangled tumours of teeth and hair and bone that she and Lou used to terrify themselves with.

She didn't hear what Landon said, not properly. Some cliché, intended to be harmless. She didn't try to form a reply, or to stop the tears; she simply sat and let them fall. So be it, she thought. Let it all come out now, Daniel and Henry and everything. She imagined a terrible drama, the room split apart, the paper flowers tumbling from their frames. But instead there was complete silence for a second or two, and then Lou jumping up and proposing some music and Landon agreeing, even Flora joining in. All of them feeling her distress and wanting to stop it.

Kitty didn't know whether to feel relieved or dismayed. In the hall, Lou put a hand on her arm and said, 'You look worn out, Kitty. Do you want to go to bed?' But she shook her head and pressed her hands against her eyes.

'I'm sorry,' she said. 'Being silly. Let's go and sing.'

They found Schubert's *Winterreise*, an edition in the right key for Landon. While Kitty buried herself in an armchair Lou set the score on the piano and flicked through the opening pages.

'I can manage the first one, at least,' she said. 'Let's have a go.'

How long was it, Kitty wondered, since Lou had played the piano? It was a long time since Kitty had heard these songs too, the gentle precision of their unhappiness designed for just such a setting as this, a few people gathered in a room at the end of a day. Lou might be out of practice but she played well, better than well, with the confident placing of phrases that Kitty remembered. And if Landon felt put upon, if he would have preferred not to sing, there was no evidence of it. From the first note his voice was miraculous, a thing of touch and warmth and intoxication, calling every cell of Kitty's body to attention.

When the shift to the major key came in the final verse, Kitty felt the relief and desolation of it flooding through her. How much better expressed in music than it could ever be in words, she thought, that knowledge that sorrow and happiness are inextricable, that one can't exist without the other. How perfectly and painfully that was conveyed by the dying Schubert. Landon understood it, Kitty thought; and Lou; and surely Flora.

She looked at her mother, then, and knew she couldn't tell her about Henry and Daniel. It was as if, at that moment, the whole tumultuous saga of her parents' marriage was spread before her, complex and tortured but complete. She could see the balance and the shape of it, like a symphony. Lou was wrong, she thought; Flora didn't have to know. She already knew quite enough.

And then, as the song came to an end, Flora moved a little, shifting her weight forward in the chair. Only Kitty saw her: a tiny movement, as though she was reaching for something, bracing herself. There was a pause, Lou not yet lifting her hand to turn the page and Landon still standing where the last phrase had left him, his eyes on Lou, locked into their shared performance. Kitty watched her mother, saw her chest rising and falling as though she had to remember to breathe, and waited for what was coming. Lou lifted her hand to turn the page, and then Flora spoke.

'Kitty darling,' she said – and then she faltered. 'Lou . . . Landon.'

'What is it?' Lou asked. 'Shall we stop? Sing something else?'

'It's lovely,' said Flora, 'really lovely, but I'm afraid the day's catching up with me.'

'Of course.' Lou shut the score. 'You must be exhausted. We should have thought.'

Flora didn't look exhausted, Kitty thought. She looked agitated. And Lou didn't look apologetic, either; she'd been enjoying herself and she didn't like the interruption. Her expression reminded Kitty suddenly, sharply, of Henry.

'Don't stop,' said Flora, 'there's no need to stop' – but there was a hiatus now, a breach in the flow of the evening. Kitty had the sense that four invisible currents had been brought to a sudden halt, four luxuriant tumbles of thought reeling up against a breakwater. She could feel petulance rising where something nobler had been a moment before. None of them met each other's eyes.

313

Flora stood up.

'Do go on,' she said, with even less conviction.

Kitty hesitated. It was her name Flora had started with. Surely she hadn't imagined that, or mistaken the sense that some irresistible momentum had caused her mother to speak it? And then Flora's gaze cut across to her, and before another conscious thought could interpose itself Kitty got to her feet and followed her out of the room.

44

She had the advantage, Flora thought, of having heard Landon sing only a few days before. She was glad of that, of not coming to this impromptu recital completely raw, but even so there was more to take in, more to think about in this little scene than she could quite bear. Kitty curled in an armchair, her face marbled with weeping and her hair a golden tumble. Lou at the piano, an entirely unexpected twist. Landon, taller and more distinguished in this little space than he had seemed on stage. All three of them, Flora realised, sharing something she lacked: an instinctive understanding of the music.

It wasn't that Landon's performance left her unmoved; far from it. It was more that it felt like listening to a foreign language, enjoying the sounds but not knowing what lay beneath them. The song was in German, of course, but it was the musical language she badly wanted to grasp: the emotions generated by the pattern of notes. Watching the others, she wished her education hadn't been so narrow. But perhaps this was an innate ability she lacked – a missing link in her brain?

And then something changed in the music: a shift of mood, like a brightening in the sky. Suddenly there was a suggestion of hope to mitigate the sadness – or perhaps, Flora realised, listening intently now, a reminder that pleasure is possible even in the depths of misery, and that misery is all the more acute for the knowledge of pleasure. Those were things the summer should have taught her. The summer, and four decades with Henry. She looked at her daughters, each bearing their burden of grief, and then at Landon, and she saw in his face something sadder still: his forbearance, his kindness, his dignity. As the music came to an end she realised that she had to speak now, before the spell was broken.

'Kitty darling,' she said, when the silence had held for a second or two – but then she stopped. The words she'd hoped would follow had dried in her throat. This wasn't the right way; she couldn't do it in public. Dear God, how could she misjudge this moment after keeping her secret so carefully for so long? How could she of all people be seduced by a song into thinking this was a good idea?

'Lou,' she said, scrambling to cover herself, 'Landon . . .'

The girls were both looking at her; not Landon.

'What is it?' Lou asked.

'I'm afraid the day is catching up with me,' Flora heard herself say.

'Of course; you must be exhausted,' said Lou. 'We should have thought.' The words were sympathetic, but there was something else in her face that caused Flora pain.

'Don't stop.' Flora smiled, hoping to reassure, to defuse. She might have waited, she thought; but she knew she couldn't have done. She hesitated for a moment longer, fearful that the opening she'd created would be wasted, the singing stopped for nothing, and then she stood up. 'Do go on,' she said. She glanced at Kitty – and to her joy and terror Kitty got to her feet too.

'Me too,' she said. 'It's been a long day.'

At that moment Landon met Flora's eyes at last, and his expression almost floored her. He raised his eyebrows, just very slightly, and Flora nodded: two tiny movements, each impossible to be sure of.

Landon turned to Lou then. 'Well,' he said, 'are you game for one more number?'

Crossing the few yards to the door, Flora didn't quite dare to believe that Kitty had followed her deliberately. But when they reached the bottom of the stairs Kitty stopped.

'Do you want some tea?' she asked. 'I could make us some.'

August 1991

August, thinks Flora, as she and Henry make the long journey down to the West Country before the funeral, is not a time for mourning. How typical of her mother to die when there are no sharp winds to drive home the chill of mortality, just balmy skies by day and the smell of hay lingering in the air even at night.

Flora's operating list overran today, so they are late. Lou is fast asleep in the back of the car as the road winds away from them, stubble gleaming in the moonlight on each side. It's after eleven when they arrive, but Jean is on the doorstep when the car pulls up, smart in a skirt and jacket, a dark silk scarf at her neck.

'That woman has the hearing of a cat,' Henry says.

His voice is jovial, relaxed, but Flora isn't deceived: not by his tone, nor by her sister's smile. Henry has barely spoken since they left home, and Jean was expecting them at eight. As they pull through the gate, she thinks with longing of the shining cool of the operating theatre.

Henry parks behind Jean and Derek's Volkswagen and opens the car door.

'Hello, Jean,' he says. 'Good of you to wait up.'

'Little mite,' says Jean, peering through the window into the back seat. 'Her bed's all made up.'

Flora feels little connection with this grey stone house their mother moved to three years ago, but Jean has been a frequent visitor: she has its cupboards and crannies well under control. She raises her eyebrows when they refuse the soup she has kept warm on the back of the Aga.

'I didn't think you'd have time to stop for food,' she says, to show that she knows they did, and that they've kept her up, therefore, later than they needed to.

'A cup of tea would be very welcome,' says Henry. 'You must put us to work tomorrow, Jean. We're behindhand, I know.'

This is partly, Flora knows, an attempt to protect her – getting in before Jean does, he'd call it – but it's also setting the tone, making it clear that he has no intention of letting their squabble (his preferred term) spill over into the serious family business of the funeral.

Infuriatingly, Jean smiles at him. She has always been susceptible to Henry's charm, despite her undeviating conviction that he's a wastrel, and no more than Flora deserves.

'Don't worry,' she says. 'There's plenty still to do.'

The next morning Flora wakes early, and she slips downstairs and lets herself out of the back door before anyone else appears. Compounding her sins, she knows, but she needs to let things settle in her head, and there certainly won't be any peace later on.

The village is quiet, swathed by the gauzy mist of a late summer morning, and the air is sweet. Filled with the satisfaction of an early harvest, Flora thinks fancifully, and she laughs at herself and feels a little better. She passes the pub and the Post Office, then halts at the corner to look at the church. She hadn't meant to go in, but gazing up at the square tower and the broad flanks of the transepts she feels herself drawn through the lych gate, and then pushing at the door, which – to her surprise – is open.

She has been asking herself why her mother chose to move down here when the cancer must already have been well established, but it strikes her now, standing in the empty nave, that the prospect of an elegant funeral in this extraordinary church must have occurred to her; must have appealed. A ludicrous explanation, of course, but there is something utterly recognisable in it that pierces the calm surface of Flora's grief. She can picture her mother sitting in one of these pews, wearing the same kind of scarf as Jean. She can hear her confiding with defiant wit that she'd been mindful of the quality of her funeral when she chose this village. There was always something barbaric beneath that cultured exterior, Flora thinks, and she feels tears and laughter catching in the back of her throat.

Sliding into a pew, Flora leans back against the smooth wood. Her mother didn't tell anyone about her illness until near the end. She gave them very little notice: just a straightforward summons a few days before she died, which Jean answered at once and Flora too late. Flora, who is used to death and familiar with its forms, was nevertheless startled by the sight of her mother's stillness against the pillows; grateful and angry that the body had been left where it was until she finally arrived. She shuts her eyes now, remembering. She came straight from the hospital, driving through the night to get down here and back again before morning, in time for a list that included a case she couldn't leave to her Registrar. And for what? For the paying of respects; the marking of dues. For some primitive need to see her mother dead.

She's not sure whether her mother was a believer. Her life, Flora thinks, was governed by precepts rather than beliefs. Christianity was part of the framework she lived by – but looking up at the surprising angels gazing down from the roof, Flora admits that she knows almost nothing of what her mother thought, about God or anything else. Did she take pride in Flora's accomplishments, for instance? Did she admire the balancing of marriage and motherhood with a surgical career, or regard it as an evil she had to accept? No opinion was ever ventured, after Flora's marriage. Her mother surely expected her to stop work after Lou's birth, but she never said so; never expressed surprise or reproach when Flora went back to the hospital six weeks later. She must have meant this as a gift, Flora thinks, but she wishes she knew what her mother really thought. No doubt Jean would have an opinion, but Flora is sure her mother would not have spoken to Jean about it. She realises, now, that there are things she and her mother had in common: fortitude, determination, a sense of honour. Sitting in a patch of morning sunshine that falls without warmth from the clerestory windows, Flora feels the first tears rising in her eyes.

Henry is washing up breakfast dishes when she gets back to the house, and Jean is on the phone. Lou is sitting at the table in her pyjamas, finishing a piece of toast.

'I walked to the church,' Flora says, when Jean puts the phone down, although she knows it looks defensive to account for her movements before her sister has asked where she's been.

'Derek's gone to the florist,' Jean says. 'I wasn't sure whether you'd want to have a say.'

'In the wreath?'

'And the church flowers.' Jean frowns. 'There will have to be flowers in the church.'

There will have to be flowers in the church. Were those exactly her mother's words, before her wedding? Flora smiles, despite herself. 'There are flowers in the church,' she says. She takes a plate and a knife from the rack by the sink and sits down opposite her daughter. 'Rather nice flowers, I thought.'

Jean hasn't moved from the phone. She leans against the dresser, her face tight.

'I had hoped,' she says, 'that we could work together, just for a few days. Would that be too much to ask?'

Flora doesn't see Landon until the wake. She hadn't even thought about whether he might be among the hordes of friends and strangers who have shown up for the funeral, but when she goes into the kitchen to check on the caterers there he is, standing by the back door, as though he's just arrived or is wondering about leaving again. He swings round when she comes in, and beams at her.

'I thought this might be the place to catch you,' he says.

Flora has forgotten his speaking voice, the hint of the operatic baritone about certain vowels. She looks at him for a moment before moving forward to accept his embrace.

'It's lovely to see you,' she says, her voice tremulous. 'It's been a long time.'

'My poor Flora.' Landon's tone is cheerful for the caterers, but he clasps her more tightly than he needs to. Flora can tell that he understands; that he knows, at least, that there is a good deal to understand.

'Henry's out there somewhere,' she says. 'Everyone's out there. Jean and Derek.'

Landon lifts her gently away from his shoulder and holds her at arm's length, studying her face. Flora notices his clothes for the first time, the extravagant cravat and the dark red carnation in the lapel of his linen jacket. This is how she remembers him, always a little larger than life. 'How are you, Flora?'

'I'm a Consultant,' she says. 'Did you know?'

'I did. The first female surgeon at St Backwards.'

She laughs. 'And I heard you on the radio last week.'

'Wagner?' he asks. 'How did it sound?'

'Compelling.'

She heard him singing, in fact, the night she drove down to see her mother lying dead. She won't tell him that, Flora thinks. She isn't sure that she could explain what it meant to hear him on that particular night. She was just glad Henry wasn't with her, Henry who loves Wagner so much.

Flora's smile is still in place, but she can feel herself quivering, as though something is struggling to burst through. The caterers finish loading their platters with canapés and bustle out of the room.

'I'm sorry,' Flora says, as tears spill down her cheeks. She didn't cry in the service. Jean wept modestly, creditably, into a handkerchief, while Flora sat dry-eyed and hatless, with Lou beside her.

Landon draws her towards him again. 'Has it been horrid?'

'Completely.'

'Tell me.'

Flora sniffs; almost a laugh, but more a sob. 'I hardly know where to start.'

'Try.'

'Oh . . .' Flora wipes her eyes, but the tears start up again as soon as she tries to speak. 'Later,' she says. 'I must go back. So many people. Are you leaving?'

'Absolutely not.' Landon squeezes her shoulder. 'Here till the bitter end.'

'There you are!' Jean's voice is exasperated and triumphant, as though Flora is a lost dog. 'I wondered what had happened to you.'

'I'm just coming,' Flora says. 'Landon's here.'

'So I see. How nice of you to come, Landon.'

'Hello, Jean.' Landon holds out a hand, his manners impeccable. 'I'm so sorry about your mother.'

The last stragglers don't leave until six o'clock: hanging on, Jean says with a quick shake of her head, in the hope of being offered supper.

'I hardly think so,' Flora says. 'They've come a long way, some of them.'

'They'd want to get back on the road, then.' Jean doesn't meet her eyes: she's at the sink, filling the kettle. Always busy, Flora thinks viciously, with some productive task.

'A wonderful turnout, anyway,' says Henry. 'I hope I can rustle up that many mourners.' He leans back in his chair, looks at his watch, sighs. 'I must get going,' he says.

Flora swings round. 'Going?'

Jean has turned too. Henry puts on his rueful face, running his stubby fingers through his hair. 'I'm covering the late night prom. I'm sure I told you.'

'For God's sake, Henry: tonight? Surely you didn't have to. Surely someone else . . .'

'It's the première of Mikhail's cello concerto,' Henry says. Flora has heard this tone of voice so often: the reasonableness, the patience, the self-justification. It incites suspicion as an instant reflex.

'What about the car?' she says. 'How am I supposed to get home?'

Henry smiles, all amiability. 'I can come back for you tomorrow.'

'I'll give you a lift.' Landon is standing in the doorway. He smiles, and Flora feels a little jump in her throat.

'Are you staying, then?' she asks.

'He means he'll take Henry,' says Jean. 'Don't you, Landon? Then Flora can keep the car.'

Landon demurs. 'I meant . . .'

'We might need Flora's car tomorrow,' Jean says firmly. 'And we wouldn't want to put you to any trouble, Landon.'

Henry gets to his feet. 'Well, that's great,' he says. 'Thanks, me old mucker. Good opportunity for a chinwag on the way.'

Landon stands very still for a moment – like an actor, Flora thinks, pausing before his next line – and then he smiles again. 'Albert Hall by ten?' he says. 'We'd better get on the road.'

That night Flora lies beside Lou, drifting in and out of sleep. In the dark, she can smell the slight, sweet scent of buttered teacakes from the high tea provided, without consultation, by Jean. Lou has been angelic all day, Flora thinks. She replays images in her mind, to help keep at bay the tumult of emotion that threatens to burst out from the safe corner where she has confined it: Lou sitting obediently on Great Aunt Liza's knee; talking politely to the vicar; answering the same questions over and over again with her sweetest smile.

Jean and Derek are sleeping on the top floor, and they have been in bed since ten thirty, so when Flora hears footsteps coming up the stairs she knows it isn't either of them. She glances at the alarm clock with its blobs of luminous paint: it's almost two o'clock. Sharply awake now, she listens for another step, and another. After a moment a figure appears, silhouetted in the doorway.

'Flora?'

'Landon?' Her voice is louder than she intended, inflated by surprise. 'What on earth are you doing here?'

'I said we'd talk later. You looked as though you needed it.'

In outline he looks taller than usual, a slender statue framed by the light from the bathroom. 'How did you get in?'

'Through a window. I planned to serenade you, if I couldn't find one open.' He begins to sing, very softly: '*Deh! Vieni alla finestra, o mio tesoro . . .*'

'Everyone's asleep,' Flora says. She wants to laugh, and to cry. She wants him to go on singing, but only to her. 'Jean and Derek are upstairs.'

'Don't they like Don Giovanni? I've always thought Jean would make an excellent Donna Anna, up her own arse with righteous indignation. Whereas you –'

The next moment he catches her in his arms. Flora isn't quite sure how it happened, whether she fell or flung herself at him, but the sensation is extraordinary: a sudden yielding to gravity. Nothing mattering in quite the same way anymore because all the usual landmarks have vanished.

'Did you really drive all the way to London and back?' she asks. 'You could have dropped him at the station.'

She can hear his voice in her chest when he speaks. 'Better this way,' he says. 'No one needs to know.'

They have never slept together before. All the years they've known each other, Flora thinks; all that time her mother hoped Landon might prevail, if Flora wouldn't have one of those army officers or stockbrokers. Why has she never realised before that she wanted him? Even that night, years ago now, when she first came back from the hospital to find Henry . . . But there is, now, an overwhelming, a magnificent sense of inevitability.

'Not here,' she says, as he runs a hand down her back. 'Come to my room.'

She and Henry have been billeted in the little room her mother used for sewing. The curtains aren't closed, and the moon transfigures the neatly folded stacks of fabric, the Singer sewing machine hunched like a fertility symbol under the window. Flora shuts the door behind them and slips her dressing gown off her shoulders.

'I'm not Don Giovanni,' Landon says. 'I came back so you could talk to me.'

'Later,' Flora says. 'Please don't start having scruples now.'

'By no means.' He smiles as she lifts her nightdress over her head.

He is gentler than Henry, and more expert. Flora is aware, at some depth, of the irony of this, but mostly she is aware of the sheer reckless pleasure of making love to a man who isn't her husband – the only other man she has ever made love to – on the floor of her mother's sewing room, on the night of her funeral. She cries, not for her mother but for herself, and for the shock and solace of this extraordinary turn of events.

Afterwards, they lie in silence. It's still dark, but the first birds are singing in the garden and a tiny breeze ruffles the edges of the sheet Landon has pulled over them.

'Better?' he says, eventually.

'Yes.'

'You poor thing.' He strokes her cheek with his finger, and Flora shivers. 'Is it Henry?'

'Not just Henry,' she says. 'It's my mother, and Jean, and the job, and Lou . . .'

'But it's what you want, the job?'

'It's what I want, but it's hard. You have no idea how hard. Sometimes I wonder . . .'

She falls silent again. No use, she thinks. She isn't going to turn back now. Better not to talk about it.

'There's someone new,' she says. 'For Henry. Someone much more important this time.'

'Do you know who she is?'

'A musician, I think. Has he talked to you about her?'

'No. He knows better than that.'

Flora studies his face in the moonlight. 'Does it bother you, talking about Henry's infidelity when we've just . . .?'

He smiles at her, and shakes his head, but she can see there's something on his mind.

'What is it?' she asks. 'Tell me.'

'I'm getting married,' he says.

Flora freezes. 'What?'

'It's not someone you know,' he says. 'I met her – oh, quite recently, actually, but . . .'

'For God's sake!' Flora sits up, pulling the sheet around her. Cuckolding Henry is one thing, but another woman's fiancé . . . 'Why didn't you tell me? What on earth were you thinking?'

'Please don't,' he says. 'We could have done this a long time ago. Perhaps we should have done.'

'But we didn't,' Flora says. 'We did it now. Right now. I can't believe . . .'

'Rosanna will never know,' he says. 'It'll never . . .'

'Too right it'll never happen again.' Flora can feel tears rising again, and this time she won't let herself think what they mean. Her brain spins, grasping at practicalities. Landon has already driven for hours, so she can hardly throw him out into the night, but the thought of Jean finding him here is more than she can bear.

'I'll go,' he says, as though he's read her mind. 'There's a Travelodge at the motorway exit. I can sleep there. I'm sorry – I'm very sorry that you feel . . .'

'Don't,' says Flora, 'don't say anything else.'

But she's glad that he doesn't move at once.

'It's my only weapon,' she says after a few moments. 'Fidelity. Knowing I'm beyond reproach.'

'You don't need a weapon,' Landon says. His voice is gentle; there's no hint of umbrage. 'I don't know quite what you need, Flora, but it's not a weapon.' He leans across and kisses her on the forehead before he gets up. There are no more apologies, no more explanations.

For a long time after he leaves Flora lies awake, feeling nothing at all. Perhaps she will never sleep again, she thinks. Perhaps there will be no peace for her now. But then she feels Lou's hand on her cheek, and sun is flooding into the room.

'Good morning, Mummy,' Lou says. 'Did you sleep well?'

For a doctor, Flora is vague about physiology. She doesn't mark the calendar or record dates. The absence of menstruation might have passed unnoticed for some time, except that the tiny thing which has taken root inside her asserts its presence more forcefully than its sister ever did. Leaning over the operating table one morning, she feels a paralysing rush of nausea.

'Canteen curry?' quips her Registrar, when they meet in the staff-room afterwards, and Flora smiles primly and leaves him to finish the list.

She has never gone home in the middle of the day before. On the way she stops to buy a pregnancy test, although she knows what the result will be. She sits in the kitchen with the white strip beside her, shaking with the enormity of what's happening to her. This is definitely not Henry's baby – although she has slept with Henry since the funeral, a fact she clings to now with fervent gratitude, despite the taint of contamination that shadowed the event – because the timing, although close enough to spare Henry's suspicions, is wrong. And Henry, of course, is an unlikely candidate for fatherhood, although stranger things have happened. Stranger things such as this one.

Having ignored the evidence in front of her for several weeks, Flora draws around her now her knowledge of biology, of chorion and amnion and cell division, hoping that the surgeon's uncompromising logic might serve her better than the woman's instincts. There is still plenty of time to make a decision. She presents the dilemma to herself: the arguments for and against keeping the baby. She couldn't bear Henry to guess that it isn't his – but assuming she can keep that secret, does she want to give him the pleasure of another child, especially just now when his affections are so securely engaged elsewhere? A baby might win him back, of course – but could she stand the indignity of that? Then there's her career: she might have a Consultancy now, but that's not the end of the road. Does she want to handicap herself further?

Henry's Catholicism is honoured more in the breach than the observance, but he would nonetheless be horrified by the idea of an abortion, if he ever caught a whiff of it. But she must consult her own feelings, Flora thinks, not his. She can't be swayed by the idea of angering him any more than of pleasing him. Surely it's possible to establish what she feels, what she wants.

She isn't in the habit of listening to the radio, but the house is so quiet that her thoughts seem to echo gratingly in the empty space. On impulse, she reaches over and turns on the set Henry keeps in the kitchen, and Radio 3 fills the room. At first she hardly hears the music; she's simply aware of people singing. And then there's just one man singing, and singing something she has heard before, heard recently. A lilting love song of a melody, designed to entice a woman to bed: *Deh! Vieni alla finestra, o mio tesoro.*

Landon's career is blossoming just now, and he's often on the radio. It's more of a surprise that she should be listening than that he should be singing, but even so the coincidence clutches her tight. She sits perfectly still until the aria finishes, and at the end of it several things set themselves out quite clearly in her mind.

It isn't quite true that she has always been in love with Landon, but it could have been.

She can't keep this baby as a reminder of him, but thinking of love seems to light a fire inside her, something vastly more powerful than she felt before Lou was born. Perhaps that's because she knows better, now, what's coming, but whatever the reason, she knows for certain that she will keep the baby, and that its conception wasn't inauspicious but an extraordinary felicity.

And if she needs a reason to allow Henry the pleasure of fatherhood again, then let it be in recompense for the circumstances that led to it.

45

They had hardly got into the kitchen before Flora stopped, her hand on the edge of the table. For a moment Kitty wondered whether she had mistaken her mother's intentions – perhaps after all she had meant to go to bed? – but then Flora began to speak, with the same uncharacteristic surge of words that had caught Kitty's attention a few moments before.

'My darling,' she said. 'There's something I need to tell you. Something about your father.'

Kitty's heart leapt with fear and relief. So Flora knew, she thought. Questions rushed at her, tripping each other up. How long had she known? Did she realise it was Daniel?

'If it's to do with –' she began.

'The thing is,' Flora said, 'that he's not your father. I'm so sorry: it's a terrible thing to spring on you.'

Kitty stared at her: the words didn't seem to make sense.

'Who's not my father?'

'Henry,' said Flora. Her face had dissolved, all its strong lines blurred. 'At least – he was in every respect except . . .'

There was silence then, complete silence except for a cascade of semiquavers in Kitty's head.

'Who is, then?' Kitty asked. 'Who is my father?'

'Landon,' said Flora. 'It was . . .'

'Landon?' said Kitty. '*Landon?*'

The semiquavers had halted on an agonising suspension that drew itself out and out and wouldn't resolve. For the moment Kitty couldn't look at Flora. It was odd how at moments like this, when your mind ought to be filled with one thing to the exclusion of everything else, it distracted itself with incidentals. Not just the discord ringing in her ears, but the flickering of the ceiling light and the sweet, astringent scent of the rhubarb stalks on the table. Anything to avoid taking in what her mother was saying.

'I'm sorry, Kitty,' Flora said. 'This isn't the way to tell you. I'm sorry to have . . . to have . . .'

Kitty could feel her mother's eyes on her, waiting for a response. She cast about for a part of her brain that would commit to rational dialogue.

'Did Henry know?' she asked, at length.

'No,' said Flora. 'At least – he had no reason to suspect.' She took a deep breath, a shuddering sort of sigh. 'He loved you so much,' she said. 'I couldn't have . . . Was that very wrong of me?'

Kitty didn't answer. The rationality she had summoned a few moments before had retreated again.

'I thought and thought about it,' Flora said. 'I couldn't do it in anger. And then when he was ill, when he was dying . . . I couldn't tell you without telling him, Kitty. You do see that?'

'Does Landon know?' Kitty asked.

'I've never told him,' Flora said. 'And he's never asked.'

She was still looking at Kitty, fearful, beseeching. Between them they were bungling this horribly, Kitty thought. The insoluble cadence was fading at last and in its wake she could hear a swirl of words, but none of them seemed to belong to her: they were simply offering their services, proposing themselves as fitting to the occasion. The trouble was, she knew more than Flora after all, and she couldn't, absolutely couldn't reveal her part of it now. But it meant – it was like a prism, diffracting what Flora had told her into two separate beams. Henry wasn't her father, and so Daniel wasn't her brother. Kitty could see the two pinpoints of light they made, but she couldn't say, just yet, what they signified. She couldn't seem to feel anything at all.

'It wasn't an affair,' Flora was saying. 'It was just . . .' She looked dismayed again, as though she'd realised this wasn't the right thing to say; that there was no right thing she could say.

And then, quite suddenly, Kitty couldn't bear any more. Flora's hand reached towards her, but before her mother could touch her she pulled herself away and turned tail up the stairs.

46

Lou knocked very quietly on Kitty's door, then pushed it open.

'Kitty?' she whispered.

There was no answer. Lou tiptoed to the bed and tweaked back the covers, but Kitty wasn't there. Strange. She hesitated for a second, then crossed the landing to her own room.

'Kitty?'

This time she saw a movement under the sheet. Shutting the door quietly behind her, she crossed the room and sat down beside the curled form of her sister.

'Darling girl,' she said, 'are you OK?'

Kitty didn't respond. After a moment Lou lay down. This must have been what Kitty intended, she thought. She must have wanted to make sure Lou would find her.

'Mum filled me in,' Lou said. 'Quite a shock.'

Kitty said nothing, but she moved her legs to make room for Lou. There were no insects chanting tonight, and no rain or wind anymore, just the occasional sighing creaks of the house and the whiff of wood smoke drifting up through the floorboards.

Lou remembered then what this reminded her of – what it was supposed to remind her of, perhaps. Or had Kitty forgotten?

Kitty must have been eight, and Lou, at seventeen, had been in love for the first time – not with someone who loved her back in quite the same way, but even so the joy and immensity of it had been more than she could keep to herself. One night, when their parents were out and she and Kitty were watching a film together, she'd poured it all out in an ad break: how she was in love with a girl at school; how Kitty must have wondered why she'd never had a boyfriend. Kitty had listened – old enough to understand, Lou had assumed, and perhaps even to have guessed. But when the film started again, Kitty had got up without a word and left the room.

Lou had been devastated. She'd sat through the rest of the film alone, numb with disappointment. Then she'd gone up to her room and found Kitty curled up in her bed, fast asleep.

Lou smiled. Dear Kitty, who'd always had a way of retreating inside herself like a hedgehog at difficult moments, leaving you with no idea what she was thinking.

And, just like last time, Kitty who had discovered that there was a difference between her and her sister.

'Kits?' Lou whispered again. 'Talk to me. Say something.'

'We don't have to tell Flora now, do we?' Kitty said. 'About Daniel?'

That wasn't what Lou had expected – but of course, she thought. Of course that was where Kitty's thoughts would go first. 'We don't have to decide just now,' she said. 'But you should talk to her, Kitty.'

Kitty rolled slightly towards her.

'She should have told us,' she said.

Us. In the dark, Lou smiled. 'You can see why she didn't. I think she was probably right.'

'Easy for you to say,' said Kitty. Lou squeezed her hand. After a moment Kitty said, 'She never told Henry.'

'No. And that's why she didn't tell us. She said nothing, all this time, for Henry's sake.'

'Or because she didn't want to admit about Landon.'

'I'm sure that wasn't –' Lou hesitated. Flora's revelation dangled before her like a child's mobile, turning slowly to expose different sides of itself. A geometric model with a person at each vertex, a new insight from each angle: Henry-Flora-Landon-Kitty-Daniel-Henry. And Lou, suspended somewhere in the middle. Her hand moved instinctively to her belly, cradling the mound that rested between her hip bones. My child won't know her father, she thought. Who was Kitty to complain about having two?

'I wish I'd known sooner,' Kitty said. 'Before –'

'I know,' Lou said.

Kitty pulled the covers tighter around her. 'I'm so tired,' she said. 'I can't think anymore.'

Lou stroked a strand of hair back from her cheek. 'Do you want to sleep here again?'

'Do you mind?'

'Of course not. But I'm not sure I can . . .'

'You can have my room,' Kitty said. 'I love you, Lou. I'm glad I've got you.'

'Promise you'll talk to Mum,' Lou said.

'I will.'

'Promise you'll tell her it's OK.'

'Yes, yes.'

When she had shut the door behind her, Lou stood for a moment on the landing.

It was Kitty, not her, who had suffered a shock this evening. But – what? Lou shook her head. There was a terrible irony in the fact that she was Henry's real daughter, not Kitty, whom he'd always loved so dearly – and who had loved him more than Lou had, too. But Kitty's opinion of Henry had been severely rocked by Martin Carver's revelation. The fairytale appearance of a long-lost father might be a saving grace for her, once she'd got over the shock of it: Lou couldn't begrudge her that. And surely it wouldn't change anything between them. No, there was nothing to regret or to resent. Just an emptiness, left behind now the excitements of the day had subsided. Just the old uncertainty, the sense of not quite fitting in, the loneliness.

God, but she missed Alice. It felt, standing there in the darkness with the stairs sweeping steeply down in front of her, as though she hadn't felt that loss fully until now, that burning absence. She could understand how people had come up with the notion of self-immolation; how misery and despair could feel strong enough to consume you.

She didn't care what it took, what terms she'd have to accept, what compromises: she just wanted Alice back. She would even – a shudder of disbelief here, but it was true, she would swear it was true – she would even give up the baby for Alice. There – that must make her an unnatural mother. But she'd been complete before, they'd been complete, and she never would be again without Alice. Let the mobile twirl, catching the light with its tantalising glints from the past and the future: what mattered to Lou was thousands of miles away.

47

'Well,' Landon said.

He didn't come any closer; that was a relief. Flora was trembling, but she couldn't bear to be consoled, least of all by Landon.

'Kitty?' he said. 'Do I understand that Kitty . . .?'

'Quite a return on a single night,' said Flora.

Landon said nothing. He looked grave, and not entirely benign, although she thought he meant to be kind.

'I'm sorry,' Flora said.

'Don't be.'

'I could have told you years ago. Henry didn't deserve her.'

'But you deserved what she brought. I understand that. You didn't have to say anything now; I'm grateful that you did. That you have.'

That speech, Flora felt, was certainly more than she deserved. She longed to sit down, but she couldn't bring herself to do that.

'I know it raises problems for you,' she said. 'And I know it's not a fair indication of your fidelity – any more than it is of mine, for the record.'

'Rosanna doesn't need to know,' Landon said. 'She has a very confined orbit.'

Registering the expression on his face, Flora felt an old ache: the pain of wondering whether his loyalty and devotion might have been dedicated to her instead. But there was another kind of pain, too. Telling him about Kitty might look, in a certain light, like a last-ditch attempt to prise Landon away from his wife, but she could see now that it would have quite the opposite effect. It might not have crossed her mind that she wished it were otherwise, but it was clear to her at this moment that, by laying her cards on the table, she was giving up her last hold on him.

Flora gripped the back of a chair, desperate to quell the shaking that was spreading through her. Possibility, she thought. That was what she'd survived on, all these years: playing hide and seek with possibility. Juggling it so skilfully that it felt all the time as though everything, anything, was within her grasp. Even after Henry died and her work was gone she'd allowed herself to believe that the world still had things to offer her. The summer had been deceptive in that respect: Fate had strung her along for a few months more. She felt as if the very last ball had fallen at her feet this evening.

Landon was looking at her with a different expression now, his long neck raised.

'Is there, by any chance,' he asked, 'some whisky in this house?'

'There's some cognac.' Flora noted with relief that her voice sounded almost normal.

'Cognac it is,' said Landon. 'Lead me to it.'

At the bottom of the stairs Flora hesitated, glancing upwards. Her maternal instincts were entirely out of their depth tonight. She didn't look at Landon. God forbid that he should think she expected his advice about Kitty – that she expected anything of him.

'Did you know?' she asked, as she took the bottle out of the cupboard. She didn't want to see his face when he answered that question; not until he'd had time to compose it.

'I wondered,' he admitted. 'I knew Henry – he told me you'd both wanted another baby. One night, in our cups. He told me it seemed to be his problem. And of course a glance at the calendar . . .'

'I see.' Astonishing that he could be so calm about it, a man who had never had a child.

Landon had found glasses; he poured them each a generous measure.

'We should have given you some of this earlier,' he said. 'An ideal treatment for near-drowning.'

Flora managed a smile. Why should she be angry, she wondered, that Landon had suspected he was Kitty's father but never troubled to confirm it, even after Henry was dead – even during these last few days, when there had been opportunity enough? Because she'd thought she was giving him something precious, and all that time he hadn't cared enough to ask for it. She turned away, clasping the cognac glass tightly.

'Flora,' Landon said, putting a hand on her elbow. 'I had no right to ask. You were married; Henry adored her. You seemed to find a kind of equilibrium, after she was born. I could enjoy Kitty at a distance. I could wonder. People do that, you know: they savour quite small things, hopes and possibilities they don't expect to see fulfilled.'

'You don't need to tell me about hopes and possibilities,' Flora said, her voice brittle now.

'I know. That's why I thought you'd understand.'

Flora took a deep breath, a sigh that started right down in the pit of her. 'I'm not very good at understanding,' she said. 'Haven't you noticed? It's not one of the things I can do.'

'What utter rubbish,' he said. 'Come here. For Heaven's sakes, don't let's argue.'

Flora wasn't sure what kind of comfort he was offering, but she held herself very still now, the kind of stillness that signifies resistance rather than acquiescence. Part of her wanted very badly to accept whatever he might give, but pride and perversity prevented her. And so much the better, she thought. She could see now that it wasn't a moral question she faced so much as a practical one; that the safe way forward would require great care and effort.

'I'm exhausted,' she said. 'I think I'll take my glass up to bed.'

48

Kitty must have slept after Lou left; certainly the room was colder when she opened her eyes again. Two or three shafts of moonlight pierced the gap between the curtains and played over the dark shapes of furniture and panelling, creating an inverted image of the daytime world. Kitty lay very still, letting her thoughts arrange themselves. Flora's news had thrown so many things into a different perspective: the implications of it rippled through her mind again now, throwing up fresh insights, fresh complications.

She had been loved by Henry, she was quite sure of that, and she had loved him back. But their relationship had never been as straight-forward as it looked. Ever since she'd begun to understand how things worked in her family, a little part of Kitty had hated herself for loving him so much – but even worse, lurking deep in the well of her con-science all those years, was the shameful knowledge that she couldn't love Henry as wholeheartedly and as unquestioningly as a daughter ought. Her childish devotion, she realised now, had been both exces-sive and insufficient, and there had been no way to bridge the gap between those equally perilous shores; no way to reconcile her to the insoluble compromises on which her life was built.

The strange thing was that this evening's discovery made all this easier, rather than harder, to bear. Shrouded in shadow, Kitty consid-ered this: another surprising fact. If Henry wasn't her father, then she owed him no more and no less than he'd earned. There was no guilt in loving someone who had loved and cared for her; no shame in not loving unreservedly someone who had caused her such distress. She needn't reproach herself for being incapable of giving more, nor Henry for not deserving more.

She shut her eyes as this insight settled into her brain. It couldn't be quite that easy, she knew. Things would look different in the morning.

But however hard she urged caution on herself it was hard to resist the idea that love needn't be as difficult as it had always seemed. And as for Daniel: did anything else matter, now, except her own feelings? If they loved each other, what difference did it make that she had been brought up believing Daniel's father to be hers? Surely her old misgivings amounted to no more than a perverse reluctance to accept what Daniel had been offering all along: to accept love.

Among the jumble of debate and justification something became clear to Kitty, and it was that she wanted Daniel here – that she could face the aftermath of today better with him beside her, and that there was no reason, now, to keep him away. She rolled over, suddenly impatient to call him, to tell him they were reprieved, to summon him to Les Violettes.

But then she stopped. In her head she could see Flora's face, contorted with anxiety. She thought about what Flora had carried with her all these years, and about what her silence had cost her. Lou was right, she thought. Lou was always right. Climbing out of bed, she padded down the stairs to find her mother.

July 2007

'My darling,' Flora says; and then she stops.

Kitty's eyes flick up to her face, but Flora can't tell whether they reveal curiosity, or anxiety, or impatience. Quite possibly none of these, she thinks. Kitty, at fifteen, is mysterious to her mother; an oddly indeterminate creature. It's as though the golden child has simply grown, without the addition of any new ingredient, into a form that doesn't suit her quite so well. She's not a difficult adolescent, unless a lack of interests or ambition counts as a difficulty, but she rarely speaks unless spoken to first, and smiles less often than she used to.

'My darling,' Flora begins again, 'I'm afraid I have some bad news for you.'

She has Kitty's attention now, and she regrets instantly the dispassionate assessment she made of her daughter a moment before. Kitty's face is all sweet concern: she even reaches a hand across the table to touch her mother's arm.

'Not me,' Flora says, and something else flashes across Kitty's face; something Flora hopes is relief. 'It's Daddy. I'm afraid he's got cancer.'

'Cancer?' This isn't what Kitty was expecting. The child of such a tempestuous marriage must always, Flora thinks guiltily, be expecting another kind of bad news. 'What kind of cancer?'

'An unusual kind,' Flora says, 'at least for men.' She hesitates. She wants to get this bit right, neither to underplay nor to overplay the stigma. 'He has breast cancer,' she says. 'It's rare in men, but not unknown – closer to one in a thousand than one in ten.'

Kitty takes her hand away from Flora – gently – and starts picking at the drips of wax on the wooden candlestick between them.

'How bad is it?' she asks.

Flora hopes it was right to have this conversation here. Perhaps it would have been easier at home, she thinks, than in a café. She chose this place with Kitty's comfort in mind rather than her own: the walls are a rather startling shade of blue and music pulses from a speaker a few feet away. At the next table there is a couple not much older than Kitty with a dozen piercings between them, in places that make Flora wince.

'Well,' she says, 'the thing is that it wasn't diagnosed as early as – often, you see, with men, they notice the lump sooner than women, because there's less tissue to conceal it.' She stops again. 'But then they're not looking for it, of course. They don't generally know it's something they can get.'

If the obvious question occurs to Kitty she doesn't ask it, and Flora is profoundly relieved. She hasn't, yet, come to terms with her own guilt on that score. Even if she can hardly be blamed for the fact that she didn't see Henry naked for more than two years after that night when he first mentioned the lump, neither her professional pride nor her conscience can forgive her for missing a critical diagnosis.

'So . . .' Kitty looks at her. 'Is it bad, then?'

'It's too early to say. He's having an operation this week, and we'll know more after that. Whether it's spread. But yes, it's serious. You can be sure, though – he's got a very good surgeon, an excellent team. The advances in female breast cancer apply to men too. There are several different kinds of treatment he can have.'

Kitty says nothing for a moment. Flora hopes she's explained things properly, in a way Kitty can understand. Too much detail, perhaps. Covering up the horror of it in a bustle of medical procedure.

'I'm very sorry, Kitty,' she says. 'It's a shock, I know.'

She can see Kitty gearing herself up to ask something, and she waits for her to say, *is he going to die?*

'Didn't he want to tell me?' Kitty asks.

There's no accusation in her tone, but even so Flora feels something deflate inside her. It was her suggestion; she who thought it would be better this way. *I'll tell her,* she said. *I'm used to talking to relatives.* Henry smiled, and said, *and you're her mother,* and she felt wrong-footed, just as she does now. A thought surfaces for a moment and registers in her mind before she can bury it again: cancer will give Henry an advantage with the children. And then she feels a flood of remorse, and she takes Kitty's hand, enclosing it in both of hers. Henry has been a good father in almost every respect. He has made it possible for Flora to do what she has done. She owes it to him to present a united front now.

'We thought it might be easier for you,' she says. 'Daddy and I discussed it, and we thought – but you can talk to him about it, of course you can. And there are other people you can speak to, if you want. Professional people.'

Kitty looks at her.

'But you're a professional person,' she says. 'You can explain things.'

'Yes, of course.' Flora is deeply touched. 'Of course I can, darling.'

There's a moment, then, when she feels that other things could be said, but she hesitates too long and suddenly the waiter is there beside them.

'Tuna salad,' he says, 'and lentil omelette.'

Flora can't recall what she ordered, but she's sure it wasn't this, which must be the least appealing item on that peculiar menu. The omelette is damp and pallid, and from between its folds oozes a greyish mass of lentils. Kitty looks at it too, and she makes a snorting sound that Flora recognises as laughter.

'Share mine,' she says. 'That looks disgusting.'

'I thought this was a place you liked,' Flora says. 'Did I get that wrong?'

'They do good cakes.' Kitty spears a chunk of tuna and holds it out to Flora. It, too, looks greyish. 'We could always just eat cake instead.'

'Why not,' says Flora. 'Throw caution to the winds.'

She feels a little dizzy now. Perhaps everything looks simpler from Kitty's point of view than hers. Perhaps it's parents who complicate matters with adolescents. It occurs to her that lurking somewhere in the shadows is a different conversation they could have had: if she turns her head a little, she might be able to see another Flora and another Kitty, sprung from the confines of their habitual manner of dealing with each other.

'It's awful about Dad,' Kitty says, and Flora can see she intends more than the words suggest. They don't have enough common language, she thinks, for Kitty to say what she really means, but at least Kitty can say something. At least she has understood.

'He's going to have a grim time, I guess,' Kitty says then, and she looks at her mother straight on.

'We all are.' The sound of that pleases Flora, the sense of them facing something together, as a family. Another insight: that good can come out of bad things. Although not often, her experience tells her. Not very often, in the long run.

49

Flora was still wide awake, despite the exhaustion that seemed to permeate deep into her bone marrow. Her brain churned, fuelled by brandy and electricity and the pent-up suspense of twenty-three years. It would keep up its restless enquiry with or without her volition, she realised, so she might as well direct it; might as well make some use of it.

What mattered most was how Kitty came out of all this, and she really couldn't tell how Kitty had taken the news. She remembered Lou's words: *It's a lot for her to take in. It's more than you realise.* It seemed to Flora that there was more for her to take in, too, than she'd dreamed of. Had she done the right thing? Would she, after all, have been better to say nothing?

She'd been famous, as a surgeon, for her decisiveness, but decisiveness wasn't the same as the ability to think through difficult issues. As in this case, surgical decisions had most often been black or white – to operate, or not to operate? – knowing that one option was reversible, and the other was not. The decision to operate was rarely criticised, at least to your face, because it was what surgeons did; and the decision not to operate, once you were too senior to be suspected of cowardice, was clothed in an almost zen-like aura of restraint. The whole business, it seemed to her now, had been designed to encourage action based on whim, dressed up as professional instinct, rather than rational analysis.

But surgery wasn't the point here, Flora reminded herself. As her mind clicked back to this evening, to her daughters, it struck her quite suddenly that she might have kept her family together, all these years, only for it to be broken apart now Henry was dead.

A whirlpool was spinning in her head now, whisking her off to a realm of unhappy sleep where accusations and betrayals loomed out of the shadows at every corner. Her heart was still beating furiously, but she was too tired to stay awake any longer; her mind was already slipping and sliding between fact and speculation, between the present and the past.

The next thing Flora was aware of – whether after seconds or hours she couldn't have said – was a knock at the door, and the squeak of a hinge.

'Hello?' she called, in a half-whisper. 'Who's that?'

'It's me.'

Kitty's voice. Flora pushed herself up on one elbow.

'Come in,' she said. 'I'm awake.'

The door squeaked again, the strip of light down the side of it widening and then narrowing again as Kitty shut it behind her.

'Hi,' she said.

'Hello.' Flora moved to the side of the bed to make room for her daughter, but Kitty sat down at the far end, right on the edge. Flora felt a pulse of – not quite disappointment, more a registering of signs; a blip on the monitor.

'So I thought we should talk,' Kitty said.

'Yes.'

'It's OK,' Kitty said next, her voice so bland – like a recorded message, Flora thought – that it was impossible to impute any meaning to the words.

'Is it?'

'It's fine. I'm fine.'

Flora nodded slowly. God, I hope that's not all, she thought. I hope we can go a little further.

'I mean,' Kitty went on after a moment, sounding not so much reluctant as uncertain, as though she were constructing a sentence from unfamiliar blocks of code, 'I mean, it's a shock, of course, but it's not . . . I needed to know.'

'Darling,' Flora said. 'My darling, I'm so sorry. I just don't know when the right time would have been to tell you.'

'Now was the right time,' Kitty said. She moved, quite suddenly, to nestle against her mother. 'I don't think you waited until Henry was dead so you could have the last laugh. I know you didn't want to hurt him.'

Flora put her arms around Kitty. 'Don't be too generous to me. I'm afraid it was mostly cowardice.'

Was that right, though? Hadn't there been times when she'd longed to say something? When the burden of secrecy had been almost more than she could bear?

'Henry had me for his whole life,' Kitty said. Her voice sounded small, and Flora's heart swelled with the sound of it. 'I loved him. But it's right to tell us now. It's . . .'

A little shudder went through her then. Flora waited for her to go on, but the silence stretched out – five seconds, ten, twenty. She felt sure there was something else, something more Kitty wanted or needed to say, but as time passed she began to think she must be wrong. She lifted her hand hesitantly to Kitty's hair, the texture of it so familiar against her fingertips, and shut her eyes. Perhaps, she thought, they could drift off to sleep like this, propped against the pillows, with Kitty's head resting on her shoulder. What bliss that would be: what a throwback to simpler times.

'I've always thought you liked Landon,' she said. 'When he came to the house, when you were a little girl.'

'I really can't think about that now,' Kitty said. 'There's too much else to . . .'

She laid her hand on Flora's, and Flora was reminded of the game they used to play sometimes when Kitty was little: piling one hand on top of another, faster and faster, until you almost couldn't tell whose hand was whose. The two of you tangled together, muddled up.

'My darling,' she said, 'I love you so much.'

Kitty's face wavered. 'I love you too, Mum,' she said. And if there was, in that moment, a glimmer of all the things that had not been said,

Flora thought, it didn't matter. This was good enough, the place they had reached, and she was more grateful than she could say.

And then – in a blink, or so it seemed – Kitty was asleep. And far from being in the embrace of motherly bliss, Flora found herself propped awkwardly against the end of the bed, neither sitting nor lying, with Kitty's head wedged in the angle of her neck. It was a horribly uncomfortable position, but Flora wouldn't have dreamed of moving. She couldn't risk waking Kitty; couldn't bear her to leave.

This was how it was as a parent, she thought. You had to savour what you could, whenever you could, and whatever the price – especially if you were there so little. The story of motherhood had been, for her, one of opportunities slipping past: occasions she'd arrived late for, or missed altogether; occasions spoiled by Henry, or when she'd been too tired or too distracted to enjoy her daughters' company. How could she have known how fast the years would pass, and how different her perspective would be at the end of them? She wished she could grasp at just a few of those vanishing threads of memory and make something different of them. How wonderful it would be to find herself back on the landing at Orchards with Lou appearing, tousle-headed, from her bed, or to leave the last case on the list to her Registrar and get home while it was still light and Kitty was playing in the garden.

And then she thought of Landon, whose whole experience of fatherhood had been stolen from him – or rather, perhaps, consciously relinquished. How had he been able to bear that, Flora wondered? Had he not felt the irresistible lure of his connection to Kitty? What kind of person did it make him if he could say nothing, do nothing for twenty years while Kitty grew up as Henry's daughter?

Landon had always been a mystery, she thought; but assembling her memories of him now as she lay awake, pins and needles radiating up her arm and across her shoulders, she understood that he was a man whose pleasures were so tightly rationed that it was almost never possible to detect any lack of fulfilment, let alone any regret. Once or

twice – on one or two obvious occasions she had seen him untram-
melled, and even then . . . She felt a shiver of something hot and cold
run through her. Did he exist, she wondered, on a knife-edge of control, or had he learned to sublimate his desires and disappointments so
thoroughly that they rarely troubled him? Did she pity him – or was
it altogether less straightforward than that? Just at this moment, she
could almost feel that she despised him. She felt a terrible pang then,
lying with the child he'd so loved curled in her arms, for Henry, who
had never suppressed anything in his life.

50

The sun was edging around the curtains when Flora woke, and she had a terrible headache. A thumping pain just like a hangover – and the analogy seemed apt, given the extraordinary recollections that pressed in on her consciousness as she lay, taking stock of her situation.

Item one: Kitty, lying crammed into the bed beside her. Kitty whom Flora had finally told – had she? – the secret she'd kept since before she was born, and who had come creeping downstairs in the middle of the night – had she? – to make her peace with her mother. Could all that be true? Certainly here she was, fast asleep, looking more like her five-year-old self than Flora would have believed possible, her hair wildly tangled and her skin sweetly flushed.

Item two: Lou, sitting at the piano last night for the first time in years, her face as rapt as her father's had been when he played. Lou weeping piteously in the garden because Alice had flown to her mother's bedside, and Lou couldn't live without her. That was a pain subtly different from any Flora had ever known, and she felt a shard of envy pricking at the soft flesh of maternal concern.

Item three: Flora herself, drenched and chilled and not a little afraid, fighting her way along an overgrown path while lightning jagged through the branches of the trees above her, then stuttering her way through an explanation as she was driven homewards through the storm-wracked countryside to a supper steeped in suspense and misapprehension.

Item four: item four Flora wasn't sure she wanted to catalogue, just now. Item four was altogether less amenable to scrutiny and interpretation, better folded away again and stuffed in the back of a drawer. Instead she began the slow, painful process of removing limbs set hard as concrete from beneath the slumbering form of her daughter. It was seven thirty: everyone else, she imagined, would sleep for hours yet.

She could bathe and dress and assemble her thoughts at leisure, a luxury which seemed, just now, both the greatest of felicities and the least she deserved.

There was still a faint smell of smoke and dampness downstairs, and the remains of supper sat where they had been left on the dining room table. On the threshold of the kitchen Flora stopped abruptly, her heart racing at the shadow of a movement in the room. A ghost, she thought, wildly. Martin's ghost, or Martin himself, just as she had met him that morning aeons ago, holding out a plate of croissants. Or no one: just a movement of air. On the far side of the room the French window stood ajar, reminding Flora that she'd forgotten to lock up last night. Her mind's eye trailed outside, wondering how the garden had fared in the storm, imagining it sullen and bedraggled this morning. A marathon of dead-heading and tidying awaited, she thought. And there would have to be an expedition to the shop. They had eaten the last tin and crust in the house last night.

An image of the next few days fell into her mind then: two or three careful, well-ordered days of activities spun into neat skeins, with elements of her old St Rémy life augmented by outings to the market in Champigny or the troglodyte caves further west; by reading in the garden and judiciously regulated conversation. Two or three evenings of more elaborate cooking than any of them really had the appetite – or indeed the skill – for, washed down with as much camaraderie as they could manage. There would not, she knew, be the kind of conversations other people might have in these circumstances. Could she bear it? Could she stand the dissembling cheerfulness, the studied disregard of subterranean currents of feeling, the surreptitious dread of saying something unguarded?

Henry would have been amused by the situation, she thought – not the matter of Kitty's paternity, of course, but it was possible, conjuring the dead in one's head, to allow for certain things to be overlooked.

No, Henry would have been entertained by the notion of the four of them circling each other, drawing together and apart, watching each other's steps. He would have had the name of some sixteenth-century courtly dance at his fingertips; a witty analogy. The thought of Henry was strangely consoling, even the wrench of grief a matter of certainty and familiarity. It made Flora feel she had something small and intangible, something unnameable, to congratulate herself for.

And then, putting a hand to the kettle, she found it hot, undoubtedly recently boiled, and her heart crashed again. It could be Lou, of course, who had made a cup of tea and taken it out through the open door, but . . .

Item four, she thought. Item four not consenting to stay hidden away in a drawer at the back of her mind after all. That elegant neck, its upper reaches left smoothly vulnerable by the pressure of the razor; that long face and Modigliani features, dark and shapely and striving for geniality. That habit of surprising her sometimes with his capacity, sometimes with his failure, to do the right thing. A man too familiar for her to have seen him properly for years.

For a few moments she stood absolutely still, letting realisation filter through to the furthest reaches of her mind and her body, to settle in her hypothalamus and dance on the nerve ends of her fingertips. No rationalising this time; no riders or defences or special pleading, but a straight line of history that began long ago with tree climbing and dinosaur bones and his amused adolescent face hearing her out as she put her case in whatever argument absorbed them that day; that trailed unswervingly through her indifference to his music and his faithful attendance at her mother's parties to his tall figure beside Henry in the church as she advanced up the aisle, and a snatch of Mozart in the middle of the night in her mother's bleak, dead house. And then sitting in her garden, just a few days ago: *for years I thought you were in love with me*, she'd said, and he had replied *I was, in a way*. She shut her eyes, remembering now not just the night that had followed that conversation, but that other night two decades ago. The one she could see, now, had altered the course of her life.

Oh God, she thought. Was this the plain and terrible truth? Was her heart's fulfilment standing out in the wet garden beyond that door, contemplating the hours, the days, the years ahead? And how did he see them? What did he hope for, beneath the tight leash of self-restraint?

Landon was standing at the far end of the garden with his back to the house, examining something in the flowerbed that ran along the back wall. For several moments Flora stood on the terrace, taking in his presence; his outline against the dull yellow of wet stone. It was no use pretending that she could walk away now. She was halfway across the garden when he turned, and then she felt sure he had known all along that she was there – that he had counted out the seconds while she stood by the door and gathered her resolve.

'You've lost some stones here,' he said, as she approached.

'What?'

'Some stones have gone from the wall.' He turned towards her. 'Given way in the storm.'

'The wall?' Flora's heart constricted, shrinking in on itself like a sea anemone. But this was the moment for courage, she told herself. This was one of those moments when life could change if you willed it hard enough.

'Landon,' she said. 'I need to talk to you. There's something I need to say.'

Landon looked at her for a moment, his head poised, and then he turned away again and pointed at the place where the top of the wall had crumbled.

'Do you have a handyman?' he asked. 'I feel sure your excellent host would wish you to do something about the damage.'

Flora shook her head. She couldn't care less about the wall, and she couldn't bear the casual cordiality of Landon's tone of voice. Just a trace of awkwardness would have been enough, but ... She had forgotten how glacial he could be; how ruthlessly imperturbable.

She told herself then that she'd never expected anything more than this, but she knew that wasn't true. She understood clearly now that last night's scene was supposed to have ushered in the final act of a comedy – *Twelfth Night,* perhaps – in which the revelation of mistaken identity and unsuspected parentage leads inevitably to joyful reconciliations and pairings off. Deep down – somewhere below the layers of justification and self-deception she had laid down over the years – she had believed that the old order would be thrown over and they would all begin anew. That other ending she had contemplated earlier, the spinning of skeins and the courtly dance: that was something from another story entirely; from the version in which her courage had failed and she had allowed the secret to sink back inside her. This – a calm inspection of the wall, an implicit message that nothing had changed between them – this wasn't at all how things were meant to be now.

But perhaps it was just a matter of perseverance. Perhaps she had to make things clearer. She took a deep breath and tried again.

'Please,' she said, 'stop talking about the wall for a moment. Please could we . . .'

Landon met her eyes, and she was sure then that he understood her, and that she understood him; and there was nothing, nothing at all, to give her encouragement.

'My dear Flora,' he said. 'Don't put me in an impossible position. I have never . . .' He stopped: too much the gentleman to plead his own virtue, Flora thought, and another rockfall of desire and regret tumbled down inside her.

'No,' she said. 'No. I'm sorry.'

'Don't be sorry,' he said. 'Don't ever be sorry. We don't need to do that to each other.'

Flora attempted a smile, but her face wasn't under her control. 'No,' she said again – a word that required almost no effort, just the tiniest eddy of breath.

'Let me make you some coffee,' Landon said. 'It's a little chilly to be outside.'

He didn't meet her eyes again as he turned back towards the house.

PART VI

Greville Auctioneers, Friday 12th December 2014

Paintings and drawings by Nicholas Comyn, from the collection of the late Henry Jones

Lot no. 6: The Triumph of Flora, 1983

This painting falls within the long tradition of artistic representations of Flora, goddess of flowers and of fertility, whose festival, held every spring, celebrated the renewal of life. Comyn's work clearly references other examples in the canon, including those by Botticelli, Titian and Rembrandt. Several of Rembrandt's Floras represent his young wife, Saskia, who is heavily pregnant in at least one portrait. The same is true of the subject of this painting – Henry Jones' wife, Flora Macintyre.

The picture was a gift for Flora, who was indeed pregnant at the time it was painted. She did not sit for the portrait, however: instead Comyn produced a celebration of an idealised Flora, drawing both on earlier representations of the goddess and on the real-life exemplar.

The radiant figure of Flora is positioned centrally in Comyn's painting. As in the famous Botticelli portrait, her hair and flowing dress are scattered with blossom and spring flowers, reminiscent of Renaissance *millefleurs* tapestries. This Flora has none of the coyness of the 1634 Rembrandt, but she does share the serenity of both Rembrandt's and Botticelli's fecund images.

Comyn's characteristically precise technique is well suited to this subject, yielding an image full of overflowing abundance and promise. The fact that it can be supposed to be a love offering adds to its potency.

51

Lou came downstairs, a few days after the storm, to find the kitchen empty. Landon had left the day before, and she imagined that Flora had resumed her habit of walking to the village to buy bread for breakfast. Lou filled the kettle and stood leaning against the work surface while it came to the boil.

Things felt different this morning: for the first time since they'd arrived, there was no hum of apprehension in the air. The last day or two had passed smoothly enough, but that had been the result of concerted effort. The Joneses were good at riding out crises, of course, and Landon, it turned out, had just the same skills of diplomacy and – Lou allowed herself a flash of emotion here – of dissimulation.

A sound from above prompted her to cast her eyes upwards briefly, but it was nothing, just the house breathing. Certainly not Kitty stirring yet: the emotional delicacy of recent days hadn't affected Kitty's capacity for sleep. Though Kitty might, Lou thought now, wake earlier today. Daniel was arriving this afternoon. The complexities of that situation seemed to have melted away with remarkable ease: in fact, Kitty's view of her relationship with Daniel seemed altogether simpler now than it had been before the Martin-Henry-Landon drama had kicked off. Lou couldn't help wondering about the legal minutiae – might Henry be named on Daniel's birth certificate, for example? – but there would be an answer to that, if it came to it. That was what lawyers were for, finding a way through complications.

The fact that Flora hadn't yet been told about Daniel's parentage caused Lou greater unease. She'd tried to persuade Kitty that introducing Daniel to Flora on false pretences was a bad idea, but Kitty had scowled and said that prejudicing Flora against Daniel before she'd even met him was a worse idea, and Lou hadn't had the strength to argue. Meanwhile, Flora seemed pleased by the prospect of an addition to their party, and Lou had to admit that she welcomed the diversion too. The ache of Alice's absence was sharper when she had nothing else on her mind, and although she felt that bearing the pain of it was a noble thing, a sacrifice she owed to Alice, some small part of her was mindful of the need for self-preservation.

Her longing to speak to Alice was still tempered by the apprehension that she had tried to express to Flora. She couldn't risk the phone, she'd concluded. She must content herself with email, and use that as sparingly as she could endure. Yesterday morning she'd written to tell Alice about the storm and to enquire after her mother. She must wait for a reply before she wrote again – and the painful pleasure of checking her email she would store up for a little while longer. Meanwhile, she decided, perhaps she'd follow Flora to the shop. She could do with a walk.

Lou was almost out of the door when the phone rang. She hesitated. Her French wasn't up to much, but perhaps it might be Daniel, confirming arrangements. She darted back to the kitchen.

'*Bonjour?*'

'Is that – Flora?'

Lou's heart bumped. Unmistakably Alice's voice, the Midwestern lilt accentuated by nervousness.

'It's Lou,' she said.

A small silence. The things she'd wanted to say, all this time, crashed and buffeted in Lou's head.

'It's –'

'I know.' Lou clutched the phone tight. 'How's your mother?'

'Better. She's coming home today.'

'I'm very glad.'

Lou waited for Alice to say, *I'm coming home too*, but she didn't. After another hesitation Alice said, 'I've written you a letter. I need to – I don't have the address.'

This was the last thing Lou had expected, but it struck her now, with a horrible plunge, that she should have guessed it was what Alice would do. She stood very still, wondering if she dared hope the letter contained anything other than the worst kind of news.

'Please, Alice,' she said. 'That isn't fair. Read me the letter now.'

There was a tiny pause, and then Alice said, 'Don't be angry.'

'I'm not angry,' Lou said – although if she hadn't been, she knew she'd be crying by now, weeping and pleading down the phone. 'What about email? Can't you send it that way?'

'No. Not email.'

Lou bit her lip. She'd always found Alice's mistrust of email touching, her conviction that words typed into a keyboard and read on a screen were too much altered to be relied upon. She preferred pen and ink, for any serious purpose. A letter as artefact, passed from one hand to another. But surely she could see that she was drawing out the agony unnecessarily. Surely it wasn't so much a scruple as a deliberate intention to . . .

'Do you have the address?' Alice asked. 'I'll send it express; it should only take a couple of days.'

'I don't know.' What if the letter went astray, Lou thought desperately? It was a long way from Fort Dodge to St Rémy: she imagined a perilous journey in lorries and aeroplanes, the slipping of seams and carelessness of baggage handlers. But if there was no other way . . .

'Hang on a minute,' she said. There was a letter for Martin Carver lying on the table in the hall, she remembered, waiting for Flora to forward it. 'I'll get it for you.'

52

This was the first time for more than a week that Flora had walked to the village alone. Now that Landon had gone she felt easier: she'd been holding her breath these last couple of days, she thought, determined to husband her dignity. It was a relief to relinquish that effort, but this morning a pervasive sadness filled the empty space in her mind. More than sadness, perhaps, but the other words she tried out had a taint of melodrama or of crisis about them that felt wrong. This was a private and a fully comprehended sadness; the kind left behind when melodrama and crisis have passed.

As she passed the familiar landmarks she was sharply aware of their poignancy, as though they had been returned to her after a period of quarantine and in the knowledge that they wouldn't be available to her forever: the row of cypresses, the field of sunflowers across the valley – and then the turning to the Abelards' farm.

Flora hadn't seen Francine since that morning when she'd appeared with the rhubarb. The story of their friendship was a strange thing, Flora thought. For a tale of such uncertain substance it contained more than its fair share of memorable images: the gift of the jam, the loan of the raincoat, the Swiss couple, the cognac, the concert. Francine had led her both to Martin and to Landon, this summer. What was she to make of that? Flora could hardly deny Francine's kindness, but she was troubled by the suspicion that she'd been part of some plan of Francine's all along. Was that entirely fanciful?

The shop was quiet this morning. Flora bought two sticks of bread, cheered by the smiled greeting and the familiar smell of the place. The sun was full in her face when she stepped outside again, and it took her a few moments to recognise the figure coming towards her.

'Hello!' she called. 'Did you guess where I'd gone?'

'I thought it was a reasonable punt,' said Lou. 'Can I carry anything?'

Flora handed her a baguette, and they fell into step along the pavement. Flora was glad to have Lou's company, and glad, too, that the charms of St Rémy seemed very obvious this morning. She wanted to draw Lou's attention to the light, the smell, the warmth: to say *I walk this way every morning; you can see why I love it.*

'Beautiful day,' she said.

'Mmm. Pretty village.'

They passed the *Hotel de Ville* and the *Café du Centre,* with its customary clique of old men sitting outside. Some not so old, Flora thought, recognising Claude Abelard among them. Poor Francine, left to hold the fort again.

'Alice rang this morning,' Lou said, as they left the little square behind them.

Flora's mind turned instantly towards her. 'Ah. Good news?'

'Her mother's better,' Lou said, 'but – Alice isn't coming home yet.'

Flora toyed with a few phrases – *what did she say? how did she sound?* – but set them aside.

'She's written me a letter,' Lou said. 'God knows what it'll say, but I can't believe it's good news.'

'Sweetheart,' Flora said. Lou was close to tears, she realised. She put a hand through her arm.

'It's OK,' Lou said. 'At least, it's not OK, but there's nothing to say.'

'No,' said Flora.

Another silence, this one less comfortable. Flora knew she was clumsy as a provider of solace, but it seemed to her suddenly that there was in fact a great deal to say, and she wished she had the happy turn of phrase, and the courage, to say it. Some of it she too might benefit from hearing spoken aloud: streams of wisdom that coursed suddenly, unexpectedly, through her head. That love almost always comes with a catch, somewhere along the line. That it can be hard to differentiate from other, more complicated, feelings. That it certainly doesn't guarantee a life of bliss. No, she couldn't say any of that to Lou, just now.

They came round the corner to the church, its steeple rising grace-fully above the village, and Flora gripped Lou's arm with sudden zeal.

'Come with me,' she said. 'There's something we should see.'

She hadn't been sure the door would be open, but it was. Inside, the church waited in the half-dark. How strange, Flora thought, that she had walked past so often and never been in.

'What is it?' Lou asked.

'A famous painting,' Flora said. 'Thirteenth century. An Annun-ciation.'

Something for a mother and a daughter to share, she had thought.

But it wasn't an Annunciation. There was Mary, wearing an expres-sion of desperate piety, but she wasn't receiving the news of her son's conception: she was cradling his dead body in her arms. Flora felt the shock of the image thud through her, an emotional depth charge planted eight hundred years ago. The wounds on Christ's hands and feet were neat and precise, unbloodied by Romantic sensibility, the pain of his mother undimmed by the centuries – no different, Flora thought, from a twenty-first-century news report from Syria or Afghanistan.

For a few moments she and Lou stood together in silence. And then, quite unexpectedly, quite shockingly, Flora started to laugh. What had she hoped for, bringing Lou in here? Some subliminal com-munication about the inalienable bond between mother and child, or the joy and responsibility of love? Well, that was all here: the very same truth she had hoped to impart. How could the terrible sadness of it seem so funny to her? The sadness of the world; of hopes unfulfilled, years passing, life expiring.

'What?' said Lou. 'What is it?'

'It's the wrong picture,' Flora said. 'A Pietà, not an Annunciation.'

'It's very beautiful.'

Lou looked bewildered – not so much by the error, Flora thought, as by her mother's inexplicable mirth – and her bewilderment made Flora laugh all the more, convulsed now with sorrow and pity and hopelessness that only seemed able to find expression in the absurdity of the situation. She was reminded of something, but she couldn't think what. Giving birth, perhaps. The wild dissociation of gas and air. She waited for Lou to join in, or for mirth to give way to tears, but there was just her laughter, echoing through the church, and the anguish of the Virgin Mary before her. Oh, thought Flora: oh, to be able to sweep away complication and misunderstanding. Lord, but life felt arduous sometimes. Would that she could sink down on one of these ancient pews and wait for peace of mind and heart to return. Would that she could sit out the summer here, among the smell of dust and incense, and let the world sail on outside. But that wasn't how it was. There was no escaping from life.

'Never mind,' she said. 'I'm sorry. Let's go home.'

Outside, the sunshine dazzled. They walked on quietly, and after a while Flora could almost believe that she'd imagined the visit to the church – except, she thought, that she felt a little stronger than she had. Perhaps that wasn't so ignoble a response, if one didn't investigate it too closely.

'It's nice to see Kitty more cheerful,' she said.

'Yes,' said Lou.

'Tell me about Daniel. Do you like him?'

'I've only met him once.'

'I thought she'd come here to get away from him,' Flora said. 'Was I wrong about that?'

'No,' said Lou. 'Not exactly. But things have – moved on.'

'She must be keen on him if she can't bear to be separated from him any longer,' Flora persisted, ignoring the side turning there, the reference to one of the ways in which things had moved on. She must talk to Lou again about Landon, but not now. There was, she thought, already too much in play.

'She is keen on him. He's a wonderful musician, she says.'

Lou shot a glance at her, apparently registering some indelicacy in that observation. Acknowledging, perhaps, the drawbacks of wonderful musicians as potential life partners: a rather touching scruple, Flora thought. She tucked her hand through Lou's arm again as they walked the last stretch along the narrow road.

53

Daniel's travel arrangements – like so many things involving his generation – seemed to have been organised almost instantaneously. He was arriving by rail: a strange choice, Kitty kept saying, since flights were cheaper and faster, but it seemed to Flora, as the three of them stood on the platform at Châtellerault and watched the TGV sweep impressively into the station, a romantic sort of entrance to make.

'There he is!' Kitty called, as the doors opened. 'Here! Daniel, I'm here!'

Any pretence at nonchalance had evaporated, Flora thought, observing her younger daughter with a mixture of amusement and fearfulness – but it was clear from their greeting that Daniel's feelings matched hers. Stocky, curly-haired, open-faced, he held his arms wide for her to run into. Clasped together on the platform, with Kitty half-hidden in his bear hug, they looked like a couple who had been separated for years rather than days. Watching them, Flora felt a powerful tug of . . . what? Envy, she supposed. Nostalgia. Emptiness. She turned away, gathering about her a protective veil of maternal gratification. Kitty was happy: what more could she want, except equal happiness for Lou?

The mood in the car was different on the way home. Daniel's scrupulous politeness to Flora made her feel a little forlorn, because it revealed an assumption that he and Kitty – and even Lou – shared a world she could never be part of. Flora couldn't help wondering whether Kitty had told him about Landon; couldn't help, then, seeing her actions through Daniel's eyes and imagining his amused distaste at the thought of her night of passion – and it was only a short step from there to feeling ridiculous in her own eyes. This morning's hysteria in the church had left its mark, too, in a slight wariness in Lou's manner and a distracting buzz in Flora's head.

Flora kept her attention firmly on the road – the long straight stretch of the *route nationale*, sweeping past villages whose names she could connect, now, to Touraine cheeses and wines and rivers. So much of it still unexplored, she thought, but even so this countryside felt familiar, and its familiarity felt comforting. The prospect of leaving France, and particularly this corner of it, filled her with sorrow, but she couldn't stay here indefinitely. She had no idea now what she'd hoped for from this summer. It seemed to her that her only motive had been to escape from what was waiting at home – the future as well as the past – and sooner or later she must, as Jean would say, go back and face the music.

A perception of herself settled on Flora then with the clarity of a perfect diagnosis. Her brain, she thought, had run rings around her all her life. She'd always been able to talk herself into or out of anything: that had been her tragedy, as well as the source of her success. She had lived all these years on the strength of her conviction, and it had been an admirable companion, ready to bend itself to the expediency of any situation – but when it failed her, she was left without a compass. She had no idea – now, for example – whether she was making things too complicated or too simple; whither she wanted to go.

And her heart had been trained so long ago to accept second billing that it had almost lost the ability to express itself. She wasn't even sure, now, whether that surge of passion for Landon that had almost overwhelmed her just a few days ago had simply been an attempt by her brain to provide a response, a solution, to the situation in which she found herself. She could believe just as readily in the revelation that she had been in love with Landon all along, and in its opposite: that she had been carried away by the intensity of the moment and a subliminal desire to tie everything up neatly.

'You're very quiet, Mum.' Lou, sitting beside her, shot a glance at her. 'Are you OK?'

'Sorry.' Flora blinked, unsure whether the itch in her eyes was the result of emotion or the strain of staring out into the sunshine. Self-pity again, she thought. Could she not be allowed a portion of self-knowledge without the scourge of self-pity in its wake?

'Shouldn't we have turned off, back there?' Lou asked. 'I saw a sign for St Rémy.'

'Oh!' Flora braked hard, and a small Fiat sounded its horn furiously before sweeping past her, the driver exclaiming expressively with his right arm.

'I might be wrong,' Lou said. 'You know these roads much better than me.'

'I wasn't concentrating,' Flora said. 'I'm sorry.'

For a moment she sat, the car stationary and her passengers silent. Had they driven along this bit of road earlier? Impossible to say. She was conscious of Daniel sitting behind her; of three pairs of eyes watching her. The road was too narrow for a three-point turn, anyway. She slid the car crossly back into gear.

'Never mind,' said Kitty, 'it's good to get lost now and then.'

The words were kindly meant, Flora knew, but it added to her humiliation that they should feel she needed reassurance. She squinted into the sun as the road unfolded in front of them, gripping the steering wheel hard. Someone's stupid mother, she thought, who can't even find her way home. God Almighty, what had she come to?

At last, out of the glare, some buildings loomed up.

'*Voilà!*' said Kitty. 'Look, we can turn there, in the garage.'

Too tense to feel relieved, Flora pulled off the road and swung the car round. This time, the miles seemed to pass at twice the speed, and almost before she'd started looking for it the sign to St Rémy appeared. She flicked on her indicator at once, to show that she'd seen it. The D road rose invitingly over a bridge, some tributary of the Vienne or the Indre dawdling beneath it, then turned east along the riverbank.

As they wound their way through the chain of villages that led back to Les Violettes, conversation in the car gradually became easier. By the time they reached St Rémy, Flora could almost feel a shred of amusement at her flusterment.

'Can you drop us in the village?' Kitty asked. 'We could walk the last bit.'

Flora bestowed her best maternal smile as Kitty and Daniel climbed out of the car. 'There's a pretty walk along the river,' she said. 'Over the bridge down there and turn left.'

Kitty smiled too, a flash of gaiety that barely concealed her impatience to be alone with Daniel. 'See you later, Mum. Thanks for the lift.'

Lou was silent as they drove off again.

'All right?' Flora asked.

'Mmm.'

Flora glanced at her. 'Hard for you, seeing Kitty with Daniel,' she said.

Lou made a little movement that was part-grimace, part-shrug. Then she said, 'I've been wondering, Ma. Something you said – are you thinking about going back to Orchards? I mean, imminently?'

'Possibly,' said Flora. 'Why?'

'I was thinking – perhaps I could come and stay for a while. I mean, if Alice isn't . . . that would be nice, wouldn't it? For you too?'

'It would be lovely,' said Flora. 'Oh, Lou, it would be absolutely lovely.'

They were passing the water tower that stood sentinel over her daily walk to the shop now. She shouldn't count any chickens, Flora told herself. Alice's letter might change everything, and of course she hoped it would, for Lou's sake – but even so it seemed to her just then that perhaps she had done some things right after all, in those years of compromise and travail. Or perhaps sometimes, occasionally, life simply delivered up more than you strictly deserved.

December 2004

This is the first Christmas for twenty-five years that Flora hasn't had to beg and barter for time off. The irony isn't lost on her – nor does it fail to remind her of that earlier occasion, so many years ago now, when the luck of the on-call rota first exposed the faultline in her marriage.

Her colleagues are each covering a day or two over Christmas and New Year, and Flora has been released for the whole stretch. She's collected enough prizes and distinctions lately that no one can doubt she's earned a certain deference: even Mark Upward, a few years younger but tireless in his bid for supremacy, has been less forceful lately. And no doubt, Flora thinks, lying in bed this first morning, their chivalrous instincts are flattered by the idea of granting her a week *en famille*. No doubt they believe, assuming her unconventional marriage is an open secret in the hospital, that she will be duly grateful.

But the truth is that there is no one else in the house as Flora begins her luxuriously extended festive break. Kitty is skiing with the school, and will soon be starting the long coach journey home, and Lou is due back from university any moment. But just now Flora is alone, and more conscious of it than she expected. More conscious of Henry's absence from her bed, though she would die rather than admit it.

She is determined to be able to report that she's made the most of her leisure, staying in bed for half the morning, but although her body remains supine her mind roams restlessly through the empty rooms, intent on noticing things she's chosen to ignore all these years. The house, she thinks, contains far more evidence of Henry's occupation than of hers. Henry's books, Henry's piano, Henry's collection of LPs ranged along a whole wall of the sitting room. And of course Henry's pictures, especially the Comyns.

She has never liked the Comyns, Flora admits. It's not an aesthetic judgement – she doesn't feel qualified to make an aesthetic judgement about them. Nor is it entirely a judgement about Nick Comyn himself. Poor Nick, dead for nearly ten years already: there is nothing she can hold against him now, and even when he was alive he was always pathetically eager to appease her, pathetically self-conscious in her presence. He had no idea, presumably, that he made her self-conscious too. That isn't something people ever think about Flora, and she's always made especially sure it isn't what Henry's friends think.

On the wall opposite the bed hangs Henry's favourite picture: that hateful portrait of her, radiantly pregnant. Flora has never wanted to recognise herself in that picture, but it would be too simplistic to say that she objects to being represented as womanly and fruitful. And also too simplistic to say that she didn't like being surprised by Henry, or that she resented his triumphant pleasure in fathering a child. None of that can fully account for her feelings about the portrait.

She forces herself to look at it now, to try to pin down what it is she resents about these pictures that hang in every room of her house. Some of them – the portrait of Elizabeth playing the cello, for example – her objection to that doesn't require an explanation, but oddly enough Flora likes that painting more than some of the others nowadays, although she was livid at the time to think that Nick Comyn had met Elizabeth; that he'd been in and out of Orchards all those years, in and out of their lives, and back and forth to Henry's mistress too. No, despite all that it's so beautiful, so striking, that she can't help feeling something for the image, for the subject, even for her recidivous husband. Though the point, surely, is that the painting reminds her of that night of drama and tragedy when she felt she understood Henry properly at last, and understood what he needed from her. It reminds her of the magnanimity she felt when she realised what he'd lost – and of the calm water that followed, the long period when she believed she'd got her reward at last. It seemed to her the night Elizabeth died that they had come through something together, breached a point of no return. She believed Henry's infidelity was in the past, or at least its capacity to hurt her.

Until three weeks ago she believed that: until the night she came back triumphant from Geneva, the night of the Chassagne-Montrachet and the fateful phone call. Her defences had been weakened, she thinks. She'd stopped suspecting that anyone could come between them.

She turns away from her portrait now, although it's innocent of any part in that deception. But there's the rub, she understands: they are all deceptions, these pictures. They are versions of the truth as Comyn saw it, or as Henry imparted it. She ponders that thought for a moment, conscious of being out of her depth in this argument, but pleased by the idea of justifying her suspicion of the paintings. But then she thinks, perhaps the point is that they do tell the truth, that they hold it there in clear sight, in perpetuity, and don't allow her any room for escape.

She throws the duvet back crossly and climbs out of bed. Perhaps what she really objects to is Henry's conviction that Comyn deserves more recognition than he got: that reminder of Henry's generosity to his friends, and his impossible certainty about his own judgement.

Perhaps today she simply minds the fact that Henry has gone, and has stayed away, as she insisted after that last debacle.

She's getting dressed when she hears the gate clink open, and then a car rolling through it. Through the window she watches Lou getting out of the third-hand Golf she insisted on having, despite Henry's eagerness to buy her something flashier, racier, more glamorous for her twenty-first birthday. When Lou comes into the hall Flora is waiting at the top of the stairs, a smile on her face.

'Hello,' Lou says. 'I wasn't sure if you were here.'

'I am. First day of my holiday.'

'Good timing, then.'

'Did you get the dissertation finished?' Flora asks, as she comes down the stairs.

Lou makes a rueful face. 'No, but it's getting there. I've trawled through most of the references, at least.'

Flora can't remember what the subject of the dissertation is, and doesn't like to ask again. 'Well done,' she says. 'You must have set off early. What do you need? Coffee? Breakfast?'

'I had breakfast before I left, but I could have more, if you're . . .'

'I've been enjoying a lie-in,' Flora says, but the statement feels less satisfying than she hoped. They all know she hates staying in bed.

'Where's Dad?' Lou asks.

'New York.'

Lou nods. She has stopped in the kitchen doorway, not quite looking at Flora.

'When's he coming home?' she asks, her voice carefully modulated.

Flora sighs – a little theatrically, she's aware of that, although she's not certain what effect she hopes to achieve. 'Well,' she says, 'I'm not quite sure.'

The weather is unseasonably mild; well on the way to a record-breaking Christmas. While the bacon cooks in the oven, Flora helps Lou bring in her luggage and carry it up to her room, and they both remark on the warmth of the day.

'You wouldn't guess it's almost Christmas,' Lou says, and then she raises an eyebrow, as if to acknowledge the other resonances of that statement. There are no decorations in the house, no food in the fridge. All that falls within Henry's purview.

Flora doesn't answer, but a little later, when the last boxes have been deposited on Lou's bedroom floor, she says, 'We could go and buy a tree this afternoon. Kitty'll be back tomorrow.'

'Sure.' Lou smiles. 'That would be nice.'

'I'm sorry I didn't warn you,' Flora says. 'About Henry, I mean. About him not being here.'

'Does Kitty know?' Lou asks.

'She knows he's in New York. Working in New York for a bit. She didn't ask, before she went off skiing –' Flora breaks off. 'I don't know whether she expects him to be home for Christmas.'

'Do you?'

Flora gives a tiny shrug. 'I threw him out,' she says, although she fears this admission will make things worse in Lou's eyes.

'For good?'

'That wasn't specified.' The conversation looms up in Flora's mind, and she pushes it away. This is ignominious, she thinks. Why should she have to justify herself to her daughter?

Lou says nothing for a while, and Flora wonders what she's thinking. But what she says comes as a surprise.

'Do you want me to speak to him?' she offers. 'If you don't want him here for Christmas that's fine, but . . .'

'It's a bit late now,' Flora says.

'To get a flight, do you mean?'

Flora nods. She feels suddenly tearful, not so much because of Henry as because of Lou: because this is the first conversation she's had with her daughter in which Lou has played the adult. She sits down on the bed, and after a moment Lou comes to sit next to her.

This is the moment, Flora thinks, when she could explain herself. She could tell Lou how it has been, all this time, and why she has done what she's done. Sentences rise in her mind and flow for a few seconds before petering out. The thing about Henry, she tells the empty space in her head, is that he needs other women: he can't settle to monogamy any more than I can settle to being a housewife. The thing is, I couldn't have walked away, because you and Kitty needed him, because I wasn't here enough, and when I had the chance to choose something different, right at the beginning, I didn't. The thing is that having him beside me all these years has meant something, and I'm in a quandary now.

She can't say any of it. It's like those pictures: if she sets it out for someone else to look at it will become the truth, a version of the truth that she'll have to stick to.

'If you have to sell yourself short, Lou,' she says eventually, 'it's better to sacrifice your heart, not your mind. That's the long and short of it. You can rely on making something of your brain, but the heart is a dicey business.'

'Words of comfort for the young woman,' says Lou, and Flora laughs. Then Lou starts laughing too, and before they know it they are clinging to each other, helpless with mirth. God knows why, thinks the bit of Flora's brain that hangs on to lucidity. God only knows what there is to laugh about, but it's an extraordinary relief. It seems to her suddenly that she hasn't laughed enough, certainly not with her daughters. Perhaps that's a better maxim: there's always a funny side, and you'll feel better if you can find it.

'I can smell burning,' Lou says, when they finally collect themselves.

'Oh Lord, the bacon!' Flora jumps up, and they race downstairs, still exhilarated, carrying with them that sumptuous feeling of easy intimacy that is so rare between them.

The bacon is rescued in the nick of time, and they sit at the kitchen table to eat it.

'Tell me about you,' Flora says, greatly daring. 'What else is going on in your life?'

'Well,' says Lou. She looks, all of a sudden, both guarded and vulnerable. That strong jawline of hers is softened by a blush that looks more like a bruise. 'Actually, there is somebody – possibly – who . . .'

Flora waits.

'It's early days,' Lou says, 'I'll keep you posted.' She smiles, a tight little smile, and looks down at her plate.

'What's she like?' Flora asks, and Lou's head shoots up again.

'I didn't think –' she begins – and then she laughs. 'I've never told you,' she says.

'Not in so many words.' Flora looks at her, thinking how beautiful Lou looks this morning, and how wise. How very much wiser than her mother, not ever to risk her happiness on a man.

54

'This is a great place,' Daniel said.

'Isn't it?'

They were up in Kitty's room, propped one at each end of her bed against the wrought-iron bedstead. If only the day could go on and on exactly like this, Kitty thought, with neither of them saying much, just looking at each other and feeling the warm, closed air of the room around them. All that beauty down by the river, the light and shade and the soft music of the water, had been almost more than she could bear.

'Weird to think this is Martin's house and he's in yours,' Daniel said.

'I don't really want to think about Martin.'

'Poor Martin. It's not his fault.'

'Even so,' Kitty said. 'Fair enough, eh?'

Daniel grinned. 'Anything's fair enough, just as long as . . .' He caught her foot and pulled, and she squealed as she slid towards him.

'Stop – I'll fall off. I'll . . .'

He was leaning over her now, the travel-smell of him filling her lungs. It felt very good to be held, to be kissed, but . . . She was like an invalid, she thought; after the last week or two she needed a little convalescence, a gentle recovery.

'Stop,' she said again. 'Not now. Not just yet.'

Daniel drew his eyebrows together, half serious and half teasing.

'Talk to me, then,' he said.

'What about?'

'About anything. Tell me about France.'

'I haven't exactly seen much of France.'

Kitty smiled, and then she took his hand, holding it against her cheek. 'Daniel, I'm happy to – I wish it meant more, but I'm happy to give him to you,' she said.

'Henry?'

'Yes.'

'You don't mean that,' he said, 'and I don't expect it. I'm just happy to have you.'

Kitty felt her eyes pricking with unexpected, inexplicable tears.

'Oh, Kitty.' Daniel moved his hand, gently, to wipe a tear off her cheek. 'I'm glad to know who my father was, but I can't feel anything more than that. I never met him.'

'You did,' Kitty said. 'Him and me. With your mother.'

Daniel stared at her, and Kitty felt another reversal of emotion: a sudden awareness of his being alone in the world, of her knowing so much more than he did.

'When he took me out on Saturdays,' she said, 'to the park, or the zoo – you and your mother were there, sometimes.'

'Do you really remember that?' Daniel asked. 'You must have been very young.'

'Four, maybe. The time I ran away – remember that story? – I did it because you were there, and I was jealous.'

Kitty felt a little breathless now.

'You can't be sure,' Daniel said. 'It could have been anyone. A friend.'

'I'm sure,' Kitty said. 'A woman with long dark hair and a little boy. I remember Henry picking him up.'

'Well, so,' said Daniel. 'But I don't remember, and when she died, he didn't see me again.'

'That was wrong,' said Kitty. 'Whatever his reasons, it was wrong. But I don't want –'

She stopped, looking at him again, every detail of his face so familiar that she couldn't disentangle the elements of it.

'Kitty,' Daniel said, 'what I've blamed him for most is making it impossible for me to have you, and now that's gone away I honestly . . .' He hesitated. 'I've done fine all these years with an invisible father who gave me money and nothing else, and now I've got a dead father with a name and a face. It's you who . . . You've lost your father twice over.' He reached out a hand to her again, tentatively this time. 'I know I'm a poor substitute.'

'You're not,' Kitty said. 'You're really not. You're more than I deserve.'

'So then marry me,' Daniel said.

'What?'

Kitty pulled away before she could stop herself. She could see from the expression on his face that Daniel regretted those words, but whether he regretted his impulsiveness or the impulse itself she couldn't tell. Her own reaction dismayed her. Surely now – they'd come through a test, she thought, worthy of *The Magic Flute*. Worthy of Tristan and Isolde. She'd wanted him with her, in the wake of all the drama: shouldn't that have swept away even the tiniest fragments of doubt and reservation? But looking up at him again, she suddenly saw how much he looked like Henry – his expression, just now, exactly Henry's. For an instant she saw Henry looking at Flora, loving, concerned, amused. Untrustworthy. Oh God. Her heart accelerated with the terror of analogy: Flora had fallen for Henry and she had fallen for Henry's son. Oh God, oh God. Had she deceived herself horribly? Got Daniel here on false pretences? That surge of joy when she'd realised she could have Daniel back – was that all bound up with Henry too?

For a moment they just looked at each other, then Daniel smiled, raised an eyebrow, and laid a finger on her nose as if to forgive her for misreading a jest. Her heart beating furiously, Kitty dragged her gaze away from him and stared out of the window. She could see the garden from here, a view of it from above, waiting in the sunshine: the intricate, laborious arrangement of box and lavender and rose, the little paths between them and the places to sit. Life was horribly complicated, she thought. More complicated for them, despite Landon, and that was all very raw, still. Perhaps it was just a question of taking a deep breath and trusting that things would work out; that you'd find a way through. Perhaps the trick was not to let the complications stop you trying.

'I'm glad you've come, Daniel,' she said. 'I'm glad you're here. But I need you need to give me a bit of time.'

'Of course,' he said. He looked relieved: there was a hint of vulnerability about him, a rare glimpse of uncertainty that moved her deeply. Henry had abandoned him, Kitty thought. The least she could do was give him a chance.

55

It was almost more than Flora could bear, seeing one daughter happy and the other miserable. It was true that Kitty's happiness since Daniel's arrival had been more muted than she'd expected – but, deducing that there had been some kind of difficulty between them, Flora was wise enough to know that it was unlikely to evaporate overnight, whatever resolution they might have reached. There was something about the two of them that gave her pause – something that niggled at her, when she saw them together – but nonetheless it was Lou who occupied most of Flora's thoughts during the day or two when they all waited for Alice's letter, and Lou's endurance began to falter.

At breakfast on the second day after Daniel's arrival, when the letter should have come but had not, Flora resolved to take action.

'What about an outing today?' she asked.

'That's a good idea.' Lou didn't quite manage a smile, but her gloom seemed to shift a little, at least. 'I was reading last night about the château of Montallon. I found a leaflet. It looks interesting: there's a maze.'

'Oh, a maze!' Kitty's face lit up. 'Let's definitely go there.'

Montallon, of all places. Flora nodded, trying not to let her dismay show. 'I've been to Montallon,' she said. 'It is interesting.'

'Oh, well, if you've already seen it –' Lou began, but Flora shook her head.

'You three go,' she said. 'I'll stay here. I've got some emails to catch up on. I haven't quite shaken off the last vestiges of the NHS yet.'

Kitty began to demur too, but Flora raised a hand to stop her.

'Really,' she said. 'You can take my car. Go. Enjoy yourselves.'

An hour later, Flora stared after the departing car with a flare of panic. Surely she hadn't meant to send them all away? She'd lost the discipline of solitude, this last week. What could she do with herself for an entire day?

For a while she drifted through the empty house, as though searching for somebody who might have stayed behind after all; searching in vain for an explanation for her perversity. Passing the door of the sitting room, she went in on impulse and sat down at the desk to check her email, hating herself for her lack of resources.

There was nothing from her usual correspondents. Lou and Kitty were here, of course, and the traffic from her colleagues had dwindled steadily. Martin had written several times, rather formal emails with some clearly flagged purpose: a list of local restaurants, or a description of something in the garden that should be flourishing just now. Looking back over his correspondence, Flora remembered his frown across the table at the end of their farewell dinner. There had at least been some nicety about that parting, she thought. Landon had seemed to feel nothing at all. How could she have imagined there was any prospect of appealing to that closely guarded heart? *We both deserved it,* he'd said. She should have listened more carefully. She should have slept with him when they were both sixteen and got it out of her system for good. But then there would have been no Kitty, and how could she ever regret that?

She scrolled on resolutely through the ranks of spam messages, deleting them one by one. And then something caught her eye: there, as though summoned by her casual reference to the NHS at breakfast, was an invitation to review an article for a surgical journal. Fuelled by idle curiosity and a fleeting waft of nostalgia, Flora clicked the link to read the paper's abstract.

A world she had almost forgotten rose up before her: a world of ethics committees and randomised controlled trials and the painstaking design of surgical equipment, as well as the blood-and-guts reality of the operating theatre. A world she had turned her back on, she told herself firmly, but before she could stop herself she had clicked the 'accept' button and downloaded the full paper.

For the next twenty minutes she read, with ghoulish fascination, an account of a multi-centre trial that she could see almost at once was flawed. Too bad, she thought, for all that time and money, all those months of human life, to be wasted on a study that couldn't advance the cause of science as it hoped because the recruitment of subjects had been badly managed, and the results were therefore hopelessly biased. Useless, in fact. Why had no one scrutinised the methodology more closely before they started?

But might it be possible . . .?

Flora had become, over the years, a proficient statistician. She grabbed a piece of paper and started skimming through the pages of text looking for numbers and details, making calculations. The results were certainly dramatic. Even with a weighty adjustment for selection bias they might still be significant, and worth a public airing.

But then she stopped. She stared out of the window at the blunt tops of the pollarded lime trees that flanked the front of the house, the heat hanging over them like a glaze. For a moment she had no idea what she was doing here. What – dragging her attention back to it – she was doing with this research paper, specifically. Was she being a wise elder, or a sentimental has-been? She pushed back her chair and went out into the garden. She was like a recovering addict, she thought, with a stab of amusement: one brief exposure to the old ways risked undermining the careful construct of her new life.

It was almost noon. The sun streamed through the vines on the terrace, throwing a wallpaper pattern across the back of the house. For a few minutes Flora surveyed the flowerbeds she had weeded, the lawn she had watered, the hedges she had clipped with Martin's secateurs. She'd better write to the editors of the journal and tell them she couldn't do the review after all. But then the paper might be reviewed by someone who would pass it without noticing the errors – or by someone who would reject it out of hand because of them. Damn and blast: why the hell had she opened it?

Perhaps, said the devil's advocate in the corner of her mind, because she needed to be needed, and it was easy to be persuaded that the world of medicine needed her. Because she could perfectly well go back to teaching or research, if not to the operating theatre, at the end of the summer. And what else did she plan to do, exactly? She might have thought she was feeling her way towards an answer to that question a week ago, but now . . .

Flora sighed, tipping back her head to let the dappled sunshine play over her face. It was vexing, the way her perspective shifted so capriciously. She'd sent her daughters away today, then wished she hadn't. She'd congratulated herself, not so long ago, on establishing a life for herself at Les Violettes, but lately she'd felt her stay here had amounted to nothing at all. The fairytale ending she didn't know she'd hoped for wasn't to be, and she couldn't stay in this sunny garden forever, keeping company with the chortling fountain and the simmering bees. Perhaps this paper had been sent, with pinpoint timing, to make her think again about the future.

Someone had suggested, after Henry's funeral, that she might go abroad, work for a medical charity somewhere, and she knew they'd thought it uncharitable of her to reject the idea out of hand. Oddly, though, it wasn't so much a matter of arrogance as of humility: Flora was well aware of her limitations. She could hardly go to sub-Saharan Africa to operate on the gastro-oesophageal junction, and it was years since she'd ventured far beyond the small intestine. She'd become too expert to be useful – not just as a surgeon, but as a person. That was what she'd thought at the time. The narrowness of her focus, the clarity of her purpose in life, had left her ill-equipped for anything else.

A little breeze wafted towards her, bringing with it the scent of the Mediterranean shrubs against the far wall; bringing, too, a waft of comfort. That light-footed association of ideas – the leap from the professional to the personal – had less conviction now, she conceded. She had learned something this summer, after all, about her capacities as mother and friend and – yes, even lover. She might not be an expert in any of those fields, but she wasn't completely inept, either. There was surely a future for her that didn't involve a retreat, a falling-back on what she knew best.

The paper was still open on her laptop, and she knew that she'd do the responsible thing: she would write a detailed report, setting out the problems with the methodology and suggesting how the data might be analysed to yield more reliable results, and then she would hand it back to the editors. She would do her bit, this time, for the furtherance of scientific knowledge, but she would not do it again.

The front doorbell rang just as she was finishing. It would be Francine, Flora supposed, bringing more rhubarb or a report on the Swiss visitors, and her spirits rose. Francine had a way of appearing when she needed a diversion.

But it wasn't Francine this time. Standing on the doorstep, and looking more than a little worse for wear, was Martin Carver.

'Martin!' Flora could keep neither the surprise nor the pleasure out of her voice. 'You look as though you've driven through the night.'

'Not quite. Very early ferry, then straight down.'

Flora gazed at him, anticipating the little thrill of presenting him to the others, later on, and they to him. Reinforcements, she thought. Evidence of some kind, or affirmation. She couldn't resist a surge of gratification.

'Come in,' she said. 'The others are all out, but – I've got quite a houseful, actually. My daughters are both here, and Kitty's boyfriend, but they –'

She broke off: something in his face raised a warning.

'I'm sorry,' he said. 'I should have rung.'

Flora stared at him, trying to decipher his expression. Stupid, she thought, to rush in, rush on, like that. 'What's the matter?' she asked. 'Has something happened?'

'Actually, it has,' he said. 'Claude Abelard's had a heart attack. He – I've come to . . .'

His voice trailed off then, but that was enough; the rest Flora could deduce. It wasn't her he'd come to see, but Francine. That would be fine, a commendable service for an old friend, except that it was painfully clear that even this brief conversation with Flora was making him deeply uncomfortable. It came to Flora in a giddy rush that she should never have underestimated the decades of history Martin had dismissed so lightly when he spoke of Francine.

Come on, she told herself; brace up. What possible reason was there for thinking that Martin would drive five hundred miles, without advance warning, to see her? She couldn't, surely, have nurtured subconscious hopes about this man at the same time as stumbling upon a lifelong passion for another? The score had always been perfectly clear with Martin: a dalliance, no more.

'I saw Claude a couple of days ago in the village,' she said, her tone assiduously professional. 'Poor Francine. Is he in a bad way?'

She knew the answer to that question before she asked it – why else would Martin be here, if not to claim Francine back when widowhood released her?

'It's touch and go, I gather.' Martin was still standing outside. 'I should have rung,' he said again, 'but could I possibly –'

'Of course.' Flora stepped back from the door. 'I'm sorry. What would you like: a shower? Something to eat? The others will be back soon; the girls and Daniel. We could all . . .'

A stricken expression crossed his face again, and despite herself Flora was touched. He hadn't meant to hurt her feelings, she thought. He'd hoped to avoid that. 'It's your house, after all,' she went on, her voice less brisk.

'You're very kind,' he said. 'I'd better get up to the hospital. I might stay with – but would you mind if I took a key, so that . . .'

Flora turned away. Really, she thought, she ought to be inured to this sort of thing: the discomfiture, and the dark humour of it. At least Henry had managed himself less clumsily. There was somehow less shame in being duped by a man who took the trouble to cultivate some expertise in it. She was grateful that no one else was here to witness her humiliation.

'Please,' she said, 'make yourself at home.'

56

When she had finished reading the letter, Lou folded it carefully and put it back in the envelope. It was written on the thick cartridge paper Alice used for sketching, and felt plumply substantial – more like a medieval peace treaty than a twenty-first century lover's account of her history.

The others had vanished the moment the postman handed the letter over, and Lou had taken it into the garden. She wondered now whether they were waiting inside, or whether they'd all gone out somewhere. She couldn't have said whether she wanted company or not, but the sense of finding herself in an unexpected place was accentuated by the silence and the stillness. It was as if this garden, enclosed by its high walls, could have been anywhere, set down on a far-off planet or at the edge of a foreign sea. Perhaps if she opened that locked door at the back she would walk out into the road that ran past Veronica Villa, or even into the dusty yard of the farm a hundred miles north-west of Des Moines where Alice was now.

For a while she simply sat, letting what Alice had written sink in, and then she took the letter inside and up to her room. Stretching out on the bed, she unfolded it again.

Dear Lou, *Alice began*, I know you will think it's cowardly to write this in a letter, but I want it to come out the right way and this is my best chance.

Lou sighed, smoothing the paper flat against the pillow and wondering if the words would mean the same thing the second time round, or if she'd find she had somehow misunderstood them. That used to happen sometimes with the notes and cards she'd hoarded as a teenager – thank yous for birthday presents or invitations to parties – but back then she'd known she was deliberately reading more into them than was really there. Was she still capable of the same self-deception? Shaking her head to shut out everything but Alice's voice, she let herself devour the whole letter once more.

I should have told you all this sooner, but I hoped it wouldn't matter if I didn't. When I met you I felt what had happened before wasn't important anymore, and I guess I was ashamed, too. I didn't want you to think less of me – and you know, we never talked about men. You never asked me, so I never told you.

When I was in high school and everyone talked about boys, I went along with it. It was a small world, and you had to fit in. You could say no to one boy, or two, but you couldn't go on saying no. And then a strange thing happened to me. I wasn't a beauty, and I never made the same effort other girls did, but – maybe because I was different and I didn't care as much – the boy everyone wanted fell for me. He was a nice boy, kind of arrogant but confident enough that he didn't need to be aggressive, and clever too. The only one who wasn't going to be a farmer.

So you can guess what happened. Halfway through twelfth grade, just when I'd figured out how to get out of Webster County and go to art school, I got pregnant. He offered to marry me. We were both seventeen, and he said he'd give up on college and stay on his Dad's farm just like everyone wanted him to. I let him think, for a bit, that I might go along with it, although I knew the me that said those things to him wasn't the person I really was, not the me who lay awake at night and felt as if the walls were closing in on me. It would have made my parents happy, and his, and there was some comfort in knowing exactly how my life would unroll, but not enough.

The baby would have been due just before I graduated from high school. I never told my parents. Never told anyone but him. There was a clinic in Fort Dodge that did things quietly. We said we were going away for the weekend, and they didn't turn a hair, just made some jokes that were the opposite of what really happened. I went away pregnant and came back not. He stayed with me all weekend, and for those few days I really did love him. I'd like to say we stayed friends, but we didn't. The next semester he started going out with my friend Grace, and after he left for college I never saw him again.

I've thought sometimes that it would have been better if I'd let the baby be adopted, so I could know that my child was out there somewhere and might come and find me one day, but I couldn't have managed that at the time. It hasn't troubled me much, especially not since I met you and found out how to be happy. Not since my career got going and I could tell myself all that would never have happened if I'd had a baby ten years ago.

You can guess the next bit too, I'm sure. I won't say it took me by surprise, because I had a pretty good idea it would be difficult, and that's why I was reluctant about the whole plan. Why I was upset you went ahead without telling me, and why I couldn't be happy for you in the way you wanted. It wasn't just the fact of you being pregnant: it was knowing exactly how you were feeling, and not saying anything. It was seeing the pleasure in your face that I couldn't share, because although you said it was our baby, I knew in my heart it was yours, and I knew I didn't deserve it. It was feeling you slipping away from me, putting the baby first even before it was born. I guess those things would have been hard anyway, but the abortion made it worse. I did my best to look after you and not let you see how I was feeling. I could see you were going through more than you expected too, and I hoped we'd come through it together, but all the time I was afraid we'd lost something we couldn't get back.

The weekend we went to Parnells you were thirteen weeks pregnant, exactly the time I lost my baby. All that day, while we were walking around, I tried to psych myself up to tell you. I thought if I could do it, maybe that would sort everything out, but I was so scared of telling you I'd killed a baby the same age as yours. As ours. And then I said something that upset you and – I know neither of us meant all those things we said, but they still hurt. The truth is, my Mom's accident wasn't so bad, but it was a reason to come home, and that's what I needed. I needed some time to sort things out in my head, and some distance between us. I don't know if you'll understand, or if you'll forgive me, but at least now you know the worst.

With my best love,
Alice

57

Alice's letter hadn't had the effect Kitty anticipated. She'd thought they'd get back from the shop to find Lou either ecstatic or desolate, but it was almost impossible to tell what she was feeling when they came face to face in the hallway. She seemed, Kitty thought, both agitated and listless, as though the situation required some great energy that she couldn't summon.

In the kitchen, Flora was busy arranging baguettes in the tall bread bin, and Daniel was staring out through the back door like someone used to making himself inconspicuous. Watching her sister fiddle with one thing then another – glancing at a postcard, touching the blade of a knife – Kitty had to stop herself grabbing Lou's hand.

'Please tell us, Looby,' she said – hearing the long-forgotten nickname with surprise, as though it was a younger, less tactful version of herself who had spoken. 'Is it good or bad?'

Lou turned, and Kitty took a step back. 'Sorry,' she said. 'Of course you don't have to say anything if you . . .'

'Alice had an abortion,' Lou said. 'Years ago. When she was still at school.'

Kitty waited. She saw Lou glance towards Flora.

'That's it, really,' Lou said. 'I mean – it was hard for her, seeing me pregnant. It brought it all back. She didn't want me to do it in the first place. I should have . . .'

'Should have what?' said Kitty, and at the same moment Flora said, 'Lou, darling –'

'I should have thought more about her,' Lou said. 'I hardly thought at all about what it felt like for her. I wanted her to think about me. I can't believe how selfish . . .'

'That's what pregnancy does,' Flora said. 'That's what it's meant to do.'

Kitty looked at her: she'd got used to hearing her mother sounding less assured this last week, but this was the old forthright Flora, certain of her ground.

'Don't,' said Lou. 'Excuses won't help.'

'It's not an excuse,' said Flora, 'it's a fact. Pregnancy is meant to make you selfish. There's an evolutionary advantage to all those hormones buffering you from the world, you and the baby. It's the supreme moment of self-justification for a woman, biologically. I suppose the difficulty . . .'

She stopped. Lou looked at her, and Flora looked back.

'What would I know,' Flora said. 'But of course Alice is a woman too. It must be . . .'

She took Lou in her arms then, and Kitty saw Lou's shoulders sag, and heard a muffled sound of distress coming from deep in her sister's chest. She glanced at Daniel, and the two of them slipped out of the room.

By mutual assent Kitty and Daniel set off towards the river, down the dusty, deserted road. Since the storm there had hardly been a cloud in the sky: Kitty could see how you might long for rain by the end of summer.

'She's quite something, your mum,' Daniel said.

'She's had to be.'

'In what way?'

Kitty hesitated. Perhaps this wasn't the right thing to say, but she couldn't veer away from it now she'd started. She wished suddenly that she'd stayed with Lou and her mother.

'To live with Henry,' she said. 'He was a pretty lousy husband.'

The phrase hung between them, weighted by the unfamiliar adjective. Little tracks of dialogue sprung from it in Kitty's head, like a crack spreading, crazing over the surface of a plate.

'We don't have to tell her, you know,' Daniel said.

'What?'

'Your mother. We don't have to tell her that I'm . . .'

Kitty bit her lip. She had said the same thing, to Lou, but . . .

'Never, you mean?'

'Not necessarily.'

Kitty shook her head. The crack had reached the edge of the plate now: in her mind's eye, she saw it split into pieces, jagged but distinct.

'I can't deceive her.'

'I didn't mean –'

Just then, a car appeared as if from nowhere, and it swerved so sharply as it approached that Kitty was sure the sight of them at the side of the road had startled the driver.

'Dangerous drivers, the French,' Daniel said, as they stepped back onto the verge.

'Wait,' said Kitty. 'Wait, Daniel. I'm sure I . . . Fucking hell, that was Martin Carver.'

58

Flora and Lou were sitting together on one of Les Violettes' more uncomfortable sofas when the doorbell rang.

'Damn,' Flora said. 'Let's leave it. It won't be anyone important.'

'It might be,' said Lou. Something flashed across her face that tore at Flora's heart: Heavens, she thinks it might be Alice, she thought. Alice thinking better of leaving matters in Lou's hands, hurtling across the Atlantic after her letter. Flora put a hand on Lou's knee and got to her feet. Not Francine this time, she thought, and not Martin either; they'd both be up at the hospital. Who else, choosing such a bad moment?

But it was Martin. And not just Martin, but Kitty and Daniel, who had slipped out of the house only a few minutes before, rushing back up the path now as though some disaster had occurred. Flora's heart plummeted. But then she thought: Kitty must have seen Martin arriving and leapt to the wrong conclusion – imagined a catastrophe at Orchards, perhaps.

'It's OK,' she said, as Kitty bolted towards her. 'Martin's come from visiting Claude.'

'Who's Claude?' Kitty stopped just behind Martin, staring at Flora without comprehension.

'A friend who's had a heart attack,' Flora said. 'The reason Martin's here. He's Francine's husband. I stayed with them when I first arrived here.'

Flora was conscious, as she spoke, of something strange happening to her words. It was as if they were metamorphosing into a language no one else understood: the same feeling as when you wake from a dream saying things that make no sense to anyone around you, and whose meaning soon eludes you, too. But she knew what was happening here, of course. This confusion was just a trick of the light. She looked at Kitty and then at Martin, summoning a reassuring smile.

'Mum,' said Kitty. 'Shall we come in?' Urgency and anxiety were etched across her face still.

'Yes, of course.' Flora stood back from the doorway and they all came past her, Kitty and then Martin and then Daniel. Things looked just fractionally different from how they had a beat or two ago, her grasp on the situation less certain.

'What is it, Kitty?' she asked. 'What's the matter?'

Martin looked at Kitty, then at Flora.

'What's going on?' Flora asked. 'Is there something. . .?'

Daniel cleared his throat. 'This really isn't the right way to do this,' he said.

Flora looked at him then, his face charged with agitation – but an agitation masked by misjudged nonchalance. That expression, she thought – and then recognition flared in her mind's eye. My God, could he . . .? The resemblance was uncanny. How had she not seen it before, she who was trained to seek clues in face and gait and gesture? At the same time she heard Martin's voice, several weeks ago: *Miranda knew Henry. Their paths crossed. Some family business.*

'Good Lord,' she said. 'You're Henry's son, aren't you. Is that why. . .?'

She remembered Kitty's unexplained misery, and the rapprochement with Daniel that had come so soon after the revelation about her own parentage. My God, what had Kitty been through?

'Yes,' Daniel said.

'I'm sorry.' Kitty looked utterly stricken. 'I'm so sorry, Mum. We weren't – we meant . . . Martin doesn't know about Landon, you see. He doesn't know Henry wasn't my father.'

59

Kitty's eyes flicked from her mother to Martin and back again. Try as she might, she couldn't bring herself to look at Daniel. Hovering just out of her field of view, just behind Daniel, was her father. Or rather, not her father. Daniel's father.

'I'm so sorry,' she said again. 'We would have told you. It just seemed . . . I didn't think there was any rush.'

She looked at Martin again then, a gaze of fierce accusation. Martin looked more miserable than anyone; he had that sagging, forlorn look that big square men get when things go badly wrong, as though they've suddenly realised they're taller and wider and more conspicuous than anyone else and wish they could fold in on themselves. Not that any of this was his fault, Kitty admitted. It was just that he was the only person left to blame, with Henry resoundingly absent and the rest of them, in one way or another, casualties of the situation.

'I can't think how I didn't see the likeness,' Flora said. 'Everything but the voice.' She stopped, and Kitty glanced at her, afraid that her composure might fracture. 'Do you know, I never even suspected there might be a child,' Flora said. 'It never occurred to me. Isn't that odd? Despite – Kitty.'

Kitty wanted to say something – *he should have told you,* or *it wasn't the same thing* – but she could see that it was, at least in her mother's mind. Except that she hadn't been left fatherless, of course. Flora was looking at Daniel still – how strange it was, the way their five pairs of eyes kept moving from one person to another, like a game of wink murder – and Kitty wondered whether she was thinking the same thing, blaming Henry for his negligence. This, she thought, was exactly what she'd hoped to spare her mother: thinking worse of Henry than she already did. Piling up fresh evidence against him, when Flora had made her peace, at last, with the rest of it. But then she wondered whether Flora had gone further than that – whether she'd come to see herself as the guilty party. Might this discovery lift a burden, when the shock had ebbed away?

'Well,' said Lou. 'I think a cup of tea is called for.'

The echo of Jean's voice must be deliberate, Kitty thought; either way, it introduced a spark of humour that fizzed for a moment and then died. But Martin leapt to attention.

'Yes,' he said. 'Tea. Let me make it.'

The making and drinking of tea served a vital purpose in English life, Kitty thought: it was the thing you could always do when there was nothing else to be done, and you needed to pass a little time, laying down a measure of it like a coat of paint over something raw and rough-edged. But even if you all understood what was happening, it was still quite possible to suffer agonies of embarrassment and awkwardness through it. Poor Martin, bringing beautiful tea cups from a cupboard in the sitting room and fussing over strainers and milk jugs, was ill-suited to the role of geisha, and more than once during the enactment of the charade (*English expatriates drinking tea in Indre-et-Loire,* she thought; Beryl Cook after Monet, perhaps) Kitty had the sense that any one of them might succumb to either mirth or despair at their own clumsiness.

Lou gave up first. They all looked at her with envy when she pushed back her chair.

'I'm going to have a rest,' she said. 'I'll see you later.'

Kitty shot a rather wild look at Daniel, who caught her eye and gave a barely perceptible nod, and then she glanced guiltily at Flora. Really, she thought, they should have found more to say, between them. Perhaps later, when Martin had gone. . .

'Well,' said Daniel, responding to his cue. 'Kitty and I were just off for a walk. Shall we . . .?'

It seemed important, as they set off, that they had somewhere to head for.

'Flora mentioned a painting in the church,' Kitty said. 'It's very old, apparently. Shall we go and look at it?'

'Sure.'

'We always used to –' She stopped. Everything felt loaded now; anything they might say to each other too momentous for the fragility of the situation. She was grateful that Daniel didn't attempt to pick up the thread of conversation. They walked in silence along the road, barely noticing the scenery, the houses and trees and the empty sky, but the further they went the more the things that weren't being said seemed to press in on them. There was no music in her head today – too much else filling it up, Kitty thought – but that seemed suddenly a topic less freighted than anything else.

'I've been thinking about writing another song cycle,' she said. That wasn't entirely true, but Landon had talked to her about singing the Ted Hughes cycle at Henry's memorial concert – unless you want to write something else, he'd said, and Kitty had thought perhaps she could, perhaps she should. And there had been an email from Janet Davidson this morning, forgotten until now among the drama of Alice's letter and Martin's appearance, confirming her PhD place for next year, and that would mean – well, she'd have to write lots for that. Lots and lots.

'Like the other one?' Daniel asked.

'I don't know. Elizabeth Jennings poems, maybe. I haven't read many, though.'

'I can be your great interpreter,' Daniel said. 'We can be like Benjamin Britten and Peter Pears.'

Kitty's heart jolted. She heard Daniel's voice in her head again: *So then marry me.* This wasn't quite the same statement, but . . . Didn't she want him to play her music, to share it with her?

'The thing is,' she said, 'that I need – space for my music.'

'Of course.' He looked bewildered. 'Of course you do.'

She wanted to say, *I can't write when you're around*, but she knew he'd have an answer for that too, or at least . . . Oh, she needed to be careful. Not only because of what they'd just come through, the effortful untangling of connections and assumptions and where it left them, but also because her music, and her belief in it, wasn't an easy topic after all. It was just taking shape inside her as a thing that could occupy her life; that she could devote herself to, and that might make sense of her. It felt like a tiny baby – tender, flawless, fragile – and she felt, suddenly, like a tigress who might do irrevocable damage defending it.

Perhaps Daniel understood some of that, because he didn't say any more about music. Instead, when he spoke again it was to say, 'I don't have a family, Kitty, so I –'

'So you want to be part of mine.' And that was another thing that shouldn't have been said; that she should have guarded against.

'No,' he said. 'No. It's just you I want. I like your mother and your sister, but that's not what I want from you. I'm glad the – secret is out of the way now, but only because . . .'

He stopped, looking at her with a sort of desperation she hadn't seen in his face before. They had reached the church now: beside them, a flight of white steps led up to the heavy door. If they could just get up them, Kitty thought, they could be absorbed by the blessed coolness, the blessed darkness of the interior. They could look at the painting that had been there for centuries, and breathe in the safe, sequestered air.

'It's no good, is it?' Daniel said. 'There's just too much stacked against us. We'll never be like other people.'

Kitty stared at him. She ought to feel something now, relief or sorrow – she ought to know which side her feelings fell, at least – but there was nothing. Just the whiteness of the sky all around her, the echoing silence in her head.

'Perhaps we won't,' she said. It seemed a little thing to say, but she knew it wasn't: that she was allowing that great ballast of certainty inside Daniel to be vaporised. It was a shame, when it had survived so much, when she could see now that it was heartfelt, but she couldn't stop it. He was right, she thought. How could they ever be like other people? How could she?

'I'm sorry,' said Daniel. 'I feel I've been a fool, but I haven't meant to be. I haven't meant anything except . . . It's just bad luck, isn't it? That we . . .' He tried to smile. 'Listen, Kitty, I don't want to be in the way. I think it would be better . . . I'll get a bus, or something. A train.'

'I can drive you,' Kitty said. 'I can take you to the station.' She meant to be kind, helpful, but she could see from his face that he saw it only as eagerness to be rid of him. For a terrible moment she thought he might be going to cry. 'Or else you could . . .' she began. 'There's no rush. You can stay.'

'No.' He looked almost angry now. He didn't have much money, Kitty thought; she wondered if he'd have to buy another ticket. Into the cavern inside her guilt and pity were begin to seep, like rainwater filtered down through layers and layers of rock. 'No, I'll go. There's a – I might catch the last Eurostar tonight.'

60

The afternoon was just beginning to slide towards evening, the light modulating from silver to gold. Flora and Martin turned right out of the front door, away from the village, and he led her down the road and through a gate with two rough stripes, red and white, painted on the post.

'Have you identified the *randonnée* signs?' he asked. 'I should have explained them to you. There are lots of paths around here.'

'Yes,' said Flora. 'I've found plenty of places to walk.'

'This is part of a much longer trail,' Martin said. He glanced at her, a look shot through with concern, inexpertly veiled. 'People are fanatical about keeping up these routes.'

Flora nodded, glad that the footpath obliged them, at this point, to fall into single file. It ran along the edge of a wood, with a field of maize tall and bright on the other side. The air smelled slightly sweet and slightly woody, and in the narrow space between vegetation and vegetation everything was close and still.

This had been a generous suggestion of Martin's, Flora thought. It was clear that he felt responsible, in some way, for the shock she'd had, and was eager to make amends – and it was true that after that extraordinary scene in the hall at Les Violettes, after the cup of tea Martin had insisted on making and no one had wanted to drink, her daughters had both melted away: Lou to lie down, and Kitty out, somewhere, with Daniel. Neither of them could be blamed for disappearing, any more than they could be blamed for the news, or the manner of its breaking, but Flora was grateful that Martin hadn't fled immediately back to Francine.

'How's Claude?' she asked.

'Better,' said Martin. 'Much better. Out of the woods, they think.'

'I'm glad.' Although, Flora thought, if she felt anything about Claude Abelard's survival it was a fleeting sense of pity for Martin and Francine, denied their happy ending.

'Flora,' Martin said, 'I feel I've got off on the wrong foot with you. I feel . . .'

'Please don't worry,' she said. 'You're not to blame. If there's been any misunderstanding, it's not your fault.'

It would be wrong to say that she'd taken the news in her stride; no one with any feeling could have managed that. But her self-reliance, her splendid rationality: this was the moment for their grand entrance, Flora thought. It hadn't taken long to weigh up the hiding of Daniel's existence from her against the hiding of Kitty's paternity from Henry – nor, indeed, to acknowledge that Daniel was merely living proof of an attachment she had understood all too well, years and years ago. And there was something singularly apt about the way the circle had been closed: Henry's infidelity had produced Daniel, and Flora's had removed the barrier to his liaison with Kitty. It was, after all, the last act of a comedy, she thought, the final episode in this bizarre saga of coincidence and misapprehension, with everything falling at last into its rightful place.

What troubled her most was the fear of history repeating itself: of Kitty, precious Kitty, involving herself with Henry's son; risking the same trail of reversals and betrayals as her mother. But if she couldn't bear that prospect for Kitty, she could hardly deny that she rued her own choice. Was that, then, where it ended, this tit for tat of revelations? Did it lead her inevitably to regret, after all?

It was odd: these big questions felt somehow less overwhelming than they should. Flora had often observed, among her patients and their relatives, the human brain's merciful ability to scale down profound emotions at moments of crisis. Was that what was happening to her, she wondered, or had her rage and grief for Henry, for everything connected to Henry, simply burned itself out?

Looking up and seeing Martin ahead of her as they rounded a corner, it struck her, with a glimmer of amusement, that being alone with him aroused more pressing feelings just now than the great upheavals that had racked her family. She dreaded any attempt on Martin's part to explain himself – which she rather feared might be the purpose of this outing. Dreaded it not because their encounter earlier in the summer didn't merit re-examination: her feelings for him had been real enough, she admitted, but she didn't much care, after the rigours of the last few days, to have them resurrected now in the name of absolution and remission for Martin.

But as the minutes passed and Martin said nothing more, Flora began to relax. Perhaps after all this was just a walk: Martin's idea of a civilised resolution, without the wearying business of explaining themselves to each other. She watched his back retreating in front of her, taller than Henry and more solid than Landon, his summer jacket creased and casually worn. She hardly knew him, she thought. It was a mistake to imagine that that back was familiar, or that it might elicit any authentic response in her. It was all shadows and fancy. The summer would pass and all these memories would be bound up as a curiosity, the narrative of a trip she would never take again. She felt her perspective take wing and soar up into the sky so that she could look down on the pair of them, climbing slowly up the hill, with the clear sight of a hawk.

When the path widened and Martin fell back to walk next to her, she accepted his presence at her side without a flicker.

'This part is rather dull,' he said. 'In a moment it opens up. There's a bit of a climb and then a lovely view before the drop down to the mill.'

'Very good,' said Flora. She meant only to sound composed, but she heard an echo of Jean's sharpness in her voice and was sorry for it. 'Look at the flowers,' she said. 'So pretty, growing along the edge of the corn.' She'd noticed them elsewhere, these strips of colour fringing fields and roads: poppies and cornflowers and several others she couldn't name, in rainbow shades of red and blue and startling yellow.

'They keep down the pests,' Martin said, 'or so my mother always said. Like roses in the vineyard.'

'Not just for the benefit of walkers, then,' said Flora.

'No.'

The path turned quite steeply uphill then, the maize rising ahead of them in a sweep of gold. It was rather hot for exertion, Flora thought, even though the afternoon was nearly over. For a while they climbed in silence.

And then, abruptly, Martin spoke again. 'You talked about mis-understanding,' he said. 'I'm a simpler soul than you, I'm afraid, so if there's any misunderstanding I suspect . . .' He broke off for a moment, breathless either from the gradient or from the rush of words. Flora felt her heart drop – and then leap in wonder.

'Oh!' she said. The top of the hill was suddenly upon them, and in the evening light the valley flared with colour. A mythic landscape, she thought. Surely this was the point of the excursion, and of the evening – a fitting conclusion to their little tale?

Martin stood beside her, but Flora could sense that his mind was on what he'd been saying, not on the marvels laid out below, and after a while she realised he was speaking again. His words flitted around her head like birds that wouldn't settle for long enough to be identified; she wanted to flap them away.

'I realise I've made a mess of things,' he said. 'I thought . . .' *Oh, there's Champigny*, Flora thought, *and the lake* . . . 'I was concerned for you,' Martin went on, 'and I wanted very much to . . .' *And is that Montallon, on the horizon? There are so many châteaux, of course* . . .

'Flora.' Martin's voice was suddenly insistent. 'Please let me explain. I'd heard from Francine that you had your daughters staying, and – well, I assumed – your . . .'

'My what?' said Flora, turning to him at last.

'Your lover, I imagined.'

Flora stared at him, and Martin lifted a hand to his forehead in a gesture of self-derision.

'How I could have thought that of you, I really . . .'

Flora was bewildered. He was mortified to have impugned her honour – was that it? To have suspected her of something that was in fact perfectly true, although perhaps it wouldn't be necessary to admit to that, or to explain the complications and limitations of her relationship with Landon. There was enough burlesque in the situation already.

'Please don't worry,' she said. 'Not on my behalf. It doesn't matter.'

'Don't say that.' Martin looked miserably at the ground now. 'I'm no good at making myself understood, that's the trouble. No good at understanding people, either, although I thought . . .'

'What?' asked Flora. Stranger and stranger, she thought. She felt like sitting him down in a consulting room and taking him through his story step by step. *When did you first notice the pain? Is it there all the time?*

'Oh, bloody hell,' he said. 'I should never have gone back to England, but I was too much of a fool to think about changing my plans. It all happened so quickly, and I thought a bit of time, a bit of space – and at least I knew where you were; I knew you were at Les Violettes.'

'What?' said Flora again – or something like that. She hardly knew whether she'd said anything at all.

'It was all a bit much for me, to be honest. Behaved like a bloody teenager. But I thought you'd got the gist, before I left. I thought my emails – then finding out that I knew something so terrible about your family . . . When there was an excuse to come back, I just leapt in the car and came.'

'But what about Francine?' Flora said, before she could stop herself. 'Surely you came back for Francine?'

'Yes, of course; of course.' He looked troubled again, but there was a spark of hope in his eyes now; a glimmer of possibility. 'But not . . . After a fashion, yes, but as a friend, not . . .'

'That was my misunderstanding,' said Flora.

Another sentence she couldn't help speaking: her mind at work again, unravelling the confusion, laying the bones of the story straight. But then suddenly there it was, set out between them, and Flora felt a horrible chill, as though solving the puzzle had unleashed a genie whose presence was the last thing she needed. Martin had thought she'd moved her lover into Les Violettes, and she had thought he'd come home to claim his, and both of them had been miserable. Which meant . . .

She couldn't move, couldn't look away, but she could feel the blood racing through her head in protest. Whatever it was, the story of this summer, whatever it might turn out to be, it wasn't a love story. If it had been, it would have had a different ending: the ending that had ducked away from her the morning after the storm, and which she felt suddenly, perversely, glad to have escaped. It certainly wouldn't have brought her here, her and Martin, to the top of this hill, with the setting sun and the breathtaking beauty of the valley below – no, dammit, this was pure hyperbole, pure parody, an example of hideously poor taste on the part of whatever deity they might look to for deliverance.

'Martin,' she said. Oh God; she could see now that he wanted to kiss her, that he thought that was what was going to happen next. 'Listen, Martin, I can't . . .'

The hand that had strayed towards her flew away now, lifting itself in a gesture of apology and self-restraint.

'I do want you to understand,' he said. 'I want you to know what my feelings are; that they are – can one still say honourable?'

Honourable. Henry, surely, had used that word. Or had he? Henry seemed suddenly hazy, along with everything else. And what did one say, Flora wondered, what did one do, faced with a declaration one didn't want: with a diagnosis one wasn't equipped to manage?

'I won't press you,' Martin said now. 'I haven't forgotten – it's only a few months, I know, since – but if you could – when you're ready – perhaps we could be here together for a while, and see – or at Orchards, even, if you . . .'

'Martin,' she said again, 'I can't – it wouldn't be fair. It's better for me just to say no.'

'Really?' The look on his face was piteous.

'Really,' she said. At least she had some courage left. 'I'm sorry. But it's better to be honest, don't you think?'

'Of course,' he said. 'Of course. You really are – you're a marvellous person, Flora. Of course I can quite see that I – but I'm very glad to have met you. I hope perhaps sometime we might see each other . . .'

'Perhaps,' agreed Flora. Thank God, at least, for the Englishman's restraint. She smiled at him now. 'I'm glad to have met you too,' she said.

61

The walk home passed in a burble of purposeless conversation, as though neither of them dared to allow silence to settle for more than a second or two. To Flora's immense relief, Martin drew his keys out of his pocket as they approached the front gate and climbed into his car without even coming into the house, muttering something about the hospital, friends to visit, apologies to the rest of the party, before driving off with an uncharacteristic squeal of tyres – which was, thought Flora, the most honest expression of his feelings since they had turned for home at the top of the hill.

Flora passed through the house with the odd sense that she had returned to being a visitor at Les Violettes. The engravings on the walls, the hall chest, the familiar tableaux glimpsed through doorways and windows all seemed to hang back from her, to retreat towards the shadowy domain of memory; sighs and whispers in the waxed air seemed to debate her right to be here. She had no idea, now, how much longer she would stay. She dreaded the thought of discussing with Martin whether he wished to go back to Orchards or to stay here; she dreaded his hopeful face suggesting that there was no reason they couldn't share the house, even if . . . She had never been in the position of splitting possessions, negotiating over access, and it felt ignominious to enter that territory now, on such a slight justification.

Out in the garden she was surprised to see Kitty bending over a flowerbed. She was still wearing the white sleeveless dress she'd had on earlier, and it was clear from its appearance that she'd been labouring for some time. Flora stood for a moment in the doorway, watching her pulling viciously at the weeds that had taken hold in the last week or two, then breaking off to empty a can of water over the parched earth. She recognised the satisfaction of the physical labour, but the gusto with which Kitty was applying herself to the task raised a warning too.

'Hello,' she called.

Kitty straightened up, and sure enough there was an expression of grim determination on her face, as well as a good deal of dust. A large basket of thwarted shoots wilting in the sun in the middle of the terrace testified to her accomplishments.

'I didn't know you were a gardener,' Flora said.

'I'm not,' Kitty said. 'I haven't any idea if I've pulled up the right things. I just felt like . . .'

'It's very therapeutic, isn't it?' said Flora. 'I've got rather behind with the weeding.'

'I'm afraid you're not meant to water plants in the middle of the day, though,' Kitty said. 'I've just remembered. It makes their pores open up, and then the sun fries them.'

Flora looked around at the shrubs, sturdily luxuriant despite her inexpert management. 'I didn't know that,' she said. 'So much for my nurturing instincts, eh? But it's not the middle of the day. It's almost seven o'clock.'

Kitty stared at her for a moment.

'Shall I make some tea?' Flora said. 'Or pour you a glass of wine? You look as though you could do with a rest.'

'There's still lots to do,' Kitty said. 'There's –'

'Come on,' said Flora. 'Come in and have a drink.'

Lou, Flora supposed, was still asleep upstairs, but where was . . .? While she was wondering how to raise this question, Kitty answered it for her.

'Daniel's gone,' she said, as she ran her hands under the kitchen tap. Her voice didn't sound as nonchalant as she'd clearly hoped it would. She shook her hands violently and water flew around the room. 'He's going home.'

Flora hesitated. 'Not because of me, I hope?'

'No. Because of me. Because we – because he – because it's no good, any of it.'

Flora watched her face flatten, the tell-tale tension in her cheeks that presaged tears. She put her arms around Kitty, and felt her chest heave and sink again.

'Oh, my darling,' she said.

'I can't even –' Kitty began, her voice muffled by Flora's blouse. 'We went to see that picture in the church that you – after Martin, and everything – but on the way we were talking, and suddenly . . .'

Flora lifted a hand to Kitty's hair: such a tender gesture always, smoothing her turbulent curls.

'The thing is,' Kitty said. 'I can't compose when I'm with him, and that's no good, is it? I can't give that up.'

'No.'

'And . . .' Kitty sniffed fiercely. 'Even if Daniel's not – a blood relation, you know, I grew up with Henry as my father, and it feels . . .' She stopped. 'I wonder if that's what – if I recognised Henry in him, and that's why . . .'

Flora said nothing. Who knew, she thought. She could certainly testify to Henry's attractions – she would be the chief witness, wouldn't she, to their power? If Daniel had inherited some of that charisma, that chutzpah, perhaps it wasn't so much Kitty seeing her father in him as . . .

'And I grew up with Henry as my example of a husband, too,' Kitty said, with a final dash of bravado. 'How could I marry his son?'

She kept her face buried in Flora's neck, as though she didn't dare to look at her. Poor Daniel, Flora thought, unacknowledged by his father and left motherless by a car crash. But poor Kitty, too; poor, poor Kitty, so entangled in the consequences of her father's behaviour. At least her upbringing had given Kitty realistic expectations, though. And a sense of caution: that was something her mother had taken sixty years to learn. But . . .

'Do you love him?' she asked, eventually.

She could feel Kitty's heart knocking against her chest; both their hearts beating together.

'I don't know. I'd know, wouldn't I, if I did?' Kitty made a little sound of sorrow and confusion. 'I hated him going, but . . . What's the matter with me that I don't know what I feel?'

'There's nothing the matter with you,' Flora said. 'Goodness, Kitty, none of us . . .' She stopped. She wanted badly to tell Kitty about Martin now, to frame that story in her mind by speaking it aloud, but this felt like the wrong moment, the wrong context. Even so, she found herself saying, 'I had a similar experience this afternoon.'

She hadn't expected Kitty to take any notice, but she lifted her head. 'What do you mean?'

'Just – an unexpected encounter.'

'With who?' Kitty asked.

Her own suffering seemed to have been nudged aside for a moment: how resilient the young were, Flora thought. She felt a little shy, now the story had been built up like this.

'With Martin,' she said.

'Martin Carver?'

'Yes.'

'And did you . . .?'

'Certainly not,' said Flora.

'But why not?' Kitty's face was eager now, despite the streaking of tears. Flora was touched, but also a little appalled. 'Maybe not – in haste, if you feel the widow's weeds . . . But think about being able to stay here whenever you wanted! Can't he cook, and everything?'

'I don't need a man to do my cooking,' said Flora, more tartly than she intended – the reference to widow's weeds had struck a tender spot – but Kitty laughed, and Flora was glad. She saw them suddenly as two of a kind, she and her daughter: two women standing their ground. She would have liked to say this to Kitty, but she was afraid it would sound contrived. While she hesitated, there was a noise on the stairs and Lou appeared, drowsy with sleep.

'Hello,' she said. 'Is it really seven o'clock?'

'It is.' Flora smiled. In her crumpled T-shirt Lou looked about fourteen, despite the protuberance of her belly. 'Do you feel better? You must have slept a long time.'

'I feel a bit odd.'

'Kitty and I were debating whether to have tea or wine,' Flora said. 'What do you fancy?'

'I'll put the kettle on.' Lou put a hand on Kitty's shoulder as she passed, then stopped. 'What have you been doing?' she asked. 'Where's Daniel?'

'We've been having a bit of an Oprah moment,' Kitty said.

'Opera or Oprah?' asked Lou.

'Either, actually,' Kitty said.

'That sounds more like wine than tea,' Lou said. 'Maybe I could allow myself half a glass. Is there any in the fridge?'

It occurred to Flora, as she opened a bottle of Vouvray, that this was the first time the three of them had been alone together since Lou and Kitty had arrived in France: that all these men had done nothing but complicate things, these last few weeks. How nice it would be, now, to whisk her girls away to some pleasant little restaurant for supper, to escape Daniel and Martin and anyone else who might arrive on the doorstep. But that, perhaps, would be problematic; too strong a statement. Well then, hers not to wish for more, but to savour the moment.

62

As they stood in the kitchen holding a glass of wine apiece, Lou had the sudden feeling that she and Flora and Kitty were part of a carefully stage-managed set piece. The Joneses often behaved self-consciously when they were together, as if playing parts that didn't come entirely naturally, but this was different. It felt as though they'd just realised they were approaching the final curtain of the drama they'd been part of this last week, and it wasn't ending quite as they'd anticipated. She imagined them following the audience back outside into the cool light of day with a slight sense of anticlimax, and she wished that it could be otherwise: that Flora, especially, could exit through a different door, into a different kind of life. That, surely, was what she'd hoped for from the summer?

'So,' she said, 'what's been happening?'

'I've been falling out with Daniel,' Kitty said, with a quavering attempt at insouciance, 'and Mum has been rejecting Prince Charming.'

'Good Heavens.' Perhaps she'd been wrong, then, to imagine an anticlimax? 'Tell me more.'

'There's not much to tell,' said Flora, 'at least not on my side.'

'Martin Carver has been holding a candle,' Kitty said, 'but Mum has snuffed it out.'

'I see.' Lou looked at her mother curiously. Her cheeks were flushed, but a sharp glint in her eyes warned off further questions. 'What about you, Kitty?' Lou asked instead. 'Trouble in Paradise?' But she could see at once that this levity was ill-judged. 'Oh, darling Kits, I'm sorry.'

'No,' said Kitty. 'It's my own fault. Or at least – I don't know. I think – he wants too much of me. He wants to be Peter Pears to my Benjamin Britten.'

That sounded rather sweet, Lou thought, rather a generous notion, even if . . . But it was more complicated than that, of course. She looked at her mother and her sister: every one of them in a muddle, she thought. She certainly hadn't worked out yet how Alice's letter left her, and even her own feelings seemed less clear than they had been. Not because she minded about the abortion, or blamed Alice for not telling her; not for any reason she could identify. It felt as though she'd lost her grip on real life, Lou thought. No wonder she could imagine an invisible director calling the shots, having no truck with the actors' hopes and desires.

'What a bunch we are,' she said. 'Not a happy ending between us.'

'You'll have one,' said Kitty.

'I don't know.'

'Of course you will. Alice will come back and everything will be fine.'

It certainly wouldn't be that easy, Lou thought. But perhaps . . . She took a sip of wine, the first she'd drunk for a couple of months, and felt the savour of it fill her senses for a moment: a forgotten pleasure, and with it a sudden release.

Perhaps at least she was beginning to understand things a little better, she thought. She could see now that neither the romantic ideal nor the clumsy chain of deceit was the whole story – and that neither simple adoration nor a dispassionate appraisal of cause and impediment would suffice, either. The truth about Alice – about love – was more elusive. Seeking it out among the murk of daily life might be an occupation to last a lifetime. Like a pig snuffing out truffles, Lou thought, remembering an article from one of the guide books she'd perused this week, and she laughed suddenly.

'Maybe,' she said.

'A nunnery might be the best place for me,' said Kitty. 'I could compose to my heart's content in a silent order.'

'Not much scope for performance, though,' said Lou. 'Nor for various other things you might miss.'

She caught her mother's eye then, and something in Flora's expression made her check herself. Time together *à trois* was too precious to be wasted in banter. They had always been good at saying nothing of consequence: the occasions when they'd managed more than that were rare.

'Shall I do something about supper?' Kitty said, as though she too felt the conversation had taken a wrong turning.

'We can all help,' said Lou, but Kitty shook her head.

'You go outside and I'll bring it to you. I'll just throw some things on a tray.'

'There's some salad in the fridge,' Flora said. 'And lots of bread.' She looked a little doubtfully at Kitty. 'We don't need much, do we?'

63

Left alone in the kitchen, Kitty soon discovered that there wasn't very much at all that could be thrown together for supper. Some things didn't change, she thought. Even here in France, with a shop ten minutes away that sold *foie gras* and any amount of wonderful cheese, they couldn't manage the knack of filling the fridge. But she wasn't sorry to have an excuse to linger for a few minutes. They might be on the brink of the kind of conversation she couldn't remember them ever having before, she and Flora and Lou. Her heart bumped as she thought about it; about truth and dare and consequences.

So it was good to have a little time to gather herself, and to let the last echoes of the scene with Daniel die away. She would gladly have gone on weeding for several more hours, working out her feelings to the plangent accompaniment of the woodwind all those Mediterranean shrubs seemed to call up: oboes for the eucalyptus, flutes for the lavender, a bassoon for the juniper bush with its boot-leather berries. A wind trio, she thought, to play *grave affettuoso* to soothe her guilt and confusion, *vivace con brio* to boost her courage, *dolce semplice* to restore her peace of mind.

But now she had the *marcato* of the kitchen knife and the *dolente* of the bare cupboards to give shape to her thoughts. She took her time over washing lettuce and chopping tomatoes, and she found some olive oil and vinegar and a scraping of mustard left in a jar to make a dressing with. She sliced yesterday's bread and toasted it under the grill, then found a tin of sardines that she arranged on a plate – and right at the back of a cupboard a small jar of tapenade, dark and pungent. That would do, she thought. That could almost be made to look like an elegantly casual *al fresco* lunch concocted by Henry's heroine, Elizabeth David. As she stacked food and plates and cutlery on a tray, she remembered the meals Henry had conjured in unpromising circumstances:

his cold collations and surprise stews, or baked beans on toast with a twist. She had a vague memory of being in the kitchen with Flora too, once upon a time, but she couldn't think when that could have been. A casserole provokingly full of lumps of flour, she remembered.

On the threshold Kitty halted for a moment, dazzled briefly by the scene. A drift of cloud was strung across the sky, fringed with the coral and carnation of approaching dusk, and below it the garden basked in a sweet wash of tremolo strings. Flora and Lou sat in the middle of the lawn, their low chatter and the chink of their wine glasses merging with the cicadas and the trickle of the fountain. There was an evening smell of warm earth, and of leaves and blossom yielding up the day's scent. It felt, Kitty thought, like a moment complete unto itself; a memory perfectly formed in an instant.

Walking across the grass she felt briefly like a trespasser, and as she set the tray down on the stone table the sardines and the French toast seemed de trop, in her eyes, but Lou's eyes widened.

'Goodness,' she said. 'How did you rustle up all this?'

'It's not much,' said Kitty. She sat down opposite her mother. If there had been a conversation, it died away now. They were both looking at her, all three of them looking at each other.

'I feel as though I ought to make a speech,' said Flora. 'This feels like a special occasion.'

'It is,' said Lou. 'Just the three of us.'

Flora sighed – not a sorrowful sigh, Kitty thought, although there was suddenly a rather serious look on her mother's face. Perhaps this was the moment for the debrief, she thought; for them to talk about Henry and Daniel and Landon. But when her mother spoke she wasn't surprised that all that was left aside. Just the three of them, she thought. That was how it should be. For now, that was what mattered.

'It's been lovely to have you both here,' Flora said. 'It hasn't exactly been a carefree holiday, I know, but I hope it's been good for you. In some ways, at least.'

'It's not over yet,' Kitty said. 'Martin hasn't come to claim his house back, has he?'

'No,' said Flora. 'But – I'm going to go home soon, I think. I could imagine staying and staying when I first came here, but. . .'

'None of us will forget this place, I'm sure,' Lou said. 'Nor this summer.'

Her voice sounded odd – too formal for the occasion, Kitty thought. Flora's eyes rested on Lou with a look of enquiry, perhaps of expectation, and then she shot a glance at Kitty. They had been talking about her, Kitty realised, while she was inside.

'What is it?' she asked. 'What are you saying?'

There was a little pause, and then Lou said, 'It's Britten whose name people remember. Don't forget that.'

Kitty stared. She could feel her heart beating, a little warm fluttering thing in her chest trying to get out into the evening air. 'What do you mean?'

'That art is special,' Lou said. 'That you're right to take your music seriously.'

'But?' said Kitty. 'It sounds as though there's a but.'

'No more than for any of us,' said Flora. 'Life interrupts and compromises, but – well, that's part of the point. But for you – if you've got something to say, something to give the world . . .'

Kitty was astonished. 'I never thought you felt like that about music,' she said. 'About art. I never thought –'

Flora smiled. 'I fell in love with Henry,' she said. 'I lived with him for nearly forty years.'

'That might have made you hate music.'

Kitty felt painfully moved, not just by her mother's affirmation but also by the sense that Flora saw her following the same path, facing the same struggle for – identity, Kitty thought. For answers. Part of her wanted badly to go on talking about her music, to tell them how it grew inside her, what it felt like, but she'd never done that before. Not even with Janet Davidson. Not even with Daniel, she thought suddenly, with a little wrenching pain of guilt and doubt which she smothered as best she could. But it was enough, almost, what had been said. Enough to acknowledge the existence of that spark of talent and vocation, to recognise its importance to her. There were other answers she needed, other questions she desperately wanted to ask, and this was the moment for them. Truth and dare and consequences. She took a deep breath.

'If you had your time over again,' she asked, 'would you marry Henry?'

For a long time Flora said nothing – so long that Kitty began to be afraid she was angry.

'I'm sorry,' she said, 'I shouldn't . . .'

'No,' said Flora, 'it's an entirely reasonable thing to ask.'

Kitty followed Flora's gaze to the lavender, thick with bees. Lou was watching her mother intently too, her hands toying with her empty wine glass.

'I can see it's a question I should be able to answer,' Flora said at last. 'Admitting to regret, or defending Henry. Giving a final judgement one way or the other. I've thought about it a lot, this summer. But you know, I can't. It's like being asked to weigh up forty years of solid history against a – a film script no one's even written. You can't know in advance what the effect of your choices will be, of course, but I did think there might be an answer at the end. A thumbs up or down. But there isn't. Not about Henry, anyway.' She smiled; a slightly cautious, characteristically Flora kind of smile.

They both waited for her to go on, but she seemed to have run out of words, for the moment.

'But if you hadn't married Henry,' Kitty asked, mustering her courage again, 'would you have married Landon instead?'

'Landon never asked me,' Flora said.

'He was so sad, those last few days,' said Lou. 'I think he wishes he could now.'

'Do you really?' Flora looked astonished; she frowned, apparently considering this. 'He's stuck to what he chose,' she said. 'Through thick and thin.'

'Is that always the right thing to do?' Lou asked. Her expression tugged at Kitty; the way she hung on Flora's answer.

'I honestly don't know,' said Flora. 'I can't tell you how to choose, or when to stick or twist. All I can say is that you can't avoid choosing. Not if you want to make anything of life. I almost think – perhaps the choosing itself matters as much as the choice you make. Picking a path and seeing where it takes you.'

'But you chose surgery, too,' Kitty said. 'You didn't just choose Henry.'

'I did,' said Flora. 'And I certainly don't regret that, even if it made me a second rate mother. No, don't answer that. The last thing I can expect from either of you is absolution.'

'Don't be ridiculous,' said Lou. 'The last thing you need is absolution. The last thing any of us need is blame, when we . . .'

Kitty looked carefully at her mother. 'They'll certainly remember your name, Mum,' she said. 'All those prizes. All those lives you saved.'

Flora shook her head. 'It's Henry they're having the memorial concert for,' she said, 'but that's not really the point.'

'What is, then?' Kitty asked.

Flora hesitated again. 'Do you remember me saying something, once,' she said, 'about not selling yourself short? About the heart and the mind?'

'No,' said Kitty, although she wished very badly that she could say yes. It seemed vitally important, just now, to follow every turn Flora took. 'I don't think I do.'

'It was me,' said Lou. 'Kitty was away skiing.'

'Of course. Of course she was.'

'Tell me now,' said Kitty.

'It was one of my moments of wisdom,' Flora said. 'Not that I've had many, as far as maternal guidance is concerned. It was – well, one of the times Henry was misbehaving. That Christmas, do you remember? When he was in New York?'

'Yes,' said Kitty. Her mother looked very young, suddenly: just like those photographs of her honeymoon.

'The gist of it,' Flora went on, 'was that if you had to decide, it was better to sacrifice your heart, not your mind. Rather surprising advice, perhaps, given what that philosophy had cost me, but I meant it. I meant that if you have a brain and you use it, you can achieve something, but the things you do for love . . .'

'Are they the things you're gonna treasure?' said Kitty.

Lou and Flora both looked at her.

'It's a song,' she said. 'By Mia van Arlen. "The things you do for love – are they the things you're gonna treasure?"'

'Hmm,' said Flora. She leaned back in her chair, and the look she settled on Kitty made the hairs stand up on her arms. 'It seems obvious to me now,' she said, 'that they are. I wasn't convinced, back then. That Christmas. I had a pretty firm conviction in the opposite direction. I feel rather embarrassed about that, now.'

Only her mother, Kitty thought, could talk about love using words like 'opposite' and 'conviction', but it was clear, in the silence that followed this speech, that it amounted to a declaration of love. She felt her eyes filling with tears as she floundered in search of a response, but before she could find one Lou spoke instead.

'I almost envy you, Ma, having got to where you are. I'm sure that's a terrible thing to say, but I wish sometimes that I could fast-forward through the next . . .'

'Don't wish the future away.' Flora's voice was gentle, but it was full of her old certainty too. 'No one should do that.'

'Even you,' said Kitty.

'Even me,' Flora said. 'Away with the past, and on with the future. Pastures new.'

Kitty felt a sudden stab of apprehension. 'But you're not ...' she began. 'You're not thinking of selling Orchards, are you? I mean, of course –'

'Not Orchards,' said Flora. 'No, not Orchards. But I think – Dad's paintings. Nicholas Comyn's paintings. I'd like to sell those. I'm not sure whether I can explain it to you, but ...'

'Away with the past?' said Lou.

'Not exactly,' said Flora. 'They're just not quite how I remember the past. How I want to remember the past. We get to choose that, too.'

The sun had been hidden for the last few minutes, and Kitty had had a strange sense that they were all waiting for it to come out – for some sort of vindication. But when, just then, sunlight spilled suddenly through a gap in the clouds, she felt not relief nor reassurance but an inexplicable sadness. She wanted something more for her mother, she understood. Not a conventional happy ending, perhaps, but – the things you do for love, she thought. The things that turn out to be more important than you think.

'What about Martin?' she asked. 'Couldn't you – I know you don't need a man to do your cooking, or for anything else, but even so, it might be nice to ...'

And then she felt foolish. Flora hardly knew Martin, she told herself. And Flora, of all people, knew how troublesome and perplexing love could be. She could just as well say the same thing to Kitty – in fact, perhaps that was exactly the point Flora had been making, she realised now, however hedged about it was. Perhaps she meant to encourage Kitty to be single-minded, but also ...

'I'm sorry,' she said. 'What do I know about anything?'

But Flora smiled at her, and glanced down at the tray which still sat, untouched, in the middle of the table.

'Dear Kitty,' she said. 'Don't be sorry. Look at all this delicious food you've found. Let's eat.'

New Year's Eve, 1977–8

This is not, Flora thinks, a party her mother would approve of. That much was clear from the moment they arrived – she and Landon, an escort her mother can hardly object to, whatever her suspicions about the evening's entertainment. Looking around her now with a sort of awe, Flora tries out the words that might be applied to this gathering and finds them deliciously evocative: louche, debauched, sybaritic. Even the sound of them speaks of things she hasn't encountered before.

The party is in a glittering basement club, decked out with silk hangings and fairy lights. The invitation specified fancy dress, and Flora is wearing an old ball gown of her mother's (a cunning idea on several counts) in which, with a few additions and alterations, she passes muster as Marie Antoinette – not entirely right for the occasion, but Flora is used to the idea of not quite fitting in. Landon is a highwayman, somehow more respectable than reprobate, but closer to the mark. There are several Tarzans, a few bunny girls, a selection of priests and nurses and the odd pirate.

Henry, whom Flora hasn't seen for a week, is ravishing in drag. His unruly hair is hidden beneath a black page-boy wig, the angles of his body all too clearly outlined by a grey silk flapper's dress. Framed by sleek wings of hair and lent emphasis by red lipstick and mascara, his face is barely recognisable but his allure is unmistakable. Seeing him across the room, Flora feels a tug of impatience and exhilaration and fear that threatens to overturn all semblance of decorum. This, too, is something new, something greater even than the broil of longing she has lived with for the past few weeks.

'Not a man for modest understatement,' says Landon, following Flora's gaze. 'Shall I get you a drink before we battle our way over?'

'Gin and tonic,' says Flora, not taking her eyes off Henry. 'Thank you. Who are those people?'

'With Henry? Nick Comyn is the tall chap. The flying ace, if that's what he's meant to be in those goggles. We were at Oxford together, Nick and Henry and I.'

'And the others?' The others are girls. Flora is more interested in them than the men; in their claims on Henry.

'No idea. That might be Nick's cousin Pru in the pink. Let's grab that drink.'

In the event neither Pru in pink (determinedly attached to her fiancé, a semi-clad pirate whose eyes wander more and more freely as his blood alcohol level rises) nor any of the rest cause Flora more than a flutter of anxiety in the course of the evening. Henry seems intent on asserting his claim on her, which Flora finds more agreeable than she could have believed. She's introduced to several of his friends (the majority dismissed by Henry in an amusing whisper as soon as they turn away) but doesn't retain their names. Nick Comyn lodges in her mind, however – gangling, drawling, awkward, he strikes a chord in her. She can tell that his unsmiling countenance is not a sign of hostility, or even unfriendliness, but even so she doesn't warm to him. He is, it seems, a painter, gaining a modest reputation in certain circles, as he puts it. He's also, Landon tells her, an aristocrat – a fact Flora registers as counting in Henry's favour with her parents, although the painting might not.

The music is loud, much of it familiar – Abba, Status Quo, Showad-dywaddy – and alternates tantalisingly between catchy rhythms and beseeching tunes that resonate deep in Flora's belly.

'Shall we dance?' Henry asks, sliding up to her ear as she exchanges a stilted sentence or two with Nick. Flora smiles, makes the little self-conscious curtsey that seems required by her costume, and takes his hand. Nick watches them move away; Flora is aware of his scrutiny, of being with Henry in the public eye. She lifts her head, feels her feet moving like a swan's beneath the wide hem of her dress. As they make their way to the dance floor, the room melts in a blur of colour and sound, a cocktail of sensations so rich and delicious that she wants never to forget them. Her mother's warnings about being left on the shelf echo in her head, roundly trounced. Here, Flora thinks, is the payoff for all those exams, all those hours in theatre: the opportunity to be her own woman, and make her own choices. Here is the glory of having it all; the prize she was waiting for.

And now, as she tries to move her body in time to the music, she realises that she is drunk, slipping willingly towards an irrevocable change. She can feel Henry's body against her, the slippery silk surface of him and the press of bone and muscle beneath. She dares herself to look up at his face, and finds his eyes, deliciously underlined with kohl, already fixed on hers. The music changes from the jigging beat of 'Tiger Feet' to the croon of 'I don't want to talk about it', and Henry draws her in close.

'You've seen the worst of me now,' he murmurs in her ear. 'Do you think you could marry me?'

Flora freezes, hanging in his arms. For several moments she says nothing, waiting for the white noise in her head to quieten, for Henry to say those words again. Her face is buried in his neck, and his hands are on her back, resting on the tight bodice of her dress.

'No?' he says, his tone gentle, amused. 'Sensible girl. Not a good prospect.'

'Yes,' she says, with a surge of laughing panic. Surely the offer can't be withdrawn so soon? Surely he can read the rapture in her silence? 'Of course yes. Absolutely.'

His hands move up to her head, and he lifts it gently away from him. 'Are you sure?' he says, looking into her eyes again. 'Do you love me enough?'

'Do you?' she asks.

'Oh yes,' he says. 'Oh yes, I do. And I love the idea of being married to a surgeon. I love the idea of you operating all day and coming home to me at night. We'll be such a couple.'

*

'Engaged?' says Landon.

He looks astonished; aghast even. Below the great wash of happiness, Flora feels a prick of petulance. He's supposed to be thrilled for her, and for Henry too.

'Yes,' she says. 'We're getting married. People do, you know. Even me.'

'To Henry.'

It's more a statement than a question, but even so there's a strain of disbelief in his voice which causes her, now, a flicker of disquiet.

'Yes,' she says again. 'Why not to Henry?'

And then she understands. She should have realised, should have seen the signs, she thinks, however discreetly they have been veiled all this time. She reaches out her hand and takes his, the words of an apology hovering on her lips. She can't quite speak them, though; can't quite bring what hangs between them into the open. For his sake, she thinks. For all their sakes.

Landon frowns. His face doesn't do what she expects: there's no softening, no lightening. Surely he wants her to be happy, Flora thinks.

And then Henry looms out of the crowd, larger than life, eyeshadow streaking his cheekbones. He looks like a Harlequin, Flora thinks, or a tart. Her chest fills with elation and pride, an extraordinary pressure of happiness.

'Here he is,' she says. 'My fiancé.'

September 2014

The autumn had set in gently. In the garden at Orchards the apple trees that had given the house its name stooped a little closer to the ground every day, and nearer the house the delphiniums she and Henry had planted the year before made a startling display – the sort of miracle, Flora knew, that other people took for granted. Looking out of the kitchen window this morning, her eye was drawn irresistibly to the wide swathe of cerulean blue, which seemed to resolve, as she gazed, into the complex architecture the flowers revealed at close hand: the tiered rosettes making up those spikes of colour, and the overlapping layers of petals that formed each bloom. Many more layers than were needed: proof, surely, of the extravagant overabundance of nature. Beyond the flowerbed, the lawn stretched away towards sheep-strewn fields and the ring of low hills that rose to meet the cool lightness of the English sky.

Flora turned away from the window when she heard the sound of a car rounding the corner, and by the time she reached the front door it had pulled into the drive. She waited a second or two before she turned the handle, so Landon was there on the threshold when the door opened.

'Good morning,' she said. He was dressed – as he had always been, it seemed to Flora – more elaborately than the occasion demanded, in a blazer that was showing its age but would have been made for him, once upon a time, and cavalry twill trousers the colour of paper left out too long in the sun.

'Hello,' he said. 'I do have the right day, then.'

An old joke, offered as a token of something. A password.

Flora stood back to let him in. It was only a few weeks since she'd seen him, since he'd left St Rémy, but it felt much longer. It felt as though they had been catapulted backward, skipping over that whole episode.

'It looks bare without them,' Landon said, stopping for a moment in the hall.

'I don't notice,' said Flora.

Landon said nothing, and Flora regretted overstating her case so early. She'd hoped this morning wouldn't be entirely about the pictures.

'Coffee?' she offered, as he followed her into the kitchen.

'Goodness,' he said.

'Haven't you seen it since we changed things round?' she asked. 'Yes, of course you have.'

Landon had visited just before Henry died – a briefer visit than Henry would have liked, awkward for reasons Flora had found hard to fathom. Some people can't bear death, Henry had said afterwards, and she'd held his hand and said, you're not dead yet, and poured him a glass of Scotch, although she'd known he'd only take a sip.

'It's an improvement,' Landon said. 'I never knew how you lived with that squalid kitchen.'

'It wasn't squalid,' Flora said. 'We liked it.'

She'd left the coffee pot ready on the stove, and she spent the time while it was brewing wondering where they should drink it. In the end, Landon solved the dilemma for her.

'Shall we go outside?' he asked. 'That little terrace was made for days like this.'

He smiled, the perfectly amiable guest, perfectly familiar old friend.

So Flora put the cups on a tray and Landon held the door open for her – the new French window she and Henry had put in so that they could get outside easily from the new kitchen. It was true that this sheltered corner was balmy even on colder autumn days than this one. A suntrap, Henry had called it. Before the French window had been installed it had been out of sight of anyone inside the house, and people used to hide there. Flora hadn't realised that before, but she could see now that that was precisely what it had been used for. Finding the girls playing here, Lou curled in a deckchair with a book and Kitty arranging stones and flowers at her feet, she must have known it was no accident that they were out here while she and Henry were arguing inside – nor that Henry should be discovered nonchalantly absorbed by the newspaper when, in Flora's mind, he had some case to answer. Perhaps the new door had had more significance than she'd realised, opening up one of the corners that had harboured their secrets and divisions.

'Lovely,' said Landon. The table and chairs were new too, positioned to catch the sun and give a view of the apple trees. The delphiniums were in plain sight, but Landon gave them no more than a glance. 'How are you finding it?' he asked. 'Being back here, after . . .'

'It's fine,' Flora said; and then, because her tone sounded a little defensive, 'Les Violettes was delightful, of course, but not for ever.'

Landon's eyes rested on her, and she wondered if he detected the quiver of – no, she wouldn't call it regret – that passed through her then.

'Have you heard from your tenant?' he asked now. 'Or perhaps I should say your landlord?'

Flora let a second pass, placing her reply on the right beat.

'We've kept in touch,' she said.

If Landon noticed the trace of deception he said nothing.

'I'm glad you've come home,' he said. 'Come back here, I mean.'

Flora's first instinct was to resent this remark – none of his business, she wanted to think – but her indignation fizzled out before it gathered any force. She could allow him to care about what happened to her, she thought; she should let him have that satisfaction. And he was right that being at Orchards was important. The past had a way of circulating here, replaying itself with different inflections, by turns uncomfortable, pleasurable and mysterious. She liked the sense that the story wasn't finished with: that there were still different ways of telling it.

'The girls are pleased too,' she said.

'How are they?' Landon asked.

'Both well,' said Flora. 'Lou's getting bigger and bigger.' Perversity, she knew, not to mention Kitty first.

'And Alice is back?'

'Yes. Some weeks ago now.' Flora looked up at his face, his familiar, noble face, and relented. 'And Kitty is . . . Kitty.' She stopped. 'Funny how she doesn't look like either of us.'

'She looks like my mother,' Landon said. He reached into his inside pocket and produced his wallet. On one side was Rosanna, young and beautiful, and on the other someone else: someone whom Flora was certain at first glance must be Kitty, dressed in the close-fitting bodice of the 1930s.

'Good heavens.' Flora took the wallet from him and stared at the photograph. She'd known this woman for years: how had she never seen the resemblance?

'She was older when you knew her,' Landon said. 'People of her generation aged faster. It would be difficult to keep a photograph of Kitty in there, but you see . . .'

'She'd like to know you better,' Flora said. She'd said just the same to Kitty: no one could accuse her of not promoting the relationship.

'There's the concert,' Landon said.

'Julia Hoxton's concert?'

Landon cocked his head. 'Henry's concert, she'd call it. I'm singing Kitty's songs. We'll rehearse them together, I hope.'

Suddenly, the business Landon had really come to talk about seemed less disagreeable than she'd thought, and Flora's resolve stronger. She leaned across to pour the remains of the coffee into their empty cups.

'We should talk about the Comyns,' she said. 'I know you've come to lobby me, but I've got a plan I think you'll have to approve of.'

Epilogue

December 2014

In the wide atrium of the concert hall guests glittered and twittered, gaggled and regrouped, circling with glasses rarely less than half full. Around them on the walls hung Nicholas Comyn's pictures, numbered and annotated ready for the auction that would form part of the evening's proceedings. Alice, who knew almost no one beyond the family, hovered at the edge of the crowd, keeping company with the paintings.

It was odd to see them all together again. Both the people and the pictures, she meant: the living and the dead, if you wanted to be fanciful about it. The sale brochure had been nicely produced and Comyn's work hung with care. Greville's had made no bones about the importance of the collection, and everyone was keen, of course, to make the most of the sale for the benefit of the memorial fund. The variety of style and material was striking, Alice thought – portraits, landscapes, interiors – but so too was the familiarity of the pictures, even to her.

'There are more of them than I thought,' said a voice near her ear, and she turned to see Lou standing beside her.

'More people or more paintings?'

'Both.'

The baby was due in a few weeks, and Lou didn't move like an ordinary person anymore. She had turned out not to be one of those women who can carry a baby hitched casually to her like a rucksack: pregnancy had taken her over, rather than being accommodated within her. Alice's eyes traced the deep curve of her back, a calligrapher's flourish, and she felt something inside her twist itself into the same shape.

They were standing beside one of the larger paintings, a still life that strayed as close as Nicholas Comyn ever went towards the abstract, the outlines of flowers and fruit (pomegranates, according to the notes) merging and blurring into stylised shapes.

'"This work,"' Lou read, from the catalogue in her hand, '"represents a departure from the artist's more familiar style. Some commentators have linked this phase of experimentation in the summer of 1986 to a period of personal turbulence." We're meant to know what that means, I suppose. Henry would have known.'

'Tricky,' Alice said. 'Always tempting to make too much of the link between art and life.'

'It's our lives too,' Lou said. 'That's the weird thing. They've always been there, around the house. We're even in some of them.'

'I know.'

Alice took her hand. It was too late, of course, and it wasn't for her to interfere – but she wished now that she'd said something. Once they're sold, she should have warned Lou, part of your history will be gone, and with it your power to interpret it, or come to terms with it.

'Henry would like the idea of them helping to fund scholarships in his name,' Lou said, as though she knew what was on Alice's mind. 'Along with Kitty's song cycle, and all this auld acquaintance.' She gestured round the room, making the statement more theatrical than it needed to be. 'He'd love the idea of having a stake in the future.'

'I can see that,' Alice said. 'I just wonder . . .'

She could see in Lou's eyes a hint of the apprehension she still betrayed, sometimes, and which they both pretended not to notice.

'It's what Mum wants, too,' Lou said, in a gentler voice than Alice expected. 'And even . . .' She had moved on, now, to stand in front of the sketch that had appeared, so mysteriously, a few days before. The sketch of a family: of Henry and Flora and Lou and Kitty, oddly faceless but unmistakable, all the same, to those who knew them. 'Even Landon,' she said. 'In the end, even Landon.'

'Are you sure it was him?' Alice asked.

'Who else?' Lou smiled. 'It's awfully touching that he had a picture of us all, all this time. Of Kitty, especially. And that he's given it up, now. I wonder – do you think his reasons were the same as Flora's?'

Alice was pondering a reply when her attention was caught by Flora, separating from the hubbub to look at a picture hanging a little way away from them: the pastel portrait of Henry as a young man that had always hung in the hall at Orchards.

'Look,' she said.

Lou turned. Flora hadn't seen them, but from here they could see both Flora and the picture clearly.

'Do you –' Alice began – but then Flora turned abruptly, and they saw that someone had greeted her; that a man was coming towards her, smiling.

'You made it,' they heard Flora say. It was impossible to tell from her tone of voice, or the slight tilt of her head, whether she was overjoyed, or merely politely appreciative. 'I wasn't sure you were going to.'

'I said I would,' he replied.

'Well, good,' said Flora. 'Come and say hello to Kitty. She'll be pleased to see you.'

As she disappeared back into the crowd, Lou and Alice stood side by side and watched her. And from a few yards away, Henry watched her too, the light of life bright in his eyes.

Greville Auctioneers, Friday 12th December 2014

Paintings and drawings by Nicholas Comyn, from the collection of the late Henry Jones

Lot no. 7: Portrait of Henry Jones, 1967

This pastel is among the earliest of Comyn's surviving works, having been completed when he and Jones were both nineteen – probably during the course of the summer after their first year at Oxford, when they travelled through Europe for several months with their mutual friend Landon Peverell. The setting of this portrait is not known, but the outlines of terracotta roofs in the background are suggestive of Tuscany.

Although it is in a medium Comyn rarely used again, except for preliminary sketches, this work shows several characteristics of his mature work. The physiognomic accuracy with which Jones' face is rendered, and the vivid sense of personality it reveals, are reminiscent of Comyn's later portraits.

This piece is of particular interest among Henry Jones' collection of Comyn's work. Although Jones remained a close friend of the artist until his death in 1995, and was his most important patron, Comyn never produced another portrait of him.

Jones' assertive posture, challenging the viewer's gaze, and Comyn's use of vibrant tones, both contribute to the sense of a strong and self-assured personality. However, there is an intimacy to this portrait – created partly by the medium and the relatively 'unworked' nature of the piece – which sets it apart. It reveals something of the public man Jones would become, but above all it speaks of the optimism and vigour of a young man at an early and carefree stage of his life.

Acknowledgements

I am always and profoundly grateful to my husband, Richard Pleming, for his support and encouragement, and for regarding it as a privilege to live with someone whose head is so often full of other things. Also to my parents and to my wonderful children for making life so interesting and rewarding, and to the various people who have helped to keep us afloat while this book was being written, especially Tracey Matulka. Among the many friends who have generously read various drafts Bryony Bethell deserves a special mention, and Wendy Osgerby's expert assistance with the descriptions of Nicholas Comyn's paintings was invaluable.

I've been fortunate to have input from several wise editors, including Sarah Willans, Gillian Stern, Sophie Wilson – and especially Joel Richardson at Bonnier Zaffre, whose judgement and tact are unsurpassed. I've also been immensely lucky in my brilliant and dedicated agent, Patrick Walsh. No one could hope for a better advocate and advisor, nor such a good friend.

Finally, I would like to thank all the people who have unknowingly helped to shape this story: the many impressive, ambitious women I have known and worked with, many of whom have juggled demanding careers with child-raising, creativity and much else, and whose inspiration and example infuse this book.